Formerly a vid⋯⋯⋯⋯⋯⋯⋯⋯⋯⋯⋯⋯**ellen**
now spends he⋯⋯⋯⋯⋯⋯⋯⋯⋯⋯⋯⋯
seductive roma⋯⋯⋯⋯⋯⋯⋯⋯⋯⋯⋯e
found enjoying⋯⋯⋯⋯⋯⋯⋯⋯⋯⋯ren,
walking for ple⋯⋯⋯⋯⋯⋯⋯⋯⋯⋯
deepest secrets and desires. Christy loves to hear from
readers. You can get hold of her at christymckellen.com.

Avril Tremayne is an award-winning author of sexy,
modern, urban romances, featuring heroes strong enough
to make any woman swoon and stronger heroines who
nevertheless refuse to do so. She took a circuitous route
to becoming a writer, via careers in nursing, teaching,
public relations and corporate affairs—most recently in
global aviation, which gave her a voracious appetite for
travel. She currently lives in Sydney, Australia, but is
feverishly plotting to move her family to Italy for half
of every year. When she's not reading or writing Avril
can be found dining to excess, drinking lots of wine and
obsessing over shoes. Find her at avriltremayne.com, on
Facebook at avril.tremayne, on Twitter, @AvrilTremayne,
or on Instagram, @avril_tremayne.

If you liked *Wild Child* and *Getting Even*
why not try

Worth the Risk by Zara Cox
Legal Desire by Lisa Childs

Discover more at millsandboon.co.uk.

WILD CHILD

CHRISTY McKELLEN

GETTING EVEN

AVRIL TREMAYNE

MILLS & BOON

First Published in Great Britain 2018
by Mills & Boon, an imprint of HarperCollins*Publishers*
1 London Bridge Street, London, SE1 9GF

Wild Child © 2018 Christy McKellen

Getting Even © 2018 Belinda De Rome

ISBN: 978-0-263-26656-6

MIX
Paper from
responsible sources
FSC® C007454

This book is produced from independently certified FSC™ paper
to ensure responsible forest management.
For more information visit www.harpercollins.co.uk/green.

Printed and bound in Spain
by CPI, Barcelona

WILD CHILD

CHRISTY McKELLEN

MILLS & BOON

Tom, you're the *boss*.

CHAPTER ONE

Maya

THE FIRST TIME I laid eyes on Benedict Chivers I was on the brink of orgasm.

It had been a long, gruelling day at the office—my arsehole of a father's office, to be precise—and I'd been yearning to step into a hot, soothing bubble bath from the moment I'd escaped that hellhole.

Luxuriating in a bath has always been a turn-on for me. It's something about the heat swirling between my thighs, and the way the soapy water makes my skin so slick and touchable, so I was right in the middle of one of my favourite sexual fantasies when a powerfully built, mouth-wateringly handsome man strode in through the unlocked bathroom door and caught me with my fingers working my clit and my body primed for much-needed release.

I must point out here that he hadn't just randomly wandered in off the street and into my flat. I was staying at my father's house in Kensington for a couple of weeks, while I was having the shonky old electrics overhauled at my place. I'd planned to crash with my friend Bella, but my father had insisted I stay with him instead—and when he insists on something, you damn well do it.

I swear it was a genuine mistake, forgetting to lock that door—but I can't say I was sorry that I had right at that moment.

The expression in the stranger's piercing pewter-grey eyes when they locked with mine was mesmerising, making my breath stutter in my throat and my heart-rate soar, flooding my body with dopamine as I gazed back at him.

He just stood there, with his firm lips slightly parted and his striking eyes narrowed and looked at me. Really *looked* at me. Like there was nothing else on earth but me, naked in that bath.

Spurred on by the captivation I saw in his face, I began to move my stilled fingers again, bathing in his intense, penetrating gaze, feeling the heat of his wanton attention right down to my bones.

Over the gentle splash of the water I could hear his breath as it scythed in and out of his throat, and through the haze of my need to finish what I'd started I saw his shoulders tense and his hands bunch rigidly at his sides, as if he was fighting to keep them there—to stop himself from reaching down into the water and touching me.

That thought took me right to the edge, and as I began to hit my peak, greedy, unconcealed desire flashed across his face, tipping me over. I came in intense waves, a loud groan of pleasure rasping through my throat as my release rushed to my head, blurring my vision.

My noisy declaration of pleasure seemed to shock him out of his shameless voyeurism, and as my world came back to rights I saw him take a step backwards, his brow furrowed into a deep frown, blinking as if he'd just come to his senses.

As I caught my breath and fought past the lingering waves of ecstasy that gripped me all I could do was laugh.

It was a pretty ridiculous situation after all.

'Nice to meet you. Thanks for the visual stimulation,' I managed to say through my giggles.

But instead of finding the humour of the situation too, he gave me a cool stare that made the laugher die in my throat, then turned on his heel and strode quickly out of the room, slamming the door shut behind him.

Shrugging off my discomfort, I smiled to myself, replaying the expression in his eyes right before I'd climaxed. He'd *wanted* to see me come. He hadn't been able to look away—even though he was clearly frustrated with himself for not doing so now.

The pleasure for me hadn't been about the illicit thrill of him catching me masturbating, though, it was the knowledge that he could have turned and walked away immediately but he hadn't. He'd stood there and watched—as if he hadn't been able to help himself.

I loved the thought of that—of having that kind of power over him. This handsome, beguiling stranger.

I wondered who he was and what he was doing here in my father's house at six o'clock in the evening. My father never came home before seven, and most nights it was more like nine o'clock before he made an appearance. This guy had to be someone special for my father to come back early and meet him here in his home.

Getting out of the bath, I dried my still tingling skin with one of the soft fluffy towels the housekeeper provides in abundance and went back to my room to get dressed, half hoping to bump into the mysterious dark-eyed visitor on the way.

But it was not to be. The sound of muffled voices floated up from downstairs—two men, I thought, and almost certainly one of them was my father, judging by the deep timbre of his voice—so it seemed likely that my mystery man had returned to whatever kind of meeting they were having down there.

I dressed quickly, pulling on a vest top and my oldest, most comfortable jeans, and made my way downstairs.

'Maya—come in here, please,' my father barked as I tiptoed past the sitting room door in an attempt to make it to the kitchen undetected and knock back a large glass of wine before suppertime.

While I was staying here he insisted I join him to

eat, and I definitely needed to be tipsy before facing him over a meal, when it would be just the two of us avoiding each other's eyes in silence.

Reluctantly, I turned back and approached the sitting room doorway, wondering what the hell I was about to walk into. My father rarely introduced me to his associates. It was always my older sister, April, the golden child of the family, whom he touted in front of them. I was merely the shady black sheep against her pristine white pedigree.

Had the guy told my father what had just happened upstairs?

Surely not.

He'd come out of it looking just as bad as me, if not worse, and my father was not a man to mess with in regards to his family. I'd heard of him destroying men—in a business sense, that is—for far less than walking in on one of his daughters in the bath.

I sauntered into the room with my head held high, determined not to be cowed by either of the intense, powerfully present men, and gave my father the kind of subservient smile that clearly made him suspicious, if his return scowl was anything to go by.

'This is Benedict Chivers. He's agreed to let you work for him at his company, Ergo-i Software, for the next few weeks while I'm away in New York.'

He gestured towards the man who had been watching me make myself come not ten minutes ago, who was now standing ramrod-straight in my father's sitting room, with a large glass of ten-year-old Scotch clutched in his large hand.

It struck me with force once again what an attractive man he was, with a square-jawed, dark-eyed handsomeness that was impossible to tear my gaze away from.

There was no grey in his thick jet-black hair, which he wore swept away from his angular, high-cheekboned face, so I guessed he was pretty young to be company director. I put him in his early thirties. He was big too. The guy must have been at least six foot four, and with a broad-shouldered, long limbed body that made me want to climb up it and rub myself against him, just to experience his visceral power up close and personal.

'You'll be there to help out with whatever he needs,' my father continued, clearly oblivious of what had gone on right under his nose upstairs— thank God. It would be such a shame to ruin the sexily enigmatic Mr Chivers at this point.

'Taking notes, organising his schedule—that sort of thing—while his executive assistant is recovering from an operation. He'll have other PAs looking after him too, so they'll be able to help you if you have any questions.'

I turned back from staring intently at Benedict Chivers—who, I was irked to note, was looking back at me as if he'd never laid eyes on me before in his life—and offered my father a demure smile.

'It'll be good for you to see how another company

runs its day-to-day business,' he said, ignoring what must have seemed like abnormally respectable behaviour coming from me. 'Especially if you really are determined to establish your own enterprise.'

He said 'enterprise' as if I was planning on setting up a seedy brothel or a gun-running cartel.

Irritation clawed up my spine.

In actual fact, my plan is to grow a custom-made jewellery business—an idea I've toyed with for ages. I'll be the first to admit I've not exactly been focussed before this point in my life, and have perhaps spent a bit too much time partying, but I had an epiphany after my twenty-third birthday, when I realised my friends were all moving on with their lives and I wasn't, and I've worked hard to refocus my goals since then.

Trouble is, a start-up jewellery business is going to need a hell of a lot of capital to get it off the ground and a lot of commercial savvy to run it profitably— the latter of which I've been working on, with the help of a night school class for the past year. My tutor thinks I'll do well, but I know my business skills are still somewhat lacking.

My father has finally agreed to give me control of my trust fund if I can prove I can be business-minded, so I can invest that money in getting my venture off the ground—precious stones and metals don't come cheap, after all. Despite the fact he's a billionaire, he's always been incredibly tight with the allowance he gives me and my two sisters, wanting us to 'learn the real value of money'.

He's particularly hard on me about it after the designer knickers debacle. But that's another story.

So, in exchange for this benevolence, I've promised him six months of my life learning the ropes from the bottom up at the family business. Not that he's entrusted me with anything important so far. All I've done is fetch endless cups of coffee and scan, then shred, about a million old files full of papers from ten years ago which have been languishing in some dusty basement. I'm pretty sure it's not actually a necessary job and he's only invented it to try and kill my spirit.

And now it seemed he wanted this guy to babysit me while he was off in the States—as if he didn't trust me to keep my promise to work hard and curb my partying when he's not around.

I decided I'd be happy for Benedict Chivers to boss me around, though. In fact, I could imagine rather enjoying it. But I wasn't going to just take it lying down—unless he suggested the sort of lying down I'd be happy to partake in, of course. It had definitely seemed as if he'd be into that when he was standing there, watching me pleasure myself in the bathroom. Even if he was pretending it hadn't happened now.

I decided, on balance, that it might actually prove to be quite entertaining to have a bit of fun with this guy, so I forced my face into a bland, respectful expression and turned to face my new boss—who knew what I looked like when I orgasmed.

'It's lovely to meet you, Mr Chivers. I'm looking forward to *coming* for you.' I shook my head and wrinkled my nose, pretending I'd misspoken by accident. 'Coming *to work* for you.'

I flashed him my most innocent smile, popping my dimple, but I could tell from the way his scowl deepened and an expression of wry acuity ghosted across his face that he knew exactly what I was doing. I got the feeling he'd make me pay for it later. At least I hoped he would.

'Good to meet you too, Maya. I look forward to having you on board,' he said smoothly.

Even though he was careful to keep any hint of innuendo out of his voice, the sound of his deep, husky voice saying those words sent a delicious shiver across my skin, and I swear I nearly came again on the spot.

Maintaining my cool in front of this guy was clearly going to be a challenge.

'I hope you'll find your time at Ergo-i rewarding. We run a tight ship, but from what your father's told me you'll be able to handle it once you've been shown the ropes,' he said, the expression in his eyes as hard as the hundred-and-fifty-million-year-old fossil on my father's mantelpiece.

A shiver of frustration ran through me. Was that really how they both saw me? As someone who needed instructions on how to make hot drinks and shuffle paper around?

'Okay…well, if that's all you need from me, there's a glass of wine with my name on it waiting for me in the kitchen,' I said coolly, feeling a sudden urge to get out of there. Being around this guy was seriously disturbing my equilibrium.

I gave them both a nod, then quickly scarpered out of the room, rushing down the hallway towards the safety of the kitchen.

Before I could reach my safe haven I heard heavy footsteps behind me and felt my father's vice-like fingers wrap around my arm, bringing me to an abrupt halt. Reluctantly, I turned back to face him, wondering what further humiliation I was to be subjected to this evening.

'I expect to hear from Benedict that you're displaying exemplary behaviour while you're working for him,' he murmured in that icy-cold tone he uses when he wants people to pay attention to what he's saying.

Not that anyone would ever dare do otherwise.

'I'd like to hope that he and April will hit it off once she gets back from China. He's a very smart and ambitious man and his company is going places. Amalgamating the two families would be very good for business. So please, for the love of God, don't do anything to put our family's reputation in jeopardy while you're working there.'

The herd of elephants that is always in the room

whenever my father and I are together stamped their feet.

I hate the way he always talks to me like I'm fourteen, instead of twenty-four. Mind you, it's a miracle he talks to me at all, after the way the fourteen-year-old me behaved… Behaviour that changed all our lives irrevocably. Particularly my mother's.

I pushed away the sting of guilt-threaded grief that's plagued me ever since that horrific day and pasted on my carefree smile. I'm a master at conjuring it at will now—even when I feel like I'm dying inside.

'I won't be dining with you this evening,' he added. 'I'm taking Benedict round the corner to the club.'

He was talking about the men-only, elitist old boys' private club where he's on the board. A place I wouldn't be seen dead in even if I *wasn't* the proud owner of a vagina.

'Have a marvellous time,' I muttered, shaking off my father's hold on me and giving him a cursory nod.

Then I turned away and headed back towards the kitchen, the need for that numbing glass of wine stronger than ever now.

Perhaps it'll actually be a good experience working for Benedict Chivers, I told myself as I took down the largest wine glass I could find from the cupboard and filled it to the brim with Sancerre from the industrial-sized fridge. It would certainly brighten up my day having him around to look at. Maybe if we got close one evening, while we were working late and everyone else had gone home, something might spark between us and melt the wall of ice he appeared to have so hastily thrown up.

Something good. Something exciting and illicit.

The best kind of something.

It would be so damn satisfying to stick it to my perfect sister too—knowing I've already had the man she's destined for. She's almost as bad as my father some days, with her judgement about the way I choose to live my life.

According to her, our family would have been better off if I'd never been born. She actually said that to me when we were younger. To my face. I laughed it off, but a small part of me died inside. Even now she still treats me as if I'm scum on her shoe, and she and my father are always on my back about something.

It's like being tag-teamed by the fun police.

If it weren't for my little sister, Juno, whom my father barely acknowledges exists most of the time—probably because she keeps her head down and hardly says a word when he's around—I'd avoid all family gatherings.

Juno's very different from the rest of the Darlington-Hume family, though—sensitive and studious, as opposed to worldly-wise and bullish—and I've always had an innate instinct to protect her because of it. She has a tendency to stand with her shoulders pulled in a little towards her chest and her head slightly bowed, as if she's constantly ducking people's attention.

I think that started in her tweens, when she suddenly put on a lot of weight and got acne. I know she was bullied for it at school—until I stepped in and put those bitches right, that was.

No one treats the people I care about badly.

No one.

So, anyway, that's the story of how I've come to find myself now staring at Benedict Chivers's smug, handsome face over a highly polished meeting room table at his multi-million-pound software company, while everyone talks numbers and he steadfastly ignores me.

I've been here nearly a week now, and he's barely said a word to me, scarcely even looked my way, getting one of his other PAs to instruct me in what he wants instead of connecting with me directly.

Yes, it fucking rankles.

I *hate* being treated like I'm beneath someone's notice. I've had to put up with enough of that over the years from my father, and I don't intend to take it from Benedict Chivers as well.

It wasn't as if I *planned* to masturbate in front of him, but from the cool way he's acted towards me since I've arrived here you'd think I did it deliberately to embarrass him. But then I suppose I *do* have a reputation for being a little wild.

The only reason I'm putting up with this torture for the next few months is so I can prove to the world

that I'm more than just a party girl. That I'm someone who deserves respect. All the drudgery and
sucking up will be worth it if I get to be my own
boss one day. Maybe I'll even impress my father by
making a success of my life.

Stranger things have happened.

I'm not banking on it, of course. The man has
an emotional wall so high it's impossible to see the
top, let alone scale it. I should know—I've tried hard
enough over the years.

But enough of that. I've never been one to feel
sorry for myself and I don't intend to start now.
I'm the master of my own destiny and I'm going to
bloody well make it a good one.

I watch my new boss now, as he leads the meeting
with hypnotising control, garnering the full attention and respect of his minions as he determinedly
works through every point on the agenda. He con-
ducts himself beautifully, with a grace and confidence that sends little thrills of awe chasing around
my body. They collect together in an erotic thrum at
the juncture of my thighs, making my skin prickle
with awareness.

Despite the fact that he acts as if he's got a dildo
permanently shoved up his behind whenever he's
around me—or maybe because of it—I find him
fascinating.

'Would you like me to fetch you anything, Mr
Chivers? A cup of tea, perhaps?' I ask him, to make
sure he has to look me directly in the eye during a

short pause in the meeting. We've not made full eye contact since I started here, and I'll be damned if I don't at least get a couple of seconds' worth of attention from him before we break for the weekend.

'No, thank you, Maya,' he says, and I hold my breath, waiting for those dark, sensual eyes to lock onto mine.

But they don't. Instead he looks down at his tablet with the meeting notes on it that I so painstakingly prepared for him, as if my presence here doesn't have any impact on him whatsoever.

Well, *fuck* that.

I excuse myself, going the long way round the table, past where he sits at the head, and making sure to bump my hip gently against his shoulder as I pretend to squeeze past him, and stride off to the bathroom.

Once in there, I stare at myself in the mirror, wondering whether I'm really brave enough to do the thing that's been racing round my mind since I realised I'd be forced to endure the whole meeting being patronised by Benedict and his fawning associates. They're talking about company pensions and I have to take what must be entirely pointless notes.

It seems Benedict Chivers is following my father's lead and trying to subdue my life force by subjecting me to endless spreadsheets and slide presentations.

I'll be lucky if I even get to the point of setting up my own business at this point. There's a good chance I'll have died of boredom before then.

So hell, yes, I *have* got the guts to do this, I tell myself, reaching up under my skirt and sliding down my knickers, then stepping out of them and hiding them in the small utility cupboard under the sink. After smoothing my skirt down, I give myself one last daring smile in the mirror, then exit the bathroom.

I return to the meeting room, feeling the cool air from the air-con unit swirling around my pussy, which only adds to the thrum of arousal that started as soon as the idea shimmied into my head.

Let's see how easy it is to ignore me now, Mr Chivers.

I go back to a different place at the table, right next to Benedict, and subtly shift my chair as I sit down so he'll have a full view of me—but no one else will—when he looks directly my way. I cross my legs primly and try not to smile as I see his gaze dart quickly towards the movement I make, then away again, as if he's training himself not to look.

I don't do it straight away. I wait until one of the associates is droning on about hybrid schemes and then make a bit of a show of shifting in my chair. Then I sigh gently, so the others won't be alerted to what I'm doing but Benedict will, and raise my foot, propping the heel of my shoe on the front bar of my chair so my knee is in the air, which forces my legs to open a little, parting my skirt.

In my peripheral vision I see Benedict's head turn and hear his sharp intake of breath as he clearly spots my 'accidental' indiscretion. I'm full-on flashing him now, and as I turn my head to look at him our gazes finally lock and I see exactly what I've been waiting for since that moment when he couldn't tear his eyes away from me in the bathroom.

Desire.

Hot, fierce need.

But before I can even smile he looks away again and asks his colleague a question, as if nothing has happened.

As if I don't exist.

He's ignoring me again.

A wave of burning frustration floods through me and I drop my foot from the chair and cross my legs again, determinedly keeping a blank expression on my face in case he looks at me again. No way will I ever show Benedict Chivers how much he's hurting me with his disregard.

The meeting seems to go on for another couple of hours—though according to my watch, when I check it at the end, it's only eighteen minutes. Eighteen pain-filled, life-sucking minutes.

The others get up from their chairs on Benedict's say-so, and I gather my pad and pen together and make to stand up, smoothing my skirt down over my legs.

'Maya, come with me. I want to see you in my office. Right now.'

The vehemence in Benedict's last two words leaves me in no doubt that I'm in for it. It just remains to be seen exactly what he has in mind by way of punishment.

The thought of that breaks through my aggravation and wet heat floods between my thighs as I follow him to his office on trembling legs, hearing him call to his other PAs that he's not to be disturbed.

I shut the door behind me with a shaky hand and turn to face him, my breath coming quickly but my head held high.

I am *not* going to let this guy get the better of me.

CHAPTER TWO

Benedict

MAYA DARLINGTON-HUME IS bad news. Everybody knows that.

Like everyone, I've seen the gossip articles showing her falling out of nightclubs on the arm of the latest It Boy and giving the finger to the camera, both of them clearly drunk or high, as well as those grainy long-lensed shots of her slouching around Primrose Hill in the late afternoon, wearing dark glasses and with a takeaway coffee clutched in her hand, after a reportedly wild party at her place the night before.

The whole thing churns my stomach. Not because women shouldn't be allowed to enjoy themselves, but because I've had a lot of experience with spoilt, bored, rich girls throughout my life, so I know one when I see one.

In my teens I worked as a maintenance guy at Tinderly, the most famous and moneyed of all the private girls' schools in the country. It was only a few miles away from where I grew up, in a rundown post-war prefab house on a rough estate on the edge of Oxford, but those girls' lives were a million miles away from my own tough upbringing.

I worked at that school throughout my late teens, saving every penny I could so I'd finally be able escape the life I'd been desperate to leave behind since I was old enough to realise that I had a waste of space, sociopathic drunk for a father and that I needed to earn enough money to rescue and rehouse my mother so we'd never have to see that piece of shit again.

That's how I was able to stick it out at Tinderly—carefully navigating my way through a dangerous minefield of adolescent girls' boredom and lust. I swear to God, I never met a single pupil there I believed would go on to make any meaningful contribution to society. It was clear they'd all end up living off either their parents' vast fortunes or their self-satisfied aristocratic future spouses'.

From my inferior position of servitude I experienced it all from those girls: abuse from the privileged, the occasional veiled but thankfully not acted upon threats to have me fired when I wouldn't give in to their sexual demands—as if I was just some plaything put there for their entertainment—and their cruelty and scorn when I refused to engage with them on *any* kind of level.

That school was a terrifying microcosm of a pampered, obtuse and corrupt society that I've tried hard to avoid during my working life.

Unfortunately, in order to maintain my software company's position as market leader, I now find myself having to associate with exactly those sorts of people. Including, it seems, Maya Darlington-Hume, who personifies everything I've come to hate about rich people: the petulant, entitled behaviour, the narcissism and, most of all, the goddamn self-indulgence.

She might be the most beautiful woman I've ever seen, with a charisma that makes it virtually impossible to keep my eyes from being drawn to her, but I'm no fool. As hard as it is to ignore her after that intensely erotic moment we shared in her father's bathroom the other week, I know I have to.

The trouble is I've not been able to stop thinking about her ever since I unashamedly watched her beautiful body writhing in the water as she brought herself to orgasm.

Fuck.

I've thought about it a thousand times since then, even though I've told myself not to.

The expression in her eyes as she came in front of me, seeming to see inside my mind and *know* that I couldn't bring myself to look away, has haunted me ever since.

I've spent more time in the gym since she's been working here than I normally would in a whole month, battling to drain the energy out of my sexual urges, trying not to picture what it would be like to have her lying writhing and needy beneath me as I thrust into her, teasing that beautiful, spirited face into the same expression of ecstasy I saw that day.

And now here she is in the flesh, looking at me with those defiant, perceptive eyes, waiting to see how I'm going to punish her for deliberately flashing me.

It's as if she senses it in me—the urge to dominate her and to take pleasure in it that I've fought against since she first started working here.

But I can't let myself do it. I can't get involved with her.

I need to keep her father sweet if I'm going to use his influence to get what I want: his agreement to sit on my executive board and exert his not insubstantial influence over the money men, so that the business I've strived so hard to build from scratch has a real chance of survival in an increasingly competitive marketplace.

We're getting our biggest product—a piece of Customer Relations Management software, or CRM as it's more commonly known, which organises and logs client contacts—into a lot of key British companies, but there's another supplier on our tail who's starting to win some of the business we've pitched for recently. Trouble is, *this* competitor is run by a guy who comes from one of London's most powerful society families, and he's getting a lot of help from the Old Boy Network.

Which is where Maxim Darlington-Hume comes in. I may not have a rich and powerful family of my own to call on, but Maxim's backing is as good as, if not better than, the next best thing. Word of mouth and personal recommendation are powerful beasts, and if Maxim will agree to play his part in convincing the majority of companies to go with us the rest will hopefully follow.

So, much as I hate it, Maxim Darlington-Hume has the ability to make or break the company I've built with my blood, sweat and tears over the last ten years, and I need to play the game in order to gain his benevolence.

That's the only reason I agreed to let Maya work here for the next few weeks—not that I'll be trusting her with anything important.

Unfortunately, it seems she's determined to make it impossible for me to ignore her until her time's up, and deciding how best to deal with her obvious cry for attention now puts me in a real quandary.

I know what I'd *like* to do—put her over my knee and give her a wake-up call she won't forget in a hurry—but of course I'm not going to do that.

I scowl at the tall, willowy temptress standing before me in my office, who gazes back coolly, her full lips pursed and her bright blue eyes meeting mine with a fortitude I feel all the way down to my cock—which twitches disobediently. She's clipped back her long, chocolate-brown hair today, and is wearing a sky-blue skirt, which skims the edge of decency with its mid-thigh hemline, and an almost see-through silk blouse under a figure-hugging jacket.

She's the very picture of an executive's wet dream.

I was acutely aware of the tense, sexually charged atmosphere between us in the room earlier—how could I not be?—and it had become glaringly apparent to me that she was going to be a real distraction whenever she was around. She has a palpable presence—a disrespectful, carelessly sexy confidence that I seem to be innately drawn to.

I'm going to have to use every reserve I have at my disposal if I'm going to keep this woman from causing me trouble I really don't need.

'Do you think that's an appropriate way to behave in a business setting?' I ask her calmly, folding my arms and frowning, determined not to let her deliberate ploy to get a rise out of me work as she backs slowly up against the desk in the middle of my office.

'I'm sorry, Mr Chivers, I have no idea what you're talking about.'

She's all innocence and big eyes, and the sheer bloody audacity of it makes my cock twitch again. She knows damn well I understand what she's up to. The woman is clearly a pro at getting what she wants and has a lust for trouble.

An awe-inspiring combination, but also a dangerous one.

'Don't think I don't know what you're doing, Maya,' I say quietly, imbuing my voice with terse authority.

She just blinks at me, but I sense the smile behind her mask of naivety.

'You were sitting in an inappropriate way in that meeting,' I say, keeping any expression in my voice to a minimum. I don't want her to know how much this chemistry between us affects me.

'You mean like this?'

Without a second's pause she sits down on my desk and raises her right leg, propping her foot on the back of one of the visitor chairs in front of it. The movement forces her legs open and her skirt to ride up her thighs, exposing her pussy to me again.

I try not to look.

Really fucking hard.

'You should wear underwear to the office.' I force the words past my suddenly dry, constricted throat. A pulse beats hard in my head and my vision swims as she gives me a wide, secretive smile.

'But I don't like wearing underwear,' she whispers huskily. 'Is it an office rule, or something?'

'No,' I say, wishing at that moment that it was, so I'd know exactly how to deal with this brain-melting situation. 'But it's indecent,' I add, which unfortunately sounds ridiculously inane when said out loud.

I silently curse myself for letting her see my obvious stumble from dispassion into prudishness.

Her eyebrows shoot up. 'Indecent? Well, perhaps you should punish me for it, then,' she suggests, with amusement in her voice.

She's laughing at me—and the knowledge makes me drag in a ragged, incensed breath.

Something wicked flares in her eyes and I feel the control I've been determinedly clinging on to for the last week start to slip.

'What are you expecting to happen here?' I ask her, fighting for nonchalance.

She shrugs, completely unapologetic. 'I have no idea. I just wondered what you'd do if I misbehaved. Perhaps you'll just stare meaningfully at me again. You seemed to enjoy doing that the last time my pussy was on show.'

I swallow hard, but don't rise to her teasing provocation. I just continue to look at her steadily. This woman has danger written all over her. I'm going to have to be firm here—let her know I'm not going to put up with her shit.

As if she's read my mind she says, 'Perhaps you should discipline me so I don't do it again.'

I raise an eyebrow, determined not to give her the pleasure of an emotional response to that. 'Discipline you how?'

Her chest is rising and falling rapidly now, as if the idea of it thrills her. Which, of course, thrills me right back.

'I don't know. How would you *like* to do it?' she says, as if she's asking me how I take my coffee.

Clearly she's enjoying playing with me. Like a cat would play with a mouse.

I can imagine how sharp her claws might be if she

got me cornered, though, so I say, 'Perhaps I should send you home for the day. To think about the consequences of your actions.'

Surprise and disappointment flash in her eyes. She doesn't like it that I'm not playing the game.

'But I'll just come back tomorrow and do it again.' Her mouth lifts in a crooked smile, her bright, intelligent eyes boring into mine. 'Perhaps you should take your frustration out on the thing that's most disturbing you.'

She lifts her other leg, putting her foot onto the chair to her left, and her skirt rides further up her thighs, fully exposing her beautiful pussy, glistening with arousal. She has to brace both hands on the surface of my desk to keep upright.

'Right here,' she says roughly, narrowing her eyes.

Something dark and compelling takes over me, and before I can check myself I take two deliberate steps forward so I'm standing between her spread legs.

I could touch her right now if I let myself. My right hand is hovering only inches away, as if magnetically drawn. My heartbeat thuds in my ears as I breathe in the sweet, arousing scent of her. I wonder fleetingly how she'd taste and feel against my tongue, but push the idea away. I can't go down on her here in my office.

I can't.

'You *know* I deserve to be taught a lesson. Otherwise it's probably not going to stop.' She smiles, her full, rosy-pink lips pulled tightly across her perfect white teeth. 'And you don't have to worry…nobody will hear anything about it from me,' she murmurs. 'It'll be our sexy little secret.'

She flashes me such a provocative look my insides rush with heat.

I swallow past my parched throat. 'I don't get involved with people I work with.'

'That's a shame,' she says, shaking her head sadly. 'Because it would make my time here a lot more entertaining—for both of us.'

I can't help but let out a snort of mirth at her audacity.

'Anyway, we're not *getting involved*,' she says. 'You're just disciplining me for my *terrible* behaviour earlier—as any good boss would,' she murmurs.

I open my mouth to tell her it's not going to happen, but for some reason the words won't come. They're stuck at the back of my throat.

Seeming to sense my weakness, she slides forward on the desk, her eyes flashing with mischief, pushing herself against my hand. I feel the slickness of her arousal coat my fingertips and the heat of her on my palm. I drag in a frustrated breath, knowing I should pull my hand away, but finding I can't do it. That I don't want to.

All the reasons why I shouldn't be letting this happen fly around my head at a dizzying rate—then completely vanish as she lets out a husky breath of satisfaction and rocks her hips a little, rubbing her

slick folds against my fingers, groaning with pleasure as the tip of my middle finger slides over her
clitoris.

'I think you *like* naughty women,' she rasps, lowering herself back onto her elbows, so she's practically lying across my desk. 'Women who like to
touch themselves in front of you and who know how
to make you come so hard your eyes roll back in
your head.'

'You're enjoying taunting me, aren't you?' I growl
back at her. 'You're getting off on it.'

I'm completely captivated by her determination
to get what she wants. I've never met anyone with
so much pluck.

'Yessss,' she hisses as I push my hand harder
against her, my fingers pressing into her hot flesh.

'I *should* punish you for that,' I say, totally losing the last vestige of my control. But I don't care. In
fact I'm so far beyond caring it's ridiculous. I seem
to be on autopilot, my craving for her driving me on
without my brain needing to engage.

'Yes…' she says again, her voice shaking as she
nods her head.

She's so wet it's easy for my finger to slip inside
her. I draw it back and forth, just inside the entrance
to her vagina, and she gives me the response I'm
looking for, dragging in a stuttering kind of breath
as if I've hit a sensitive spot.

My cock, which is as hard as a rock now, presses
distractingly against my trousers—as if it has a life

of its own and is trying to escape its confines. But there's no way I'm getting it out right now. I want to feel power over her, like she had over me that day at her father's house, but I also need to see her come again so badly it's blurring all other thoughts in my head.

I slip another finger inside her, pushing them both deep and feeling her slick arousal run down my hand. Finding the rough pad of her G-spot, I curl my fingers and make a beckoning motion against it, seeing her twitch and jerk in response to the pressure I put there.

'Oh, fuck!' she whispers, scratching her nails against the polished surface of my desk, her breasts heaving beneath the thin material of her blouse.

I brace my other hand on the edge of the desk and lean in towards her, taking care to keep my body from touching her. I sense if my cock gets any kind of friction against it right now I'm going to lose my mind.

'More…give me more,' she begs, writhing against my hand.

After taking a moment to tease her, pretending I'm deciding whether or not to give her what she needs, I thrust another finger inside her, feeling her stretch to take it.

'Ungh!' she moans, her beautiful face contracted in a concentrated frown.

But she obviously likes what I'm doing to her because she bucks her hips, pressing herself harder into my hand. Lifting her head, she looks me directly in the eyes, her expression intensely challenging and such a turn-on I nearly come without her even touching me.

'Is that all you've got?' she mutters in a voice broken with need.

So I add another finger and see a pleasure-pain-tinged frown flash across her face, quickly followed by an ecstatic widening of her eyes as she stretches more to take my intrusion. Her mouth drops open and a long, low sigh of pleasure whispers out of her throat as I push in deeper.

Sensing she's close now, I bring my thumb into play, sliding it over her clit in tight circles, taking immense pleasure in seeing her legs tremble on either side of me.

'Yes, I'm so close…make me come,' she gasps, her spine arching away from the desk.

But I'm not going to let her call the shots. *I'm* in control here, and I need her to understand that. I didn't get to the position I'm in today by letting other people dictate the play.

I still the motion of my hand, drawing my fingers out of her a little way.

She lets out a shout of distress. 'No—no! Don't stop now. Please! Keep going!'

I smile to myself, a sense of power surging through me. 'Only if you promise not to act up at work again. And you have to wear underwear to the office from now on.'

She nods wildly, trying to push herself onto my hand again, seemingly desperate. 'Okay, okay—I promise.'

'And don't make any noise when you come,' I demand—partly because I don't want the people on the other side of the door to hear her, but mostly because I want to *own* this orgasm. I want her to do as I fucking well say in order to get it.

She nods again, seemingly unable to form any words in her state of frantic need, and I begin the deep push-pull of my fingers inside her again, increasing the pressure on her clit with my thumb with each stroke.

I half expect her to defy me, and groan out loud when she orgasms, but I'm surprised and elated when I see her jerk beneath me, biting down hard on her bottom lip and screwing her eyes shut as she starts to come around my hand. I feel her internal muscles spasming, squeezing me hard, and I experience a sort of brain orgasm at the sight of her losing herself but obeying my command.

My whole body heats at the sight of it, sending a wave of profound satisfaction through me as she keeps on jerking against my fingers, as if the greedy sensations have her entirely in their grip and are refusing to let go.

It takes a long time for her to stop moving and sink heavily against the table, as though her bones have melted, and when she does I'm finally able to tear my eyes away from the most erotic sight I've ever experienced and breathe again.

And that's when it hits me—what I've just done.

I withdraw my hand, hearing her drag in a breath of surprise as if we've become one and I've torn away a part of her. I want to get the hell out of there, away from her compelling presence, but I know I can't do that. I *won't* do that. So instead I lift her feet off the chairs and tug down her skirt to cover her.

She sits up, propping her hands on either side of her. 'Thanks, I needed that,' she murmurs.

I don't look at her. I can't. If I do I think I might say something I'll regret later. Instead I nod, then walk away, skirting the desk, and sit down in my chair.

She slides off the table and turns to look at me, her head held high as if nothing untoward has happened. As if I haven't just taken advantage of her in the most lewd way possible.

'You can leave now. Remember what you promised me,' I say to her, determinedly keeping my voice steady.

I fold my arms again, so she doesn't see how much my hands are shaking. I'm sure she's going to get angry, tell me I'm a monster to dismiss her so coldly after what has just happened between us, but she doesn't. Instead she pushes back her shoulders and gives me an obedient nod.

'Yes, sir, Mr Chivers,' she breathes in that delicious husky voice of hers.

Turning gracefully on the spot, she heads for the door—but before she leaves she turns back and flashes me one last guileful smile, letting me know that this thing isn't over between us, then lets herself out of my office, closing the door quietly behind her.

I drop my head into my hands and let out a low groan.

Well, *that* didn't exactly go as I planned.

Fuck!

I'm supposed to be looking out for her while her father's in New York. He specifically warned me not to let her get into my head and twist me around her little finger and I laughed, telling him there was no way that would happen, thinking I could handle her.

Well, I guess I *did* handle her. Just not in the way I intended.

We've crossed a line now, though, and I know there's no going back. But at least I know what I'm up against.

Anyway, she won't be working here for long, and judging by her reputation for short, sharp relationships she isn't looking for anything serious from me.

I certainly don't want a serious relationship right now—not that she's the type of woman I'd expect to settle down with anyway…if I ever do.

That's not to say I didn't enjoy what just happened between us. She certainly is a fascinating woman…

I rub my hands over my scalp, feeling frustration flood through me.

She's the very last person I should be letting get

under my skin right now. It's okay for her—playing at working here, then swanning off to fritter away her trust fund on some vanity project—but it's my career and reputation at stake and I have to put my business first.

If she thinks I'm going to carry on playing her sexy little power games she can bloody well think again.

CHAPTER THREE

Maya

I PUT A brave face on it as I saunter out of Benedict's office, pretending I'm still in control of the situation and my response to him—but, *Jesus*, what happened back there has rattled me well and good.

I went in there intending to get his attention, but I had no idea just how far I was willing to go in order to get it until the intensely erotic promise of the situation seduced me into total abandon.

That was pretty extreme, though. Even for me.

Not that I didn't love every single second of it…

The rest of my afternoon is spent in a brain-addled haze, and I stumble home feeling the kind of euphoria I can normally only procure from a dealer.

I'm not usually one for repeat performances—famous for it, in fact—but as I sit in my father's kitchen, gulping down a humongous glass of wine like it's water, I can't get Benedict Chivers out of my head.

That should be enough for me—that breathtakingly sexy culmination of our mutual attraction. It should be, but it isn't. Because he demonstrated something I've been looking for for a long time—a strength and self-possession I've been unable to find before now. Normally when I force my admittedly sometimes overwhelming personality on a man he either turns into a gibbering wreck or blows it by getting selfish and carried away with a sense of his own importance. But not Benedict Chivers. He somehow managed to give me exactly what I most needed. Despite him maintaining strict control over the situation I still felt powerful, wanted and majorly fucking sexy.

And sitting here, humming with echoes of the pleasure he gave me, I know for sure that I definitely want to feel like that again.

Unfortunately, it seems we're not on the same page where that particular want is concerned.

I turn up at the office the next day, looking my absolute sex bomb best, only to find to my screaming frustration that he's not in, and all my tasks are to be passed on through tersely worded emails or by word of mouth from one of his other PAs.

By the time I get home I seriously wonder whether I'm going to spontaneously combust from sexual tension. Is that a thing? Is it possible my body will actually catch fire and I'll be found in the morning, just a pile of ash and false eyelashes?

It's not as if I don't have other options to satisfy this weirdly consuming need. I've cultivated a comprehensive book of contacts for fun, no-strings sex over the years and, believe me, I'm not afraid to use it. So I call up Freddie Valentine—a semi-regular hook-up of mine who fronts the indie band Blues and Dues, who've been getting a lot of press lately for their wild partying.

Mercifully, he's free and tells me to, 'Come right over and sit on my face, babe.'

But for some reason, it's not happening for me, and when he leans in to kiss me and slides his hands around my waist, pulling me against his rock-hard body, I freeze.

Usually I love having sex, because in those moments I can dodge the strange restlessness that follows me around like a toxic cloud and escape into pure, beautiful sensation. My thoughts are centred entirely on how my body is being worshipped, and of course my interest in my partner's—no one could ever accuse me of being a selfish lover—but not, it seems, today.

There's nothing there. Not even a spark of desire.

Despite my acute awareness of the guy's sharp looks and rocking body, I feel nothing. So, ignoring his huffy baffled protests I tell him I've changed my mind and I'm not in the mood after all and practically run out of his apartment.

I sit on my bed at home, wondering what the hell has happened to me.

I toss the question around my mind for the next couple of days, growing increasingly frustrated and not a little bit worried by the weird infatuation I seem to have developed for my boss.

My boss who is once again acting as if I mean absolutely nothing to him.

Friday morning I finally get an opportunity to be in a room with him alone as I take him the coffee that the other PAs are too busy to fetch. Despite my family name and social status I'm still the last in when it comes to employment here, so I'm considered the bottom of the pile. I'm sure my father must have insisted on that being enforced too. He's a wily bastard like that. Luckily, his irreverence actually benefits me today, which gives me an extra little kick of satisfaction.

I walk into Benedict's office, making my strides long and confident as I cover the floor between the door and his desk. The memory of what happened on that thing the last time I was in here makes my whole body flush with heat as I approach it.

He looks up from what he's doing at his computer and fixes me with a hard, distant stare.

'What can I do for you, Maya?'

'I thought you might be thirsty, Mr Chivers,' I say, offering up the large mug of strong black coffee.

'Thank you. You can put it right there.' He gestures to a space on the desk before turning his gaze back to his computer, effectively dismissing me.

'Can I do anything else for you?' My voice is all

smooth and warm. I'm determined not to let him snub me, and I wait until he looks up at me again and flash him a coy smile.

'No. Thank you.' The expression in his eyes is hard, but I swear I see a twinkle of something wicked behind his nonchalance.

'This is a nice desk you have here. Sturdy.' I give it a gentle tap with my fingertips. 'I meant to say that the last time I was in here,' I add, with a provocative raise of my eyebrows.

A muscle twitches in his jaw and his eyes widen infinitesimally, as if he's thinking about what happened here too. 'I'm glad you think so, Maya. I chose it myself.'

'You have good taste.'

'Thank you.' He steeples his fingers and rests his chin on the apex of them, whilst maintaining his penetrating stare.

I think about the way he used those fingers on me—*in* me—and I feel echoes of the sensory memory of it all the way inside, which only increases the inescapable erotic hum of arousal I've been suffering ever since that day.

'I hear you're getting on well with the tasks you've been given,' he says.

I experience a sting of annoyance at his change in subject, but front it out.

'Yeah, well, I pride myself on doing a good job.'

He nods, then asks, 'And are you finding being here *stimulating*?'

There's a definite twinkle in his eye now.

He's flirting with me. Finally!

I move closer to the desk and perch one bum cheek on the edge of it, looking down at him, holding his gaze. The air is thick with tension and desire crackles through me. There's unquestionably something still going on between us. I can *feel* it. I long for him to reach out and pull me towards him. Kiss me like he'd stop breathing if he didn't. To prove he's as desperate for my touch as I am for his.

'Some days more so than others,' I murmur. 'It really depends on who's around.' I lean in closer to him, holding his intense gaze with my own.

My whole body is humming with awareness, as if I can feel every nerve-ending in my skin. My leg and buttock feel ultra-sensitive where they're pressed against the hard wood of the desk.

Does he know what he's doing to me?

Will he touch me again?

I want him to. So much I ache with it. In fact I'm having enormous trouble keeping my seat and not jumping into his lap.

But I need to be cool about this. Benedict Chivers is clearly not a man to tolerate lascivious behaviour. Unless he's the one perpetrating it, of course.

My breath is thick and shallow, and I have to swallow hard past the dryness in my throat as I wait for his next move.

'Well, I'm glad you're getting on well,' he says abruptly, sitting back in his chair as if he's suddenly bored with the conversation and keen to get back to work. 'Your father will be pleased.'

I stare at him in confusion. Why the hell is he bringing my father into the room with us? Is he mad? It's the ultimate bucket of cold water on my lust and I drag in a sharp breath as if I've just been slapped in the face.

'Anyway, Maya, thanks again for the coffee. I have a meeting with the head of marketing now, so if you could show her in when you leave I'd appreciate it.'

He's looking back at his computer as he says this, all businesslike again.

If it weren't for the cold tone in his voice I'd suspect he was still playing the scene, but as he glances up at me I see with a lurch of sickening disappointment that he's not joking. He's deadly serious. He's calling a halt to this scenario.

My skin rushes with icy mortification.

I stand up shakily and brush down my skirt to give my trembling fingers something to do.

'Yes, sir,' I manage to force through my gritted teeth, and I turn and walk away from him, acutely aware of how stiffly I'm moving but not able to do a damn thing about it.

The distance from his desk to the door feels like acres, and I breathe a sigh of relief as I'm finally able to grab the handle and let myself out.

He's not just going to let me have what I want when I want it. I get that now.

'He's ready for you,' I mutter to the marketing manager as I pass her, striding back towards my desk with my mind racing.

This thing between us isn't over yet, though.

Not even close.

I shake out the tension in my shoulders.

To be honest, I'm actually pleased he's making it hard for me. It'll be much more satisfying if I have to work for it—I like a challenge.

But this particular situation, I realise, calls for some seriously creative thinking.

Friday night I end up working late at the office, chasing confirmation for a conference call with clients in the US, and I'm just about to pack up for the night when Rosie, one of the other PAs, comes tripping across to my desk in a flap, her normally porcelain-pale cheeks flushed with colour.

'Oh, God, Maya, I need your help!' she pants at me. 'I'm so late for my dinner with Nico and I'm supposed to drop this package round to Benedict's house. Apparently he's been waiting for it for ages and wants it right away.'

'What is it?' I ask, intrigued, eying the large padded envelope in her hand.

She shrugs. 'I'm not sure. Laura didn't say when she thrust it at me and ordered me to take it to him. The bitch. She thinks her position here trumps mine because she's slightly more senior, so I always end up saddled with the after-hours errands.' She wrinkles her nose in disgust. 'From the size and weight of it, I'd guess it's a new mobile phone or something.'

I give her a supportive eye-roll. Laura *is* a bitch, and she takes the piss with everyone, though she seems to particularly pick on Rosie—perhaps because Rosie seems so happy and settled with her boyfriend who, as she excitedly whispered to me at lunchtime a couple of days ago, may be about to pop the question. Perhaps even tonight.

I hold out my hand. 'Give it to me. I'll take it to him. You shouldn't have to be late for your dinner date just so he can have his new toy to play with.'

'Don't you have somewhere you need to be too?' she asks with a guilty look in her eye.

'Nah. I'm free as a bird tonight,' I reply, flashing her a reassuring smile.

I'm actually genuinely happy to help her out. She's the only PA here who's treated me like a person rather than Maxim Darlington-Hume's nepotistically advantaged daughter. She's also saved my arse a couple of times, catching silly mistakes I made in my first few days here, and has since taken me under her wing, giving up time during her lunch breaks to show me exactly how our perfectionist boss likes things done.

'You're an absolute angel!' she says, relief lightening her voice.

She passes me the parcel, then a Post-it note with a handwritten address on it. Benedict's handwriting? I wonder. It's neat and cursive, with a confident upstroke. Whoever wrote it was pressing the pen down firmly onto the paper, because as I run my fingers along the back I can feel the indentation of the words.

'Enjoy your night,' I add with a smile, before pulling on my coat.

I certainly intend to enjoy mine.

Back at my father's house, I steam open the envelope and extract the small, neat box containing the newest release of the world's most popular mobile phone, scoffing at his unoriginality.

Going up to my bedroom, I toss the phone onto my bedside table, then pull open the bottom drawer of my chest of drawers. I rummage around until I find what I'm looking for, unable to suppress a grin as I imagine how he's going to react when I deliver this into his large, *capable* hands.

The thought arouses me so much I have to sit on my bed and take a few deep, calming breaths, feeling the insistent throb between my legs that's been ever-present since that first incident on his desk intensify. My stomach jumps with nerves at the thought of what I'm about to do, but I fight the urge to chicken out.

Instead I stand up and tuck the package firmly under my arm.

Whatever happens from this point on, I'm pretty sure this is going to be a night I won't ever forget.

Benedict's house isn't far away from my father's, on one of the picturesque leafy green squares in Kensington, and I walk quickly and confidently—

despite my nerves—up the black-and-white che-quered tile steps and ring the large brass buzzer. Like my father, he appears to own the entire house.

By himself? I wonder, as it suddenly occurs to me that he might not be on his own this evening. Perhaps he has a housekeeper or a butler who will insist on taking the package to him, so I won't get to hand it over myself.

But before I can formulate an alternative plan the door swings open to reveal the man himself in all his glory. He's dressed casually, in faded jeans and a black shirt that fits snugly across his broad shoulders. There are definitely some well-sculpted muscles hiding under there, I think as I stare up at him, my attention trapped by this vision of male perfection.

Goosebumps rush across my skin as I take a moment to fully appreciate the magnificence of him. There's something inherently virile about him—as if he oozes sex and power from every pore. I'm surprised he doesn't have women throwing themselves at him everywhere he goes.

But then, maybe he does.

The thought sends a prickle of alarm up my spine, for some reason.

'Maya. What can I do for you?' he asks. He sounds a little wary, as if he thinks I'm here to cause mischief.

Smart man.

I reach under my arm and pull out the package I've carefully stuck back together to make it look as if it hasn't been opened. 'I have an urgent delivery from the office for you. I offered to bring it because I live so close,' I say.

He eyes me for a moment longer, as if waiting for the punchline, but when I don't provide one he nods and holds out his hand. 'Thank you.'

'You're welcome,' I say, realising with a thump of fear that he might just take it and dismiss me on the doorstep—which means I'll miss all the fun.

'Could I use your bathroom?' I ask hurriedly, making pleading eyes at him. 'I've come straight from the office and I'm bursting.'

I do a little jiggle for good measure, like a little kid might when she's desperate for the loo. He doesn't answer for a second, but then he seems to decide that he can't be rude and refuse me entry—or perhaps he just doesn't want me peeing myself on his doorstep—and steps back to let me inside.

Accidentally on purpose, I forget to hand him the package on my mercy dash to the downstairs bathroom—which he shouts is the second door on the right—under the grand sweeping staircase. I scoot inside and lock the door, taking a few moments to calm my erratic breathing and check my reflection in the mirror.

You're strong, you're in control, you're capable of getting what you want, I tell myself, practising a composed smile in the mirror before flushing the loo and washing my hands, in case he's listening out for it.

I have a moment of terror as I contemplate what I'm about to do, but I know there's no going back now. I want to go through with this. I need to.

Okay. Show-time.

Benedict

I wait in my kitchen for Maya to reappear, not wanting her to find me hanging around in the hallway as if her presence here is unsettling me.

Even though it is.

What's she playing at, turning up at my house like this? I'm uncomfortable with her being here in my personal sanctuary without any prior warning—especially since I seem to be having so much trouble keeping her out of my head when we're at work.

Not that I'm going to let *her* know that.

I hear her footsteps and the bang of the door as she leaves the bathroom.

'I'm in the kitchen,' I shout, not wanting her to have an excuse to go snooping around my house.

'Nice place,' she coos as she enters, the parcel swinging loosely in her hand.

'Can I have my package now?' I ask with a wry smile, holding out my hand for it.

'Sure.' Holding it up, she wiggles it at me and wrinkles her nose, as if she's only just realised she's still holding it, and then strolls casually over to where I'm standing, thrusting it towards me when we're close enough for it to pass between us.

'It says "urgent" on the front, so it's probably best if you open it right away,' she points out.

I swear I hear a slight hitch in her voice and I lock eyes with her, trying to read her expression for a sign of what kind of game she's playing. My heart stutters in my chest as a whole host of unnerving possibilities rush through my head.

'Just doing my job as your PA,' she says breezily, though I'm sure she's keenly aware of my suspicion that she's here to do more than just fulfil an errand.

'It'd be neglecting of my duties if I didn't make sure you were fully aware of all the relevant information,' she adds with a serene smile.

It's the smile that makes me most wary. I know she's up to something, but I can't quite figure out what and it's making me nervous.

The last thing I want is for her to think she can waltz into my house and make a fool of me.

I rip open the top of the package and upend the contents onto the work surface. My whole body tenses as I take in the shocking sight of the three items she's obviously substituted in place of my new phone.

A bullet-shaped vibrator, a tube of lube and a butt plug.

'Oh!' she says, clearly feigning shock. 'Perhaps I shouldn't have been here when you opened such a personal parcel.'

Heat rushes over my skin as disbelief chases

amusement, which chases a dangerous kind of hunger.

I turn slowly and fix her with a hard stare, to let her know I'm not going to let her get away with trying to humiliate me like this.

To my frustration, she doesn't even flinch.

Pretending not to notice my ire, she picks up the metal butt plug and examines it. 'What do you use this for?' she asks, all innocent.

She's a cool customer all right.

'Ooh, it's so cold,' she says, making big eyes at me when I meet her gaze.

Determined not to let her wrestle away control of the situation, I take it from her and weigh it in my hand. It's very heavy. And, like she says, cold. The sensation of the smooth metal on my palm sends a wave of arousal straight up my spine.

The corner of her lips twitch, but the expression in her eyes is still feigned naiveté.

As if.

'Perhaps we should put it somewhere to warm it up,' I suggest, just to see whether she's really willing to go that far, or if this is all just a ruse to get one over on me.

'Where?' she asks, lifting her hands in a pseudo baffled gesture.

Okay, then, I guess she really is determined to push this as far as she can.

But am I?

My heart hits my ribs. Hard.

There's a beat of silence while we study each other, looking for weakness in each other's poise, and my whole body becomes one hot pulse of blood.

'Why don't you take off your underwear and I'll show you exactly where I'm thinking of putting it?' I murmur.

'I'm not wearing any,' she states boldly, though her voice has a raspy quality to it now, as though she's struggling to get her words out.

Judging by her high colour and the size of her pupils, she's just as turned on by this as I am.

'You said I only have to wear knickers to the office,' she adds, when I frown at her in mock consternation, 'and we're not in the office right now.'

Ah, so we're still playing *that* game, are we?

Well, that's fine by me.

'Show me,' I order roughly.

She doesn't hesitate, but does exactly as I demand, lifting her skirt to prove she's not lying to me.

My breath rattles in my throat as I take in the enticing sight of her naked lower body. She's standing with her feet slightly apart and I catch a glint of wet arousal between her thighs.

Okay, this woman is seriously fucking with my self-control.

It's not like me to be swayed by this kind of provocation, but the desire and the self-assurance I see in her eyes has driven me right to the edge. For a few moments I seriously consider using those toys on her, and then burying myself inside her.

I want it so much my whole body is vibrating with the stress of holding myself back.

But I can't. I have to stay in control of this.

'When you're with me you should consider yourself still at work,' I say roughly, taking a deliberate step away from her and folding my arms—to show her that I'm not about to hand her what she wants and also to give myself a chance to get my raging need for her under control. 'And since you've deliberately chosen to misinterpret my rule about underwear I'm going to have to punish you by confiscating your toys.'

She stares at me with a small frown pinching her brow, as if she's not sure she's heard me correctly.

Without another word I hold up the butt plug and make a big show of dropping it into the pocket of my trousers. 'It should stay nice and warm in there,' I say.

She blinks at me, then opens her mouth, perhaps to ask whether that's a promise that I'll use it on her some time in the future, but then she closes it again. Maybe she's scared I'll say no. At least this way she can pretend there's still a game at play.

She lets go of the hem of her skirt and it and glides down to cover her thighs again.

Part of me grieves for the loss of the alluring sight of her beautiful naked body and the pleasure we could have given each other, but the other part knows this is the right thing to do. If I give in to this now I'm toast.

'Make sure you take good care of that,' she mutters. Her voice sounds rough and uneven. 'It's one of my favourites.'

'I will,' I reply calmly, though I feel anything but. 'As long as you bring my phone into the office on Monday morning. I expect to see it sitting on my desk—the phone that is, Maya, not you—when I get in first thing.'

'Or what?' she demands in a husky voice.

'Or I'll have to start legal proceedings towards you for theft of company property.'

I take a deliberate step towards her, then regret it when the heady scent of her hits my senses.

'I don't fuck around, Maya,' I murmur, only just managing to hang on to my composure—but I need to, I have to. 'As you'll come to realise. Business is business.'

She visibly swallows. 'Fine—but you don't know what you're missing,' is all she says in response, and with a cool nod of her head she stalks past me and out of the room.

I hear her quick footsteps in the hall, then the creak of the front door opening and the slam of it closing as she leaves.

I breathe out and collapse onto one of the nearby kitchen chairs, every muscle in my body throbbing with pent-up frustration.

Thank God she left when she did, because I'm not sure I'd have been able to maintain my rapidly failing grip on control if she'd stayed much longer.

I've never met anyone with such self-possession or so much gumption, and it's fucking *dazzling*. Whenever she's around I feel things I've never experienced before. Things that make my heart race and my brain fizz with a compelling desire to get to know more about her. To find out what's really going on in that inventive head of hers.

But, as much as I want to act on the fierce attraction between us, I know I can't do it. Not when I'm so painfully aware of the potential damage it could do to my business relationship with Maxim. If he thinks for a second that I've taken advantage of his daughter in any way, especially after he made it *very* clear how he'd feel about that, I can kiss his beneficence and therefore quite possibly my company's future goodbye.

So I'm going to have to keep Maya at arm's length. Because if I give in to this dangerous fascination I'm developing for her it could fucking destroy me.

CHAPTER FOUR

Maya

I STUMBLE HOME, barely registering my surroundings, and let myself in through my father's front door with a shaking hand.

I can't believe this is happening to me. I've *never* been turned down for sex before—especially not kinky sex—and I'm utterly bewildered by his rejection.

Going straight upstairs, I sit on the edge of my bed and stare in disbelief at the reflection of my flushed face in the dressing table mirror.

I'm in shock. Total and utter shock.

He's somehow managed to take away the one thing I thought I had absolute power over in my life.

And he's probably laughing at me right now whilst chucking my favourite toys in the bin.

Taking a couple of deep breaths, I begin to put myself back together.

I'm not going to let this break me. No fucking way.

Way worse things have happened to me than being rejected by a man I barely even know, and I'm still here—living my life, fighting for my future.

I ball my hands into fists, feeling my nails bite into my palms, and take some more steadying breaths, aware of the blood starting to rush through my veins again.

Nothing could ever compare to the horror of losing my mother in the shockingly pointless and life-changing way she was taken from me.

Or to the heart-rending guilt I carry with me every day because of it.

So I can damn well handle something as inconsequential as a knock-back from a man who means absolutely nothing to me.

My nails bite deeper.

Yeah, I'll be okay. I know I will. I'm well-practised in burying my feelings and getting on with my life. No one gets past the composed indifference I've so successfully shielded myself with over the years.

So if Benedict Chivers thinks he's broken me he's got another think coming.

On Monday, after a weekend during which I've barely slept because the scene in Benedict's kitchen seems to have got stuck in my mind, playing over and over again like a broken record, I'm making my way to my desk after lunch when Rosie comes dashing over, looking as if she's about to throw up.

'Oh, God, Maya, I've made a real mess of Ben's

diary. A prospective client's here in Reception to meet with him, but apparently he's still out at a meeting with his lawyer and he's not answering his phone.' Her hands are trembling and her breathing is erratic.

'Whoa—calm down. I'm sure it's nothing to get too panicked about,' I soothe.

She shakes her head as if she doesn't agree. 'This will be the third thing I've got wrong in as many weeks. He's already warned me I'm on dangerous ground if I don't pull my socks up. He's going to fire me when he finds out,' she whispers, her voice breaking.

Instinctively I pull her into a hug, feeling her slight frame shaking against my chest as she begins to cry. 'It'll be okay, Rosie,' I assure her, alarmed by the terror I see in my friend's eyes. Surely Benedict won't fire her over something like this?

I think back to the cold-hearted way he's dealt with me so far.

Then again, maybe he will.

No. I'm not letting it happen. Not to someone who's shown me so much kindness. Loyalty and friendship are the things I value most in this world.

'Nobody's getting fired today,' I say, drawing back to look her dead in the eyes. 'Look, why don't you go to the bathroom and take a few minutes to compose yourself? I'll handle this. What's the name of the client?'

'Hugo W-Wynn Jones. He's come over for a

s-site visit. He's interested in some t-tailor-made CRM software,' she says through her hiccoughing sobs.

'Okay. Fine. I'll give him the tour and keep him entertained until Benedict gets back.'

'Are you s-sure? What if Ben's angry with you for doing that w-without checking with him first? I think this guy's a really b-big deal,' she whispers, her eyes wide with anxiety.

'Don't worry about me. I can look after myself.'

I flash her a smile, which I hope comes across as blasé, even though my insides feel totally knotted.

She still looks a little uncertain, so I shrug and say, 'I'm a Darlington-Hume—what's the worst that can happen to me? I'll be quietly asked to leave and my father will arrange for me to go and make coffee for one of his other business cronies.'

I try not to think about how much this might set me back in my quest for respect from my father as I stare boldly back at her.

I'll just have to make sure I don't mess it up, that's all.

'Okay, if you're s-sure—'

'Totally sure. I'll be fine,' I say, with a confidence I have to drag up from my gut. 'Now, go and put yourself back together,' I say, putting my hands on her shoulders and giving her an encouraging push out of the cubicle.

I make sure Rosie is heading towards the ladies' bathroom before turning on my heel and striding towards Reception. Well, my father always says the only the reason I get away with so much of my shit is because I'm a master at charming people. So I'm going to use that skill for good today.

Like a motherfucking PA superhero.

I crack my knuckles.

Okay, Hugo Wynn Jones, prepare to be charmed.

Benedict

I walk back to my office after the meeting with my lawyer, aware of a strange hum of nerves in the pit of my stomach as I wonder what I'll find when I get there.

Will Maya have ignored my demand for only my new phone to be waiting for me on my desk and be ready for another round of *hold your nerve*?

Memories of her lying across my desk, her legs spread for me, makes me immediately hard, and I have to pull my suit jacket closed to hide the evidence of my arousal from one of my PAs, Laura, who for some reason is standing right outside my office door, as if she's waiting for me.

When she sees me she rushes over with a stressed look on her face.

'Ben, thank goodness you're back. Hugo Wynn Jones is here to see you about the CRM system.'

My pulse quickens. 'What? *Now?*'

Laura looks a little pale. 'Actually, he's been here for half an hour already. It wasn't me who got the date wrong, I swear,' she adds hurriedly. 'Rosie was looking after your diary when the meeting request came in and she put it in for the wrong day.'

Blood pumps hard in my temple as I think about how offended Hugo must be, having been made to wait for me. I mutter a sting of curses under my breath. I've already spent a hell of a lot of hours perfecting a proposal to try and win his business, and I'd hoped to impress him in person when he came in to meet me and take a look around the office.

'Where have you put him?' I ask, aware that my voice sounds terse. But I really don't have time for niceties right now. The longer I keep him waiting the more opportunity there is for this situation to get away from me.

'Maya's shown him around and introduced him to key members of the team, and she's just taken him into the meeting room,' Laura answers, her voice breathy with stress. 'I didn't know she was doing that until I saw her with him,' she adds, obviously trying to save her own arse.

I turn to frown at her, dismay sinking through me. 'Wait—did you say *Maya*'s looking after him?'

Jesus, who knows what she's saying to him right now?

The throb in my temple becomes painful. Surely she wouldn't badmouth me to Hugo.

Would she?

We didn't exactly part on good terms the last time

we saw each other, so it's quite possible she might be using this opportunity to get back at me.

Cold alarm sinks through me as I consider the terrible potential damage she might be causing.

I barge into the meeting room to find Hugo sitting in one of the large leather swivel chairs with a cup of coffee in his hand, laughing his head off at something Maya's just said.

'Hugo, I'm so sorry I'm late. Apparently we've had a diary miscommunication,' I say, trying to imbue my voice with calm control, even though I don't feel much of it right now.

When I glance at Maya she flashes me a bold but composed smile—which, despite the seriousness of the situation, makes something flip in my chest.

What the hell did she say to him to make him laugh like that? I wonder wildly.

'No problem at all,' Hugo says with a dismissive wave of his hand. 'Maya's been good enough to show me around. Great set-up you have here. Very impressive. And she's been keeping me entertained with tales of the office,' he adds, with a warm smile in her direction.

I'm surprised to feel a sting of jealousy at the atmosphere of camaraderie they seem to have built between them. I stare at them both for a couple of beats, trying to figure out whether she's been telling him negative stories about me, but when Hugo continues to smile in what seems to be genuine approval I tell myself to relax.

'Okay, great—well, if you're happy with what Maya's shown you perhaps we can talk about how you see the project moving forward?' I say, taking a seat on the opposite side of the table. 'Thank you, Maya,' I add, giving her a nod of gratitude mostly for Hugo's benefit—I'm reserving judgement as to whether I really am grateful for her help till after this meeting concludes and I'm confident she's not done any damage.

I wait until she's left the room before giving my full attention to the matter at hand: securing this business.

An hour and, to be perfectly frank, some highly skilled glad-handing later, Wynn Jones is on his way out of the building, after once again lavishing me with compliments about the business and with a firm assurance that he'll be back in touch soon with a signed contract.

The place is nearly deserted, because it's now the end of the day, and I head straight for my office to send a couple of emails that need attending to urgently.

As I walk towards my desk there's a knock on the door and Maya comes striding in.

'Don't fire Rosie,' she says, as soon as the door closes behind her.

She walks over to where I'm standing, her hands clenched at her sides. To my surprise, the ever-present mischievous twinkle in her eyes is noticeably absent.

'Why not?' I ask, sitting back on the edge of my desk, intrigued by her unusual switch to sincerity.

'Because it was a total accident; it could have happened to any of us,' she says fiercely.

I blink, surprised by her vehemence. 'Why do *you* care what happens to her?'

She folds her arms and her stance becomes more aggressive, as if she's keying up for a fight with me.

'Because I like her. She's the only person here who's actually been nice to me since I started—she hasn't judged me or pigeonholed me like everyone else.'

She tilts her head pointedly and raises an eyebrow, as if to suggest she includes me in that grouping.

There's an infinitesimal pause, during which she continues to stare at me with that same challenging expression, then she adds, 'And she's a smart, hardworking and loyal person who's an asset to your business. You'd be crazy to let her go.'

I don't know how it's possible, but my body is responding to *businesslike* Maya even more than to *flirty* Maya.

She's really fucking arresting when she's being serious.

Despite this added inconvenience, I look back at her steadily.

I have to say I'm surprised and a little bemused to see Maya Darlington-Hume standing up for a woman she barely knows—I really wasn't expecting that kind of altruistic behaviour from her. For all she knows she could be making real trouble for herself, with both me *and* her father, but she's standing her ground anyway.

And I like that.

'I'm not going to fire her.' The words leave my mouth before I've had time to properly consider what I'm saying. 'But she'll be given a written warning,' I add quickly.

She lets out a low sigh, as if she's been holding her breath, waiting for my decision, and then she clasps both hands together in an appreciative gesture.

'Thank you,' she says, sounding as if she's genuinely grateful.

Warmth pools in my chest—which also takes me by surprise. Is it because I feel as if I've just seen another side to her? A more genuine side? One she normally hides from me? Not that I should let that seduce me into letting down my guard. I get the feeling she's a master manipulator, and I'm hyper aware that she's been playing games with me from the moment we met.

'It's good to know that you're not quite the cold-hearted business-bastard I had you pegged as,' she says, flashing me a teasing grin now.

'Yes, well, perhaps you should be a little more concerned about your own behaviour if you're going to convince people you're actually serious about running a business,' I bite back, more aggressively than I mean to.

Her comment has made me uncomfortable. Do I really come across like that? I know I can be stern with my staff when I want something done well, but I'd hoped they saw me as being a firm but fair boss.

Taking a defensive step backwards, she loosens her stance and her body language becomes suddenly indolent—like she actually doesn't give a shit *what* I think. It's as if she's realised she mustn't show me her real feelings in case I use them against her. It reminds me of the way she acted towards her father when we were in his sitting room together the day we met. Despite my lingering annoyance about her comment, I can't help but feel for her. It must be pretty taxing having Maxim for a father, after all.

'Actually, I think you'll find Mr Wynn Jones was very impressed with my behaviour today,' she retorts, before I can say something to soften my response. 'He particularly liked my jokes.'

Her meaningful smirk makes me tense.

'What did you say to him just before I walked in?' I ask carefully. It's been bugging me ever since I saw the two of them turn to look at me with broad grins across their faces.

She takes a couple of sauntering steps back towards me, bringing her sweet floral scent with her. I try not to breathe it in—my body is already responding alarmingly to the shortening of the space between us.

'Don't worry, I didn't say anything bad about you, *boss*. I know where my loyalties lie.'

'You mean you're afraid I'll badmouth you to your father if you do anything to piss me off,' I say, immediately kicking myself internally for my crassness. Her proximity is *really* messing with my composure.

She doesn't recoil, though; instead she takes another step closer to me, so we're only a couple of feet apart now. So close I could reach out and touch her if I wanted to.

The air throbs between us.

'I'm only playing my father's game so I can finally be independent from him,' she says with a hard kind of resolve in her expression. 'Once I've done my time at his company—and yours—I'm taking full control of my life and my money. Despite what everyone thinks, I'm serious about making a success of my business.'

Interesting. So I'm not the only one needing to keep Maxim sweet to get what I want. It seems we have something in common. I have to admit I'm surprised to find she's actually serious about setting up her own company. I'd assumed it was just a ruse to placate her father and keep her funds flowing.

'Well, I applaud you,' I say sincerely. I suspect she'll have the tenacity and smarts to achieve what she wants too. 'And, yes, you did do a good job, showing Wynn Jones around,' I go on, before she has time to respond to my switch in attitude. 'He was impressed with how knowledgeable you are about the business. It seems you've picked up a lot in the short space of time you've been working here.'

'I'm sure you find it hard to believe, but I *am* capable of more than just making coffee.'

Her smile is wry, but I sense indignation behind it—which makes my stomach lurch. Does she really believe I think so poorly of her? But then, to be fair, I've never let her know I've noticed how hard she's been working.

'I don't find that difficult to believe at all,' I say calmly. 'You strike me as a very shrewd and enterprising woman, and I appreciate your ability to think quickly and keep a cool head. You saved the day—and the deal.'

She's looking at me now as if I've just grown another nose.

'Oh, okay…well, good. I'm glad to have helped.' The antagonism in her stance finally slips away and her arms relax by her sides.

'You really did.'

I push myself to my feet, so now we're standing only inches apart. A hazy kind of look steals over her eyes as I stare into them and her lips part as she draws in a quivering breath.

I can't help but glance down at her mouth, wondering how it would feel under mine, how it would open for me, how sweet she would taste.

The air seems to hum between us with a dangerous sort of tension. The sort I really shouldn't be allowing myself to feel.

I know that getting closer to her right now would be entirely inappropriate. And potentially incredibly dangerous. I know it, but I don't seem to be able to get the idea of it out of my head.

'Perhaps I deserve some kind of reward for saving the day?' she murmurs, flashing me a provocative smile.

My cock hardens as I think about how I'd *like* to reward her: with a replay of the first time I summoned her into my office. But I quash the idea quickly. I mustn't give in to this.

'I guess so,' I say gruffly. 'I'll be sure to let your father know what an asset you've been to the business today.'

I think I see disappointment flash across her face, but only for a second before she quickly reins it in and gives me a cool, gratified nod.

'Well, if that's everything you need from me today, Mr Chivers, I'm going to head off home.'

Her mouth widens into a bright, seductive smile, then she swivels on the spot and strides away from me on those beautiful long legs of hers, her head high, her shoulders back. Ever the picture of cool confidence.

Pausing at the door, she raises her hand to give a backwards wave with her fingers.

She knows I'm still watching her.

'See you tomorrow,' she calls over her shoulder, and then disappears out of my office, leaving the air humming with promise in her wake.

Slumping back against the desk, I try to reconcile all the thoughts rushing through my mind.

Maya Darlington-Hume is not the person I thought she was.

I realise now that everything I assumed I knew about her has come from the stories I've read about her in the press, which all paint her as being a vacuous, self-centred party girl. But from what I've seen first-hand today, that doesn't seem to be true at all.

Unease ripples through me.

Thinking about it now, every piece of work she's done for me so far has been carried out with accuracy and a flair I wasn't expecting. I tried to put it down to the other PAs helping her, but I know, deep down, that's it's all her. I just didn't want to accept it before. After her last couple of stunts I wanted her to be less than she obviously is: to make it easier to deny myself and not have to accept how much I want her.

I stand up and start to pace the floor, my whole body vibrating with a need I can't deny any more.

Fuck it.

There's clearly no point in trying to ignore my attraction to her. This thing between us is too strong to resist. We're both adults—we know the score. No one's going to get hurt. It'll only be a short-term thing anyway. Just a bit of fun to pass the time. Our sexy little secret.

I turn and head for the door.

Maya

I stride towards the lifts feeling thoroughly confused.

Something changed between us in that office—after he told me I'd done a good job with Hugo and complimented me on the work I've been doing for him. It was as if he saw me as a real person for the very first time, and I felt so elated by his praise I wanted to kiss him for it.

I didn't, though, because the last thing I need right now is him rejecting me again.

What I want is for him to come to *me*—to not be able to resist me. Then we'll be on an even footing.

The office is deserted. The rest of the staff always seem to leave on the dot of six, so it's quiet as I stroll through Reception.

I'm just about to press the button for the lift when I hear heavy footsteps coming towards me across the marble floor.

I know it's him.

I just know it.

I can't explain how, but every molecule in my body reacts—as if there's some weird cosmic connection between us.

I turn to face him, preparing to make a smart quip about him needing me to stay behind to 'polish his paperweight'. But before I can utter a word he strides straight up to me, his dark eyes full of an intent that makes my stomach swoop with excitement, and his mouth crashes down onto mine.

I take a couple of stumbling steps backwards and feel my back meeting the wall behind me.

Without a pause his lips brutally force mine open, so he can slide his tongue into my mouth. It's as if he's punishing me for something—perhaps for turning him on and snapping his control when he's been working so hard to resist this dangerous connection between us.

But, oh, it feels so fucking good.

God, the taste of him: it's like power and testosterone and sex mixed into a heady, addictive elixir.

It's everything I imagined—and so much more—and I revel in the darkly sensual essence of him as it twists through my senses.

His kisses are so demanding I have no choice but to sink into them, allowing him to fully take the lead, and as his mouth moves roughly over mine and his tongue slides into me I can't help but let out a moan of satisfaction.

The noise I make causes him to still, and I cry out in frustration as he pulls away from me, his dark eyes flashing with barely controlled desire.

'Don't stop now,' I bite out, the frantic need for this to reach completion throbbing through my body like an insistent heartbeat.

Staring into my eyes, he lets his fingers find the hem of my skirt and roughly pushes it up my thighs. Then he cups my pussy, grinding the heel of his hand against me. I drag in a breath at the shocking, intimate touch, and curse the flimsy material of my

knickers that prevents his fingertips from dipping
inside me.

He leans towards me, his breath hot on my neck.
'You think you should have a reward, do you?' he
mutters into my ear.

'Yes. I want one. I *deserve* one,' I hiss back. The
delicious sensations of his touch are tipping me into
a near frantic state of longing.

'I don't know if you do...' he teases in a low
growl, and I almost punch him in frustration.

'Please, please!' I moan as he starts to make firm
circling motions with his hand. It feels amazing, but
I need more. Much more.

He puts his hand on my jaw and turns my face
towards him, so I'm forced to look him in the eye
as he continues the maddening rhythm of his hand
against me. It's so intimate, so immediate, that I feel
myself start to shake with anticipation.

We both freeze as the sound of footsteps rings
out in the stairwell next to where he has me pressed
against the wall.

I swear in frustration as he slides his hand away
from my needy body. He's not going to stop this now,
is he? Please, God, *no*.

But it seems my fear is unwarranted, because
he doesn't move away. Instead he slides his hands
under my thighs and lifts me up, holding me against
his powerful body and carrying me into a meeting
room. After kicking the door shut he presses me

back against the wall while he turns the lock, his eyes never leaving mine.

And it's on, baby.

It's fucking *on*.

Benedict

I put my finger to my lips. If we're going to do this we'll have to be quiet about it.

She nods her understanding.

I kiss her again, hard, loving the feeling of her soft, pliant mouth under mine.

Her breath is coming fast and thickly, and as I slide my hands up her thighs and twist my fingers into the soaked material of her knickers I hear it hitch in her throat. She lowers her legs from where she has them wrapped around my waist, so I can tug the flimsy scrap of silk down her thighs, and she steps out of them as they fall to the floor at our feet.

'Hmm, now…how should I reward you?' I murmur, feeling her body tremble against me. I pull back to scan her face and the arousal I see in her eyes makes my cock throb against the confines of my trousers.

'You could fuck me. Right now,' she whispers against my lips, with that trademark audacity of hers.

And I find I like that suggestion. A lot.

Shoving my hand into my pocket, I fish out the condom I stashed in my wallet this morning on a whim. Not because I was expecting anything to happen between us today—in fact as I travelled in I was pretty certain I wouldn't let anything happen between us ever again. But I'm mightily glad I put it there now.

As soon as she sees what I'm holding between my fingers she lets out a hiss of triumph through her teeth and immediately goes to undo my belt.

'No need to rush,' I mutter, raising a chastising eyebrow at her eagerness. But she ignores me, tugging the button of my trousers open and sliding down my fly.

'Yes, there is,' she grinds out. 'I've been thinking about this for weeks, and I think I'm going to explode if you don't stick your cock in me right fucking *now*.'

I can't help but laugh, but I'm immediately silenced as she slides her hand into my boxers and takes a firm hold of my dick. Desire lances me, and I have to take a deep breath to centre myself.

She's not the only one who's about ready to explode with sexual frustration. Despite telling myself over and over that I have to stay away from her, my body is keen to remind me just what I've been holding out on. I need to give in to this mad urge to be inside her, to fuck her swiftly and greedily, until I've finally satisfied the hunger that's been growing in me ever since I laid eyes on her in that bathtub.

But I'm also intensely aware that I need to keep my wits about me. This could all go horribly wrong if I'm not careful.

Tearing open the packet, I remove the condom with shaking fingers. Her hand is moving swiftly up and down my cock now, and I have to forcibly knock it away so I can roll the condom on.

Once it's in place I slide one hand under her thigh and lift her leg, encouraging her to lock it around my waist, then I take a moment to tease her, swiping the head of my cock back and forth over her swollen clit, playing between her folds as I stare into her eyes. I can feel how engorged she is and it's clear she's *very* ready for me.

This observation is proved right when she lets out a quiet moan of frustration and whispers, 'Please, please, *please*! Just fucking *do* it!'

Her eyes are wild with need as I push inside her, taking it slowly at first, moving inch by pleasurable inch, and the sensation of her clenching around my cock nearly blows my mind.

I'm pleased to see her jaws clamp together, as if she's holding back her groan. She's obeying my command not to make any noise, and this realisation sends a shot of fiery adrenaline straight down my spine.

I'm in charge here and she's letting me know it. She's mine to control, this feisty, fascinating woman. All mine. The knowledge of this is so powerful I actually have to think about something bland and unsexy to stop myself from coming right then.

Once I'm sure she's comfortably stretched to take me, I throw off my leisureliness and begin to pound into her hard, feeling her grasp my arms as my thrusts push her up the wall.

Her breath pants out of her and her grip tightens as I change position, so that I'm hitting her sweet spot each time I thrust. I can tell she's close to orgasm because she starts to bite her lip, and her breathing quietens as if she's concentrating hard on not allowing herself to cry out, and a few strokes later she comes hard around my cock, burying her mouth against my shoulder to stifle her moans.

I waste no more time holding back and finally let myself go, slamming into her hard and feeling the waves of my own orgasm overtake me, dragging me under into a world of mindless sensation.

Maya

Afterwards, he watches me with hooded eyes as I smooth my skirt back down my legs, then attempt to flatten my rumpled hair.

There's a weird sort of tautness in the air between us now—that awkward transition between the end of sex and leaving. The playfulness of our previous encounters isn't there any more. Things feel suddenly more serious between us—perhaps because we now know how amazing fucking each other can be.

There's no point denying it any more: we're good together.

Despite loving every second of what we just did, I realise I'm strangely edgy. I've never felt like this after sex before. It's always been about the pure pleasure of the climax, but this time it's different. I feel more emotionally connected to him, somehow. I guess because I actually like him.

I *really* like him.

'I should go,' I say, not wanting to think too hard about this disturbing revelation.

He just nods and unlocks the door, peering out to check the coast is clear before making a gesture for me to exit the room.

On shaky legs I walk to the lift and press the 'down' button, feeling his dominating presence at my back.

The lift arrives immediately and I step inside, then turn around to flash him a nonchalant grin as the doors begin to close between us.

'Who knew you could be so wild, Mr Chivers?' I say. Though of course I'd known he was capable of it all along. That's why I'd wanted to break him so much. To finally be allowed to experience it.

He slams his hand against the doors, halting their progress. 'Don't call me Mr Chivers,' he bites out with a frown. 'Not now.'

'So what do you *want* me to call you then? Sir?' I tease.

'Ben. Just call me Ben.'

'So we're finally on first-name terms, after sexual encounter number four.'

To my dismay I'm awarded another frown for that.

'Look, I'm sorry,' he says, rubbing a hand over

his jaw, 'but I don't feel comfortable with the boss-employee dynamic after what we've just done.'

His expression is so serious my stomach does a strange nervous roll. Surely he's not going to call a halt to this *now*? Not when I know how good it can be with him? I'll go mad.

I flap a hand at him. 'Look, it's okay. I wanted this. I pretty much begged you for it.' The grin I shoot him is rueful. 'And, anyway, you're not really my boss. You don't pay me a wage and I can walk away any time I like,' I point out.

There's a small weighted pause before he nods, then says, 'Are you okay with this being a casual, discreet fling? Just till your time here is up? I'm not in the market for a relationship at the moment.'

Is *that* what he's worried about? That I'll boil his bunny if he refuses to be my boyfriend?

'Absolutely fine by me. I'm not exactly the serious relationship type myself,' I say with a reassuring smile—though for some reason I'm actually feeling a bit wobbly about agreeing to a definite end date to this. Or am I spun because he's so keen to keep me a secret?

I force myself to shake off my concern. If there's no likelihood of it lasting past my time here why should I care anyway?

I see relief cross his face—which only increases my insecurity.

'Good,' he says.

'Well, if that's everything, I'll see you tomorrow,

Ben,' I say, dredging up a grin and nodding pointedly towards where his hand is still holding the lift doors open.

I have the strongest urge to be on my own now—to clear my head and get my racing heartbeat under control.

'Looking forward to it, Maya,' he replies smoothly, and I'm relieved to finally see a twinkle of warmth in his dark eyes as he releases his grip on the doors and they slide closed between us.

CHAPTER FIVE

Benedict

THE NEXT MORNING I have to drag myself out of bed after a night of hyper intense, gratuitously explicit sex dreams involving Maya that have left me exhausted.

I hoped that by giving in to the need that had been stubbornly coursing through me for the past couple of weeks I'd finally get her out of my head and be able to think about something else for a change.

How wrong I was.

I go through my morning routine, only deviating from it by having a wank in the shower to get my irrepressible hard-on to finally disappear. I don't seem to be able to get the alluring scent of her out of my nostrils and it's making me crazy.

I stride into my office with the blood pulsing hot through my veins in anticipation of seeing her again.

Despite it only being hours, it feels as though days have passed since we were alone together in the boardroom. The memory of what we did in there comes back to smack me hard in the chest and I sit down heavily in my office chair as my whole body tightens with an acute desire to do it all over again.

Right fucking now.

Jesus. I'm really going to have to watch myself. If her father gets wind of what's happening between us...

As if she's sensed that I've been thinking about her there's a confident knock on the door and Maya strides in, her head held high and her slender hips swaying provocatively as she walks towards where I'm sitting.

She's wearing the barely decent skirt suit again.

'Is there anything I can I do for you this morning, *Ben*?' she asks me in that gorgeous smoky voice of hers.

I just look at her steadily as all the things I'd like her to do for me right now spin through my mind. But I know I shouldn't be entertaining them—not with the rest of my staff right outside the door.

Not that it stopped me before, after the flashing incident.

And it is my company after all.

I'm the *boss*.

Something seems to break inside me as I think this, and a strange kind of lightness ripples through my body.

I hear myself say, 'Lock the door, then come over here.'

She doesn't hesitate. Turning on the spot, she strides back to the door and flips the lock, then saunters over to where I'm now standing with my arms folded, her eyes shining with excitement and her full mouth pulled into an eager grin.

'Have I done something wrong?' she asks, and from the tone of her voice I can tell she's hoping I'll say yes. It seems she's just as keen as me to get right back to where we left off last night.

'I don't know, Maya. Have you?' I demand, more than happy to play along.

'I do seem to have forgotten to put on my underwear again,' she says with a pseudo remorseful look on her face. 'Look.'

And she slides her skirt up her slim, shapely legs to show me.

'So I see,' I reply with a suddenly dry mouth. 'Well, I'm deeply disappointed in you.' I take a couple of steps towards her, close enough that I can feel the heat radiating from her body. 'You know I'm going to have to discipline you for that?' I murmur.

She nods, sitting back on the desk and spreading her legs for me. 'I was hoping you were going to say that.'

Oh, man, there's no way this is stopping now.

Not a hope in hell.

Later that day I call one of my account managers in to the office and ask her to let Maya shadow her for a couple of days, with a view to her assisting with some of the projects and clients she manages. After seeing how well Maya handled the situation with Hugo I'm determined to give her as much useful experience here at Ergo-i as possible.

She deserves it after using her initiative to help save that business opportunity.

Not that it's an entirely altruistic move on my part; I'm pretty damn sure she'll do a great job of project management—she's most definitely a people person, and very organised—and she'll be much more useful in that role than in aiding the other PAs who, in truth, already have all the bases covered.

Unfortunately, there aren't many other opportunities for us to be alone during the rest of the week, because we're busy getting ready for an important new product launch, and I find myself fielding constant questions from my marketing and PR team during the day, then ending up staying late each night with the programmers. But I still manage to think of a couple of excuses to get Maya to come into my office.

One time it's to bring in a paper copy of a contract, which I go over in detail, taking great pleasure in making her wait impatiently for me to sign it before getting up from behind my desk and pushing her into my chair, securing her promise not to make any noise before making her come with my mouth.

Afterwards she gleefully returns the favour by getting to her knees, dragging open my fly and sucking my rock-hard cock eagerly into her mouth.

She was right. I totally appreciate a woman who knows exactly how to make a man's eyes roll back in his head.

It's after seven o'clock on Friday when I come up for air after a ridiculously busy day, so I'm surprised to find Maya still sitting at her desk in her cubicle, with books and papers spread out in front of her. There are lots of colourful hand-drawn designs in an open notebook to the left of her laptop, and a complicated-looking page of graphs open on the screen.

'What are you working on?' I ask as I walk up behind her to look more closely at what she's doing.

She jumps in surprise, then turns to flash me a sheepish smile, as if I've caught her doing something illicit. 'You're still here?' she asks breathily, hurriedly closing her laptop and flipping her notebook closed.

'Yeah, I'll be working late again tonight and all weekend. The team need more time to test the software before we release it on Monday morning and I want to be around to sign it off,' I say, moving round to prop one elbow on the wall of her cubicle. 'Is that something for Ergo-i?' I press, though I know it can't be.

She looks at me for a second without speaking, as if she's weighing up whether she wants to talk to me about it or not. Her enthusiasm for the project obviously wins through, though, because she says, 'No, it's for my jewellery business.'

'Can I see?' I ask, nodding at the notebook, intrigued to see what she's planning to do.

After a second's pause she nods and hands it over.

I flip it open to a page of hand-drawn designs. One is for an intricately woven silver necklace. It looks like a web and has a red gemstone set into it, which I suddenly realise is the body of a spider, with delicate silvery legs. The other is of what I guess is an engagement ring, which has very fine twisted silver strands making up the body of it and tiny shapes like hands holding the diamond in the middle. They're unusual, but strikingly beautiful pieces.

'These are amazing,' I say, genuinely impressed.

The pleasure I see in her smile—and is that relief?—makes my chest contract.

'Thanks. I've been working on the designs for weeks now, and I'm nearly ready to start making them as sample pieces.'

'You're going to make the jewellery yourself?' I ask, surprised again.

'Sure am. To begin with, at least. I've already completed a couple of night classes in silverwork and gem setting, and I've got another coming up soon for some more off-the-wall techniques.'

'I can see these selling really well,' I say, meaning it.

'I hope so. I think there's a market for them. I'm still slogging away on my business plan at the moment, though. I want to make sure it's in as good a shape as possible before showing it to my father. It's going to have to be watertight if it's going to satisfy him it has the potential to make money so he'll finally let me have access to my trust fund. Then I can invest in the materials I need and get it underway.'

I'm surprised by her earnestness, though I don't know why I should be. She's shown a lot of dedication to the work she's taken on at my company recently, and she's clearly a smart and very driven woman.

'Well, knowing how determined you are to get what you want, I expect you'll be very successful at whatever you put your mind to,' I say with a grin.

'God, I hope so,' she says, her expression turning a little beleaguered. 'I don't exactly have a great track record.' She leans back and crosses her arms, flashing me an awkward smile. 'I wasn't very focussed at school. My social life was more important to me than my education in my teens, and I kind of lost the plot and ended up flunking all my exams, so it's been quite a steep learning curve.' She shrugs, her gaze not quite meeting mine. 'It's going to be a challenge, breaking into such a competitive market, but I'm going to give it my best shot.'

'You'll do it if you keep working hard and refuse to give up. That's what worked for me,' I say.

She smiles at me now, the expression in her eyes more animated than I've ever seen it, and my stomach does a slow dive at the resolve I see there.

'Yeah, well, I'll be spending most of my evenings

and weekends on it for the foreseeable future—when I'm not out living up to my wild child reputation, that is,' she adds, tipping me a roguish wink.

Blood rushes to my head and the crazy thought that *I* want to be the only one to give her pleasure pops unwittingly into my head.

But I know I'm being an idiot. I'm probably only reacting like that because I'm knackered after such an intense week. Having to keep my sexual urges in check and my mind off her and on the job has been exhausting.

'Want me to take a look at your business plan?' I ask, in an attempt to refocus my thoughts—although I genuinely like the idea of being able to use my experience to help her if I can.

'Really? Would you do that?' she asks, sounding surprised, but gratified.

'Sure. I'd be happy to once we've got this product launched.'

'Okay. I'll email it to you then.'

'Do that,' I say with a nod. 'And I'll get back to you with some thoughts as soon as I can'.

'Thanks, Ben, that would be really great.' She quirks an eyebrow. 'You can be totally honest with me about it, you know. I can take it.'

'I know.' And I feel as if I do—as if I'm beginning to *get* her.

'Ben?'

To my annoyance, my head developer has come

over to interrupt us. He's shuffling from foot to foot, looking thoroughly agitated.

'We need you. There's a problem with some of the code,' he says tetchily.

'I'll be there in a minute,' I tell him.

He gives me a tight smile and bustles off.

'I'd better go,' I say to her, backing away reluctantly. I'm frustrated about having to cut our conversation short, just when I'm starting to get to know the real Maya. 'See you on Monday.'

'Yeah, have a good weekend.'

'What weekend?' I say with a wry smile, knowing I'll be working all the hours here in the office till the launch on Monday.

She grimaces in sympathy. 'Well, we'll just have to find a fun way to celebrate once the product's gone live,' she says, tipping me another saucy wink.

I groan low in my throat, wishing I had a time machine so I could skip forward to Monday, when I'll be stripping off her clothes. Grabbing that reward firmly in both hands, then picking up this conversation where we left off.

The temptation to suggest we slip off to my office right now is so strong I can actually taste the tang of need in my mouth. But I'm not going to give in to it.

Business has to come first. I've not worked this hard for this long to let my standards slip now.

'Looking forward to it already,' I say, frustration making my voice rough as I turn and force myself to walk away from her.

* * *

The weekend drags like nothing I've ever experienced before.

It's not uncommon for me to work through both Saturday and Sunday. I did it for years whilst building up my business to the position it's in today—pulling all-nighters to get proposals written and completing projects to deadline—so it's strange to actually feel I'm missing out on something by being in the office.

Not that I actually *am* missing out on anything. I've not made any plans to see friends this weekend, and this fling with Maya has been entirely confined to office hours, but I still have the strangest craving to be anywhere but here right now. It's almost as if I need something other than work to fully engage me for once.

So on Monday morning, as soon as the software's gone live, I go straight to find Maya and scratch that itch.

'I guess congratulations are in order,' she says with a knowing smirk as I stride towards her desk.

'They are,' I say with a firm nod. 'In fact I'm just off to get a celebratory brunch. Fancy *coming*, Maya?' I ask, giving her a meaningful look.

'I absolutely do, Ben,' she says with a grin, getting up and hurriedly pulling on her suit jacket.

I've booked a room in a hotel a couple of streets away, because the thought of inviting her to my house made me uneasy. It felt too intimate, somehow, too personal—and the last thing I need right now is for my private space to be invaded by something I don't want to attach any meaning to.

We're barely through the door of the hotel suite before we're tearing each other's clothes off and kissing as if we've not seen each other for weeks. It's as incredible as I've been imagining it will be all weekend. The woman knows how to push all my buttons, both with her words and her actions, and I lose myself in her, pressing her hard into the bed as I thrust inside her, feeling her nails bite into my back and welcoming the pain along with the pleasure.

I take my time, taking her to the brink of orgasm then pulling back, teasing and testing, changing position to hit new highs of pleasure until we're both reeling with the need to come. Only then do I let myself go and give in to the raging need I've been bottling up for the last couple of days.

'So, have you always had a penchant for pushing your sexual boundaries?' I ask with a smile as we lie in a sweaty, sticky heap the next lunchtime, after a fun and filthy session in which the fruit platter she ordered from room service had taken a starring role.

'Well, I've always loved sex, and I'm a very *creative* person, so I guess it was inevitable,' she replies, rolling on top of me, her naked body hot and slick against mine.

Her grin is infectious.

'How about you?' she asks, sliding down my body so she can rest her head on my chest.

I stiffen, uncomfortable about revealing too many personal details to her. While I don't think she'd go talking to all and sundry about my private life, I do feel an innate instinct to protect myself. It's always been like that for me, after growing up in such an unstable environment.

'I've had my fair share of sexual experiences,' I say, hoping that will suffice.

She raises her head and gives me a look of impatience. 'Go on—tell me more. You can't tease me with that, then leave me hanging. It's pure cruelty.'

I sigh, realising she's not going to let me wriggle out of this conversation. 'I was a bit of a late bloomer, because I didn't have a lot of time for socialising when I was in my teens or early twenties. I had to work all the time to cover both the rent and my college fees, so there wasn't a lot of time or opportunity to explore my sexual fetishes.'

'That's too bad,' she says, idly running her fingertip around my nipple. 'So what kind of job did you have? Please say pool boy or tennis coach and bring all my teenage fantasies to life.'

'I was a caretaker at Tinderly,' I say, distracted by the way the merest touch from her can make my dick spring fully to attention, even though we've only just had sex.

'I bet those pubescent girls *loved* you,' she teases.

'Yeah. A little too much sometimes. And, no, before you ask, I never succumbed. I like to think I have more pride and better taste than to take up with one of those types of girls.'

'So, what? You're slumming it here with me?' she says glibly, though I catch a note of challenge in her voice.

'Hardly,' I reply, keeping my tone level and flippant, though I feel a sting of shame about how I originally lumped her in with my opinion about those girls.

'I'm guessing you've had plenty of opportunities to get down and dirty with an array of willing women since then, though, being such a hotshot business tycoon.' She looks up and waggles her eyebrows suggestively.

I shrug. 'I've had a few sexual relationships over the years, but nothing long-term. I've been too busy with the business to give my personal life the kind of attention it needs to conduct a serious relationship.'

'So just kinky flings, then?' she prompts with a grin.

I let out a snort. 'No. You're my first kinky fling.'

'Really?' she says, her surprise evident.

'Yeah,' I admit. 'My sex life's been pretty straight up till now. I like to be in charge—as I'm sure you've noticed—but that's about the extent of it.'

'Oh, goody—that leaves lots more for us to explore, then,' she murmurs, her eyes shining with excitement.

I smile back, but I'm actually a little uncomfort-

able with the direction this conversation is heading—
it implies that this thing between us could become
more serious than we agreed. But I don't want to
wreck the mood, so instead I roll over, flipping her
onto her back and kissing her hard.

When we come up for air she smiles at me, her
eyes hazy with desire.

'Have you ever had a serious relationship?' I ask,
feeling an urge to know more about her, to even
things up.

She pauses for a few moments, and wrinkles her
nose as if seriously considering my question. 'Yeah,
one—in my teens. I thought I was in love with the
first guy I ever slept with.'

'Oh…?' I prompt, noting a strange sinking feeling in my gut, but not able to pinpoint exactly what's
bothering me about that statement.

'It didn't last long, though. My father found out
and basically ruined him, so he had to leave the
country and get a job in America.'

'Jesus!' I say, shocked by the thought of Maxim
doing something so extreme to someone who must
have been just a kid. It makes me wonder what he'd
do to me if he found out what we were doing right
now under his nose.

'Yeah, well, my father's protective like that. He
doesn't take well to his friends fucking his daughters.'

I gape at her, feeling more rattled by the second.
'His *friends*?'

'Yeah… Jack used to come over to our house all the time, to hang out with my father. He was really kind to me, and I guess I fell for him because he was the only person who was nice to me at that point in my life.' There's a short pause while she stares up at the ceiling, then she adds, 'I was a bit of a bratty teenager.'

'Was he the same age as your father?' I feel sickened by the thought of the guy taking advantage of a young, vulnerable Maya.

'Nah. He was in his mid-twenties. He was a real financial whizz, and my father basically headhunted him from one of his rivals and took him under his wing. I think he thought he'd be his protégé, since we Darlington-Hume offspring had all failed him by turning out to be female.'

Her focus becomes distant, as if her thoughts are being sucked into the past.

'I didn't sleep with him until I was seventeen, though. Well, I basically seduced him. He wasn't that keen to do anything behind my father's back—and for good reason, as it it turns out. He never contacted me again once he'd left the country. I think he's doing well in the States, though. I hear he's running his own multi-million-dollar business over there, so I guess I wasn't all bad for him. I like to think I actually gave him that opportunity.'

She lets out a low chuckle, but it doesn't have any real joy in it.

My heart goes out to her as I consider how difficult it must be for her to conduct relationships with the threat of an overbearing father like Maxim looking over her shoulder all the time. The guys she dates must be really reluctant to get too close to her.

It's a good job she's so spirited, otherwise she'd probably never have any fun at all.

The heavy feeling of foreboding this thought conjures in me makes my gut tense, so I try to distance myself from the story she's just told me, reassuring myself this thing between us isn't the same situation at all. Even so, it brings home to me once again the fact that I really shouldn't be risking the future of my business for a fling. Even with someone as captivating as Maya.

As if she's thinking the same thing, she suddenly says, 'Hey, did you hear? My father's going to be back in England next week.'

I turn to look at her, my stomach doing a strange, uncomfortable roll.

We both agreed that this would only last until she stopped working for me, and I wonder whether she's now hoping he'll not want her back right away.

Am I too?

But instead of addressing this troubling question I say, 'Yeah, I know. He's invited me to his birthday party next Wednesday.'

'Are you going to go?' she asks, sounding suspiciously as if she's pretending she doesn't care one way or the other.

'I thought I'd make an appearance, yes. He's keen

for me to attend, and it'll be a good networking opportunity.'

The mention of her father has killed the mood, so I sit up and swing my legs off the bed, feeling jumpy and agitated.

'We should probably get back before we're missed,' I say, getting up and making for the shower.

'Yeah, we wouldn't want to be the subject of salacious office gossip,' she teases, but I sense a sting of hurt in her words.

I turn back to see that she's now sitting with her knees pulled in towards her chest and her arms wrapped tightly around them.

'Look, it's nothing personal, keeping this quiet,' I say gruffly. 'I just have a thing about keeping my sex life away from the office.'

She just shrugs. 'Well, don't worry—nobody will hear a thing about it from me.'

A strange sort of lightness lifts through me as I see genuine honesty in her face. Something inside me warms my chest—a deep sense of relief, perhaps—and I realise it's because I believe she really means it. We're in this together.

'You can trust me,' she says, as if wanting to absolutely confirm it for me.

'I know I can,' I say, returning to sit on the edge of the bed. 'I hope you feel you can trust me too.'

I raise my hand to her face, smoothing the pad of my thumb over her cheek, and I'm gratified to feel her lean into my touch.

'I do,' she says, moving forward to kiss me lightly on the lips. 'Your overactive sense of decency is too bloody strong for you to deliberately do anything to hurt me anyway.'

I give her a tight smile, thinking again about where this might all lead, and wondering whether we should call a halt to it now, before things get too messy. But looking into those astute, captivating eyes of hers, I know for damn sure that that's not going to happen.

CHAPTER SIX

Maya

ON FRIDAY LUNCHTIME we lie entwined together in the hotel room that's become our regular haunt for the last few days. Ben decided he didn't want to risk us being seen together at the office and, while I have no problem having sex on his desk, I have to admit the super-king–size bed is a far more comfortable place to fuck.

To my surprise, the thing I've particularly come to like is lying together in bed afterwards and talking. It's not something I've really done before—usually I'm up and out before the condom's even off. But not with him. I want to stay. Which is beginning to make me nervous. I know from experience that good things don't last with me—I always manage to wreck them somehow—and it's going to be so much harder to finish this thing with him if I start getting emotionally attached. Which is why I've tried to keep the chat frivolous and upbeat till now.

'I have to get back soon. I have a lot of calls to make this afternoon,' Ben says as I run my fingers across his taut belly and then lower, to trace the delicious V-shape of his hips. The guy has an amazing body, considering how much time he spends behind a desk.

'No, don't go back yet,' I wheedle, unwilling to relinquish the feel of him under my hands and the sense of calm I have with his strong, powerful body close to mine.

'I have to,' he says with a wry smile. 'I'm the boss. I'm supposed to set a good example and actually do some work.'

'What turned you into such a goody-two-shoes workaholic?' I groan, annoyed that I won't be getting my second orgasm this lunchtime.

'Need,' he replies, sitting up and pulling away from my touch. 'I didn't start out with the same privileges in life you've had. I've had to work bloody hard to get to the position I'm in today.'

The hint of agitation in his tone sends prickles across my skin.

'Hey, I'm sorry. I didn't mean to offend you,' I say, my stomach turning over as I see the tension in his face.

'Yeah, well, it's a bit of a sore point,' he says gruffly.

I sit up and put a placating hand on his arm, deciding my determination not to get emotionally attached is pretty much null and void. It's happened anyway, despite my attempts to avoid it.

I guess I just like him too much.

'Tell me about it. I want to know more about what your life was like before I met you,' I say gently, suddenly realising that the last thing I want is for him to leave here feeling I don't give a shit about him. 'Please. Stay and talk to me.'

For a moment I think he's going to refuse, but then his frown softens and he sighs and drops his head back against the headboard, rubbing his hand over his face.

'It's not a particularly entertaining tale,' he says with a grimace.

'That's okay,' I say shrugging, fascinated to know what it is that drives him so hard.

He sighs and stares up at the ceiling. 'I grew up in a pretty poor household, because my father pissed away all our money on booze and gambling, and I spent all my spare time in my late teens working to earn enough money to try and get my mother and I the hell away from him. My mother couldn't work because she suffered with agoraphobia—probably brought on by the physical and mental abuse he dished out when he was drunk. Which was all the time.'

'Oh, Jesus, that's awful,' I say, my eyes wide with horror and my heart in my throat.

He lets out a low breath, as if he's trying to get his residual anger about it under control.

'When I was sixteen my father hit her so hard he broke her jaw. I was just getting back from work and I caught him doing it. I was bigger than him by that point, and I was so angry I kicked the shit out of him. He promised never to do it again, and at the time I thought he'd keep his word. But I found out later that my mother kept any beatings he dealt out after that a secret from me. She didn't want me to get involved again in case things went too far and one of us killed the other. She'd wanted to leave him for years but she was too scared, because he told her he'd kill both of us if she ever did.'

I put my hand gently onto his arm in a gesture of support and I'm alarmed by how tense he is.

'I felt so fucking impotent for so many years,' he bites out, 'which is why I work so hard now—so I never have to feel that powerless again.'

My heart aches for the scared, desperate little boy I imagine he used to be. There's no wonder he's so controlled in everything he does now if he had such an insecure, violent upbringing. It must have been horrendous to have to deal with all that from such a young age. Especially if he felt responsible for his mother's wellbeing.

This sentiment makes me go hot, then cold, as I think about my own mother and the awful way I treated her.

No. This is not the time to dwell on that. This is about Ben.

'So where's your father now?' I ask, attempting to get my racing pulse under control before he notices how shaky I've become.

'As far as I know he's still living in the house I

grew up in, getting shit-faced every day. To be honest, I couldn't give a toss where he is as long as he's nowhere near my mother.'

'And where is she?'

He sighs. 'Once I'd saved enough money I finally persuaded her to leave him and paid to rehouse her. I bought her a place in the Cotswolds a few years ago. She's happy living there on her own—or so she tells me.'

'Do you see much of her?' I ask. I realise I'd love to meet Ben's mother, to get to know more about his roots. Not that I'd ever suggest it. That's not the sort of thing you do when you're only having a fling with someone.

'Not as much as I should,' he says with a frown. 'I'm so busy with work I don't get many opportunities to visit her.'

He looks uncomfortable now, though, as if this is something he's been telling himself to assuage the guilt he feels about it. It makes me wonder whether he avoids seeing her because she reminds him too much of the horrors of his childhood.

'I bet she misses you,' I say quietly, wanting to reassure him in some way that he's not alone in this feeling.

He looks at me sharply, but doesn't say anything. He doesn't need to; it's all there on his face. The guilt and anger he must carry around with him every day, that he hides so well under the veneer of hard-nosed businessman.

'You should be proud of yourself for what you've achieved. I bet she is,' I say, gently squeezing his arm. 'And you're right—my father came from a wealthy background, so we all had a head start, but you've built everything you have from scratch. That's truly impressive.'

He lets out a mirthless snort. 'I was well incentivised. I promised myself I'd never go back to being on the poverty line, scrabbling to keep my head above water. Being treated like I'm nothing,' he bites out, the muscle in his jaw jumping under the pressure of his clamped teeth.

'Well, you won't have to—not now you've made such a success of Ergo-i,' I say with a supportive smile.

To my surprise he frowns and lets out a low, tired-sounding sigh. 'If only it were that simple. Unfortunately, we're facing some stiff competition from a new rival firm, so we're going to have to watch our backs. I'm trying to shore up our executive board at the moment, to give us as much reputational sway as possible.'

A light bulb suddenly goes on in my head. 'Are you hoping to use my father's influence on the board?' I ask. 'Is that why you're so keen to get into bed with him?'

He gives a jerky nod. 'If I don't get your father on-side there's a good chance we'll start losing the contracts I've been counting on to keep us at the top of the market. So, yes, I need him. Which is precisely why I shouldn't be in bed with *you*. I doubt he'd look very kindly on me fucking his daughter when I promised him I'd look after you.'

He gets up and pulls on his trousers, his movements jerky.

'I really have to get back,' he says, not looking at me as he leans down to retrieve his shirt from the floor and tug it over his head.

I slump back against the headboard, suddenly feeling overwhelmed and drained of energy.

I don't say anything as I watch him tie his shoe-laces and pull on his suit jacket—because what is there to say?

'See you back at the office,' he says, his voice edged with tension as he strides back to me and drops a kiss onto the top of my head.

I'm suddenly intensely aware of the distance between us. I don't want him to leave like this, frustrated and angry. I want to see him smile again before he goes.

'Hey, are you busy tomorrow?' I ask before he disappears. 'I'm moving back into my flat now that the electrics are finally sorted, so I thought I could make us a celebratory meal. You don't know this about me, but I'm an awesome cook—my lasagne is to die for. Or there are plenty of great pubs in Primrose Hill we can check out.'

I'm trying to keep my tone flippant, but I'm not sure I'm being very successful. I desperately want him to say yes, so we can get back to the cosy camaraderie of before.

There's a heavy pause before Ben says, 'I can't. I've arranged to visit some friends this weekend.'

A horrible sort of heavy disappointment sinks through me, starting in my throat and moving all the way down to my stomach in one sickening lurch.

'No worries,' I manage to say, through a mouth that feels like it's full of sand. 'It was only an idea—in case you were bored and looking for something to do. Or some*one*.'

I can't believe I actually said that. I sound like such a loser. A desperate one.

The sinking feeling gets worse.

He's brought up his barriers now. Is it because he regrets getting too personal and telling me about his parents? Or has our conversation made him think a bit too hard about the dangerous position he's putting himself in by associating with me?

Fuck. Why does everything have to be so complicated?

And why do I care so much anyway?

It shouldn't matter that we can't see each other this weekend; we've seen each other every day this week, after all.

It shouldn't matter, but for some reason it does.

'Look, I'm sorry, but I really have to go,' he says gruffly.

'Of course you do. All those minions aren't going to boss themselves around,' I say, forcing my lips into a cocky smile. 'I'd better get back too. I'm meeting some friends for after-work drinks later, so I need to leave on the dot,' I lie, swinging my legs off the bed. 'I suspect it'll turn into a big night out, knowing them, so I'll probably be good for nothing tomorrow anyway.'

He frowns, but doesn't say anything before giving me a curt nod and then striding out of the door, leaving me alone to wonder how things got so weird between us so fast.

But of course I know how—because of me and my big mouth.

I made myself sound too needy. As if I wanted to have a proper date—in public—and that wasn't part of our arrangement. It's just sex between us after all.

I rub at the weird tension that's making my chest ache and head straight for the shower.

Anyway, it's not as though I don't have plenty of other options. I can call up a whole host of people to come over and hang out with me if I want. In fact that's exactly what I'm going to do. It's about time I threw one of my legendary parties anyway, and now I have the perfect excuse.

I set the shower to its most powerful setting and step under the water, finding relief in the sensation of water pounding against my skin.

Yeah, that's exactly what I need. To spend some quality time with my friends and have a proper blow-out.

Excitement surges through me as I begin to plan it in my head.

This weekend is going to be *fun*.

Benedict

I told Maya that I was going to see friends this week-end as an excuse, suddenly finding I needed some headspace away from her all-consuming presence.

I've become hyper aware that things have got a bit intense with her recently, and talking to her about my past and spending cosy nights at her place is def-initely *not* the way to go if we've got any chance of keeping things light and emotion-free.

It was the genuine interest I saw in her face that made me open up and talk about my parents and my concerns for my business, though. The cosy camara-derie we share when we're in that hotel room—just the two of us, hiding out from the rest of the world—made it seem like the right thing to do. And at least now she understands how high the stakes are for me in seeing her.

I just have to hope my trust in her hasn't been mis-placed. Still, I'm uncomfortably aware that I need to be more circumspect from this point on.

I have to reset my priorities.

It's imperative I keep my head on straight and handle this fling the way I meant to from the be-ginning.

Getting home to an empty house on Friday eve-ning, though, I realise I don't want to be on my own.

I'm restless and agitated for some reason.

I think back to the conversation Maya and I had about my mother. It bothers me. I've been so caught up with work I've put off seeing her a lot over the years, but I can't in all good conscience use that as an excuse any more. Maya's right—she probably does miss me; I'm the only family she has, after all.

I really should make more of an effort to include her in my life.

So with that thought ringing through my head I pick up my phone and call my mother, feeling my heart lift at her obvious delight when I tell her I'm coming for a long overdue visit.

Maya

Despite laughing, swapping gossip and dancing till four a.m. with my friends at my party, I still spend the entire weekend thinking about Ben and wondering whether he's having a good time too.

I know I need to stay cool about this thing between us—which in all likelihood is going to end soon—but to be perfectly honest I'm finding it really bloody hard.

I think he has to be the most impressive person I've ever met—and that's saying something, because I've met a *lot* of impressive people over the years.

But none of them have got under my skin like he has.

Hearing about his horrific upbringing seems to have flipped a switch in my head and I've not been able to stop thinking about it—about him and what he's been through. It's no wonder he's so attached to the life he's built for himself if he grew up with so little and has had to fight hard for what he has now. It must be horrendous for him even to consider losing it all.

I can imagine that kind of humiliation would kill someone as proud as Ben. Not that I suspect it will ever come to that—he's too smart and resourceful to let it happen. Too careful and considered. Which is probably why this fling with me seems to be spinning him out so much.

Monday finally rolls around, and I'm frustrated to find that Ben's out at a meeting all morning. No matter how hard I try, I can't seem to settle to anything. A voice in my head keeps whispering *Perhaps it's over already*, and no matter how hard I try to shut it off it won't bloody well pipe down.

To my utter relief, a text message from him pops up on my phone at midday, asking me to meet him at our hotel, and I'm finally able to breathe again.

It seems he's just as unable to resist our illicit lunchtime rendezvous as I am.

'So, it's your father's party on Wednesday night,' Ben says as I pull on my underwear and flatten down my hair an hour later, ready to return to the office after a particularly fast and furious screw.

It appears that time apart from each other adds real fire to our fucking.

My heart does a nosedive as I contemplate what he actually means.

We're on a countdown now to the end.

I hate the fact that my father has our relationship in such a stranglehold. Just like the rest of my life.

I can't wait to be free of the bastard.

'Yeah. It's going to be quite a do. I think he's invited the whole of London high society to fawn at his feet,' I say, laying on the derision to keep my disquiet in check. 'I hope you don't expect to get any special treatment from me there, though, *boss*. I'll be off duty,' I joke with a playful smile, though I'm keenly aware of a prickle of dread beneath my skin.

He smiles back, and despite the tension in my body my heart leaps at the warmth in his eyes.

Perhaps this won't be the end?

Perhaps…

'In that case I guess we should make the most of the time we have left now,' he says, grabbing hold of me and pulling me back onto the bed, where he proceeds to remove the underwear I've just put back on.

Not that I mind one little bit.

I'd happily stay here with him, naked in bed, for every second we have left together if I could.

CHAPTER SEVEN

Maya

I SPEND A lot of time getting ready for my father's party on Wednesday night.

Not because he's celebrating his big five-o and has really pushed the boat out, inviting what seems to be the entire embarrassment of riches that constitutes London's high society, but because Ben will be there.

The last couple of days I've spent around him have been incredible, but each morning I've woken up with a deep sense of foreboding, knowing that the time we have together is rapidly coming to a close.

The party's already in full swing when I saunter into my father's house, in a little black number that hugs my body like a second skin, and I'm aware of a number of male eyes on me as I push my way through the throng, holding my head high and fixing a wide smile on my face.

I'm a pro at this kind of thing now, after years and years of being wheeled out and exhibited in front of the nobs and notables my father wants to impress.

My expensive schooling has paid off, because I know how to work a crowd, how to say the right thing, ask the right questions, slip in just the right amount of fawning compliments.

I make sure to do the dutiful daughter bit in full view of my father, so I'll be able to slink away later and actually have some fun.

With this in mind, I look around for Ben, but I can't see him amongst the well-heeled crowd. Perhaps he's decided to be fashionably late.

I try not to let the jitters in my stomach distract me as I partake in a bit of tedious small talk—flashing my winning smile and laughing at my conversationalist's jokes—until I'm suddenly aware that someone is looking at me. I can feel a gaze boring into the side of my head and I turn, heart jumping, hoping to see the one person I'm hanging all my hopes on for an entertaining night.

But it's not to be. It's a guy I've dated a couple of times, but I've not been able to summon enough interest to sleep with him. He's pretty, but boring as hell.

Unfortunately, he seems intent on go number three, and he sidles over with a glass of champagne for me, flashes me a wolfish sort of grin, then launches into some inane banter. I'm sure it works a treat on the dull dilettantes he regularly beds, then dumps for the next one in line, but it doesn't do a thing for me. He seems insubstantial and pale after Ben's dark looks and intense charisma.

Ugh, where *is* Ben?

Maybe he's changed his mind and isn't coming after all.

Frustration, quickly followed by a sick sinking feeling, rolls through me.

'Sorry, but I need to dash to the bathroom. Too much wine,' I say to wolf-boy, thrusting my now empty glass at him. Without waiting for his response I turn away and walk swiftly towards the kitchen and freedom.

I'll go and skulk away in there for a bit, with the waiting staff, and then if Ben doesn't show I'll make a bid for freedom and meet my friends at the club they're off to tonight. More booze and some wild dancing is exactly what I need right now, to blot out the hollow feeling in the pit of my stomach.

I'm just passing the door to my father's home office when I suddenly become aware of someone coming up behind me.

Dammit. Wolf-boy just doesn't want to take no for an answer.

I stop in my tracks and spin around, fixing a cool, distant expression on my face, ready to shut him down fast.

'Look, I'm very flattered, but I'm really not in the mood to...' My words peter out as I turn to face my stalker and realise it's not wolf-boy after all.

It's Ben.

My whole body comes alive at the sight of him, rushing with heat as I stare into his dark eyes, which are narrowed in amusement.

'Not in the mood to what?' he asks with a wry smile.

My insides do an ecstatic flip-flop.

'To make any more boring small talk with my father's cronies,' I reply, matching his smile.

'And do you include *me* in that grouping?'

I shake my head, my gaze remaining steady on his. 'Absolutely not, boss.'

He shoots me a reproving frown. 'I thought I wasn't getting any special treatment tonight?'

'That depends on what you mean by "special",' I murmur, gesturing for him to follow me into my father's mercifully empty office.

I shut the door firmly behind us and flip the lock, then turn back to slide my fingers into his hair and kiss him hard. I press my body up against his, delighting in the feel of his hard, muscular frame against me. We fit together so perfectly—it's as if we were made for each other. I revel in that thought, taking my time to explore the hard planes of his back with my fingertips as I kiss him, totally absorbed in my greedy inspection.

So it takes me a moment to realise that something's wrong.

He's resisting me.

Benedict

'We shouldn't do this here—not right under your father's nose,' I say, drawing away from her even though the whole of my being screams at me to keep kissing her and be damned.

But I can't do that. I mustn't. It's too damn dangerous.

She withdraws from me and smiles, then shrugs, but it looks awkward and stiff.

'Okay, but you realise I'll be out of your company and out of your life any minute anyway? Now that he's back?' she says. 'After that you can pretend I don't exist.'

'Don't say that.'

I'm hurt that she'd think I'd be so cold as to want to do that.

She shrugs. 'It's fine. I get it. I'm not the type of woman you'd be looking to settle down with. It's not my style anyway. I like the thrill of the chase, but I get bored easily.'

There's something in her face, though, when she says this, that makes me think it's a line she's reeled out to protect herself.

'Maya—'

She flaps a hand. 'Look, don't worry about my father. If by some miracle he finds out about us he'll just assume it was all my fault anyway. He knows what I'm like—he's not exactly my biggest fan.'

'What do you mean?' I ask, disturbed by how casually she says this.

'Oh, I don't know... I've always disappointed him. He and I have never seen eye to eye,' she says, turning away and walking over to a mirror on the wall to check her lipstick.

Her posture is stiff, and I get a strong sense that there's more to this than she's letting on.

But I don't push it. I can't allow myself to get emotionally involved with her. I already care about her more than is healthy for a short-term fling.

While she wipes away a bit of mascara that's smudged under her eye, I try to distract myself from the concern looming at the edge of my consciousness by walking to the bookcase on the other side of the room, which has a shelf full of framed photos, lined up in a neat row.

They're all a bit faded, so they must have been there for some time. Most of them are of Maxim with people from the social scene, but others are actors or famous politicians. It suddenly strikes me that there are no photos of his family anywhere in the room. Not even one of Maya's mother, who famously died ten years ago in a skiing accident.

'It's an impressive line-up,' I say, nodding towards the photos as she walks over to join me.

I turn to look at her and breathe in her unique, alluring scent, my skin rushing with pleasure as I inhale it deep into my lungs. It's the smell I go to sleep with in my nostrils every night. She's somehow permeated every part of my life.

'Yes, my father likes to collect people like trophies,' she says, with a cynical lift of her eyebrow.

Her comment makes my insides squirm, and I wonder for a second whether he's doing that to me.

Pushing away this disturbing thought, I say, 'I was actually looking for a photo of your mother. I've heard you look a lot like her.'

To my surprise she visibly tenses and pulls her arms across her chest.

'So I've been told. Many, many times,' she mutters.

Her voice has lost its playful edge, and if I'm not mistaken it's taken on a croak of emotion. She goes to speak, then seems to change her mind and presses her lips together again. Glancing down, I see that her hands are shaking.

Concern rattles through me. 'Sorry, I didn't mean to upset you. I must have been hard to lose her at such a young age,' I say, reaching out a hand. She steps away from it to avoid my touch. I feel stung by her rejection, but when she turns to meet my eyes again I see that there's real pain in them.

Shit. I've gone too far. Got too personal.

My stomach sinks so rapidly I feel nausea.

What can of worms have I just opened?

'Are you okay?' I ask, shocked by how pale she is, as if all the blood has drained from her face.

'I'm—' She shakes her head, as if the words won't come.

'Maya? What is it?'

I step in front of her and instinctively I put my

hands on her shoulders, gently drawing her closer to me. I want her to know she's safe here with me.

'It *was* hard,' she whispers.

She's got her arms wrapped so tightly around her body now I can see the tendons standing out in her forearms.

'I was on the skiing holiday with her…when she died. It was just her and me. It was horrendous. The most awful thing in the world.'

She takes a shuddery breath, but her eyes still don't meet mine.

'I'd accidentally got onto a difficult run that I wasn't skilled enough to be on. She followed me, then fell and bashed her head trying to catch up with me. Trying to keep me safe.'

Her voice is raw with emotion and her eyes are clouded over now, as if she's retreated far inside herself.

I remember reading about Isabella Darlington-Hume's death when it was splashed across the headlines ten years ago. It had been a front-page story at the time—the most famous socialite of that time, tragically killed in the prime of her life.

'I didn't realise you were there when it happened,' I say quietly, horrified by the anguish I see on her face.

'My father managed to keep most of the details out of the press,' she replies, speaking in an indifferent tone now, which doesn't match the look in her eyes at all. 'One of the many benefits of being rich and powerful.'

Her brow creases and I see her jaw tighten, as if she's desperately trying not to let her emotions get the better of her.

I'm about to open my mouth and say something to comfort her—not that I have any idea what could do that right now—when her body language suddenly changes and she straightens up, as if she's throwing off her melancholy and returning to her normal insouciant self.

'Anyway, there's no point in dwelling on the past, right?' she says, in an abnormally bright voice. 'Especially when there's so much to look forward to in the future.'

She smiles at me as if we've just been discussing some frivolous piece of gossip.

There's a strange atmosphere in the room now, which is making me really uncomfortable.

Something weird is going on here.

It's as if I've just seen a glimpse of her sensitive alter ego, but now the cocksure Maya has fought her way back.

We both jump as someone rattles the door handle.

'We should go back to the party before my father misses us,' she says, pushing away from the wall. 'You're right—it'd look pretty bad for the two of us to be discovered hiding out in here together.' She leans in towards me and raises her eyebrows. 'And

I wouldn't want to tarnish your *impeccable* reputation so you lose favour with him. Business is business, right?'

I can't tell whether she's joking or not, so I just give her an awkward sort of frowning nod. Clearly she's put her barriers back up now, so she doesn't have to deal with messy feelings about what she just told me.

To be perfectly honest, I'm not quite sure how to deal with what I'm feeling right now either. The thought of her carrying around the pain of losing her mother like that, every day of her life, horrifies me. But, perhaps even more frustratingly, I know there's not a damn thing I can do to help her.

Not that it's my responsibility.

Though of course I feel that it is.

Because, most worryingly, every time I find out something new about her I get pulled a little deeper into her life—care about her a little bit more.

And that definitely was *not* part of the plan.

Maya

Ben and I walk back to the party, side by side.

But not together.

There's a distance between us again—I can sense it.

Is it because I lost the plot and let him see a more vulnerable side to me?

It wouldn't surprise me. It's probably made him

want to run a mile. Weepy confessions aren't what he signed up for.

I'm a good-time girl—wild, seductive, never sentimental. Self-pity isn't sexy. It's not the sort of thing that endears you to people, which is why I never talk about my mother to anyone.

I suddenly feel sick at the thought of him knowing about it. What the hell possessed me to talk to Ben of all people about her?

I think it was the way he put his hands on my shoulders that loosened my tongue. His touch made me feel safe. Protected. I felt closer to him in those moments than I have to anyone in a very long time.

But as soon as I started my sorry tale I became aware of the weight of emotion that I was pouring into the room. I suddenly felt exposed and stupid, which is why I then put on that ridiculous show of bravado.

I wonder wildly how him knowing about this might impact on our relationship—not that you could exactly call it one. To be honest, I don't know *what* it is we have, but I do know that for a while now it's started to feel like more than just casual sex...

My train of thought is cut short as my father appears as if from nowhere, like a bad omen, and strides straight up to Ben, offering him his hand.

'Benedict—glad you made it.'

'Happy birthday, Maxim. Thanks for inviting me.' Ben takes my father's hand and gives it a firm shake.

I feel my father's eyes on me and turn to look at him.

'I was just showing Ben the photo line-up of "Society's Most Privileged" in your office,' I quip, before he can ask me where the hell I've been.

'Well, I'd appreciate it if you could share your attention around a bit and go and talk to some of our other guests,' my father says tersely. 'Your disappearance has been remarked on.'

I give him one of my fake subservient smiles, which he ignores, deliberately moving between Ben and I and turning his back on me.

Obviously Ben's the only person he deems it worth engaging with here. I feel the coldness of his actions and bite my lip against the wave of hurt it elicits. It's only because I'm still a little wobbly about what just happened in his office that I'm letting it affect me, though. Normally I don't give a shit when he stonewalls me.

'I'd like to introduce you to a few people—particularly my daughter April,' my father says to Ben, as if I'm not even there.

'She's a very impressive woman, Maxim,' Ben says, leaning a little to the side to catch my eye.

I look quickly away from him, not sure what he's playing at.

'April? Yes, she's a real asset to the business and to the family,' my father replies, glancing over his shoulder to shoot me a reproachful look, as if I should be learning something from this.

'Actually, I was talking about Maya,' Ben says smoothly. 'She stepped in and saved an important contract from hitting the skids the other week. I'm impressed with her business savvy too. I had the pleasure of seeing the proposal for her jewellery enterprise. It's inspiring. She's clearly put a lot of work into it. It's exceptionally well thought out and meticulously planned. If I were you I'd seriously consider giving her the backing she needs to get it off the ground. I can see it being a hugely successful venture. She's appears to be a chip off the old block, Maxim.'

For a second my father looks as though he can't quite believe what he's hearing, but he quickly covers it with a solicitous smile.

My heart flutters like a bird in my chest as Ben grins at me.

God, I fucking love this—he's standing up for me in front of my father. The first person who ever has.

A small voice in my head starts to whisper strange things to me. Things like, *What if there could be more to this with Ben? Something real?*

My stomach does an excited sort of roll and I have to give myself a mental slap. I'd be crazy to think like that. He's made it perfectly clear he doesn't want anything more serious than a fling with me.

My father glances between the two of us with his eyes narrowed. Does he suspect Ben and I are fucking and that that's the only reason he's complimenting me?

And is he right?

Tension twists in my chest as I consider this possibility.

But, no, surely that's not true.

'Well, that's heartening to hear,' my father says gruffly. 'I'll take a look at the paperwork this week with a view to moving it forward, then.'

He gives me a stiff nod, and if I didn't know better I'd think he was actually pleased I've done such a good job.

He turns back to Ben. 'I'm glad to hear she's been pulling her weight, but I won't need you to entertain her any longer. Now I'm back in London she'll be coming back to work at my office tomorrow morning.'

I suck in a sharp breath. So soon? I'd hoped I'd have at least the rest of the week at Ergo-i before I had to leave—before our fling was officially over.

I want to argue with my father and ask if he can spare me for a bit longer, but I'm acutely aware that that would look very suspicious. It was only ever meant to be a short secondment, with no prospect of me staying on there.

The only way it might work is if Ben steps in—perhaps citing the need for me to have a bit of time to hand over a project I've been working on.

I hold my breath, hoping he'll somehow read my thoughts, but to my utter dismay he just nods and says, 'Okay, that's fine with me.'

Disappointment, sadness and frustration take turns to throb through me, but I'm hyper aware that for Ben's sake I need to look as though I'm totally relaxed about it all.

'Thanks for having her for so long,' my father adds, as if Ben's been looking after a troublesome pet for him.

'It was my absolute pleasure to have her.'

There's no inflection or innuendo in his voice. No private joke aimed just at me. And my heart sinks.

'Let me introduce you to April,' my father says, holding up his arm as if to herd Ben in the direction he wants him to go. Away from me.

With just a nod of farewell in my direction, Ben allows my father to guide him away, through the busy throng of people.

My legs feel weirdly wobbly, so I grip hold of a nearby banister and spin myself around to lean against the newel post for support.

Through my haze of dejection I become aware of my little sister, Juno, walking over to where I'm standing.

'Hey, Jubelly—enjoying the party?' I ask her, desperately trying to pull myself together. I can't fall apart right now. That would be all kinds of bad news.

She scowls and shakes her head at me, making her beautiful chestnut hair ripple across her shoulders. It's really nice to see her wearing it down for once. She usually has it tied back in a tight knot at the base of her skull—which, as I regularly point out, is an offence against nature.

'Maya, can you please stop calling me that? I'm twenty-two years old!' she hisses.

When I turn to grin at her, glad for the distraction from Ben and what just happened, I notice her face is flushed.

'Hey, what's up?' I ask.

It's not like my little sister to get irritated. Her head is always too far up in the clouds for her to notice much of what's going on in front of her—as if she's constantly thinking about the work she'd rather be doing. *Disengaged from real life* is what my father calls it—when he bothers to pay her any attention.

I sometimes call her Professor, just to tease her, but I suspect she actually likes it. She's just started a PhD in something to do with identifying and curing heart disease at St George's, so she'll probably make it to being a real professor one day. How we ended up in the same nuclear family is an absolute mystery to me.

'I'd just rather no one hears you call me that. It makes me sound so young and—*naïve*,' she mutters.

I frown at her. 'Anyone in particular?' I ask, sensing from the stiffness of her posture that she's putting on a front for someone here.

She looks for a moment as if she battling with herself about whether or not to ask me something.

Obviously her curiosity wins out because she blurts, 'How well do you know Alessandro Ricci?'

'Are you asking whether I've slept with him?' I ask her, amused.

Sandro is minor Italian royalty and your classic shockingly handsome alpha male playboy. As far as I can tell he's totally self-absorbed, and a bit on the dim side—the last man I'd expect Juno to be interested in.

The couple of boyfriends she's had in the past have been beta, to say the least. Maybe even gamma. Juno is a very pretty woman, now that she's grown into her looks, but she's never seemed very interested in men. Being smart is much more important to her than being beautiful—and fair play to her, I say.

Juno shoots me an uncomfortable grimace. 'Well...er...yes, I suppose that is what I mean.'

She's smitten, I realise, so I decide to go easy on her.

'No, I've never slept with him—much to my regret.' I flash her a wry smile, which she has trouble returning. Her face is really flushed now, and she's not meeting my eyes.

'My friend Sara's been in love with him for years—unrequited,' I hastily add, when I see Juno's face fall, 'so I've always avoided him. Friends are much more important than a quick fling with a sexy but ultimately throwaway man.'

Juno's gaze flicks to mine, and I'm surprised to see relief in her eyes.

'You really like him, huh?' I ask gently.

She shrugs stiffly, looking really awkward now. 'He fascinates me, that's all.'

'So that uni lecturer isn't on your radar any more?' I tease.

She's talked about this guy—Adam—so much I feel like I know him, though we've never met. She's never admitted it, but it's clear Juno had a humongous crush on him for the whole of her MA year, and never plucked up the courage to ask him out.

Could this be what her questions about Sandro are about? Finding courage? Or, more pointedly, finding someone to give her some? The guy is famous for his bedroom antics, and apparently a fantastic lover, so that would fit.

She shifts on the spot, her face flushing even more, if that's possible. 'Adam…er…isn't very interested in me. He thinks I'm too young for him and—' She pauses and swallows. 'And too innocent.'

I let out a short, sharp laugh. 'Are you telling me he's knocked you back because you're a virgin?'

She definitely can't look at me now. Instead she nods her head solemnly.

'*Argh*, forget about him, Ju, he sounds like a loser. Any guy should consider himself hugely privileged to be with you. And who cares whether you're a virgin anyway? It's not like there isn't an easy fix for that.'

'For someone like you, maybe,' she mutters. 'But I have no idea how to approach a man and ask him to have sex with me.'

'Is that why you're interested in Sandro?' I ask, interested to see whether my earlier guess will be confirmed.

Juno sighs and rubs her hand over her face, as if she's exhausted by the whole thing now. 'I know. It's a ridiculous idea.'

'Not necessarily,' I say gently. 'You could ask him.' I put a reassuring hand on her arm, feeling the heat of her humiliation burning through the thin fabric of her crêpe top. 'He'd be crazy to say no. It'd be a huge privilege to sleep with someone as fabulous as you.'

She gives me a wan, wobbly smile. 'That's really kind, Maya, but I don't think I'd have the confidence to go through with it anyway.'

'Of course you could!' I say with vehemence. 'You go for what you want, Ju. You've got to get out there and make things happen for yourself, at least that's been my experience.'

I think back to the way I lay back on Ben's desk and demanded that he made me come, feeling the heat of my desire for him swoop through me. Why can't I get him out of my head? We've fucked multiple times now. Done the deed, fulfilled the need. Surely I've had enough of him now to allow me to turn my affections to someone new. It's always been the case with partners in the past.

'Maybe you're right,' she says, her voice uncertain.

I look over towards where Ben is now talking

to April. She's as elegant and together-looking as ever, with her sleek baby-blonde hair pulled into a neat chignon and her coldly beautiful face perfectly but subtly made-up. I stiffen as I watch him give her a really warm smile that makes his eyes shine. His body language is showing he's way too interested in her for my liking. My stomach lurches and I feel lightheaded as a wave of sickness washes through me.

I could never hope to compete with April— I just don't *do* refined—and she's exactly the sort of woman I'd expect someone like Ben to want as a long-term partner. I know for sure that it would please my father if the two of them got together.

'My advice though, Ju, is to stay away from powerful alpha men,' I add to my little sister. 'They're nothing but trouble.'

Juno must have heard the weird wobble in my voice because she turns to look at me.

'You okay, Maya?'

'I'm fine,' I say brightly.

Because I am.

I'm always fine.

'Time to fill my boots with forty per cent alcohol, though,' I say with a grin.

She rolls her eyes at me—she's not a drinker, my sensible little sister—and gives me a dismissive wave before wandering off.

I turn back to look over to where Ben is still talking to April, his statuesque figure standing out like a beacon in a sea of uniformity.

I'm hyper aware that there's something very wrong about the way I'm feeling. But it's okay. *I'm* okay.

I take a breath.

I don't need him. I'll be fine without him.

Absolutely fine.

CHAPTER EIGHT

Benedict

I DON'T GET any more time with Maya after Maxim commandeers me—he seems intent on introducing me to just about everyone who's attended the party, and I don't feel I can refuse him.

I wonder a few times whether I should check whether she's okay. I'd not felt it wise to contradict Maxim's wishes for her to return to work with him in case he became suspicious about my motives, but I want her to know I'm frustrated about her time at Ergo-i—and therefore our affair—ending so abruptly.

I also wonder—while I struggle to stay focussed and engaged with the business-talk going on around me—whether having this enforced end to our fling will actually turn out to be a good thing. A clean break will give me back some much-needed headspace—especially since the pain I'd seen in Maya's eyes when she told me about what had happened to her mother seems to have completely fucked with my head.

It's made me want to take her away from here and protect her from it. To try and make her happy again.

The irony that she's the last person on earth I should be feeling like that about hasn't escaped me. I've been determined to maintain a clear line between fun fling and relationship, since neither of us is interested in a future together, but despite this I've allowed myself to start caring about her.

Which means it's a good time to end it.

On the couple of occasions when I catch a glimpse of her, she's laughing and joking with someone. It seems as if she's absolutely fine.

And then she just disappears.

The party feels empty and lifeless without her, even though there have to be close to a hundred people still there, and I find it almost impossible to concentrate on the conversations I have from that point on. As the Maya-free minutes tick by it becomes increasingly clear to me that I can't leave things like this. We need to give this thing a proper ending.

So, twenty minutes later, I make an excuse to Maxim about an important call to the States—'It's imperative I make it from the office'—and finally manage to escape.

After dropping in to my house to pick up a package I've been meaning to give to Maya for a while now, I make my way over to her flat in Primrose Hill, hoping like hell that I'll catch her in.

Maya

When it comes down to it I can't stomach the thought of going out clubbing and pretending to have a good time, when my chest feels like someone's trapped it in a vice, so I go back to my flat and pour myself a very large vodka, trying not to think about Ben and April having a grand old time together at my father's party as I tip it down my throat.

Blotting out everything I'm feeling right now is definitely the only way to go tonight.

I'm just about to pour myself another shot with a shaking hand when there's a loud knock on my door.

Who the fuck thinks it's okay to come calling at eleven o'clock at night? If it's Freddie Valentine— or wolf-boy—I swear to God, I'm actually going to kill him on my doorstep.

Resisting the urge to go and select a suitable knife from the kitchen with which to perpetrate this imagined act, I march to the door and fling it open, ready to unleash a tirade of abuse on the idiot who's so foolishly decided to call on me right now.

My heart swoops up to my throat when I see that it's neither of those idiots.

It's Ben.

He's not with April; he's come here to be with me.

'What are you doing here? I thought you were set on schmoozing it up at my father's party tonight,' I say, trying not to grin like a fool as I stare into his hypnotising eyes and tendrils of lust stroke my skin.

'I've schmoozed enough for one night.' He gives me a frowning sort of smile, then says, 'Listen, I'm sorry about how I acted in front of your father, but I thought it'd look a bit suspect if I asked you to stay on with me for longer.'

I give him a forgiving nod, even though I'm still feeling bruised by the indifference I saw in his eyes when he did it. It felt horrifyingly real at the time.

'That's what I figured.'

He smiles, looking relieved, then holds up a Jiffy bag and shakes it. The items inside make a gentle clicking sound as they knock together.

'I have something I need to give you.'

I grin as the memory of the parcel I took to his house flashes through my mind.

'I hope it's what I think it is,' I say, backing up into the hallway, inviting him in with my eyes.

I walk straight into my bedroom, willing him to follow me. I don't want to waste time pussyfooting around, making small talk, when I could have him in my bed.

As soon as we get there I remember with a sting of embarrassment that I've left the room in a shocking state. There are clothes strewn all over the bed, and you can barely see the top of my dressing table for make-up.

'Sorry. I'm not the tidiest of people,' I say, hastily kicking a pair of discarded knickers into another pile of clothes on the floor.

He's seen what I've just done, and to my humiliation he stoops down and picks up the knickers between his fingertips, holds them up for a second and looks at me with one dark eyebrow raised, then tosses them into the bin by my chest of drawers.

'I hear that's where you usually deposit those fancy designer knickers of yours once you've worn them for a day. That must be an expensive habit,' he says with a shake of his head.

I can't help but laugh, even though I'm sick to death of correcting people about that fallacy. 'Urban myth,' I say, raising one derisive eyebrow. 'I did that *once*. As a joke. My idiot ex went to the tabloids with it as a story to make some fast cash and suddenly it became a fact in people's minds that I throw my knickers away every day. Even my bloody *father* believed it!'

He nods slowly, his eyes not leaving mine, but I can tell from the expression in them that he believes me. This gives me an unexpected lift of happiness, which in turn sends a twist of nerves up through my stomach.

'Hey, thanks for putting that word in for me about my business plan,' I say quickly, to distract myself.

'It was my absolute pleasure. I meant every word of it.'

'Well, I appreciate it.'

There's a heavy pause and we just look at each other. I feel my heart fluttering like mad in my chest.

'Are you okay?' he asks quietly, his expression darkening with concern. 'I was worried—after that conversation we had in your father's study.'

My stomach does an alarming lurch. I really don't want to talk about that again—not here, not now.

'I'm fine,' I say breezily. 'I was just a bit tiddly from the champagne and it made me maudlin, that's all.'

He keeps frowning at me, and then he opens his mouth to say something else, so I cut him off.

'Can I have my parcel?' I'm desperate to break the downbeat atmosphere that's developing and get back to the fun stuff. He doesn't seem to be taking advantage of the fact that he's in my bedroom, standing right next to my bed, and it's starting to worry me.

'Sure.' He moves closer, his spicy scent making my head swim with longing, and holds it up.

I take it from him with a playful smile. Reaching inside, I pull out the items I was forced to leave at his house—my vibrator, lube and butt plug—and set them on my dresser.

Hello, my old friends.

'I thought I should return them. I've had them sitting in my kitchen drawer for far too long.'

I grin as I imagine his cleaner opening the cutlery drawer to discover my butt plug nestled next to the fish knives.

'So, anyway, I wanted to come and tell you we're going to miss you at Ergo-i,' he says with a twisted smile. 'It's been educational.'

He takes a step back towards the door and alarm thuds through me as I suddenly realise he's come here to return my things—*and say goodbye.*

My pulse beats hard in my temple and my stomach rolls with panic.

No. No fucking way am I letting him just swan off like that. It can't end like this. I won't let it.

'I hope you had fun with them,' I say quickly, bringing out my most seductive smile.

His return grin is slow and amused, but I sense he's not going to let me get what I want so easily.

Good thing I'm not a quitter.

'Have you been fantasising about using them on me?' I ask, making my voice breathy. 'Because I know I have.'

He looks at me with an intensity that makes my toes curl but doesn't say anything.

A muscle flickers in his jaw.

I'm desperate for him to tell me he's not ready for this thing between us to be over yet. To say he doesn't want to let me go. That we should extend our fling.

I have no idea whether that's really how he feels, though. He's not giving anything away.

I move towards him until we're only a couple of inches apart, and the heat of his body makes the bare skin on my neck and arms prickle with awareness.

'You know, technically I'm still working for you. Until tomorrow morning, that is,' I say softly.

'Yes. Technically that's correct,' he replies, his voice rough and low.

The atmosphere is so charged now I swear I can *feel* the air throbbing between us.

He seems to feel it too, because when I take one

more step towards him, moving so close to him that I can feel the whisper of his ragged breath against my mouth, his whole body tenses, as if he's holding himself back.

'Then stay,' I murmur.

He frowns, his eyes narrowing, and I swear I can see the internal battle he's fighting reflected in them.

'I shouldn't...' he murmurs back.

I flash him a wry smile. 'Since when have you done what you *should* do instead of what you *want* to do?'

He lets out a gentle snort of frustration, then raises his hand to cup my jaw, stroking his thumb against my cheek. It's such a possessive move that I know, right then, that I've won.

This is confirmed when he lets out a low kind of growl and finally crushes his lips against mine, pulling me hard against him with his other hand.

His mouth feels like heaven on mine and I'm aware of my whole body flushing with wanton heat.

God, I want him. *So* much.

He's like a drug, pulling me under, making my head fuzzy, seducing me till I don't know which way's up.

As if he's caught in the same spell, he suddenly yanks up the skirt of my dress, exposing the flimsy material of my knickers. Hooking his fingers into the lace at the side he tugs hard. I feel it rip and give way. The remainder of my underwear falls to the floor at my feet.

'Another pair destined for the bin,' he murmurs, shaking his head in mock regret, and if I hadn't been so crazy with longing I would have laughed at the smile in his voice.

There's an excruciating pause as he takes a small step back and just looks me in the eye, his pupils fully blown in the dim light, before he slides his hand between my legs.

The sensation of his fingers on my bare skin is so intense I inhale sharply, only to slowly exhale as his fingertips explore me, drifting over my sensitive flesh, then probing and penetrating me deep inside. It's as if he's committing the feel of me to memory.

The avidity of it makes my breath stutter in my throat.

'So you've missed your toys, huh…?' he murmurs.

'Yes,' I whisper back through desire-numbed lips. 'So much.'

'Then let's get you reacquainted.'

Abruptly withdrawing his intimate touch, he puts his hands on my hips and spins me around so I'm facing my dressing table.

'Brace your hands on the top,' he instructs.

I do as I'm told. He won't get any complaints from me. I'm not going to do anything to jeopardise this. I've been fantasising about it happening for too long to have it not work out now.

The skirt of my dress is already bunched up around my waist, so he's got a clear view of my arse, which he drags a little closer to him. I'm forced to bend lower and rest my forearms on the top of the table to steady myself. Make-up scatters onto the floor as I make room to rest my arms comfortably, but I'm well beyond caring about that right now.

His long fingers slide between my legs again, parting me, then dipping inside me, catching a particularly sensitive spot. I'm so wet now they slide in easily, and I feel the transference of my silky arousal as he slips his fingertips out and moves them back towards my arsehole, leaving a slick trail in his wake.

The sensation of him touching me there makes my body hum with excitement. It's so filthily intimate and lewd I can barely stand it.

But I will.

I want this so much I think I'd die if he stopped now.

Seeming to sense how needy I am, he presses one of his fingertips against the puckered hole, then skates across and around it, teasing me into a frenzy with his intent. Mercifully, he begins to work his finger slowly inside me, then back out, then in again, until I stop resisting the gentle push-pull.

'You're very tight…you're going to have to relax more or this is going to hurt.'

'Just use a lot of lube,' I demand brazenly, not caring at all what he thinks of me right at this moment.

A laugh rumbles out of him. I hear the snap and squirt of the tube, then a cold, slippery sensation against my hole that makes me suck in a sharp breath. It feels like magic. Then a solid cold object presses into me. He pushes it in slowly, moving back fractionally when I resist, then forward again until it finally slides past the tight ring of muscle and settles inside me. There's a good burning sensation, then a delicious fullness as it seats itself properly.

I stand there frozen, trembling with anticipation, hyper aware of my heartbeat as it throbs in my throat, my head, between my legs.

'What's going to happen now?' I blurt out, unable to keep my cool any longer.

He doesn't reply. Instead I hear the sound of the zip on his trousers being lowered, and the crackle and snap of a condom being taken out of its packet and put on.

And then he slides deep inside me, taking my breath away.

The feeling is intense and monumentally exciting.

And I like it. I like it *a lot*.

As he thrusts hard inside me the plug moves a little deeper too, and the feeling of double penetration nearly blows my mind. There's something thrillingly filthy about it, and the awareness of that turns me on even more.

I feel feverish, as if every nerve-ending in my body has come alive and is crackling with heat.

I can't help but make a raw, guttural grunt of pleasure in the back of my throat, and I bite down on my lip as he begins to drive into me hard, then slide fully out again so I feel cool air on my pussy before his cock re-enters me. Each time he thrusts into me I experience waves of euphoria like I've never felt before.

And then things get even more intense.

In my insular world of sensation I didn't notice him picking up my vibrator, but I certainly feel it as he presses it hard against my clit. It's all I can do not to scream with pleasure as the vibrations intensify the peaking throb between my legs.

A few more thrusts and I'm gone, spiralling into a world of pleasure, barely aware of my surroundings as my whole body convulses in orgasm.

It seems Ben's pretty much there too, because he drops the vibrator, grips my hips again and begins to slam into me as if he's finally allowing himself to let go and take what he wants.

'Fuck, you're so tight with this thing inside you,' he mutters, and two strokes later he comes, thrusting hard into me and letting out a low growl of satisfaction, which sends echoes of my orgasm through me.

I'm in heaven. Absolute heaven.

And I know exactly why.

Because he stayed when he should have walked away. He couldn't resist me.

And I love it that I have that power over him.

Fucking *love* it.

Benedict

When the world finally comes back into focus I find myself pressed up hard to Maya, my thighs flush with hers and my hands firmly gripping her hips. I can feel the quick rise and fall of her breathing under me and the steadying sensation of it centres me enough to regain my scattered composure.

I've never felt as out of control of a situation before. *Never.* And, to be honest, it's scaring the shit out of me.

Carefully I draw away from her and dispose of the condom, depositing it in the much-discussed bin while she visits the bathroom.

I sit down heavily on the edge of the bed and wait for her to return. I know this should be the end, but I'm having trouble reconciling myself to that fact.

I shouldn't have let it happen. I came here to say goodbye. But it seems that whenever I'm around Maya something takes me over and I find it impossible to resist her. She was right, of course. I have been fantasising about doing what I've just done to her. And more. Much more. My time with her has given me a real taste for exploring my sexual fantasies. And she knows exactly how to make them all come true.

'You okay?' she asks me as she walks back into the room.

'I'm fine,' I lie, then take a steadying breath and say, 'You know we can't do this any more.'

'I know,' she says, sliding into bed, 'but we're going to anyway, right?'

I don't answer. I can't. I just sit there, looking at her expectant face.

She lets out a low sigh. 'Look, just get into bed with me, okay? Just for a minute.'

I shouldn't do it. I know I shouldn't. If I get into that bed I'm not getting out of it again.

I know this—just like I know that continuing this fling with Maya could destroy everything I've worked for: my social standing, my business, my security.

And yet I can't walk away either. Not yet.

Being with her is the most uplifting, exhilarating—life-affirming—thing I've ever done and I'm hooked on it.

'If we do carry on seeing each other we have to be really careful,' I say, getting under the covers next to her and pulling her into my arms. 'I can't put my business in jeopardy for this.'

'I hear you,' she mumbles, kissing along my jawline and gently biting at my earlobe, sending a shiver of lust straight through me.

'I mean it, Maya. Absolute discretion.'

'Understood,' she says, her voice light with pleasure, and something else: victory, perhaps? 'We'll only carry on till one or both of us gets bored. Then we'll walk away. No questions, no regrets,' she murmurs against my neck.

'You're not making life easy for me, you know,' I grumble.

'I know,' she says, sliding her hand down my stomach. 'But, seriously, who wants easy?'

CHAPTER NINE

Benedict

SO WE KEEP seeing each other, covertly in the evenings, after we've finished at our respective offices.

After spending my entire childhood feeling unsettled and anxious and powerless, I told myself I'd never allow myself to be in that position again—so what the hell am I doing risking everything I have for a fling with the most inappropriate woman in the world?

I know I'm walking on a knife-edge, but I don't seem able to stop myself. I guess I'm actually finding the danger of it exciting—which is really unlike me. I'm normally so controlled, so strategic, but this thing with Maya is like nothing I've ever experienced before. It's both thrilling and terrifying at the same time.

And it makes me feel alive.

With these thoughts still racing through my mind, I'm just about to turn off my computer and leave the office the following Friday evening when Maxim's number shows up on my mobile's screen.

A rush of adrenaline makes my heart thump like a hammer against my ribs.

Has he found out about Maya and I?

With a dark sense of foreboding I answer the call. 'Maxim. What can I do for you?' I ask, cursing the shake in my voice.

There's a short pause on the end of the line before he says, 'I'd like to invite you over for brunch at my place tomorrow. Eleven o'clock suit you?'

Is it my imagination or does he sound more terse than usual? Or am I just projecting my anxiety about this thing with Maya onto him? Well, whatever's happening here, I know I have to turn up and face the man. Even if it means being forced to explain what the hell I'm doing messing around with his daughter.

The story Maya told me about what happened to the last associate of Maxim's who got involved with her slams right to the forefront of my mind as I think this. Not that I'll let him just push me around like he did that guy. Maya and I are adults, after all, and we can make our own decisions. But I could really do without a complication like this at the moment.

'Yes, eleven o'clock is fine,' I reply, as evenly as I can.

'Great. See you then,' Maxim says, and rings off.

I sit staring at the phone for a few seconds, wondering what the hell I'm going to walk into there.

Shrugging off my concern, I get up from my chair and, sliding my phone into my pocket, stride out of my office and lock the door behind me.

I'm not about to let Maxim Darlington-Hume intimidate me, that's for damn sure.

If that's what he's intending to do.

I shake off the final bit of tension in my shoulders as I approach the lift and stab at the button to take me down to the lobby, determined not to let it get to me. There's no point worrying about something that might never happen.

Anyway, I've faced worse and come through it fighting.

I can handle whatever life's about to throw at me next.

I turn up at eleven o'clock on the dot and am greeted at the door by Maxim himself, looking imposing in sharply tailored trousers and a dark grey shirt which is open at the neck. I think it must be impossible for Maxim Darlington-Hume to look anything but impeccably turned out, even in casual wear. I, in sharp contrast, am wearing faded jeans and a casual V-necked jumper today, but he doesn't seem to care, ushering me inside with a wave.

'Benedict, thanks for coming at such short notice.'

I shake his proffered hand—Maxim seems to be a great believer in a firm handshake—then follow him deeper into his large hallway.

'I've invited my daughters to join us today,' he

says as we walk towards the dining room. 'I think it'd be good for you to talk to April about your plans for the future of Ergo-i, since she's my right-hand woman and will be the person to contact when I'm not available.'

On the one hand this is good news, because it points towards him not having found out about me and Maya, and is therefore still on board with blessing my business with his expertise and influence, but on the other it's bad news—because 'daughters' means that Maya's here too.

We're going to have to watch ourselves, because we could easily give everything away if we're not careful.

'Ben, how lovely to see you again,' April says as we enter the room, standing up to greet me.

I shake her cool, firm hand—she's her father's daughter through and through—and return her smile, then turn to glance around the room.

There she is, Maya, sitting at the other end of the table, looking poised and beautiful. My stomach twists in knots. It's worrying how she always has such a discomposing effect on me. It isn't going to make this easy.

'Maya, good to see you,' I say amiably, hoping she'll play the game.

'Mr Chivers, marvellous to see you too,' she replies, in such an overly polite tone I'm afraid she might give us away.

'Do sit down, Ben,' April says with exaggerated

friendliness, as if to try and cancel out what she clearly thinks is her sister's rudeness.

She points to the chair next to her, which I feel forced to take.

In my peripheral vision I see Maya shift in her chair, raising her knee to prop her foot on the edge of her seat, and for one crazy moment I wonder whether she's flashing me again. My body reacts instinctively, my blood rushing hot through my veins and my cock springing to attention. I push the ridiculous idea out of my head and force myself to relax. Of course she's not going to do that with her father and sister here.

Is she?

I don't dare look.

The housekeeper comes in then, and delivers us each a plate containing a full English breakfast. I keep my focus firmly on my food, tucking in immediately at Maxim's insistence, grateful for the distraction.

There's a short silence while we all swallow down our first mouthfuls. To be honest, I'm having trouble getting the food past my throat because I'm so aware of Maya's presence to my left. She, on the other hand doesn't appear to be eating at all, I realise, when I sneak a glance at her. Instead she's staring out of one of the long picture windows, which affords a magnificent view of the lush, neatly manicured garden.

'Where's Juno? I thought you said you'd invited her,' April asks her father, who's sitting on the other side of her.

'She's in Italy,' Maya chimes in, causing us all to turn to look at her.

April responds with a scowl. 'What's she doing in Italy?'

'You mean *who's* she doing?' Maya quirks a waggish eyebrow. 'Sandro Ricci, hopefully.'

'Ugh! Maya, for goodness' sake, can you talk about something other than sex for once? Anyone would think you're fourteen, not twenty-four!' April spits back.

'Jesus, don't be such a bloody prude, April. It's just sex—everyone does it.'

There's an infinitesimal pause during which the two women glare at each other. April looks away first.

'Well, maybe not *you*,' Maya adds in an undertone that we all hear very clearly.

April rolls her eyes but I notice her shift in her chair, as if she's been made uncomfortable by the comment. Judging by the tense way April always holds herself I wonder whether Maya's comment is actually accurate. She certainly gives the impression she needs to loosen up a little.

April flashes me an apologetic smile, then proceeds to ask me a comprehensive slew of questions about my future plans for the new software we've just launched.

I spend the next twenty minutes talking about the state of the market with her, acutely aware of Maya sitting at the other side of the table, not saying a word. Maxim joins in every now and again with the conversation, and doesn't seem at all put out by Maya's silence, nor bothered by that fact she's being completely ignored by everyone.

As soon as we've all finished eating and the plates are cleared away Maya excuses herself. I watch her go out of the corner of my eye, but she doesn't look back at me.

April keeps me talking for another few minutes and I struggle to keep my agitation in check. I want to go and find Maya, smooth things over with her, but I'm not sure how I'm going to manage it with April and her father around.

I'm about to excuse myself to the bathroom and go to try and find her when the housekeeper re-enters the room and whispers something into Maxim's ear.

'I'm sorry to break up the conversation, but we've had a call from David in New York, April, and he needs to speak to us urgently.' He turns to fix me with his lofty stare. 'If you'll excuse us, Benedict? We need to take this.'

'Of course,' I say, standing up as they do, relieved for the excuse to get away. 'Thank you for inviting me over.'

Maxim gives me one last handshake and leaves the room. April shoots me a friendly but tight smile before following in his wake.

I leave straight after them and go to look for Maya. I find her in the kitchen, pouring herself a glass of water.

'You're still here, then?' she says, without looking at me.

I ignore her question, though it doesn't really sound like a question—more like an accusation.

'Sorry I didn't get an opportunity to talk to you over brunch,' I say, leaning casually against the counter next to her, watching as she pops two painkillers out of their plastic pockets and swallows them down with a gulp of water.

She lifts one shoulder in an indifferent shrug. 'Don't apologise. You and my sister clearly have a lot in common. Much more than you and I do. We just have sex, but you can talk *business* with her, right?'

Does she feel inadequate compared to her sister? I suppose I can understand why she might. April is a very successful businesswoman and Maya is only at the beginning of her journey with her own venture.

'So I take it you and April don't get on, then?' I say, injecting humour into my voice to try and lighten the mood.

'My sister is a bitch from hell,' she says bluntly, and I can tell from the sharp way she looks at me that I've hit a nerve.

'It's that bad between you?'

'Yes,' she bites out, 'it's *that* bad.'

'Is there anything in particular that rubs you up the wrong way about her?' I ask, intrigued.

I can see that April might be a little officious, but surely it's the role of the eldest child to keep the younger siblings in line?

'The fact she wishes I'd never been born probably has something to do with it,' she says, her eyes flashing with something that could be anger, or perhaps hurt.

'What? Surely she's never said that to you.'

'You wanna bet?' she says, raising her eyebrows in challenge.

Before I have a chance to push her for more information the housekeeper strides into the kitchen. Her gaze travels from where I'm lounging against the counter to where Maya is standing ramrod-straight, glaring at me with defiance in her eyes. She turns around and walks straight back out again.

Smart woman.

Maya continues to frown at me, but I'm sure I catch a hint of anguish in her expression now. My chest contracts at the sight of it and I reach for her. Despite being hyper aware of how easily we could get caught, I'm not going to just walk away from her when she's clearly feeling upset about being ignored.

Because, despite my determination not to, I care about her. She's the most gutsy, unpredictable and extraordinary woman I've ever met and she deserves better than that.

I decide a charm offensive is probably in order to smooth the tension out.

'Are you feeling okay?' I ask, pushing a loose strand of hair away from her face.

She looks at me with big, sorrowful eyes. 'Headache.'

'You know the best cure for that?' I murmur, moving in to crowd her against the kitchen counter.

Her body language is stiff, as if she's holding herself back, but the heat she radiates towards me and the seductive scent of her in my nostrils only hardens my resolve.

Her expression is all cool indifference, but I see the spark of interest in her eyes. 'Enlighten me,' she says with a bored-sounding sigh.

'An orgasm.'

Her eyebrows rise fractionally, though I can tell she's trying not to give me any reaction. She's still punishing me for ignoring me earlier.

'Oh, really? And who around here is going to give me one of those?'

Despite her annoyance with me I can tell she can't resist the challenge I'm throwing out.

'Come with me and maybe you'll find out.'

I'm just stepping away from her when I'm suddenly aware of someone walking into the kitchen behind me.

All the hairs on the back of my neck stand up, and as I turn and see who it is my stomach drops to the floor. It's Maxim.

He gives us both a look that I can't quite interpret and my body flushes hot, then cold.

Did he hear what I just said to her?

Fuck. What is *wrong* with me? How could I have been so careless? This thing with Maya has messed so thoroughly with my head that I'm taking stupid risks now.

My heart thumps hard against my chest and goosebumps flare across my skin as Maxim walks towards me.

'Benedict—glad I caught you. I wanted a quick word before you go,' he says, clapping a hand on my shoulder in a fatherly sort of gesture and making me jump a little at the force of it. 'It looked as though you and April were getting on well over brunch.'

This is said as a statement, not a question.

I stare at him in panicked confusion for a moment, before it dawns on me that he can't have heard what Maya and I were saying and is talking about something completely different.

I force myself to focus. I have to keep a cool head here or this could go very wrong.

'Yes, she and I have a lot in common,' I agree. 'Especially where our views on how to run a business are concerned. She's a very switched-on woman. You must be proud of the way she's developing her role in your company.'

I'm twitchy with the awareness that Maya is standing right there beside me, listening to every word of this—especially because I now know how much she dislikes her sister—but I also know it'd be a bad idea to try and fob Maxim off with anything but the truth right now.

He smiles, which puts me immediately on my guard. The man is not normally a smiler.

'I was going to suggest you take her out for dinner. Get to know her a bit better. Perhaps while you're there the two of you could discuss our role in your business going forward,' he says, with great emphasis on 'our'.

And I suddenly realise exactly what's going on here. He wants me to partner with April—and not just in a business sense.

In my peripheral vision I see Maya turn her head sharply to look at me, and in that moment I know that this is probably my one and only opportunity to tell Maxim about us—openly and honestly. To let this thing between us out into the world and perhaps turn it into something more than it's been allowed to be up till this point.

But do I want that?

Do I?

I know I have about two seconds to decide, and I'm on the verge of saying the words when I see something in Maxim's face that stops me—a hardness and a determination to get what he wants.

With a stab of frustration I realise I have to do as he asks if I still want him on my executive board. A wrong move now could jeopardise the company I've strived so hard to make a success of, and I can't let it all slip through my fingers.

My heart thumps wildly against my chest.

I can't do it. I can't tell him about us.

Not right now.

And it's just dinner with April at this point. Surely Maya will understand that?

Pushing a dissenting voice to the back of my mind, I give Maxim a returning smile and say, 'Yes, sure. That sounds like a good idea. I'll give her a call in the week to arrange it.'

Maxim gives me a nod of approval. 'Good. Well, thanks again for coming over today. I'm looking forward to getting to know you better as our partnership develops.'

'Me too,' I say, though my voice lacks its usual confidence.

I sound like a fucking fake.

Maxim's mobile phone begins to ring and he excuses himself with a nod of apology.

I watch him walk away, wondering how it was he came to be such a devious bastard. Maybe it's because he lost his wife at such an early age. Perhaps it damaged him more than he lets on.

As soon as he's gone I glance towards Maya, and I'm assaulted by a wave of self-reproach as I take in the shuttered expression on her face.

'Well, I guess that's you and me finished, then,' she says.

If the look in her eyes wasn't so hard I'd think she was joking. But I know her too well by now.

'It's just a business dinner with April.'

'Don't be an idiot, Ben. You *know* that's not what it really is. My father wants you and April to become a power couple—one he can control. You can't go out with her and continue this fling with me. It's too dangerous. There's no way he won't find out about us.

Not when his precious April's involved. He'll have you under such close scrutiny you won't be able to take a piss without him knowing about it.'

'I have to play his game for now—for the sake of my business,' I say with a growl of frustration.

I want to tell her how close I was to exposing us, but I can't bring myself to. Perhaps because deep down I'm ashamed of myself for not having the guts to do it, and I know what a coward it'll make me seem if I say it out loud.

And I really don't want her to think of me like that.

'I understand, Ben—really. Your business has to come first,' she says, with a cold finality that sends a shock of distress through me.

She shakes her head, making her long, silky hair shimmer across her shoulders. 'I guess I shouldn't be surprised. Money and power always win out.'

'Maya—'

But she cuts me off with a raised hand. That cool insouciance act is back.

'This thing between us always had a shelf life and I guess we've just reached it.'

I stare at her in shock. Where has the warm, playful woman I've gotten to know over these last few weeks gone?

'Look—'

Again she waves away my protest, her face so blank of emotion it's chilling.

'A word of warning, though. April dumped a man

she was actually in love with because she was afraid it'd make her look bad when word got out that his father was a money-grubbing liar, so she won't think twice about ditching you the moment you're not useful to her any more.'

She moves closer to me…so close I can smell her familiar sensual scent—which, of course, has the same discomposing effect on me that it always does.

'I recommend you watch your back. I wouldn't put it past my father to try and steal your company out from under you,' she adds. 'With April's help.'

'Wait—can we please just talk about this—?'

She shakes her head with such finality I know she's made up her mind. She's ending this.

'Bye, Ben. It's been fun. Have a nice life.'

Before I'm able to utter a word in response she turns her back on me and walks away, leaving me standing in the empty room, staring after her with the terrifying sense that I've just lost something very precious and I might never be able to get it back.

CHAPTER TEN

Maya

I HEAD STRAIGHT back to my flat in a state of cold numbness and sit determinedly flicking through the pages of my little black book, looking for someone to take away the horrible hollow ache of pain that's pressing in on my chest. But I end up throwing it at the wall in frustration. I don't want any of the people in it.

I want Ben.

But I can't have him. Not any more. Not now my father's made it clear what his plans are for him. I know exactly what will happen if he doesn't get his way and I can't expect Ben to put his future on the line for me. For a fling.

Because he made it very clear through his silence that that's really all I am to him. There was a moment back there with my father when Ben could have told him about us. But he chose not to. He chose his business interests instead.

I shouldn't be upset about that—he never promised me more—but I guess deep down I hoped…

I swallow hard, trying to clear the painful tightness in my throat.

I know I have to pull myself together, but I'm scared that the pieces of me that were shattered apart the moment Ben agreed to go on that date with April are too fragmented to heal back together.

I slam into the kitchen and pour myself a large vodka, which I neck in one go. There's a hot pressure behind my eyes that I can't shake; it's like I'm ill with some kind of fever.

Except I know I'm not ill.

It's something much worse than that.

I'm fucking *in love* with him.

But he doesn't love me back.

How have I let this happen to me? I've never let myself care this much about someone before—for this exact reason.

The irony of it is that I childishly thought I'd be getting one over on April by pursuing Ben. Looks like the joke's on me.

Obviously I don't deserve to settle down with someone as amazing as him—not after the way I've acted. My father's made this very clear, first by taking Jack away from me and now by taking Ben, which I suppose I deserve since I was instrumental in taking the woman he loved away from him.

Karma has finally caught up with me and come to mercilessly rip my heart out of my chest.

And the fundamental truth of it is that no matter how I feel about April, I know Ben will be much better off with my infinitely more palatable sister. She can give him the kind of security and social standing he's always craved. They'll make the perfect couple: business-minded, ambitious and extremely success-ful at getting exactly what they want.

And I want Ben to be happy. I really do.

So it's time for me to move on—even though the very thought of it makes me sick to my stomach.

My thoughts are derailed by a loud, determined knock on the door and my stomach lurches.

It's him. I know it is without even having to look. But I can't talk to him right now. If I do I'm afraid all my pain and heartache will come spilling out and I'll never be able to put myself back together again.

I take a deep breath.

Then another.

I can't be a coward about this. I have to face him and put an end to whatever's left between us—for both our sakes.

There's another loud knock on the door and I stomp towards it and swing it open, summoning every last reserve of strength I have in me, deter-mined not to let the sight of him break me.

'What do you want, Ben?' I ask dispassionately.

'I think we need to talk,' he says.

I let out a long sigh, loading it with as much dis-dain as I can muster. 'I thought I'd made it clear. It's over. I don't want to see you any more,' I say, and go to shut the door in his face.

But before I can get it all the way closed he's put

his arm out to stop me and pushed the door open again, propelling me back into the hallway with the force of the swing.

'Hey!' I shout in frustration.

There's a strange kind of jumpiness building in my limbs, as if I'm losing control of them, and I'm suddenly terrified I'm not going to be able to keep up this uncaring charade for much longer.

I back up into the hallway as he advances towards me.

'Fine—come in then. But I'm really not interested in anything you have to say,' I mutter, turning my back on him.

I can't let him to know how much this is hurting me. I want him to think I don't care, so he doesn't have to either.

Taking a deep breath, I march into my living room and go to stand in the middle of it with my arms tightly folded. He follows me in, shucking off his coat and laying it on the sofa before turning to fix me with his penetrating gaze.

I stare back at him coolly, with my blood racing hot through my veins and my heartbeat thumping in my throat.

'Well, go ahead, then—say your piece,' I prompt tonelessly when he doesn't immediately say anything. I can't stand the silence; it's driving me crazy.

He sighs. 'Look, he caught me off-guard, and at the time I didn't feel like I had a choice about agreeing to that date with your sister,' he says, his dark eyes intent on mine.

'I know. I get it. It's fine, Ben—seriously. But it's time we put an end to this fling now anyway. It's run its course.' My breath is coming thickly through my throat as I desperately try to keep my tears at bay.

'I wanted to tell him about us—' he begins to say.

I put my hand up to stop him. 'I don't need to hear your excuses. We don't need to drag this out. It's over.' I lay the flat of my hand against his chest and push hard. 'Just go, okay? I'm bored with this now.'

He barely moves. It's like trying to move a man-shaped block of concrete.

'Just like that?' he asks, as if he can't believe I'd be so cold as to act that way.

'Yes, just like that,' I say, ruthlessly stripping my voice of any emotion.

'We never should have got involved with each other,' he bites out in frustration, scrubbing his hand through his hair.

'No. We shouldn't. It would have saved us both a lot of trouble.'

The air is heavy now, with resentment and something else—something dark, which throbs with dangerous promise.

'Look, just fucking *leave*, will you?' I shout in frustration.

But when I go to push him one more time he wraps his fingers around my upper arms, pulling me against him, trapping me. And I'm not entirely sure how it happens, but the very next second we're kissing. One of us must have started it, but I can't for the life of me say who. But it's exactly what I want. What I need right now.

I bite at his lips, then push back hard as he kisses me deeply, forcing his tongue into my mouth. It's as if we're battling for supremacy.

And it's a battle I'm determined to win.

A surge of rage at the unfairness of it all makes me shove at him hard, propelling him backwards. His legs hit the sofa and he falls back onto it, pulling me with him.

My mouth is on his again, rough and angry, and I tear at his clothes and scratch his skin, using this lead-up to sex—because that's certainly what's going to happen here—to make him hurt like I'm hurting, even if it's only physically.

He's pulling at my clothes too—tugging up my skirt and yanking so hard on my knickers that they rip and come away in his hand.

His breath is hot and fast on my face, his eyes dark and shot with lust when I pull back to look into them.

I fight with his belt for a moment, before tugging the soft leather out of the buckle so I can move on to tearing off the button on his trousers and yanking down the zip.

Wrapping my hand around his cock, I feel how hard and ready for me he is, and without another thought in my head I move up his body and slide down onto him, taking him all the way deep inside me in one angry thrust.

We both let out guttural groans as my body meets his, and I use my arms to take my weight as I bounce up and down on his cock, feeling him hit me deep inside and loving the pleasurable pain this causes me.

I'm panting hard now, letting out low groans of satisfaction as I maintain control of the movement. I'm just using him to wank off on, I tell myself. That's all this is. I'm using him like he's used me.

Reaching up, he cups my face with his hands and begins to stroke his thumbs across my cheeks, but I shake my head fiercely, releasing myself from his grip. I don't want any kind of gentle affection right now. I want fast and rough and ugly.

I lift myself off him, before smashing down again and grinding myself against his pelvis, making sure his cock hits all the right spots inside me. Sensation coils deep inside me as I repeat the movements over and over and I begin to feel myself go. I let out a loud cry of relief as an orgasm crashes into me, the intensity of it blurring my vision and making the blood rush in my ears.

I'm taking control back.

It's mine again now. All fucking *mine*.

Lights and colours flash across my eyes as I allow myself to sink into the ecstasy of the sensations, and I'm only vaguely aware of Ben thrusting hard into me from below before letting out his own groan of completion.

We lie pressed together hard, panting, his arms wrapped around me, as we slowly come back to our senses.

And that's when the panic hits me.

I sit up, pushing at him to let go of me, to get out of me.

He draws his arms away reluctantly and I scramble off him and stand up.

'Hey, what's wrong? Are you okay?' he asks, his dark eyes narrowed with worry as he sits up.

But I don't want his concern. Not any more.

'I'm fine,' I say flippantly, though I feel anything but. I need to keep calm, keep my head, or this could all go horribly wrong for me.

Steeling myself, I turn to face him, tugging down my skirt.

'Okay, I got what I needed—closure. So feel free to move on to my sister with a clear conscience.'

'What?' He looks totally confused. 'What the hell are you talking about?'

'I'm not playing games, Ben. I'm genuinely ready to move on—and so, I think, are you.'

He stands up, tugging at his trousers, and moves towards me, holding up both hands, palms forward. 'That's not what this was and you know it.'

I make a big show of yawning loudly. 'You need to leave. I'm tired and I want to go to bed.'

He stares at me with an incredulous frown on his face for a moment, as if he's wondering whether I'm really serious. Clearly he decides that I am, because he sweeps his coat off the back of the sofa.

'Fine—if that's the way you want to play it, I'll go.'

'Good,' I say, and a mixture of relief and panicky regret swirl through me as I watch him disappear out of the room.

I catch up with him as he's opening the front door. For some reason I'm unable to just leave it at that. I need to make sure there's no way back from this.

He turns to look at me and something like relief flashes across his face—as if he thinks I've changed my mind and come to stop him leaving.

'I hope you, April and my father are happy together in your cosy little threesome. You deserve each other,' I force myself to say, trying not to react to the wounded look on his face this provokes. I have to hold the pretence together, for both our sakes. 'Now, get out of my house!'

I give him a firm push, then another, forcing him to take a stumbling step over the threshold.

'Maya—'

He begins to argue, perhaps hoping to say something that'll make it easier on us both when we're pretending to be civil to each other at all the hideous family dos we're bound to bump into each other at for many years to come.

'Don't bother,' I say coldly. 'I don't want to hear it. In fact I don't ever want to hear from you again.'

And with that I shut the door firmly in his face.

CHAPTER ELEVEN

Benedict

SHE DOESN'T OPEN the door to me again, no matter how long I stand there banging on it. So, deciding not to embarrass myself any longer, I leave her doorstep and make my way home, feeling sick to my stomach.

Is that it, then? Is it really over between us? I can't quite believe it could have ended so suddenly, but then again, I'm also not that surprised. I've been expecting something like this all along.

So why does it feel like my insides have been pulled out through my throat?

I don't hear from her again. Not that I'm expecting to after the ice-cold send-off she gave me. And on Friday night—six long, painful days after Maya cut me out of her life for good—I enter the 'restaurant of the moment' with April and pull out a chair for her at the table the maître d' shows us to.

She flashes me a grateful but cool smile.

I take a moment to pull myself together and refocus. It's not fair on my dinner companion if my thoughts are elsewhere for the entire evening.

Mind you, having said that, April is a very beautiful, smart and capable woman—the latter borne out by the fact that Maxim is happy for her to be so intrinsically involved with his business—but it seems all those glowing attributes come with an aloof distance and a disassociation from the people around her.

From what I've seen of her so far, she says all the right things at the right time—but it's as if she's playing a part. She's not really there in spirit. There's something missing. I know it sounds ridiculous, but I'd hazard a guess at it being her soul.

We make chitchat about business matters while we choose our meals and place our orders, and I try to not think about Maya for at least a few minutes. But it seems I'm incapable of it, because when there's a pause in conversation I can't stop myself from asking, 'So, how's Maya getting on with her plans for her jewellery business?'

April smiles dispassionately and leans back in her chair. 'My father seems to be impressed with her business plan so he's agreed to support her in it.'

'That's great,' I say, genuinely pleased to hear it, despite my lingering frustration with the way she ended things between us.

'I understand you had the pleasure of her company for a few weeks?' April says with a wry smile. 'That must have been challenging.'

I lean back in my chair and cross my arms, feeling defensive on Maya's behalf at the derision in April's tone.

'Actually, we got on really well,' I say, fixing April with a steady smile. 'Her work ethic really impressed me. I think she'll make a real success of her business. She's certainly got the drive and determination for it.'

April's eyebrows rise. 'Yes, *determined* is a very appropriate adjective for my sister.'

'Maya mentioned the two of you don't really get on?'

I really shouldn't keep talking about her, but I don't seem able to stop myself.

April lets out a small snort. 'That's putting it lightly. She hates my guts. Though I guess it's not surprising, considering what I said to her after our mother died.'

She gives me a calculating look, as if trying to assess from my reaction how much I already know about their story.

'What *did* you say to her?' I ask, intrigued to hear about it from April's perspective.

She swallows before she speaks. 'I basically suggested that we'd be better off without her in our family.'

'Why would you do that?' I ask, shock and horror sliding through me at hearing that Maya hadn't been exaggerating about April's cruelty.

She looks over her shoulder, as if to check whether

anyone is listening in, and when she sees that no one is she leans forward in her chair and places her hands on the table in front of her.

'Because of her self-centred behaviour—before and after we lost my mother.'

'What sort of behaviour?'

April lets out a beleaguered sigh. 'Everything always has to be about *her*.' She sits back in her chair again, her brow pinched into a frown. 'My mother was supposed to be going on a skiing trip with a friend the week she died, but she had to take Maya with her instead because she'd been expelled from school.'

'Really? What was she expelled for?'

'I don't know. Knowing Maya, it will have been something to do with boys,' April bites out.

I don't react. Even though I instinctively want to defend Maya, my need to hear more about this wins out.

'The worst thing was that my mother's death could have been avoided, but she didn't go to the hospital after her fall—I'm guessing because she didn't want to leave Maya alone.'

She shifts in her chair and glances away. I look down to see she's twisted her fingers together so tightly they're starting to turn white.

'One of the hotel employees found her unconscious on the floor of their suite the morning after the accident—Maya was still languishing in bed with a hangover,' she adds, looking back at me. 'In the panic they didn't realise Maya was there, and they arranged for my mother's transfer back to the UK. My father had to send one of my mother's friends to go and get her and bring her home the next day.'

'The next *day*? And your father didn't go for her himself?' I ask, horrified to hear this.

'No.' She frowns at me. 'I think he was too worried about my mother's condition and didn't want to leave her.'

'But he didn't mind leaving his fourteen-year-old daughter alone in another country, not knowing whether her mother was alive or dead?' My voice is unsteady with dismay.

There's a tense pause as April digests this, as if it's never occurred to her before. 'Yes, I guess so...' she says slowly.

'Jesus,' I say, shaking my head.

That's pretty fucked up. No wonder Maya thinks her father isn't her greatest fan.

It occurs to me, in a flash of sickening insight, that Maya's probably been using her wild behaviour as an escape from the horrifying belief that her family all blame her for her mother's death.

The bottle of wine we've ordered arrives then, interrupting us, and we're quiet for a moment as the waiter pours us both a glass.

'I hadn't heard about Maya's involvement in your mother's accident until very recently,' I say to April once he's walked away.

'She told you about it?' she asks sharply, apparently shocked by the idea of this.

I nod. 'She mentioned it one day, when I asked her about your mother.'

'Huh… I'm surprised. As far as I know she's never uttered a word about it to anyone. She's refused to speak to any of the counsellors I've set up appointments with over the years.'

'Yes, well, she's a proud, headstrong woman. I imagine that implying there's something wrong with her and then trying to force her to do something she doesn't want to do would be counterproductive,' I point out.

There's no wonder Maya hates being around her sister if April's constantly tried to pressure her into getting psychoanalysed. I can't imagine *that* going down well with Maya at all.

'Perhaps she just wants to bury the past so she can get on with her life?' I suggest.

'Yes, well, she's been trying to do that for the last ten years. It's clear from her headline-grabbing behaviour that something's bound to give soon, though.'

Suddenly dropping her cutlery on the side of her plate, April lets out a small, surprisingly frustrated-sounding groan and puts her head in her hands.

'Of course I regret what I said to her now. Of *course* I do. I know deep down that it was just a horrible accident.'

'But you blamed Maya for your mother's death at the time?' I prompt.

April sighs and runs a hand over her face. 'It must have seemed like that to her back then, I suppose.'

She looks directly at me, her expression pleading.

'But in my defence I was in shock and grieving, and pretty naïve at that point in my life. I was only twenty and I'd led a really sheltered life. My mother's death turned my world upside down. It turned *all* our worlds upside down.'

The look in her eyes makes me think she's asking me to forgive her.

'I accept that what I said was unforgivable, and I've tried so many times to say sorry and repair our relationship, but she shut me out that day and she's never let me back in again. Anything I do or say— any interest I show in her life—she sees as meddling. So I'm afraid I've just given up trying.'

I nod and politely look away as she blinks rapidly. She takes a breath before she speaks again.

'My father was devastated after my mother died. He seemed to completely close down emotionally, so I ended up pretty much taking over as carer for my sisters once I'd graduated from university.'

She takes another long, audible breath.

'One of the worst things about that time was that I was in love with a guy I'd got together with in my final year. Jamie de Montford…' She tilts her head, as if asking whether I know him. 'He's a professional tennis player.'

I've heard of him—how could I not have? He's a very successful sports personality—but I don't know him personally, so I shake my head.

'I'd hoped to carry on my relationship with him after graduating, but my father…asked me—' there's an infinitesimal pause before the word 'asked', as if she's struggling not to say something different, '—to finish it with him, because apparently Jamie's father had planned a hostile takeover of our company right after my mother's death.'

She pauses to take a big gulp of her wine.

'The worst thing was, Jamie's father and mine had been good friends since their school days.' She takes another sip. 'My father doesn't take kindly to any kind of betrayal—especially not from people he thinks he can trust.'

Raising her eyebrows at me, she shakes her head as if in warning.

'Cross my father once and you'll never have the opportunity to do it again. He can be a hard bastard when he wants to be.'

She sighs, then waves a hand, as if annoyed with herself for deviating from her point.

'Anyway, he'd made it his life's mission to ruin Jamie's father financially, and he made me promise never to see Jamie again—which Jamie saw as me putting my father's wishes ahead of his. Let's just say he's never forgiven me for it. I think he actually believes I helped my father destroy his—or at least that I didn't try to stop him—even though I knew it would hurt Jamie too. Unfortunately, we run in similar social circles, and often bump into each other at parties and events. He clearly hates me now, and is vile every time I see him.'

'But you still love him? Is that what you're trying to tell me?' I interject, sensing that this story might hold the secret to her lost soul.

I see the same kind of closed look steal over her face that Maya gets when she's battling her feelings.

'No. Not any more. Not after the horrible way he treated me after the break-up.'

Picking up her knife and fork again, she stabs her steak and begins sawing at it, the motion uncharacteristically jerky. After a moment, she shakes her head, as if annoyed with herself for losing her cool, and forces herself to calm the movement.

'Anyway, that's all in the past. I like to live in the present. Speaking of which—it seems my father is a big fan of yours, and he thinks you and your company have an exciting journey ahead of you.'

'I'm pleased he's considering taking a position on my executive board,' I say, though from what I've just heard, added to the warning Maya gave me about him, I'm beginning to wonder whether I really want anything to do with the mercenary bastard.

'So you should be. He has a lot of influence around here.'

She glances around the restaurant, as if looking for specific examples of the sort of people he can bend to his will, then turns back to take another gulp of wine from her nearly empty glass.

'You realise he's keen for the two of us to partner up?' Her smile is wide, but a little forced. 'Personally, I mean, not just in a business sense.'

'I got that impression, yes,' I say carefully.

I don't want to say the wrong thing here and destroy a possibly beneficial alliance. Despite having heard Maya's complaints about April, I find I actually like her. She's a little cold and uptight, but now I know why I've warmed to her.

'So what do you think?' she asks me, her expression assertive and direct.

'About what?'

'About a partnership of convenience. I wouldn't be averse to marrying you if it would be mutually convenient to our business interests. It could be a purely platonic relationship, if you'd prefer.'

I gape at her, lost for words. Has she really just asked me to marry her? Looking at her expression of cool attentiveness, I realise that she has.

Intellectually, I recognise that in business terms it would be a very good move. Being a part of the Darlington-Hume family would open all sorts of doors. So I'm surprised by how violently against the idea I am. A disgusted voice in my head is telling me not even to consider it. It sounds suspiciously like Maya's voice and it won't bloody shut up.

The memory of the utter contempt on her face the very last time I saw her comes back to me like a punch to the chest, and I'm suddenly aware of a weird, painful sort of tightness there.

'That's an interesting offer, and I'm hugely grateful for the opportunity to consider it,' I say carefully, keeping my gaze steady with hers. 'But I'm not sure I'm in a position to accept right now.'

She sits back in her chair and fixes me with a discerning stare.

'Are you in love with Maya?'

The bluntness of the question takes me by surprise, and it's a full few seconds before I'm able to reply.

'No. Of course not.'

Still she assesses me with one eyebrow quirked, as if she's not convinced I'm telling her the truth.

'Are you sure? Because you've not stopped asking about her all evening.'

I frown and cross my arms, finding it hard to look her in the eye for some reason. 'Yes, I'm sure.'

Which of course I *am*.

Aren't I?

I'm not in love with Maya. I can't be. I don't do serious relationships and neither does she.

April nods curtly, but the look on her face tells me she's not convinced by my blustering denial.

'Okay. Well, I'm going to Morocco for the weekend, but perhaps we could talk again once I'm back,' she says, in a gentle sort of voice that makes me think she's actually a little concerned about me.

Not that she needs to be.

I'm fine. Totally fine.

We get up from the table and I give April a kiss on the cheek before seeing her to the chauffeur-driven Bentley that's waiting for her outside.

After that I'm too restless to go home, so instead I head to a nearby bar and sit sipping whisky while thoughts of what I've just learned about Maya spin through my head.

The more I drink, the more intense the disturbing, heavy sinking feeling in my chest gets.

If I'm totally honest with myself—and I know that it's probably time I am—I'm ashamed of myself for treating Maya with so little respect, so little care for her feelings. Especially now I know what happened to her in her youth.

No one should have to live with something like that hanging over them. No wonder she acts the way she does, as if she couldn't give a shit what people think of her. She must have to in order to deal with the horror of believing that the people she loves most hate her. And I imagine she must hate herself too, to some degree—even if her mother's death was just a terrible accident.

And now she's shut me out too, after I failed to give her the loyalty she needed. I told her she could trust me, but when I put her father's wishes above hers I proved without a doubt that she couldn't.

After seeing the coldness in her eyes, I can't imagine her ever trusting me again.

It shocked me just how callous she was at the end too—as if she'd already expelled me from her heart.

If I was ever there in the first place.

But then, haven't I also been repressing the feelings I have for her?

After spending my whole childhood hiding my emotions from my father, so as not to give him the pleasure of having any kind of power over me, I've become used to keeping myself aloof and distant. To stopping myself from loving anyone in case they use it against me. In case they finally break me.

I realise, as I sit staring in disgust at the now half-empty bottle of whisky I ordered, that the pain I've been feeling in my chest is my heart, which is missing a piece that Maya's been filling. A hole I didn't want to acknowledge existed before. And I know I can't go on pretending to myself that she means nothing to me.

It's time I accepted the feelings I have for her—to acknowledge that the time I've spent with her has woken me up from the emotionless half-life I was living until I met her.

There's no point denying it any longer.

April's right. I'm in love with Maya.

And I want a real relationship with her. One in which I get to take care of her and make her happy. Because she deserves that.

But it seems my revelation has come too late. Because she's made it perfectly clear that she definitely doesn't feel the same way.

CHAPTER TWELVE

Maya

AFTER A WEEK of excruciatingly long days at my father's office, when I stumble in and perform my mundane tasks in a numb daze, followed by long, restless nights which leave me shattered and drained, I spend all of Saturday in bed with my phone resolutely turned off, blankly watching old action thrillers back to back, finding some sick solace in the gory bloodshed they supply.

More than once I imagine it's actually my father on the receiving end of the violence, instead of the poor innocent bad guys who haven't done anything nearly as bad as he has.

Despite a stupid niggling hope that Ben won't be able to live without me, he hasn't called or turned up on my doorstep again, or shown any sign of missing me at all.

So it seems he believed my self-centred bitch performance was real and it truly is over between us.

When I wake up late on Sunday, after another night of fitful sleep, during which I had to force myself to leave my phone turned off so I wouldn't constantly check it on the off-chance that Ben had texted or called and I'd missed it, I'm momentarily confused to see about twenty voicemail messages showing up when I finally turn it on again.

Someone's been trying very hard to get hold of me.

When I open up the app with a trembling finger I see the calls started a couple of hours ago.

And they're all from April.

I almost delete them without listening to them, assuming she's calling to give me her usual kind of talking-to about some kind of bad behaviour I've supposedly perpetrated, but some sixth sense kicks in and I stop myself. She wouldn't call me that many times unless it was really important.

With my heart thumping in my ears, I click on the first message and listen to it. My sister's voice comes through loud and clear, though it's not quite the together April I'm used to hearing. In fact she sounds breathy and worried.

'Maya, it's me. Listen, don't panic, but Dad's been in a bad accident on the motorway. According to the police, another driver had a heart attack at the wheel and crashed into him. His car flipped over a few times.'

She pauses here for a second and I hear a cacophony of sound in the background, like lots of people chattering.

Her words swim through my mind and it's as if I'm hearing them from afar—as if I'm only dreaming this and it's not really happening.

And I'm calm. Calmer than I've ever been in my entire life.

'He's been helicoptered to St John's Wood Hospital,' she goes on. 'I'm in bloody Morocco and I can't get a flight back—'

Her voice becomes even more stressed-sounding at this point, and through the thick fog in my head I picture her standing at an airport desk, glowering at some poor woman who's just told my formidable sister she can't help her.

'There's a baggage handlers' strike, or some such shit,' she goes on.

Yep, she's definitely stressed if she's swearing, I think abstractedly.

'Hopefully they'll get themselves organised soon, but in the meantime I'm going to wait here at the airport. I've tried to get our private jet to come for me, but apparently one of Dad's executives has got it in Australia at the moment.'

There's the sound of a child crying in the background, then a frustrated sigh from my sister as she apparently moves away from the human nuisance.

'Anyway… Can you go to the hospital to be with him till I get there? The doctors can't—or won't— give me much information about his condition over the phone, but apparently he's in Theatre—'

It's at this point that she really starts to lose it, and

I hear what sounds like a hiccough on the end of the line. When she speaks again to sign off the call it's clear she's trying not to cry.

The sound of my sister's distress hits me hard, finally breaking through my strange dissociation and stealing the breath from my lungs.

Oh, my God, my father's in the hospital.

All on his own, judging by the other calls April has made to my phone and I've not answered. I click through them frantically, listening to the beginning of each message. Yep, she's still stuck in Morocco, and apparently Juno's still in Italy and having the same sort of problem getting a flight back.

It's up to me to handle this.

My head swims and I have to sit down and take some deep breaths till the feeling passes.

But I'm frighteningly conscious that I'm wasting time.

My father needs me.

I have to get over there right fucking *now*.

Somehow I manage to pull myself together and drag on some clothes with shaking hands, shove my feet into some shoes and grab my coat and bag.

I'm not entirely sure how I get to the hospital. It's all a blur of taxis and panic.

When I finally locate my father's ward I'm enraged not to be able to find someone to help me right away. Don't they know this is a fucking emergency? What if my father's dying alone? I can't let that happen.

Pushing that awful thought out of my head—I think I'll go insane if I even entertain it—I finally find a nurse to help me and she pages my father's doctor. When he arrives, he patiently explains that my father's pretty messed up, with broken ribs, a collapsed lung and head injuries. He's in surgery and will be for the next hour or so.

I feel as though I'm not actually present in my body as I watch him walk away to see to another patient, as if my father's accident is only one of the many routine things he has to deal with today— which is probably sadly accurate.

For me, though, it's like standing at the edge of the world. One false step now and I'll plunge into blackness.

Memories of the horror and panic I felt the morning after I childishly ignored my mother's pleas to let her into my locked hotel bedroom at the ski resort so we could talk come slamming into my head. Not seeing her on my way down, I'd convinced myself she hadn't cared enough to follow me down that treacherous ski slope. Then I'd woken up from a deep, booze-induced sleep to find the apartment empty and the door wide open, as if she'd left in a hurry.

It fell to the poor hotel receptionist to tell me she'd been found unconscious on the living room floor and rushed off to hospital in a helicopter. They hadn't even realised I was there, because I'd somehow slept through the whole ruckus and the information hadn't been passed on properly in the panic to get my mother medical care quickly.

After being unable to reach my father I went back to the suite and waited there. And waited. I paced up and down, feeling as though I was going mad, wanting my dad so badly I felt sick with it.

Thirteen horrifying hours later my mother's friend Sylvie came to get me and take me home. She was the one who told me my mother was dead.

Her expression was full of abject grief, and also what I came to realise was reproach for the central part I'd played in the tragedy. It stayed with me for a long time after that, haunting my dreams.

And now here I am again—only this time it's my father whose life is in the balance.

And once again I'm alone.

There's an empty sort of ache in my chest, and I have a weird sense that I desperately need something to fill it or I'll go crazy.

I know what it is I need, of course. Or rather who.

Ben.

It's Ben.

I want his warm, reassuring presence here with me, to keep me calm and sane. I want him to hold me and tell me it's all going to be okay.

But I know he won't come, even if I call him. Why would he? I made sure he'd never want to see me ever again.

I'm pacing the hallway, trying to keep panic at

bay, not sure what to do with myself, when a familiar figure appears at the end of the corridor.

I stare at him, wondering whether I'm seeing things in my fucked-up state.

But I know by the way my stomach plunges and my heart starts to race that I'm not.

He's really here.

Ben's here.

But why?

'I came as soon as I heard,' he says in a worried voice as he reaches me. 'Are you okay?'

'Me?' I ask stupidly. 'It's my father who was in the accident.'

He frowns, as if I'm talking nonsense. 'I know that. April called me. She told me what happened.'

The elation I felt at seeing him instantly dissolves, leaving behind a heavy, hot ache of jealousy. So he's here for April, then.

'April's not here yet. She's stuck in Morocco.' I somehow manage to force the words past my constricted throat.

'I'm not here for April,' he says, shaking his head in exasperation. 'I'm here for *you*.'

'Me?' I say again, sure my ears must be playing tricks on me. He can't be here for me. Why would he be?

Unless…

I'm suddenly hyper aware of a tremble, starting deep inside my body and radiating outwards, making my flesh prickle as it hits my skin.

'She said she's not been able to get hold of you so I went over to your flat,' I hear Ben say through the strange, distancing fog in my head. 'When you weren't there I assumed you must be here already. At least I hoped so.' He takes a breath and frowns. 'I wanted to make sure you're okay.'

'Why would you do that?' I mutter.

He sighs, as if I'm being obtuse. 'Because I care about you, no matter what you might believe, and I didn't want you to be alone.'

A wave of sensation passes all the way through my body from my toes to my head, like a rushing surge of electricity, quickly followed by panic as I realise I'm about to cry in front of him. My whole body begins to shake uncontrollably with the stress of holding it back.

And then suddenly everything gets even more weird and distant, and I'm vaguely aware of Ben putting his arms around me and pulling me tightly against him. I rest my head on his shoulder, experiencing blessed relief in the way this makes me feel so safe.

'It's okay,' he murmurs. 'I've got you.'

I can feel his breath on the skin of my neck and the warmth and strength of his arms around me. It's the most wonderful thing in the world and I finally allow myself to sink into it and let go.

'I'm here for you, Maya,' he murmurs into my ear. 'I'm not going to leave you on your own to deal with this.'

Benedict

She looks terrible.

My heart stutters in my chest as I take in how pale she is, how dark the circles are under her eyes, as if she's not slept for a long time.

I manage to get the attention of a passing nurse and she shows us to a quiet private room where we can sit down. I guide Maya to a sofa and take the seat next to her.

'Are you okay?' I ask. I feel ridiculous for asking such a stupid question, but I want her to know that I'm concerned about her. That I genuinely care. Even if she doesn't want me to.

'I can't stop thinking that it's all my fault,' she blurts out, turning to look at me with haunted eyes.

'What are you talking about?' I ask, frowning in confusion.

'I was so angry with my father for taking you away from me. I wished—' She stops, as if the words are too painful to say out loud. She clears her throat and shakes her head, trying to pull herself together. 'I wished he was dead so he'd stop meddling in my life. But I didn't really mean it.'

I can practically feel her need for forgiveness.

'And now he's lying in a hospital bed. If he doesn't make it…' She pauses again and the air throbs with her angst.

'It's not your fault,' I say, cupping her jaw in my

hand so she's forced to look at me. I'm desperate to reassure her.

'But I fuck everything up, Ben.'

Her voice sounds so broken with pain it physically hurts me to hear it.

'What are you talking about? Of course you don't.'

'I do! It was my fault that my mum died,' she says angrily, confirming my fear that this must be bringing back all her old feelings of guilt and grief.

She starts to cry, her whole body convulsing with the force of her anguish, and I pull her into my arms, feeling her shuddering against me. All I can do is stroke her hair and whisper soothing words until her sobs finally slow and she sinks against me.

'Shit. I'm so sorry,' she whispers against my shoulder.

'No need to be sorry.'

'You must think I'm a such an awful, pathetic person.'

I shake my head. 'I don't, Maya.'

'You will once I tell you the truth,' she says. 'I didn't tell you the worst bit. I doubt you'll want anything to do with me ever again once you know what a selfish bitch I am.'

I see shame and pain flash across her face, so I lay my hand gently on her arm to show my support, feeling her tremble under my touch.

'Let me be the judge of that.'

I hold my breath, my heart beating hard as I wait

for her to continue. But she seems to be struggling to let the words out.

'It's okay, Maya. It won't change how I feel about you. Just say it.'

I can tell she doesn't fully believe me, but I also see that she's warring with herself about not telling me. She feels the need to confess, that's obvious, if she's going to move on. If *we're* going to move on.

She takes a shaky-sounding breath, then blows it out before speaking in a quiet, tear-strangled voice.

'I deliberately went onto that ski slope to scare her—even though I knew neither of us were skilled enough to ski on it.'

There's a tense, ringing silence while she stares down at her trembling hands and twists her fingers together.

'Why did you do that?' I ask, sensing her need for me to push her to keep talking. It's clear from the tense way she's holding herself that she doesn't usually allow herself to talk about it at all.

'I was angry and selfish and stupid,' she says in a rush.

She sucks in a steadying breath, then lets it out slowly before speaking again.

'I'd been expelled from school for cutting class to go and smoke weed on the recreational ground with some boys, so she'd taken me on that skiing holiday for us to have some girl-time. She was supposed to be going with a friend, but she cancelled on her so we could go together instead. I was really excited about it because we'd been close in my younger years, but as I got older she backed away from me. She always seemed to have something on her mind, and I felt like she'd stopped listening to me—or caring about me. That's why I started acting up at school. Because it would always get her attention. My father was always too busy with work to talk, and I wasn't academically brilliant like my sisters so he wasn't very interested in me anyway—I don't think he knew who I was most of the time. It was her I went to when I had a problem. She always showed me the love and affection I craved. Until she stopped being available.'

She shakes her head. Her eyes look glassy, as if she's imagining being back at the scene.

'We had a row about my bad behaviour and I decided to punish her—to test her love, I guess—by threatening to ski down that run. It was notoriously difficult, and people had died trying to do it, so she made me promise not to go on it.'

She closes her eyes and her shoulders seem to draw in towards her chest.

'She acted like she didn't care. I was so angry with her I skied down it in defiance and then went and got drunk in a local bar. I didn't realise she'd followed me down until the next day.'

She takes a ragged-sounding breath.

'My father hates me for it. He's never let me talk to him about what happened. I've tried so many times, but he refuses to discuss it. And now he's going to die before I can tell him that I'm sorry.'

There's an awful pause and I search desperately for the right thing to say. But what the hell *is* that? What could possibly make her feel better right now?

'I'm sure he doesn't hate you, Maya. You were just a child when it happened, and your mother was responsible for her own decisions. It sounds like it was just a terrible accident,' I reassure her. 'And you'll get to have that conversation with your father once he's better. He's getting the best care here, and as we know he's a tough bastard. He's not going to let something as inconsequential as a car accident do him in.'

I'm relieved to hear her laugh at that, even though it sounds strained.

She finally turns to look at me and I see hope in her face. And trust. And fear.

'Why are you here? After the awful way I treated you the other day I thought you'd never want anything to do with me ever again.'

I sigh and run my hand over my face, knowing it's time I was completely honest with her. 'Because it was never just a fling, what we had. You mean more to me than that. I tried to pretend to myself that I didn't care about you, but I do. I *do* care.'

'Really?' She's looking at me as if she can't quite believe it.

I let out a frustrated groan. 'I never should have agreed to go on that date with April. It was a gutless thing to do. Totally selfish. I told myself I was putting my concern about jeopardising my business relationship with your father first. But the truth is I was afraid of how I really felt about you, so I took the easy way out when it was offered to me, pretending to myself that I didn't have a choice. But of course I did.'

I reach out and cup her face again, so she can't look away.

'I want to have a proper relationship with you.' I swallow hard. 'Because I'm in love with you.'

Her eyes pool with tears and she lets out a hiccoughing sort of laugh.

'Thank *God*, because I love you too.'

I lean forward and kiss her gently, savouring the incredible, wonderfully familiar, taste of her in my mouth.

'You'd be better off with April, though, you know,' she says, her voice wobbling with emotion when we finally break away from each other. 'I'm not refined and successful, or a good person like she is.' She looks down, breaking eye contact with me. 'I'm afraid I don't deserve you. That's why I pushed you away.'

I nod, totally understanding that impulse.

She lets out a mirthless laugh. 'You see? I'm a fucking mess, Ben. I think it's because after my mother died I completely lost my mind. I felt completely powerless, so I made damn sure I'd never be in a position where I'd feel that vulnerable again. Until now. Until you. You crept up on me.'

She gives me a smile that nearly breaks my heart.

'You were just meant to be a bit of fun.'

I want so much to take away her pain, to set her

free from her guilt, but I know the only person who can do that is her. Hopefully with my support. Now that I'm really looking I can see that her fear of rejection has been there in her eyes the whole time I've known her—I just mistook it for insolence up till this point.

I experience a wave of shame at how badly I've misjudged her.

'None of us are perfect,' I say with a wry smile. 'You know, I always thought I hated the girls at that school where I used to work because they had such first-world problems,' I say sinking a little into her embrace, feeling her supporting me. 'They all seemed so excessively unhappy, considering their families' wealth and status. But I know now that misery breaches class boundaries. My mother and I were physically abused, but I know there are lots of types of abuse. Mental abuse, or something as simple as feeling forgotten about or ignored. Loneliness and isolation are ugly, brutal bastards. I was selfish to think you could never have any problems because of your seemingly privileged lifestyle.' I grimace at her. 'I'm sorry.'

She gives me an understanding smile and I feel reassured that she forgives me for being so obtuse and short-sighted.

'You're not the only one who's been misguided. All my bratty, headline-grabbing behaviour has been about trying to get my father's attention—to get him to care enough to talk to me so we can finally deal

with the subject of my part in my mother's death—
but I just ended up disappointing and alienating him
even more.'

She looks so tired, so utterly beaten. I pull her
into my arms and hold her tightly against me, rocking her gently.

'I should go and check how he's doing,' she says
shakily, trying to pull away from me.

'No, Maya, you need to rest. You're clearly exhausted. There's nothing you can do right now anyway. They'll come and tell us once he's out of surgery
and able to have visitors.'

Looking into her face, I can see how lost she
looks, how vulnerable, and I feel a surge of protec-
tiveness towards her.

'Here—lie down,' I say, moving off the sofa so
she can sink down onto it and stretch out.

I find a blanket on a shelf nearby and cover her
with it.

'Ben?' I hear her murmur.

'It's okay. I'm still here,' I say, sitting on the floor
next to her and stroking her hair away from her face.
'I'm not going anywhere.'

And I mean it too.

I'm staying right here with her, for as long as she
needs me.

Maya

I love this man.

He seems to genuinely understand me, and that's

worth more to me than anything. He knows every awful, humiliating thing about me now, but he's still here, sitting beside me. Listening to me. Smiling at me.

I feel as if a weight has been lifted from my chest now that he knows what I did all those years ago. He's seen through the façade I've been projecting to the rest of the world for so many years and right into the darkest part of my soul. And he's still here.

It's funny, but after telling him about it something strange happened inside me. The hardness I've grown used to living with—the hardness that keeps me upright and moving forward—started to soften and I had the strongest impulse to pull myself into a tiny ball and have Ben wrap himself around me. For me to be the core and him my shield. I've never experienced anything like it before in my life—it's as if I believe he can make me whole again.

I know—I sound like I'm on drugs. But I promise I'm not. I'm just in love.

Not that *that* doesn't scare the shit out of me.

'Ben?' I whisper.

'Yes?'

'I need to be able to love you in *my* language. I'm not sure I can do it the way other people do. I'm not all hearts and roses and eloquent declarations of love. I don't work that way,' I blurt, not entirely sure whether what I'm saying makes sense. 'But I *do* love you,' I assure him. 'More than I can express right now. Or probably ever. I'm good at glib. I'm not good at real. As long as you know that about me we'll probably be okay.' I take a breath. 'Okay?'

I must look terrified, because he clearly feels the need to reassure me.

'Of *course* it's okay!' he says, with so much force I jerk back a little.

'I mean—' he raises his hand and smooths his fingertips across my cheek '—I'll love you no matter how you choose to express yourself. I *love* that you have a different way of connecting with me because it feels like it's only meant for me. You *get* me and I *get* you. We're both totally fucked, but that's okay. We can be fucked together.'

I can't help but smile, despite the seriousness of the topic.

'My mother left this huge hole in my heart that I've never been able to fill,' I say. 'There'll always be a void there. I've tried to plug it with partying and drugs, and anything else I thought would be *substantial* enough. But I know there's nothing that could ever do that. I think I just need to find a way to live with it. It'll always be there. But it doesn't need to have the same power over my self-worth that it's had in the past. I can choose to hold the memories of her close, but not at the expense of my happiness. My mum wouldn't have wanted that for me. She loved me. I know that. And I loved her. I still do and I always will.'

'I think that's a very healthy way to look at it,' he says with a kind smile.

At some point I must have dozed off, because I

wake with a start when I hear Ben talking to someone in the room.

'Maya?' he says gently, kneeling down next to me
as I peel my heavy eyelids open.

'Hey. What's going on? How long have I been
asleep?'

'About four hours.'

I try to sit up and he helps me, sitting next to me
on the sofa and smoothing down my hair for me.

'The doctor just came in to say that your father's
awake and able to receive visitors.'

'He's okay?' I ask, my voice wobbly with relief.

'Yes. He's doing fine.'

'Oh, thank God,' I say, getting up. 'In that case
I'm going to go and see him and tell him that I love
him.'

Ben nods, then stands up too, holding out his hand
for me to take.

'What are you doing?' I ask, a little bemused.

'I'm coming with you,' he replies.

I stare at him in shock for a second, before pulling
myself together. 'But he'll know something's going
on between us if we go in there together,' I point out.

'Good. I want him to know.'

I put a trembling hand on his chest, right over
his heart.

'Are you sure? I've told you about his reputation
for destroying men who piss him off, and if you pick
me over April you can be damn sure he's going to
be pissed off.'

'I don't care,' he says roughly. 'I'm not sneaking around with you any more like I'm ashamed of what we're doing. I'm proud to be with you—proud of you.'

Thankfully he opens the door then and ushers me out, so I don't have a chance to break down in front of him again.

As we're walking down the corridor to the private room where my father is in recovery Ben gives my hand a reassuring squeeze. I squeeze it back, then wait for him to drop it before we enter the room.

He doesn't. If anything his grip tightens.

Glancing up at him, I see a look of tough resilience on his face and feel my heart flip over.

We're in this together now.

Pushing open the door, I see that my father is awake and sitting up in bed, though he's hooked up to the many machines next to him and wires trail from his arms and chest. Half of his face is swollen, but when he turns to look at us I can tell it's definitely still my father in there from the commanding expression in his eyes.

The poor nurses. I bet he's been giving them hell.

My father lets out a long-suffering sigh as we stride into the room together. 'I suspected as much,' he says, scowling down at where my hand is tightly linked with Ben's.

'I'm guessing you're not keen on the idea of Maya and I having a relationship?' Ben asks him, as if wanting it absolutely confirmed.

My father frowns—or at least half his face does.

'I'm happy for you to have closer links with our family, but if all you want is an "in" to it, Benedict, you be better off chasing after April.'

'I'm not *chasing after* anyone,' Ben replies hotly. 'And you and your family links can go to hell for all I care. I'm in love with Maya—she is the most compassionate, loving and loyal person I've ever met—and I'm prepared to give up the opportunity to have you sit on my board to be with her, no matter the consequences. She's far more important to me than any company.'

His voice has turned into an angry growl by the end of this tirade, but to my surprise, instead of getting angry back, my father slowly nods his head with a look of admiration on his face and holds up his hand as if in surrender.

'Well, Benedict, that's good enough for me.'

We both stare at him in silence for a moment, stunned by that reaction, but after a second I'm aware of Ben squeezing my hand. I turn to look at him and the smile he gives me makes my insides melt.

I allow myself to revel in the emotion I'm feeling for just a moment, poignantly aware that it's something I've not felt for a very long time.

Happiness. Pure, unadulterated happiness.

The sound of my father clearing his throat brings me back into the room and I somehow manage to pull myself together enough to say, 'I'm glad you're okay, Daddy. I was really scared when I heard about the crash.'

My father gives me a curt sort of nod, as if all the emotion swirling about the room is getting a bit beyond the pale.

'Yes, well, thanks for coming to see me.'

I swallow hard, readying myself for what I need to say to him. My throat is suddenly achy with too many years' worth of withheld emotion, and my eyes are so hot with held-back tears they're painful.

'I just wanted to tell you…to let you know…that I love you, and that I'm sorry for all the pain I've caused you,' I force out, preparing myself to hear my father brush my words aside and change the subject.

But to my surprise he reaches out a hand and beckons me towards him. Like a little girl, I walk over and take it, revelling in the warmth of his skin against mine. It's such a long time since we touched each other like this, and the realisation makes my tears spill over and run down my cheeks.

'You're so like your mother,' he says in a broken voice.

And that totally breaks me.

I lurch forward and gather him to me and he hugs me hard, his hand rubbing in soothing motions on my back like he used to do when I was a little girl and felt ill or was scared of the dark.

'I'm glad you're here,' he whispers fiercely into my hair.

I sob quietly into his shoulder for a while, letting

the waves of relief and regret and grief wash over me until I feel strong enough to let go.

Stepping back, I find Ben has moved to my side. I take his hand, and when I turn to look at him he smiles at me.

'Let me take you home now,' he says quietly.

'Yes, I'd like that.'

I turn back to my father, who's already replaced his mask of cool composure. 'I'll come and visit you again tomorrow, Daddy.'

He nods. 'Good, and then you can get me the hell out of here. I can recuperate at home. I don't need all these bloody doctors trying to tell me what to do.'

I shake my head at him—my father the tyrant.

'Okay, well, we'll discuss it tomorrow,' I say, taking Ben's hand and squeezing it to let him know I'm ready to leave.

But as we turn to go my father says, 'Make sure you take good care of my girl, Benedict.'

Ben turns back to him with a smile, then offers his hand to my father, which he shakes.

'I will, Maxim, I promise you that.'

And with the calm certainty that he really means that flowing through me, we leave the hospital.

'So, what would you like to do now?' Ben asks me as we walk out to his car.

His brow is drawn into a concerned frown, as if he's worried that the scene with my father has broken me. In fact, strangely, I find it's done the opposite—it's made me stronger.

It's going to take me some time to process and come to terms with everything I've discovered about myself recently, but I know that if Ben's with me, supporting me, it'll make it a whole lot easier.

In fact I'm almost looking forward to it.

But not right now. Not today.

Today I want to revel in the happiness I feel at being with him. Not as his kinky fling—but as his partner.

'Well, Mr Chivers, I don't know about you, but I could happily go back to bed right now and fuck until I can't remember my own name,' I say, waggling my eyebrows at him.

I see relief on his face—and something else.

Desire.

'I think I could get on board with that,' he says, sliding his arm around my shoulders and pulling me against his strong, gorgeous body.

A body I intend to stay *very* close to for the rest of my life…

* * * * *

GETTING EVEN

AVRIL TREMAYNE

MILLS & BOON

For my mother-in-law, Paula.

And with a million thanks to Kali and Mayte,

for sorting out my gorgeous Rafael's Spanish,

and to Sarah White for Scarlett-the-wonder-therapist's wisdom!

CHAPTER ONE

VERONICA WAS STARTING to think rereading *Wuthering Heights* before this trip to Yorkshire hadn't been such a good idea. She was finding it impossible not to compare Rafael Velez, sitting six pews in front of her, to Heathcliff—who was, of course, a prime asshole, albeit a magnetic one.

And once she'd started down that path, it was inevitable that she'd wonder if that made her some version of Cathy—who, sure, was intriguing, but had been stupid enough to leave the action halfway through the novel by dropping dead of a Heathcliff-inflicted broken heart. And Veronica wasn't having any of that drop-dead-of-a-broken-heart crap!

In fact, she considered herself to be walking, talking proof that a woman did *not* drop dead of a broken heart. She hadn't dropped dead seven years, two months, three weeks and five days ago when Rafael had decided the most appropriate graduation gift he could offer after living with her for three and a half fucking years was to run out on her. And she wasn't going to drop dead today, despite the bloodlust flushing through every cell in her body just because she could see the back of his damn head!

Nope. No dropping dead allowed.

At least not by her.

If *he* wanted to drop dead, he was welcome to do so. Not that she'd give him the satisfaction of *telling* him to drop dead. She might want to pulverize the bastard, but she was a Johnson, and it came naturally to Johnsons to give zero fucks in public.

Well, it came naturally to most Johnsons—others had to work at it.

All right. Okay. Fine. *She* was the only Johnson who had to work at it.

But she *did* work at it, and she'd worked at it every day since graduation when that asshole Velez had pulled the rug out from under her.

She'd worked at it *even harder* from the moment Romy had called to warn her that Rafael would not only be at the wedding but that he'd be bringing the gorgeous, scarlet-haired, only-one-name-required TV soap star Felicity as his plus-one.

Her zero-fuck-giving goal today was to go up to him and Felicity during the wedding reception—not too soon, not too late—and be utterly charming, perfectly sweet, and completely *not* brokenhearted.

She would just be someone Rafael used to date at college.

A double-divorcée with *nothing to prove*, she didn't need to bring a date to wave like a freaking banner of achievement under the nose of anyone who cared enough to look.

Wearing a hot-pink Dior dress, skyscraper Christian Louboutin heels and a coiffure secured with enough pins to set off every metal detector in the Leeds Bradford Airport, she had no intention of cowering in the background like some desperate and dateless loser.

Armed with pre-prepared lines she'd rehearsed a few thousand times to ensure their delivery carried just the right tone of dispassionate indifference to indicate she no longer gave a rat's ass about him. *Hello, Rafael. Long time no see. Congratulations on your two bestsellers—they're in my TBR pile.*

And the pièce de résistance? "The look." Straight out of her mother's playbook. Veronica had practiced it in the mirror—the eyebrows of destruction, the arched smile.

"The look" would let him know she had *no intention* of reading his tedious novels, no matter what words to the contrary were issuing from her mouth.

Her mother had given Rafael "the look" the first time she'd met him. Veronica had warned him to expect it, had assured him *all* boyfriends—hers *and* her sister Scarlett's—copped it to test their mettle, so not to take it personally. But Rafael had been only nineteen and laboring under a misapprehension that her family was an all-powerful branch of some de facto American aristocracy, and he'd shivered as though an Arctic wind had blown right through him.

Well, she looked forward to seeing how he handled "the look" now that he was twenty-nine and a ragingly successful author. If she could wring a

shiver from him *today*, she'd be downright *thankful*
he hadn't proposed to her all those years ago. It would
mean he hadn't *deserved* her. It would, in short, deliver the coup de grâce to her quest for vengeance—
a quest that had seen her block his every attempt to
contact her after he'd left her and marry not one but
two men who were everything he despised.

Just one unworthy shiver, that's all she asked.
There'd be no need, then, to tear off his head and
kick it across the Yorkshire moors—the image of
doing which had been giving her an unhealthy degree of satisfaction despite it very obviously signaling she gave *way* too many fucks. *So many* fucks. A
billion, trillion, gazillion fucking fucks.

And *breeeaaaaathe*, before she succumbed to that
thing Scarlett-the-wonder-therapist had warned her
about—vasovagal syncope. Fancy term for fainting!

Oh shit! Was that what was happening to her? Because that blood-pumping organ in her chest she'd
assumed had lapsed into a lifelong coma was palpi-
tating itself back to painful consciousness, her palms
were sweating, her skin was prickling and the breath
she'd taken in didn't seem to want to come back out.
What had Scarlett said to do? Sit so she wouldn't fall
down? Shut up so she didn't babble something stupid? Check and check—no better place to be than in
a hushed chapel. Oh, and she was supposed to *avoid
triggers*! Which meant she had to stop looking at the
back of Rafael's damn head.

But she couldn't stop looking.

Could. Not.

Only one thing to do: get out.

She darted a look to the right, where she'd already located the closest exit, which she knew led to some famous mausoleum. Surely if a girl was going to pass out, doing it among the dead—who told no tales and *certainly* weren't giving any fucks—was the way to go. She could lie on a crypt, faint, recover and be back in time for you-may-kiss-the-bride.

Deal!

She leaned close to the elderly lady sitting primly beside her in navy blue Yves Saint Laurent and whispered, "Excuse me, I need to make a phone call. May I squeeze past you?"

"Of course," came the polite reply.

She stood, waiting for room to be made for her to pass, only to watch in horror as Ms. YSL's navy blue purse, which was large enough to house a medium-size dog, slid off her lap and landed on the floor with a heavy thud.

Maybe that wouldn't have been such a disaster if not for the tube of mints that escaped its navy leather bondage and rolled out of reach, which occasioned a clearly enunciated little-old-lady "Oh fuck" that made Veronica burst out laughing. Seriously? How could she *not* laugh when an audible *Oh fuck* exploded in the anticipatory air of a chapel in an accent so posh it would do the Queen of England proud? Problem was, it was *the* laugh, the one that came with the distinctive taken-by-surprise-no-time-to-stop-it snort, a laugh Rafael would instantly connect with her because it had always made *him* laugh. Laugh…and kiss her.

The dominos started falling fast, heads turning row by row toward the commotion.

Any second now Rafael would turn, too, and see her standing like a hot-pink lighthouse complete with silver-domed roof. Vasovagal syncope would overtake her and she'd collapse in a heap, with her legs akimbo and her underwear showing, *not at all* like a zero-fuck-giving Johnson, and she'd end up in the mausoleum all right—as a *corpse*, having died of mortification!

It happened quickly—a matter of seconds only—and yet it felt like a slow-motion dream. The sights, sounds, scents of the chapel fading out of her consciousness... Rafael looking over his shoulder...seeing her...putting his hand on Felicity's shoulder... Felicity turning, staring, intent and curious, obviously knowing exactly who she was.

Bad. Bad, bad, bad.

And then, before Veronica's heart could take one more staccato rush of beats, Felicity and Rafael looked at each other, something unspoken passed between them, and as one they faced forward again, heads together.

God. God, God, God.

Veronica could hear the whoosh of her pulse in her ears, her breaths huffing in and out, smell her own vanilla scent mingling with the incense in the chapel as heat suffused her.

There was a rustle beside her; she turned mechanically toward it.

"I'm sorry about that," Ms. Navy Blue said—

choosing *now* to whisper! Her purse was retrieved, her legs slanting to the side. "Is that enough room for you?"

And Veronica's head cleared. She was in a Yorkshire chapel at the wedding of two of her college besties and she was *not going to faint*. She was *not*. Johnsons did not faint in public.

"No, *I'm* sorry," Veronica said, resuming her seat and pasting on a nice big smile. "I think I've left it too late to make my phone call—the bride's about to arrive."

A sound at the main entrance confirmed that this was not, in fact, a lie. Veronica swiveled gratefully toward that sound, and the sight of Romy, incandescently happy on her father's arm, drove all other thoughts out of her head for a blessed moment.

A pause—then music—and Romy commenced her walk up the aisle, ivory satin swishing around her ankles. The gown was simple, as chic and modern as Romy herself, hugging her generous curves and showing off her most prized possession—her baby bump. Romy had rejected the idea of wearing a veil on the basis it would obscure her view of Matt, and as Romy's unwavering gaze fixed on the man she'd loved for so long and never thought she'd have, that decision made perfect sense.

Veronica turned to see Matt's reaction. Love. Joy. And something she hadn't quite expected: rampant desire. As though he might break free of the whole wedding palaver, stride down the aisle and devour Romy in one hungry bite. Poor Teague—Veronica's

third college bestie, the harassed-looking best man—
appeared to be waging a fierce battle to keep Matt
in place via a grip on Matt's coat sleeve, but he gave
up when Romy reached Matt's side. It was obvious
nothing was going to stop Matt from hauling Romy
into his arms.

As Matt kissed the bride way too early and way,
way too passionately, the chapel erupted in laughter
and sighs.

Veronica tried to imagine either of her husbands
kissing the bride out of sequence and came up blank.
Her first husband, Piers, had still been in love with
his ex-girlfriend—he hadn't kept that a secret and
he hadn't cared that Veronica was still in love with
Rafael. And marrying Simeon had been about his
loneliness and her despair, not love. It was hardly
surprising those unions—comfort unions, she called
them—weren't exactly torrid, although both men
had given the relationships their best shot, and so
had she.

She looked again at Rafael, wondering if the reason she never felt anything warmer than tepid anymore was that she'd expended all the passion she had
to give on him in those heated three and a half years
of living together. It had been a Molotov cocktail of
a relationship. Ardent. Intensely physical. Tempestu-
ous. From the moment their eyes had locked in her
freshman year at Capitol U they hadn't been able to
keep their hands off each other.

It was disturbingly easy to imagine Rafael doing
to her what Matt was doing to Romy. Easy to imag-

ine her going one better than Romy and wrapping her legs around Rafael's waist. That would have given Ms. Yves Saint Laurent a real "Oh fuck" moment. It would have shocked Rafael, too, because as passionate as he was in the bedroom, he had a core of decorum she lacked. The kiss—yes. The legs—*Veronica, no! Think of your parents!*

Well, it was a pointless rumination since Rafael hadn't proposed the way everyone had expected him to. It would be more relevant to contemplate his wedding to *Felicity*. A can't-wait kiss between those two intensely beautiful people would have the whole population of America swooning as they read all about it in the tabloids. Given Felicity's acting career and Rafael's extraordinary critical and commercial literary success—the hot new author with a film adaptation already in the works—it would get a great spread in *US Weekly* even if the nuptials took place in Colombia instead of LA for the sake of Rafael's beloved grandparents, which he'd always hinted would happen.

Veronica's own weddings had *not* been in the tabloids. They'd been lavish New York society affairs, but very private—which was the Johnson way. Planned to the last sprig of baby's breath by her mother, who'd stepped into the breach because Veronica hadn't cared enough to plan them for herself. Veronica had just wanted them done, done, over and done…

"Today is a celebration," the minister said, the formal words reverberating in the chapel. "A celebration of love, of commitment, of friendship, of family,

and of two people who are making a choice to be together forever."

Together forever.

Forever.

Te amaré por siempre, Verónica.

Those were the last words Rafael had said to her.

I will love you forever.

Liar.

Fucking, fucking *liar*.

She was here on her own—and that changed everything.

Rafael wanted to tear his hands through his hair
to relieve some of the pressure on his skull, but he
couldn't because she'd see, and she'd guess.

Fuck.

Matt should have told him she'd be on her own.
Okay. Unfair. It was his own damn fault Matt hadn't
told him. He'd been so focused on pretending Veronica's presence—or absence—was immaterial to him
that when Matt had cautiously volunteered that she'd
sent in her RSVP, he'd laughed it off with a flippant
"Too much water under that bridge."

Matt had instantly dropped the subject. Leaving
Rafael to kick himself for not giving a more open-
ended response that might have gotten Matt to slip
up on the radio silence for once and reveal if she
was dating anyone now that her second divorce had
gone through.

The only way to find shit like that out about a
Johnson was for someone in the know to straight-out

tell you. Johnsons didn't have social media accounts, they didn't give interviews—at least not the personal kind—and when they were photographed at society events they were polished and PR'd to the hilt, not a hair or a word out of place. End result? Only the easy stuff was out there in cyberspace. Which is how he knew she was working as an acquisitions editor in the Johnson/Charles Book Group (Daddy's publishing company—no surprise there), which authors she'd signed, and the charities she supported with her ambassadorial presence as well as her dollars. He'd seen photos of her with her husbands at society parties, but no accompanying gossip.

The only romantic gossip he'd ever read about a Johnson involved Veronica's younger sister, Scarlett—and he'd only discovered that because the guy had been from some backwater town where he'd made the local paper after a drug bust. It had pissed Rafael off because Scarlett dating some lowlife druggie, even temporarily, made a mockery of his own sacrifice in leaving Veronica. Like, what were her parents thinking to let that guy within touching distance?

Digression. The important thing was that he knew nothing about the current state of Veronica's love life. The fact that she was here solo didn't mean there wasn't a boyfriend stashed somewhere, a new fiancé in the wings. It'd be just like her to have turned up alone for no other reason than to play a game with his head, as though she hadn't tortured him enough.

Veronica: *Why would I bring someone, Rafa? I can't be* bothered *to make you jealous.*

Him: *Yeah, well, I haven't been pining for you, either, and* I don't care *that you weren't pining for me. God damn you to hell, Veronica!*

He looked down at his hand, fisted on his thigh. It was vibrating with an unholy mix of impotent lust and outright rage.

Felicity put her hand over that fist. "Stop, Rafa!"

He hissed in a breath. "Don't call me that."

"Why not? I'm supposed to be in love with you, aren't I? And anyway, it's what your mom calls you."

"You're not my mother."

"I'm not *her*, you mean."

He laid a deceptively gentle hush finger over her lips for the benefit of any spectators. "Get your hand off me and shut up."

Felicity, the brat, sucked the tip of his finger into her mouth.

"Stop it," he said under his breath.

"How about I kiss you on the mouth?" she whispered back. "See what she thinks of that?"

He didn't answer. He was too irritated at himself for dragging Felicity over from Los Angeles for a performance now rendered unnecessary.

Felicity craned up to get her mouth close to his unaccommodating ear. To the uninitiated, it probably looked like she was cooing love words but what she actually said was, "How much is Matt worth, anyway? That engagement ring on Romy's finger's a whopper—I can see the sparkle from here."

Rafael's hand went instantly, instinctively, to the breast pocket of his jacket—where the ring he'd bought Veronica once upon a time, which he always carried with him, was. Nothing like Romy's ring. Or either of Veronica's. Thank God he'd spared himself the indignity of producing it all those years ago.

It was exactly the memory he needed to bring him back to the moment. "More than you and I put together times a hundred," he said.

She leaned her head against his shoulder. "You're going after her, aren't you?" she said.

He breathed in. Out. "Yep."

"Am I going to be able to stop you?"

"Nope."

CHAPTER TWO

THE WEDDING WAS over and she hadn't fainted. Yippee.

Now for the tricky part. Getting out of the chapel ahead of Rafael, fighting her way to the front of the throng of well-wishers swamping the bride and groom, and pretending she wasn't interested in Rafael's exact whereabouts while doing the kiss-and-hug routine with the wedding party.

But all it took was Romy's sympathetic voice in her ear, asking, "You okay?" to make her want to scream from nerves.

"Hello!" she said, exasperated. "I told you I'd be on my best behavior. What did you think I was going to do?"

Matt dragged her away from Romy, pulling her into a bone-crushing hug. "Hire a hit man, of course," he said.

Veronica kissed him on the cheek. "Now there's an idea!" she said as he released her. "I must call Scarlett and get the name of hers. Although I think she calls him an enforcer, not a hit man."

"What the fuck? Go, Scarlett!"

"She's not *dating* him, Matthew. She knows him in a strictly client-privilege way."

Matt swung around to beckon to Teague, who was multitasking with a piece of paper in one hand and his cell phone at his ear. "Keep an eye on Table Two tonight, will you? Do your best to stop the bloodbath V's planning."

Veronica gave a thump to one of Matt's massive shoulders. "I'll hire the enforcer to take *you* out if you're not caref—" Breaking off as the implication hit. "Hang on. What do you mean Table Two?"

"He's on Table Two," Teague chipped in, disconnecting his call and leaning in to kiss Veronica on the forehead. "*And* he's about a hundred feet away, waylaid by at least seven, eight…no, *ten* autograph hunters, who are besieging Felicity, because Romy's friends clearly have no pride. So if you want to get away, now's the moment."

Veronica turned, saw Felicity chatting animatedly and signing what Veronica assumed were Orders of Service from the wedding. Rafael was beside her, smiling benignly but looking preoccupied.

For a moment she couldn't breathe and was grateful when Teague moved her a little to the side to make room for other guests to talk to Romy and Matt.

"You look like you're going to pass out," Teague said.

She shook her head then nodded. "I need to duck back into the chapel and out the side exit. There's a mausoleum."

"Er…"

"Yeah, a mausoleum! Go figure! Tremenhill Estate really is a one-site-fits-all proposition, isn't it? Births, deaths, marriages. The chapel, the reception hall, the manor house, the cottages, the mausoleum, where I really need to be. I'm staying here, you know—or maybe you don't know. In a cottage, not a crypt. And I'm giving zero fucks, in case you hadn't noticed."

"Yeah, I can't say I've noticed zero fucks so far. You're babbling, just FYI."

"That's vasovagal syncope. I think it means I'm going to faint. So I'd better stop talking and go sit down."

"Fuck." He brought her close, his arm under hers. "How far away is your cottage?"

"Walking distance. Why?"

"Because I'll take you there."

She pulled away from him. "No! No, no, no. I'm just going to walk calmly away, call my sister and let her talk me out of murdering that bastard, while you—" giving him a little push in the direction of Romy and Matt "—do your duty, smile in the wedding photos and impress everyone with your sunshine-and-light act."

"Okay, but—"

"Teague! If I was going to faint, it would have happened mid-babble. Please let me at least *pretend* to be giving zero fucks."

He gave her a searching look and then sighed. "Fine," he said. "But you come and get me if you need me."

She waited until he was back with Matt and Romy,

then gave him a quick thumbs-up of reassurance before straightening her spine and walking-not-running toward the chapel. She allowed herself a look over her shoulder as she reached the doorway to find the autographing session was finished. Felicity was now tucked under Rafael's arm as the two of them made their leisurely way over to the bride and groom. A chill of foreboding raced down her spine as Rafael's eyes landed on her and she froze like a deer in the headlights, every cell in her body quivering.

He tilted his head as though challenging her—to what, she had no idea—and she unfroze. "Oh no," she said through gritted teeth. "Zero fucks." She turned her back on him to enter the chapel, where she wasted no time making her way straight back out again through the infamous side exit she'd eschewed earlier.

She hadn't known what to expect of the mausoleum, but it was magnificent. A circular stone structure set atop a platform on a grassy hill, surrounded by a veranda whose roof was supported by a series of columns all the way round. A stone path bisecting a pristine lawn connected it to the chapel but also seemed to isolate it, which seemed kind of surreal and yet completely perfect.

As Veronica slowly made her way along the path, she had the fanciful notion that the mausoleum wasn't only a guardian of souls but a sentinel, keeping vigil over the brooding, untamed moors beyond the estate's civilized perfection. Bleak, wild and lonely on one side, manicured perfection on the other—like the two halves of her.

She laughed as she ascended the steps, imagining what Scarlett would say if she started describing herself in such terms. Something like *Stop hugging trees and get your head out of your ass!* most likely.

That was Scarlett—always talking sense. And, by God, Veronica was ready to hear it!

She took her cell phone out of her purse, brought up her sister's number and stabbed at the call button.

Scarlett answered on the second ring as though she'd been expecting the call. "So you've seen him," she said without preamble.

"Yes."

"And?"

"I'm scared when I talk to him I'm going to lose it. Or maybe faint. Which would be worse?"

"Maaaybe try to avoid either."

"If you're saying I shouldn't talk to him, why did you let me come in the first place?"

"I didn't 'let' you. Nobody 'lets' you do anything. You just do it! As *I* recall it, I had the temerity to remind you that you still go stratospherically apeshit when someone says his name and you were the one who *insisted* you were ready for this."

"I may have been…premature in my assessment."

"So what are you going to do? Hide in the restroom all night?"

"No."

"Where are you now?"

"Outside a mausoleum."

"Hang on! The wedding's in a *cemetery*? Never would have picked Romy as a Goth!"

"Romy as a Go—? No! It's not a cemetery, just a kind of…of burial place, near the chapel."

"Ooooh, I see dead people!"

"That's *exactly* the problem!" Veronica said. "I *do* see dead people. At least, I *want* to see dead people. Correction, I want to see dead *person*. Just the one." Pausing, she thought about Felicity beneath Rafael's protective arm back at the chapel. "Okay, maybe two."

"*What* are you talking about?"

"I want to kill him! Obviously."

"Okaaay, take a breath."

"I've taken so many breaths I've used up half the oxygen in Yorkshire!"

"Well, take another and try to remember what I said about using a catastrophe scale to keep things in perspective."

"Oh, on the catastrophe scale this is a ten!"

"No, Veronica, it's *not* a ten. There are worse things than seeing your ex at a wedding, so take a moment now to think about them."

"Um, like…say…a typhoon ripping through the estate and killing all the guests?"

"Yeees. Although somewhat *unlikely*, if that makes you feel better, relatively speaking, then—"

"All the corpses in this mausoleum rising up as zombies and swarming out to kill all the guests."

"That's a little macabre but—"

"A sudden blizzard—"

"In *July*?"

"—snap-freezing the moors and killing all the guests."

"I'm sensing a theme here, Veronica."

"*Sharknado*. Herd of trampling bison. An invasion of serial killers. Everyone dead."

"Don't you think killing all the guests is a little extreme when you only really want to kill one?"

"Yes!" Veronica agreed. "And all I need to do is go back to my cottage and get a knife from the kitchen. It's close enough that I could be back in under five minutes. He'd probably still be kissing Romy and hugging Matt and shaking Teague's hand and holding on to Felicity and do not—*do not!*—tell me ever again how good she is in *This Time Forever*—and it would all be over with one downward slice."

"Okay, enough, Veronica! Nobody has to die!"

"Castration, then. I'll find a *rusty* knife."

"Can't you just castrate the voodoo doll?" Scarlett said, and started laughing. "I can't believe I'm telling you to castrate a voodoo doll like it's an actual solution!"

"Don't joke about my doll!" Veronica said. "Sticking pins in him has helped me a lot."

"Okay, I surrender! Kill Rafael! Go ahead! Do it! Just don't leave any DNA 'cuz Mom will freak out if you get caught. And if we're talking catastrophe scale… Well, let's just say I'd back her over the typhoon. The sharks, as well. *Definitely* the bison wouldn't stand a chance."

"Zombies?"

"Pfft. Child's play. *And* she'd out-frost the July

snap-freeze. I'm pretty sure she'd even give the serial killers a run for their money." Pause. "You know, you really could just give up on achieving closure—or at least postpone it—and keep your distance."

"Downside?"

"Being bitter and twisted forever."

"You're not being very helpful."

"Okay then, how's this? *Don't* stab Rafael *or* castrate him, unless you want to be either in jail or in therapy for a thousand years! Maybe try going up to the guy exactly as you'd planned and talking about his books and being civilized and burying the hatchet somewhere other than in his skull and moving the fuck on."

"We were never civilized before, what made me think I could be now?"

"That was then, this is now. College kids—mature adults. Get it?"

"Okay, but I haven't read the books. *His* books. You know why."

"So read his damn books! Who knows, you might learn something that will help you consign him to the past—or the devil—whichever. Now hang up before *I* need therapy!"

"Not. Helpful."

"I'm hanging up, Veronica," Scarlett said, singsong style—and the line went dead.

"Read his damn books," Veronica muttered as she all but threw her phone into her purse. "As *if*!" She'd read the damn *blurbs*—they were enough to tell her she shouldn't read his damn *books*. Rich girl/poor boy. Bitch girl/proud boy. Romeo/Juliet. Unhappily-ever-after. She was a book editor—she knew how to read between the lines of a blurb. *She* knew he was writing about her, even if nobody else did.

Well, she guessed that counted as a forever—immortalized in literature. Just not the *Till death do us part* kind of forever she'd envisaged when he'd said *Te amaré por siempre, Verónica* that day in the garage of their DC town house.

"Till death do us part," she said softly, thinking of the souls inside the mausoleum who were traveling into eternity together. She'd heard there was a married couple laid to rest in there who'd been together sixty years and died a day apart. *That* was what forever was.

She'd felt envious hearing Romy and Matt repeating the "till death do us part" vow in the chapel today. She'd hadn't made that vow at either of her weddings—appropriately, as it turned out, since one marriage had lasted a mere twelve months and the other only twenty months. The idea of being interred with either Piers or Simeon for eternity in a place like this would never have entered her head. That kind of commitment belonged to a different kind of love. A consuming love. A *Wuthering Heights* kind of love. The kind that made Heathcliff bribe the sexton to remove the side of Cathy's coffin so that when he was buried beside her, in a coffin identically opened, their remains would mingle in death.

"'I wish I were a girl again, half savage and hardy, and free...'" she murmured, and the wistfulness of that quote from *Wuthering Heights* had her eyes rolling. "Get out of my head, Cathy," she called out to the moors, "and take Heathcliff with you!"

She listened for an echo but instead she heard a gravelly voice with the barest hint of an accent say behind her, "Rereading *Wuthering Heights*, Veronica? *Again?*"

She turned...and there he was.

CHAPTER THREE

RAFAEL NOTED THE way her eyes went wide, the way her nostrils flared, the uptick in her breathing, the tension that ran through her, the flare of rage.

And then she drew herself in, tipped up her chin, arched her eyebrows and controlled the flame. She was like ice water drip-dripping onto hot coals—a hiss, a sizzle, no more. "You know what a sucker I am for a doomed love story," she drawled.

"I'm sorry Piers and Simeon didn't live up to your expectations," he said, out-drawling her, "but 'doomed' seems a little harsh."

Drip, drip of ice—but the steam was rising from those coals and it was only a matter of time before the ice melted. "Hmm, yes, I suppose it *is* a little harsh," she agreed. "At least they had the courage to *try*, right?"

"Try...but fail."

"I don't think you're the man to talk to me about marriage failures when you've never actually made it to the altar."

"Is that a proposal?"

"It could be...the day hell freezes over."

"Maybe that's just as well, given the three and a half years you had with me lasted longer than both your marriages combined. Marriage obviously doesn't agree with you. I wonder why…?"

She laughed—a long, fake peal of it. "How about you explore my marriages in your next book?"

He smiled, left it hanging there for a heartbeat and then said, "What do you mean my *next* book?"

He saw her chest rise with the breath she slowly drew in, then fall as she let it out. Oh, she'd definitely learned some methods to maintain her self-control over the years. A pity.

"So you've skewered them already, have you?" she said, and he might have believed she was bored if not for the scalding heat in her eyes.

"You tell me."

Another of those peals of fake laughter. "I don't see how I can since I haven't read your books."

Okay, that threw him. Enough that he had to actively work to keep his face impassive. His books had both been number one *New York Times* bestsellers, and she was an editor at Johnson/Charles—one of the most prestigious midsize publishers in America. Those two facts should have guaranteed a read for both books, even without their personal history. "Can I assume that means you're still blocking me? After all these years? A more egotistical man might think you weren't over him."

The flare of anger, the tamping down, the slow breath. "Tell you what—" pulling her cell phone out of her purse "—how about I download them now?

Old times' sake and all that. You were always so particular about how I spent my money, but I assume you have no objection to me slinging you a few bucks this way."

"By all means sling away, since it's money I've earned," he said smoothly, admiring her nerve while simultaneously wanting to shake it out of her. "Maybe we can get together sometime and you can tell me what you think."

"Sure," she said—but her eyes told him he could drop dead. "Can you give me the titles?"

He bit back a laugh at the sheer arrogance of her. "The first one is called *Catch, Tag, Release*."

"Ah, yes," she said, tapping away at her phone. "As in hooking some poor fish, whacking an invasive tag through its fin, then throwing it back in the sea."

"My second book—*Liar, Liar* if you're really clicking—looks at what that fish does when it gets its new lease on life."

"How uplifting that sounds—*Liar, Liar*."

"I'm sure you'll find both books...instructive."

"Oh joy!" she said, and rolled her eyes, which had him vowing to make her eyes roll all the way back in her head for him before the night was over. "Just what I look for in a novel—to be *instructed*!" She put her cell phone away. "Right. All set. Now, I'm sure you're anxious to return to Felicity—must have been painful, unjoining yourself from her hip!"

Oh God, it was *so hard* not to laugh. "Jealous, Veronica?"

"Jealous? Please!" She spluttered that out. "I assure you, you have my permission to fuck whomever you want to fuck."

He stepped in close, crowding into her space, and the vanilla scent of her flooded his senses. She dabbed that special oil everywhere, even between her legs—and the taste memory of licking it from her was so vivid, he had to swallow because his mouth had flooded with saliva. "You sure about that?"

"Most certainly."

"Then that is very good to know."

"If that's all, I have husband number three waiting in the wings for me at the reception."

He took her left hand in his, rubbed his thumb along her ring finger without taking his eyes from her face, found nothing there. Good. The photos he'd seen of her with her husbands, the massive diamond engagement rings they'd given her flashing in the camera lights, had caused him to break two expensive cell phones throwing them against the wall. Time for her to pay for what seeing those rings had done to him.

He smiled at her—made it as chillingly seductive as he could. "I know you came on your own, Veronica, and I can make a good guess as to why."

She snatched her hand back. "Husband number three is a work in progress but it's going to happen, I promise you that."

"Then I look forward to being introduced to him."

"And I look forward to meeting your conjoined twin just as soon as you've reattached yourself," she said, and stalked past him.

* * *

Veronica stormed her way across the lawn, furious with herself.

So much for coming on her own—he'd seen right through her.

So much for her rehearsed lines—he'd gotten in first about the books.

So much for being charming and sweet—she'd been snide and venomous.

So much for her intimidating eyebrows—he'd looked ready to lick them back down into place.

And, oh God, her entire traitorous body was in eruption mode. She wanted to stab him and...and *kiss* him, damn it! Taste him once more. Touch him. *Feel* something.

So much for closure, then!

Third husband? Where was she going to get one of those? Out of her ass?

She'd just have to hope there was a single man at the reception she could attach herself to. A single man who wasn't going to trip over his tongue when Veronica dragged him into Felicity's orbit.

"Yeah, good luck with that," she muttered as she tramped through gardens and across more lawns en route to what was known as Tremenhill Hall but was really a repurposed mansion.

Okay, time to dust off the catastrophe scale. She needed something brutally dystopian if she was to emerge from her next encounter with Rafael with any dignity. Too bad nothing sprang readily to mind.

She should have gone for the damn knife, screw the

DNA evidence! Her mother could have shipped her off to a country that didn't have an extradition treaty with the United States. Like…she didn't know…did India have one? She could go and live on an ashram. Now *there* was a catastrophe she could get behind! Telling her mother she was gifting her trust fund to an ashram in India.

"Yeah, no thanks," she said, and giggled suddenly as the marquee set up for welcome drinks outside the hall came into view. Like…*giggled*! Well, who knew? The catastrophe scale actually worked!

She whooshed out what felt like her first normal breath of the day as she crossed yet another lawn toward what was a very *bridal* confection. Garlands of white blooms not only festooned the marquee's upper edge but also anchored billowing swathes of silky white fabric around the support poles. She looked down at her hot-pink dress, feeling every bit as conspicuous as she had during that "Oh fuck" moment in the chapel. But after her dare-you encounter with Rafael at the mausoleum, she was okay with that.

Or she would be, just as soon as she made sure she wasn't on Table Two with Rafael and Felicity, because that would be taking the whole zero fucks mantra too far. Not that she really believed Romy and Matt would put her in that awkward position, but it was always better to be safe than sorry. And if she *was* on Table Two? Well, the bride and groom would be the first victims of the ensuing bloodbath, that's all. It would be her *Carrie* moment!

She'd been to enough gala events to predict the

seating plans would be at the hall entrance, so she walked straight through the marquee—and bingo! Two gold easels were set up alongside potted plants on either side of a center set of double doors. She headed for one of the easels and scanned the list for Table Two.

Brief close of her eyes—relief!—to find Rafael and Felicity listed but not her, before locating her name on Table Seven.

The room layout pinned below the table lists showed Tables Two and Seven were on opposite sides of the dance floor, but she decided she'd feel more confident of her ability to keep it together if she went inside and got the picture in 3D.

Through the full-height Palladian windows on either side of the entrance, she could see staff tweaking table settings. She hoped they wouldn't shoo her out when she barged in early or she might lose her shit, but figured if she walked in like she owned the place—channeling her smiling-assassin mother and crossing that with the intimidating countenance so often worn by the headmistress of the Koller Finishing School in Switzerland—nobody would dare.

"Don't fuck with me, people," she said under her breath, stepping up and over the stoop to swing open the heavy double doors.

Within seconds she was threading her hot-pink, unchallenged way to Table Two. She sat in the spot reserved for Rafael Velez, then in the one for Felicity, and checked their line of sight to all the other tables before making her way to Table Seven. There she found that although she wouldn't be facing them, she'd definitely be visible to them in profile.

That was going to have to change. Depositing her purse on her seat, she walked slowly around her table, stopping at each seat for a fresh assessment.

And then she heard her name. "Veronica Johnson."

Male. British accent.

"'Oh fuck' from the chapel," he added.

"I wonder how many times people are going to mention that to me tonight," she said…and turned… and *yes*! Early thirties. Handsome. Impeccably suited—*with tie*, unlike Rafael Velez.

"I'll be your knight in shining armor and defend you from attack," he said.

"Hey, *I* didn't say it, all I did was laugh."

"And how could you not?"

"Exactly!" she said, and smiled her best smile at him. "But I'm in the market for a Sir Galahad tonight, as it turns out."

"Ah! Well, in that case, let's put you—" picking up her place card and bringing it to where she was standing "—here—" putting it down at the seat to her left "—next to me!"

She laughed as she squinted at his place card. "Why thank you, Phillip Castle." She nodded at the extra card jostling for space beside her own. "But what will Sally Paulson say about it?"

"Ah, well, as to that…" He plucked Sally off the table and carried it around the table to put it where Veronica used to be. "I happen to know Sally Paulson fancies Romy's cousin, Lloyd Allen—your erstwhile dining companion. So we're sorted."

A lightning-fast look across to Table Two told her she'd now be showing Rafael her back. "Seems we are," she said, and decided to test the water vis-à-vis his susceptibility to Felicity. "You're not disappointed you won't be gazing across at the famous Felicity all night?"

He looked around as though Felicity had just materialized. Bad sign. "How do you know that?"

"I had a quick look around all the tables and found her on Table Two."

"Ah! *Maybe* we need to do a few more place card swaps in that case—trade Sally and Lloyd for her and Rafael Velez."

"A fan, are you?" Veronica said, abandoning hope of using him as her Husband No. 3 masquerader.

"Of hers? No. Of his? Most definitely."

Damn, definitely *no use to me,* she thought, then wondered if she'd said those words out loud because Phillip laughed. "No, I'm not gay," he said. "I just want his next book, *Stomp.*"

"His next...? Ah! You're in *publishing*!"

"I am! Smythe & Lowe."

"Me, too—Johnson/Charles. That explains why Romy has us on the same table."

He looked her up and down, plucked her card back up off the table and read the name. "You're *that* Veronica Johnson?"

"If you mean Veronica Johnson, editor, then yes."

"More than an editor with that surname."

"The name doesn't carry as much weight as you'd think—and definitely not since the merger."

"Do I scent dissatisfaction? If you're contemplating a move, we're looking for a Publishing Director for our new romance imprint."

"That's two moves—presuming it's in London?"

"You'd love London."

"I *do* love London." Veronica laughed. "So thank you—I'll take that under advisement."

"I mean it!"

"So do I."

"No you don't—you New Yorkers are bloody hard to extract—but I'm a firm believer in the old adage 'there's many a slip twixt cup and lip,' so I'm not giving up." He put her card back on the table. "So—shall we do the card swap?"

"Hmm…" she said, pretending to think about it. "It would mean crossing out and rewriting names on Romy's seating plan or there'd be pandemonium in here. If you're willing to do that when Romy's had the thing done by a calligrapher in gold ink, you're much braver than I am!"

"Gah! Okay, stand down. Romy's such a stickler for…"

But Veronica knew all Romy's stickler-isms and tuned out to estimate how long it had been since she'd left Rafael at the mausoleum. Surely he and Felicity had to have made it to the marquee by now.

She tuned back into Philip to catch "…and that way we can leave the seating plan as is—so what do you say, shall we risk it?"

"No, I think it's a recipe for disaster," she said, assuming he'd come back to the subject of place card tampering. And then she smiled sweetly at him. At least, was it sweet? Her smile? She hoped it wasn't as *Sharknado*-ish as she felt. "But if you escort me to the marquee for a glass of champagne, I'll introduce you to Rafael."

Phillip blinked at her. "You *know* him?"

"I do."

"But he's published with—"

"I know him *personally* not professionally. Johnson/Charles isn't interested in publishing him."

Phillip was looking at her curiously now. "So you're not interested in acquiring his next book? It's going to go to number one on the *New York Times* bestseller list without even trying, you know."

"You mean *Stomp*? But I thought that was already—"

"Nope. I hear his deal has just fallen through."

"Oh. Well. I see. But still…no," she said. When Phillip blinked at her in disbelief, she added, "We're over-inventoried. In that…er…area."

"In the unbelievably fantastic, must-read, going-to-make-a-fortune area?"

She had no answer to that. Her boss, Melissa Charles—nickname "the Attack Dog"—would never understand a withered romance getting in the way of business. Veronica had had to lie when Melissa had asked her if she'd known Rafael at Capitol U. Melissa had been desperate to land *Liar, Liar* for Johnson/Charles and Veronica had known that any *hint* of familiarity let alone a full-blown, live-in love affair would have seen her pimped out to get it PDQ.

She hated to think what her reception would have been. She had, after all, refused to take his calls then blocked him, burned the letter he'd sent her via Matt and banned their mutual friends from telling him anything about her (and she knew he knew about that ban because she'd dispatched Teague to tell him so). So for her to come sniffing around begging for his book...?

No.

No, no, no.

She tried another smile—knew this one was definitely struggling to get anywhere near sweet. "If you'd rather I *don't* introduce you, that's fine by me. You can ask Romy to get you two together."

"*Romy* knows him, too?"

"Romy, Matt, Rafael and I went to Capitol University together. We shared a house."

"Good God! Why hasn't she ever introduced me?"

"Maybe because he lives in LA," she said through slightly gritted teeth. Did he want to meet Rafael or stand around talking about him? "But he's here, and we're here, so the offer's...there...?"

He held out his arm. "An offer I can't refuse."

CHAPTER FOUR

"WELL, FUCK," RAFAEL SAID under his breath as a triumphant-looking Veronica headed for him, accompanied by a guy who was a carbon copy of both her trust-fund-lugging husbands.

She stopped to take a glass from a passing waiter, then laughed at something Preppy Boy said as he grabbed his own glass. And in that instant Rafael may as well have been nineteen again, in that first year at college, about to go feral because some random dick of a guy had hit on her.

His hand jerked, champagne sloshing out of the glass and onto his shoe. Ordinarily he wouldn't have been able to stop himself from cleaning that off, but the thought that Veronica would spot it, and in the process see that his shoes were handmade, stopped him. Not that he wanted to show off—she had a whole *closet* full of designer shoes—he just wanted to show her that he'd come a long, proud way, and the shoes were a symbol she'd understand.

Felicity gave his arm a warning squeeze. "You're not going to strangle the poor man, are you?"

His lips twisted—half smile, half grimace. "I'm more likely to wring *her* neck."

"You guys must have had fun at college if she can't even walk beside another man without winding you up! Get it together, will you?"

And then Veronica was there, flashing a smile—what she called her finishing school smile—and he wanted to grab her by the arms and shake her and tell her not to use that smile on him. He wanted to kiss her, rip those uptight pins from her perfectly coiffed silver-blond hair and tear off her perfect dress and rattle her easy grace. He used to be able to do it. Make her as desperate and deranged as he was. Strip the cool off her just by touching her, so that she was hot and disheveled and gasping and throbbing.

And by God, he was going to do it again.

But to get her to lose her cool meant keeping his. So he quirked up an amused eyebrow, inclined his head toward the guy she thought she was waving in his face like a victory flag, and said, "Number three?"

"How's the hip?" she quipped back, inclining her head toward Felicity.

"Unattached," he said. "Needing a replacement. Interested?"

"Is it the *balls* giving you trouble?"

"It's the socket. I need a new one, but I can use an old one in the meantime."

At which point Felicity cleared her throat and he became conscious that he and Veronica were exuding enough heat to light a furnace.

Veronica stepped forward, that smile replastered

to her face as she held out her hand to Felicity. "I'm Veronica Johnson, an old college friend of Rafael's."

Felicity gave her fake smile for fake smile as she took that hand, shook it. "Felicity."

"Oh, I know who you are—my sister, Scarlett, is your biggest fan!" Veronica laughed—like sweet bells on a clear night—but it was as fake as her smile; he knew because there was no snort to it. "*Not*, I promise you, in a Stephen King *Misery* kind of way." She pulled Preppy Boy fully into the circle. "And this is Phillip Castle." Back to Rafael, with her eyebrows set to go-fuck-yourself. "You know how we were talking about your next book? *Stamp*, is it?"

"Close enough," Rafael said as Phillip choked on his champagne.

"Well, Phillip's with Smythe & Lowe, and *he's* very interested."

"Oh, *he* is, is he?"

"Yes—go figure. And since you seemed so keen to tell me about your books when we had that delightful chat earlier, I knew you'd jump at the chance to speak to someone…impartial? Meanwhile, if you can spare Felicity—" turning to Felicity "—I hope she'll regale me with all the salacious details about what happens next with Beth and Braxton in *This Time Forever* so I can fill Scarlett in once I'm back home in New York."

Felicity waved an airy hand. "Oh, Beth's going to have a wonderfully tragic soapy end I'm afraid," she said, and narrowed her eyes ever so slightly. "I'm leaving the show to play Julie in *Catch, Tag, Release*—didn't Rafa tell you?"

Veronica's smile slipped, which told Rafael she didn't like what she'd just heard. The news, or the name, or both? No time to work it out, because the slip was microscopic and transient and Veronica was bouncing right back hard.

"Oh well, I'm *dying* to hear all about *that*," she said and, before he knew it, the women were separated from the men. *She'd* done it, of course. A society-girl skill of hers he'd never been able to demystify. Correction—he'd never *had* to demystify, because she'd never used it against him before.

Well, whatever she'd done, it had worked: he was out of earshot.

Phillip—poor, clueless bastard—was paying the price for that, because valiantly though he tried to engage Rafael in conversation, Rafael simply didn't give enough of a fuck to listen. The guy deserved better than monosyllabic nonresponses but that's what he got. He had to know something was seriously awry by this point, but Rafael was too busy straining his ears toward Veronica to care.

Rafael finally shot Felicity a look he hoped she'd interpret correctly as *Get Veronica back here now*.

Felicity double-blinked at him—her way of saying she understood—and not only steered Veronica back into the circle but, like the trouper she was, engaged Phillip in a conversation about *Liar, Liar*.

He saw that Veronica's champagne flute was empty and reached out to take it—just one second too late to stop a passing waiter from stopping beside her and proffering his tray. She smiled at the waiter, swapped her empty glass for a full one, then angled her body away to say something to a nearby guest.

Shit!

He kept his lips curved in a slight smile, pretending to listen to Felicity and Phillip while his nerve endings zapped, his blood simmered and his scalp twitched at the proximity of Veronica's small, slender fingers, which used to twine tightly in his hair when she came. Unbearable to have her so close after all this time and not be able to touch her.

She timed, perfectly, the return of her attention to when there was a lull in the conversation between Felicity and Phillip, casting a sweeping glance around the marquee and saying, "Everyone's moving in." She made a graceful hand gesture. "See? The doors are open." She turned to Phillip. "Shall we, Sir Galahad?"

"We shall indeed, milady," Phillip responded promptly, and gallantly held out his arm for her to take.

She flashed her *Stepford Wives* smile somewhere between Rafael and Felicity. "Maybe we'll run into each other on the dance floor later."

And that was it. She was gone.

"Run into each other on the dance floor?" Felicity said. "*That'll* be interesting!"

"Don't worry, it won't happen. She's already made her point."

"Which was?"

"That she's over me."

"So what are you going to do?"

"Prove that she's not."

CHAPTER FIVE

THE FOOD WAS FABULOUS. The wine excellent. Teague's
best-man speech was a triumph of gentle wit. Romy
and Matt's jointly delivered response weaving super-
heroes, damsels in distress and mere-mortal babies
into a love story was flat-out adorable. And Veronica
prayed for the night to be over so she could go to bed
with a bottle of gin.

She'd been feeling so proud of herself out in the
marquee. Parading Phillip under his nose, exuding
fan-girl charm all over Felicity, resisting the urge to
smash a champagne flute and stab Rafael through
the heart when Felicity dropped that bombshell about
playing Julie—playing *her*—in *Catch, Tag, Release*
and called him "Rafa" like she owned him.

She'd entered the hall and taken her seat and told
herself that elusive thing called closure was almost
within her grasp.

And then Rafael had strolled in, arm-in-arm with
Felicity, and sent her a look of such smugness she was
all the way back to fury again.

Which had obviously made her a diabolically bad

companion for Phillip, who kept disappearing whenever he wasn't required to sit at the table to eat.

Rafael couldn't have been much of a companion
for Felicity, either, because when *he* wasn't sitting
at his table to eat, he spent his time gloating at Veronica from various vantage points. Yes, gloating!
There was no other way to describe his secretive,
self-satisfied smile.

If she hadn't been giving zero fucks, she would
have been tempted to go up to him and smack it off
his face. As it was, all she could do was *not* look
at him. Which was easier said than done because
it required her to keep him in her peripheral vision
to make sure she didn't do it by accident while simultaneously directing her eyes elsewhere wearing
an I-am-fascinated expression. And maintaining her
eyebrows in a perpetual go-fuck-yourself arch while
performing those ocular gymnastics had given her a
crick in her neck and a headache.

Worst of all, the joy she felt for Romy and Matt
had been tainted by a bone-deep envy she hadn't been
expecting and they didn't deserve.

It was just that she'd somehow assumed Romy and
Matt would be the way they'd been in the old days—
together but not *especially* together; tactile but more
like the way you physically interacted with your best
friend; joking around but inviting the rest of the gang
in for a laugh. She'd been so certain their marriage
would be predicated on a position of *Hey, why* not
do it? since they were both single and were going to
have the kid Romy needed anyway. That would have

meant today was more college reunion than wedding, with Veronica and Rafael tag-teaming the group hugs to avoid any partisanship.

But the reality was vastly different from her expectations. The way Matt and Romy had looked at each other in the chapel was the first indication. Then Matt's at-the-altar kiss. And the jolts had been coming thick and fast ever since, making it abundantly clear the Romy and Matt partnership was nothing like the way it used to be. Oh, there was a glimmer of their old friendship in there, but it was embedded deep in something much more visceral.

Matt looked at Romy like he was hungry for her. He touched her like he was dying for want of her. His fingers had lingered at her lips after he'd fed her the obligatory piece of wedding cake as though they had their own taste buds and she was some kind of divine nectar. Even the smallest kiss was imbued with a sense of sexual urgency that made Veronica feel like a voyeur.

And the bridal waltz they were currently performing? It was like nothing Veronica had ever seen. Certainly nothing like either of her own, which had been carefully choreographed and perfectly executed but completely devoid of the barely tethered lust that pulsed between Romy and Matt as they glided across the floor.

They finished the dance with a bedroom kiss. The way she imagined Rafael ending *their* bridal waltz, and the envy inside her morphed into a boa constrictor, wrapping itself around her internal organs and squeezing tighter and tighter until she thought one of them might burst through her skin in some *Alien*-like horror moment.

She watched as Romy's parents joined Romy and Matt on the dance floor—Romy going into her father's arms, Matt dancing with Romy's mother. A few minutes later Teague—doing duty as MC as well as everything else—invited *all* the guests to join in. But Veronica couldn't bear the thought of it. Even if Phillip miraculously reappeared to ask her, she'd say no. *Maybe* she would have roused herself for Teague, but he was standing on the other side of the dance floor looking as though the idea of dancing after that sensual display was as nauseating to him as it was to her.

Well, that was something she *could* do: try to cheer Teague up.

But when Veronica's impetuous steps took her to the edge of the dance floor, she saw that Rafael had beaten her there. God! He was turning into her nemesis!

As she watched, Rafael slung a casual arm around Teague's shoulders and said something that made Teague throw back his head and laugh. It was the first time she'd seen Teague laugh all night and her heart softened, her hostility automatically depressurizing.

But it was a bittersweet moment.

In the old days she would have thought nothing of joining Rafael and Teague. The fact that now she couldn't brought the truth home to her: her old life was in pieces that could never be put back together.

It didn't make any difference to tell herself it was

normal for some groups to splinter and others to form, for individuals to unexpectedly pair up and couples to split up, that that was what was *supposed* to happen when college students moved into the big, wide world and got jobs and changed lifestyles. Because despite knowing that intellectually, in her heart it was different. In her *heart*, in her *soul*, she'd been waiting in limbo for this moment to come…and then go. The moment when she'd accept that Rafael would never again be hers. Only now it was here, it suddenly seemed wrong for the world to keep spinning as though nothing had changed.

A spinning world invalidated the baffled suffering she'd endured since Rafael had left her. It made a mockery of her attempts to protect herself by burying her memories of him, banning herself from asking questions about him, stopping herself from reading his books, from searching online for news of him.

A spinning world told her everyone had moved on except her.

Was she really supposed to accept that life would go on the way it had been going on for the past seven years, two months, three weeks and five days? Did she have to keep *enduring*, with this barren rage choked inside her, this desperate desire for something too nebulous to name except to say that it was more than love, what she'd once had, what she'd lost?

Yes—that had to be the answer to those questions. Yes, she had to accept, she had to endure, she had to live…because the world kept spinning even if *she* had stopped.

She imagined this was how it would feel to be shut in a coffin with the lid nailed down but to still be breathing. Buried alive, screaming for someone to set you free, but nobody hearing you and life outside your airless cocoon going on without you. It's how she'd felt growing up a Johnson, like she was stifling. How she'd felt at that finishing school she'd been sent to for a year when she'd been expelled from high school during her rebellious phase. How she'd felt when college finished and Rafael had left her and she'd gone back to New York to pick up her old life because what else was she supposed to do?

Oh God, she needed to move, needed air and peace and quiet. But her feet stayed rooted to the spot, longing for something else, unable to bear that this really was that final moment and she'd never see him again.

The decision was made almost without conscious thought—that if that were true, if she really was never to see him again, she would look her fill and add the last view of him to all those memories she couldn't bear to resurrect. It was safe to look, from here—the crowded dance floor a perfect filter. People moving together, drawing apart. Now-you-see-him-now-you-don't. Flashpoint vignettes so brief he'd have to know she was there to catch her at it.

And so she drank in the sight of him. The black hair, the so-white smile against his gold-bronze skin, his lean elegance in that perfectly tailored suit and *of course* he didn't need the constraint of a tie…

She closed her eyes, the better to file the picture

away. Enough. Surely that was enough. But it *wasn't* enough, so she opened her eyes to see him once more…and found him staring at her from across the dance floor.

Now you see me.

Oh God, had he known she was there all along?

The crowd on the dance floor moved.

Now you don't.

Go! Get out! That was the voice of reason in her head screaming at her. But her feet wouldn't obey the order. It was as though a string connected her to Rafael despite the viewing channel having closed.

Sixty seconds…dancers shifting…her pulse thundering in her ears, her breaths coming short and shallow.

Now you see me.

And Rafael was *still staring at her*, like he'd been x-raying through the blood, bone and sinew of the gyrating bodies on the floor to watch her.

The dancers on the floor drew close together again, the line of sight narrowed and was gone, the music changed to something slow and romantic. Couples music.

Veronica imagined Rafael going to find Felicity, leading Felicity onto the dance floor, and the spell holding her there broke so that she was moving at last, weaving between the tables…exiting the hall… through the marquee…crossing the lawn. And she didn't care that Johnsons never ran away, she just needed to breathe.

She was glad it was still light enough for her to see

even though it was past nine o'clock, but she wouldn't have long before she was stumbling around in the dark.

If only Rafael would leave early! Take Felicity and go. But, oh God, that would mean they'd soon be in bed together. He'd kiss her the moment they were alone. Peel off her skintight teal dress. He'd whisper to her that she was beautiful. *Eres hermosa.* That he loved her. *Te amo.* That he'd love her forever. *Te amaré por siempre*—

No! Not that! Not that he'd love her forever! He couldn't say that, he *couldn't*. The mere *thought* of him saying that to another woman made Veronica want to throw up.

Oh how she wished she could time-travel back to five minutes before he'd turned around in the chapel so she could escape through that side exit, go to her cottage, pack her things, drive to the airport and board the first plane out.

Or go further back to the day the wedding invitation had arrived and decline it.

Go *all the way back* to the night she'd met Rafael Velez and not fall in love at first sight.

It was the most potent of all her memories, the night they'd met, and she'd been suppressing it for so long, trying *so hard* to seal it off in the vault, and it wasn't fair that it could ache in her chest now like a fresh, jagged wound.

End of first semester. Finals over. Planning one last night out with Romy before Christmas break. Deciding on Flick's—a favorite student hangout because the drinks were cheap and nobody ever got asked for ID. Thirty seconds in, noticing a tall, hunky guy surrounded by women. Matt. But it was the lean, intense man with Matt who'd caught Veronica's attention. Rafael.

Rafael's dark eyes had landed on her from across the room and she'd instantly made up her mind that that was the night she'd finally go all the way. He'd leaned close to Matt, whispered something, and Matt had looked at her, his vivid green eyes undressing Veronica like a bolt of fast lightning before moving on to Romy. Matt had cocked his head to the side—presumably assessing Romy's fuckability—given a why-not shrug, and the two of them had headed over.

Perfect, perfect night. Talking to Rafael about nothing in particular and yet everything. Matt and Romy laughing in the background. Having only one Kir Royale—her favorite cocktail—before switching to water because she wanted to *remember* losing her virginity. None of them wanting to call it a night at closing time. Going back to the three-bedroom town house Veronica's father had bought to see her through university. Dumping coats and scarves, kicking off shoes.

She had a vague memory of Matt and Romy on the couch together, waging a battle over the sex life of Captain America. But the only sex life of interest to Veronica that night was her own, so she'd taken Rafael boldly by the hand and led him to her bedroom.

Almost before the door had closed, she'd been in his arms being kissed. She remembered him draw-

ing back, asking her, "All right?" and waiting for her
ardent "Yes" before removing her clothes. Kissing
her mouth as each item came off. Murmuring to her
in English and Spanish. Telling her how lovely she
was—*encantadora que eres.* That he'd wanted her
his whole life—*yo te he querido toda mi vida.* That
he'd never felt so wild for anyone—*nunca había sen-
tido esto por nadie.*

Then one more kiss. "Are you sure?" he'd asked
and she'd taken his hands, put them on her breasts
and nodded because her throat was too tight to speak.

He'd run his fingers over her skin—gently, rever-
ently, as though he'd known it was her first time—before letting them settle between her thighs, stroking
her there until she'd come. His tongue next, travers-
ing the path his fingers had taken until he'd dropped
to his knees to lick her, holding her hips steady as
she trembled through the orgasm that took her over
like a warm wave.

Only once the very last ripple had receded did he
get to his feet. He'd stripped then—no fanfare, just
getting his clothes out of her way. And then he'd taken
her hands in his and put them on his lightly haired
chest, mirroring the trust with which she'd placed his
hands on her breasts, inviting her to touch anywhere
she wanted—as much or as little, as hard or as soft,
as fast or as slow. And while she did that, the pads of
her fingers roaming at will, *his* fingers had returned
to that throbbing place between her legs, slipped inside her, stretching her, preparing her.

Not until she'd sent her fingers down the narrow

trail of hair below his navel and taken the hot girth of his cock in her hand did he stop her, his hand over hers. "No more until you're ready for me to take you, *mi vida*," he'd said, and she'd told him she *was* ready, so ready, so very ready.

He'd retrieved a condom from his discarded jeans, sheathed himself, taken her in his arms for a quivering moment before walking her backward to the bed, kissing her, kissing her, kissing her. And he'd pulled her down with him, taking her weight before rolling her beneath him, his legs going between hers, not to push hers open but to let her know, give her time, wait through it while he paused at the entrance to her body. He'd said he was sorry, so sorry, for the pain he would cause, and then he'd slowly entered her, his mouth covering hers to catch her gasp, to drink it in.

He'd thought it was a gasp of pain that had escaped her and he'd wanted to absorb that pain for her. But he'd been wrong. It was awe, wonder, reverence even—not pain. She'd felt so lucky, because she'd heard a million horror stories from other women about first sexual encounters—fumbling, impatience, discomfort, brutality, disgust—whereas Rafael had made it slow and beautiful for her. Empowering, too, so that she hadn't been shy about telling him she wanted him again that night, and the next morning. And each time he'd given her something more than she'd known it was possible to want.

They'd spent Christmas texting and calling each other. When she'd arrived back in DC, he'd been waiting on her doorstep to tell her he loved her.

He'd moved in that night. An hour after that they'd had their first fight when he'd found out (a) her parents owned the place and (b) she wasn't going to charge him rent.

The only way she'd been able to think of to get him to stay was to talk Romy and Matt into sharing the house, as well, so the rent could be split four ways to enable Rafael to afford what he deemed an equitable share of the market rate.

He hadn't alluded to it again, even though she knew it burned him up that Romy had only moved in for her sake and Matt for his—which was crazy, because those two had become inseparable. (And, hello, look at them today!)

But if *that* crisis had been averted, the pattern of their first argument was to repeat itself over and over again. Disagreements about money and lifestyle squalling out of nowhere, passionate reconciliations, a cessation in hostilities, the war inevitably restarting. All the way through to the last night they'd spent together, the night before graduation, when they'd had a fight over *nothing*—a bottle of champagne and a teeny, tiny jar of caviar she'd wanted just the two of them to share before the full-on mania of graduation day when her parents and his mother would be in town.

"Why not hang a gigolo sign around my neck?" he'd demanded. "It's what your parents think."

The fight had spiraled, because she was tired of him misjudging her parents so willfully. She'd told him what her parents *really* thought was that unless he found a way to come to terms with her money, they were going to end up fighting their whole lives! In turn, he'd refused to accept her parents' invitation for him to bring his mother to a celebratory dinner with them and Scarlett at Catch of the Day, because it was the most expensive restaurant in town. He couldn't afford it, and he was damned if he was going to be paid for.

Veronica *knew* his mother had thought he was being a dick (definitely *not* his mother's word but true nonetheless) because she'd not only called Veronica's mother to apologize but told Veronica she'd raised him to be proud, not rude, and she hoped Veronica's impeccable manners would rub off on him soon. (Luckily, Mrs. Velez hadn't been able to see inside her not-so-impeccable head at that moment.)

They'd smoothed it over that night, repapered the same crack they'd repaired so many times before, and he'd made love to her as though he was escaping the demons of hell while simultaneously soaring toward heaven. And the next day—just before they'd left for Capitol U—she'd seen him slip a small jeweler's box in his pocket.

She'd known then he was going to propose to her, and she'd *glowed* throughout the graduation ceremony, despite a burgeoning unease over the extravagant graduation present she'd bought him. He'd have to see that the gift was perfect for the way they'd start their life together—soaring free.

A dry sob yanked her back to the present. It had come from her, that anguished sound. She'd let her guard down, which was what always happened when she aired those memories. Good reason not to remember.

She shook her head as though she could shake the memory back from whence it came and blew out a cleansing breath as she looked around. She'd walked all the way back to the mausoleum. Ha! She was sure Scarlett would have something to say about that. Her subconscious taking over, telling her she still wanted the whole *till death do us part* deal, despite the fact her real love, her overwhelming, passionate, first and only love, hadn't made it past college.

She ascended the steps to the platform and contemplated going inside this time if she could get in, wanting to read the inscriptions, hoping to be convinced it was possible to find a love that would last beyond forever. She actually went so far as to put her hand on the door handle but something stopped her. It seemed too private, too sacred, to poison the resting place of that long-married couple with her bitterness. She was better off out here, looking at the moors and dreaming of Brontë-esque separated soulmates and thwarted passion…

She heard a sound behind her and whirled, her heart in her mouth—only to splutter out a laugh. "Teague Hamilton! You scared the crap out of me! What are you doing here?"

"Looking for you, doofus."

He joined her then reeled back with a "Whoa" when he saw she had her hand poised on the handle.

"If you're going in, I'll wait here for you. I don't do graves, as you know."

She gave a sound that was between a laugh and a sigh as she took his hand. "No, I'm not going in. Let's get our Brontë on and look at the view instead."

"I think the Brontës went a little further than looking at the view, V, and actually lived it," he said as she led him away.

"We'll be secondary characters, not the romantic leads. More calm contemplation, less tumultuous thrashing through the heather."

He laughed as they stopped and stood side by side. "That's good! Much as I'd like to go all Edward Fairfax Rochester and brood across the moors, I'm too tired to go full-on romantic hero," he said. "Why did nobody warn me how onerous it was to double as best man for the groom and maid of honor for the bride? Maid of honor! God, I can't believe I'm actually using that phrase."

"Nobody warned you because you might have backed out—and where would the bride and groom have been then?"

"Hmm, Matt had two other options. My choice would have been Artie, though, so you could have been maid of honor without risk of a blood-drenched 'Red Wedding' scenario."

"My need to murder Rafael aside, I think two husbands knocks me out of contention for that role."

He examined her, mouth pursed thoughtfully. "For someone who's been married twice, you have a distinctly unmarried look about you. I don't think your bouquet-catching days are over."

She slanted him a sideways, eyelash-batting smile. "Is that a proposal, because I should warn you I'm on the hunt for husband number three."

He draped an arm across her shoulders. "Do you want it to be?"

"It'd make my parents happy."

"Oh, well then, that's a perfect enticement, isn't it?"

She rubbed her head against his shoulder. "And maybe it would make me happy, too."

"And maybe…not?"

"Maybe not," she conceded. "But I wish we'd been the ones to fall in love back then."

"That was never going to happen. You were already taken by the time I met you and I…" He hesitated but then shrugged and continued. "I was hoping for Romy as we all know, even if we don't talk about it. But she was already taken, too, as it turns out. And who could ever compete with Matt?"

"You could compete with anyone, Teague, for the right woman. I wish it *had* been me. We're so much alike it would have been…uncomplicated."

"*Are* we so much alike?"

"*Aren't* we?"

"The whole scion-of-the-family thing, maybe." He shrugged. "But as for what lies beneath…?"

"Are you saying you have mysterious depths?"

"Maybe I'm saying you do. Rafael thought so. It wasn't the scion he wanted, you know."

"No, he *definitely* didn't want that part of me!" Silence as she wound her arm behind his back. "Tough, today, huh? But of course you handled it like a champ because you're perfect."

"Beneath this urbane exterior is a seething mass of violent contradiction, ready to go on an imperfect rampage."

"It's a shame you never got together with Frankie in that case."

"Frankie?"

"Frankie—sexy Aussie, Flick's boozer whisperer by day, exotic dancer by night."

"Yeah right!" he scoffed.

"Why not?"

"Because… Just because."

She snuggled into his side—half in sympathy, half needing the comfort for herself. "You know, we *could* give marriage a shot, T-Man."

"Thanks but no thanks. It's my turn to be looked at the way Romy looks at Matt. The way you always, *always* looked at Rafael." He tugged her in a little closer, tightening his arm around her. "Speaking of whom…?"

"Speaking of whom…it's done. Over. I'm ready to sell that motorcycle, which has been doing *nobody* any good stashed out of sight in the garage in Kentucky since graduation."

"A 1952 Vincent Black Shadow isn't a mere motorcycle."

"It is to me. But to him… Well, I *thought* it was his dream bike."

"Hmm."

"What?"

"Just that he never let you buy him so much as a cup of coffee, so I'm not sure what made you think he'd accept a motorcycle that cost the earth."

"Oh, only that we'd ride off into the sunset on it."

"Living on your dime." He laughed. "Delusional."

"He was supposed to propose to me."

Teague turned her into his arms, held her silently for a minute. "And if he had, what did you think would happen? His personality would suddenly change and he'd happily retire to live off your trust fund?"

"If we'd married, my money would have become *our* money, and that would have made it…made it okay for him to write full-time. That's not the same as retiring."

"Jesus, V! You spent three and a half years wrapped around him—*literally* wrapped around him. You had to know him better than that…" Pause, as he searched her face. "Which makes me wonder why you did it. There had to be a reason."

"Maybe I should ask Scarlett—not that it matters now. It's over. It's too late."

"I'm not sure Rafael sees it that way. He's certainly coming for you full steam ahead."

"I don't think the few minutes' conversation we've had this evening qualifies as full steam ahead."

"I mean literally, at this moment, walking toward us."

Her eyes went wide, her heart leaped, her body

went rigid. "Is F-Felicity w-with him?" Oh God, she was stuttering.

"Nope."

"H-he'll leave. He'll leave n-now he's seen I'm here."

"I don't think leaving's high on his list of things to do in Yorkshire," Teague said dryly. "Now—" repositioning her so she was standing beside him and tucking her hand into the crook of his arm "—stop cowering and face him head-on the way you always did."

Veronica's breath caught painfully at the sight of Rafael treading up the steps. He looked like he belonged here, caught between the wild moors and the elegant lawn of the estate, with dusk approaching. Heathcliff on a mission. And she'd opened the way for him to achieve that mission because she'd been unable to resist staring at him across a dance floor.

"You looking for me, Rafe?" Teague asked cheerfully as Rafael came to a stop in front of them.

"No," Rafael said, unequivocal.

"Just needed some air, peace, quiet? We're leaving anyway, so we'll concede the field. If you could just edge over so we can get past…?"

Rafael stayed where he was. "You're welcome to leave, Teague. Veronica, however, is not." He nodded at Veronica's hand on Teague's arm. "Let him go."

She swallowed. "And if I don't?"

Rafael gave a half shrug, almost apologetic. "I'll break his arm."

"Okaaay," Teague said, looking at Veronica to see what she wanted.

She had to swallow again but then she nodded and released her hold. "Tell Romy I'll be there for the bouquet toss."

Teague looked from her to Rafael, back to her. "If you need me…" he said.

"She won't need you," Rafael said. He stepped aside to let Teague pass but then stopped him. "And, Teague, don't worry—she's the bloodthirsty one, not me."

Teague laughed softly. "You two do my head in."

Veronica waited until Teague was halfway across the lawn then gave Rafael what she hoped was an approximation of "the look."

"A broken-armed best man might have been a little awkward to explain to Matt and Romy."

"Good thing I didn't break it then."

"Question is, why did you want to?"

"I *didn't* want to. I like Teague. As you know, since you watched me talk to him for twenty minutes. But you needed to stay and he needed to know he's not going to be husband number three. At least, not yet. I'm not waiting through another marriage to get what's between us finished, Veronica."

"Whatever was between us was finished when you walked out on me without giving me the courtesy of telling me it was over."

"You're the one who made it over."

She laughed then. A desperate laugh, the cadence of which she couldn't control. "Your memory is faulty, Rafael. Not that who did what to whom matters after all this time. Who cares?"

"Who cares? You apparently. So go ahead and be the one to tell me it's over. Say goodbye, formally and officially."

She adjusted her stance, planting her feet, ready for a fight. "Do you think I won't?"

"I think you *can't*," he said. "I think that's why you blocked me. I think that's why you didn't read my books. I think that's why you've been a pain in the ass all night."

"I've barely *looked* at you all night!"

"Hence—pain in the ass. We could have built up to this if you had, but now we're out of time, and all I have to go on is the way you looked at me across the dance floor. So if you want to say goodbye, that's fine. But I want you to touch me as you say it."

"Touch you?" she asked, incredulous.

"Touch me. Carte blanche to choose any body part you want—a fingernail if that's all you can bear."

"Just because I touched you once upon a time doesn't mean I want to do so now. It doesn't work like that."

He said nothing—just waited.

She took a steadying breath and raised her eyes to his face, hoping to find something there that would stop her. This was different from when she'd been alone with him out here earlier, different from the time in the marquee. They'd been fencing then, with face masks and buttons on their sword tips. But looking at him now, cataloging the changes time had wrought in him, she knew this wasn't a safe sport.

There were tiny lines at the corners of his eyes;

a new gauntness in his cheeks and a hardness to his sensual mouth. His expression was cynical in a way it never had been—as though he'd finally seen everything he wanted to see. The thick black hair was longer today than he'd ever worn it, signaling he'd stopped giving a damn about looking like the Teagues of the world.

He'd always been a soulfully beautiful man, and now he was breathtakingly so. Tougher, maybe even ruthless. He wasn't an unknown boy who could steal your heart with one melting look across a crowded bar; he was a man who could steal your will and make you want what he *told* you to want. And that's exactly what he was doing, because despite telling herself she owed him nothing, that she didn't have to prove a damn thing to him, that he could go to hell without her saying one more word, her hands were moving—seemingly of their own volition.

He stood perfectly still as her hands landed on his chest, but it was as though all his senses swirled around her, connecting with hers, causing a rush of wet arousal between her thighs. Her skin itched. The tiny hairs on the back of her neck tingled. She stared at her hands as though she could see through them into his heart, which was pounding in time with her own. A hard, fast drum against her palm. Once, her hands had been allowed to roam at will over his body, no permission needed. But as Scarlett had said, that was then, this was now.

Then she'd wanted everything he'd had to give. Now all she needed from him was closure. And with one small word, just two syllables, she could have it.

A slow blink, a difficult swallow. She opened her mouth, but to her horror the word wouldn't come out.

His hands came up to cover hers where they rested on his chest. "You can't say it, can you, Veronica?"

She pulled her hands out from under his. "You've changed." Not an answer.

"True."

"So why does it matter if I say it or not? You've already moved on—you have everything you ever wanted."

"Do I?"

"Don't you?" She half turned away then turned back. "This is pointless. Felicity…"

"What about her?"

"She'll be wondering where you are."

"Felicity knows I'm with you."

"What an accommodating girlfriend."

"She's not my girlfriend."

"Then what? No—don't answer that! It's none of my business. The sun's going to set any minute and… and it's getting cold. Time to go back. Let me pass."

His answer was to remove his jacket and drape it around her shoulders. Oh, the feel of it. The warmth from him. The lemony scent of his aftershave wafting up from the collar. It was so unfair, what everything about him still did to her.

She instantly removed it, held it out to him. "We're done here."

He took the jacket and put it around her again.

"We're not done until you say goodbye. Or…there's another option. I have a proposal."

"I told you before, when hell freezes over."

"No chance of anything freezing when you and I are involved."

"Okay, look, we both know you're not the marrying kind, so how about you just tell me what your proposal actually *is*, then I can say no and we can move on."

"Moving on—that's the proposal in a nutshell. A way to move on."

"What do you *want*, Rafael?"

"Simple. I want to fuck you, Veronica. I want one night—that's all."

CHAPTER SIX

HE HADN'T MEANT to put that so baldly, so *crudely*, but he'd been caught up in a whirl of resentment at seeing her with Teague—a resentment that was both surprising and unfair.

It wasn't jealousy—at least not of the usual variety; he knew Teague and Veronica had a brother/sister relationship. Actually he'd have resented their closeness *less* if it had been romantic, because he knew he could trump that the same way he could trump what she'd had with her husbands. No, it was their easy, uncomplicated familiarity that bugged him. Their *otherness*. The polished, gilded, old-money perfection they shared, which wordlessly proclaimed that the world had always been their oyster and they were definitely its pearls, whereas he... Well, to stretch the analogy, he'd been shucked too early and polished too late; his nacre would never match the luster of those two—those *four* if you included her matching set of husbands.

Well fuck it, he was past playing tenement slum to their penthouse view. He'd say what he wanted any way he wanted. He'd write the epilogue to their romance in *his* language, and enjoy the symmetry of earning a new fortune from *Stomp* off Veronica's back. Then maybe he'd be free at last to find a new story to tell.

"Well?" he asked. "Are you going to answer me?"

Typically, Veronica refused to be intimidated by his coarse choice of words, opening her eyes innocent-wide. "Oh, that was a *question*! You're not telling me you *want* to fuck me, you're asking me if I'll *let* you! I see." She removed his jacket for the second time, held it out to him. "The answer is no. And don't give this to me again. I don't want *it*, and I don't want the fuck."

He took the jacket, shrugged into it. "Why not?"

"The jacket? Because my days of borrowing your clothes are over. The fuck?" She raised her chin, tried to look down her nose at him, but she lacked the height to do it effectively—and he'd just bet that pissed her the hell off. "I don't have to give a reason. Now, I suggest you go back to Felicity and do whatever it is you normally do with wedding dates."

"I told you, Felicity isn't my girlfriend."

"Whatever she is, she's with you and I'm not, so if that's all…"

He blocked her attempt to move past him. "She's a friend. And if you really want to know why she's with me—"

"I don't."

"—it's for protection. She's protecting me from you."

"You can *not* be serious! What did you think I'd do? Throw myself at you if you wandered in on your own?"

"I just told you straight-out I want to fuck you, Veronica, so go ahead and throw yourself at me. You can take it as a given I won't fight you off."

"The only thing I'll be *throwing* at you is a dagger after what you did to me. So, if you want to stay safe, let me pass."

"Who said I wanted to stay safe?"

She shook her head, held up a hand to ward him off.

"Ah, I see," he said, "*you* want to stay safe."

She laughed—unconvincingly. "If you think you scare me—"

"I think I never *used* to…but I think I do now. Look at your hand, keeping me away even though I haven't taken one step closer."

She dropped her hand. "I'm not scared of you."

"Really? 'Cuz that's quite a fight-flight-freeze response you've got going on. Pupils dilated. Body quivering. Breaths fast and shallow." He smiled. "Oh, wait, that's not fight-flight-freeze! I've seen you like this before, haven't I? Every night for three and a half years."

She licked her lips and, God, he wanted to be the one licking them. "That was then, this is now," she said.

"Say the word and I'll be on my knees for you in a heartbeat, same as I always was."

"What you want is for *me* to be on my knees for *you*."

He took two steps back, putting some distance between them to make it harder to haul her in. "You used to be braver than this, Veronica. The night we met you said straight-out you wanted me and you were going to have me."

"And look how that turned out!"

"That turned out the way you wanted it to!"

"I didn't leave *myself* you know!"

He felt his hand clench. Fury. She *knew* what she'd done. "You left me as surely as I left you."

"Bullshit!"

"After defying your parents to live with me."

"Which didn't get me very far, did it?"

"It got you as far as you wanted to go!" he said, hating the bitterness in his voice. "It got you three and a half years of slumming it. But in the end you had to go and stick one price tag too many on me."

She tossed her head—actually tossed her damn head. "You put all those price tags on yourself!"

"You lost your nerve."

"How dare you say that!"

"What happened to you after I left, Veronica, that you couldn't even pick up the goddamn phone when I called? Did Mommy send you back to finishing school? Did they tame you after all?"

And there it was—the flare of wild heat, unmasked, as she closed the distance he'd put between them and shoved him in the chest. "You want to know what *happened* to me? *You* happened, you bastard!" Shove. "Not my mother. Not my father. Not my sister. They weren't the ones who told you to leave me.

You did that yourself!" Shove. "You *stole* whatever bravery I had when you made my money more important to you than I was." Shove. "When you told me you'd love me forever then made a fool of me by leaving me five minutes later." Shove. "When you trampled all over my pride by leaving Matt to tell me you'd gone." Shove. "And now you expect me to *fuck* you just because you say so?" Shove. "I'll get my fucks somewhere else thank you!"

"I stole your bravery? Okay, so be the old Veronica and come and get it back off me."

"I don't—"

"I made a fool of you? Come right at me and make me regret it. I trampled all over your pride? Get your steel-capped boots on and kick the shit out of me for it. Make me pay for leaving you. Make me suffer. Make me shake with lust for you the way I always did. Make me work for what I want to take from you. Make me want nothing more than to have you. You know you can do it, Veronica. You were so close to turning me into your slave last time."

"Oh! *Oh!* You were too stubborn to be *anyone's* slave, and you *certainly* were never mine."

"No? Then maybe you should prove that to me, because right about now I think you could get me to do anything you asked with one kiss."

"And if I kissed you and then asked for you to leave me *the hell* alone?"

"Then I *will* leave you the hell alone. Is it what you want? Look me in the eye and tell me."

"What I *want*…" she said breathlessly. "What I

want is…" Her eyes closed. He could feel the roiling, impotent anger rolling off her in waves. He knew it was going to break and he exulted in the anticipation of it. And then she threw back her head, pounded her fists on her pink-clad thighs. "Oh *God*," she cried to the heavens. "What I want is *not* to want you!" Pound. "I don't." Pound. "Want." Pound. "To want you!" Pound. "Don't you get it?"

"Oh, I get it," he said, and gave in at last to the need to touch her, reaching for her, dragging her into his arms. And, dear God, having her back like this was terrifyingly right. She had to be able to feel his heartbeat, maybe even hear it, galloping like a fucking horse, but he didn't care. She could feel anything she wanted, do anything to him she wanted at that moment, and he'd let her—and wasn't that a spiral back into the past! "I'm in that boat up to my ears in ballast so heavy I can't catch a breeze."

She shook her head against his chest but made no attempt to free herself. "This doesn't make sense, what you're asking for."

"We never did make sense, you and I."

"I hate you."

"I'm not asking you to love me."

"I mean *hate*. I hate you so much I made a voodoo doll of you using that lock of hair you gave me and a T-shirt you left in the laundry hamper."

"Jesus!" He laughed—crowed with it—because this was peak Veronica. Unadulterated and feisty as hell. A voodoo doll! He didn't know why he loved that so much but, God, he did. "With pins I suppose?"

"I stick them in every day."

"That explains a lot."

"Still want to fuck me?" she asked.

"Hell yes! But can you take a few pins out of its cock first?"

"No guarantees."

"What about if I perform to your satisfaction tonight? Will you take it easy on Little Rafa after we go our separate ways tomorrow?"

She laughed, only it came out like a snorting snuffle because her face was pressed into his chest. "Little Rafa? Please tell me that's not what you call your penis these days."

"Little? How can you, of all people, suggest that?" He brushed a trembling hand across the back of her neck. "What if I told you what I want is to stop whatever it is that makes you want to hurt me, and makes me want to hurt you? Not that I've gone to your artistic lengths and made a voodoo doll, despite still having the lock of hair you gave *me* and the blue silk panties I found in the back seat of my car. Ha. Remember that night when we went stargazing…?"

"I remember," she said. "And I remember that sex was never the problem, so if the goal of this proposal of yours is to fuck our way out of each other's heads in one night when we didn't manage it in three and a half years…?" She shook her head, "It's insane, Rafael."

"You're right, it's insane," he said, "up to a point."

"Up to a point?"

"We were in love then. Now we're not. So I'm betting we're going to find that sex between us will turn out to be not as special as we once thought it was, and the final goodbye will be easy."

"And if it *is* as special?"

"Then you'll have no trouble making me beg for more time—and it'll be up to you whether you give it to me or not. Revenge served hot."

"And there's the catch!" She pulled out of his arms, stepped back.

"I know you want revenge, Veronica."

"Oh, I do," she assured him. "But it's the begging I'm talking about. You don't know *how* to beg."

"What do you think I'm doing now?"

"It's not begging, what you're doing. It's negotiating, to get what you want."

Another laugh rumbled through him. "Oh…well, if you're open to negotiation, lay out your terms and conditions," he said.

She bit at her bottom lip, sucked it as though she could already taste him. "I only have one condition."

"Name it, it's yours."

"I want your new book."

He blinked.

"*Stomp*," she said.

"*Stomp*?"

She smiled. "Say hello to your new editor, Rafael."

CHAPTER SEVEN

"So...do we have a deal, Rafael?" she asked.

He looked out at the moors, as though seeking guidance, murmuring something that sounded like "symmetry" but could just as easily have been "irony." And then something in Spanish. She'd surprised him, asking for the book. Well, she'd surprised herself, too. But she knew she'd need more than one night to take her revenge. She needed something of his that was permanent, something she could control, to make up for the parts of *her* he'd used in those other books, over which she'd had no say at all. A fair trade. One book for two.

"This can stop right now if you like," she said coolly when the silence stretched too far. "You keep your book, we go back to the hall and forget we had this discussion."

"Forget?" he said, huffing out a breath that was half a laugh before bringing his eyes back to her. "I haven't forgotten anything, Veronica. Not one thing. But if we're playing hardball, I have two conditions of my own. The first is that Bryan, my agent, has to be happy with the contract."

"Of course—that's a given."

"The second? Well, we both know my book is worth more than one night, so I'll take the whole two weeks you're staying here."

"How do you know how long I'm staying here?"

"The same way I know you're on a working holiday, half the time sightseeing, the other half editing Tori Jayle's new book. The way I know you're staying in a two-bedroom cottage on the estate—I even know which one. The way I know you were intending to go on to London tomorrow and work out of Johnson/Charles's Notting Hill office, but when you arrived yesterday you liked the coziness and seclusion of the cottage so much you abandoned the London plan and extended your booking here." He smiled— very pleased with himself. "Because you told Phillip Castle."

"*Phillip?* Did you—? *What* did you do?"

"Only suggested Felicity might like to keep him occupied between courses."

She sucked in an outraged breath. "Felicity *spied* on me for you?"

"It's innocuous stuff, Veronica. As innocuous as all the other things you took such delight in banning Matt, Teague and Romy from telling me. So get over it and tell me if we have a deal."

"When do I get the book?"

"Three weeks—once you're safely back in New York. Meanwhile, I'll let Bryan know to expect a call from you."

"Not me," she said. "My boss."

"You have a *boss*? A *real* boss?"

"Why *wouldn't* I have a real boss?"

"I thought Daddy's little girl would be the one in the corner office."

"And I *will* be in the corner office—when I've *earned* that spot."

"Then let's hope *Stomp* gets you closer. That'll be...poetic."

A claw of apprehension scratched at her spine. Symmetry. Irony. Poetry. What didn't she know? "What do you mean by 'poetic'?"

"Don't worry. *Stomp* isn't a book of poetry." He huffed out one more of those half laughs, half breaths. "My one attempt at poetry wasn't exactly a roaring success."

"Why three weeks? I thought it was finished?"

"I've decided it needs an epilogue. Just need to see if—how—that comes together. But once that's done, it'll be all systems go."

She stared at him, that apprehension working its way through her entire body now.

He stared at her—implacable.

Long moments while she tried to think of questions she could ask that would settle her nerves and tell her she was doing the right thing.

"Veronica?" he prompted.

Oh for God's sake! Two weeks—her body for a book. Not the most savory way of doing business but she'd come this far, she might as well go all the way. So, "Deal," she said.

He smiled—triumph. Not reassuring.

"So here's what has to happen," he said. "You go back ahead of me and get your key slipped under the door of my room—303, third floor of the hall. I'll make my farewells, check out, get myself over to the cottage, and expect you…when? How long do you need?"

"I think…an hour? Give or take ten minutes."

"An *hour*?"

"It's the last I'll see of Romy and Matt this trip— they're going straight to Spain in the morning. And I need to at least pretend to catch the bouquet."

"If I have to wait that long, you'd better take off your underwear before you leave the reception."

He said it so conversationally, it took a moment for the words to sink in. And then she laughed in disbelief. "Negotiations are over, buddy."

"O-kay—but I warn you that anything blocking my way when you get in the door is in danger of being ripped to shreds."

Her heart kicked as the image of him ripping her underwear to shreds formed in her head. But she knew a way to make his heart kick right back. "Then how about I go one better?" she said and, keeping her eyes on his, she stepped back, reached a hand under her dress, gave a little wriggle, a tug, and within seconds had her panties down around her ankles. Such a tiny scrap of lace, a nondescript beige, but she might as well have worn that scrap especially for him because the crotch was soaking and she didn't care that he'd know. She stepped out of her panties, scooped them up, held them out.

She saw his Adam's apple bob viciously in his throat as he took them. For a moment he did nothing but hold them, and look at them, and breathe in slowly through nostrils flared wide. And then with another difficult swallow he put them in his pants' pocket.

"So tell me," he said, and nodded at her skirt, "do you still wax everything off?"

She understood from that one question that when Rafael said he wanted to fuck her, he meant he was going to fuck her *good*. And if he thought that was going to discompose her? Well, hold her beer. If this was to be a war of seduction, she was going to win it. "Yes," she said boldly. "Want to see?"

He stepped closer. "Want to touch."

Okay, she wasn't winning the war just yet because that *did* discompose her. "We're outside a mausoleum, you know that, right?"

"I know that. And I also know I'm a long way off dead."

And so, she thought, was she. She felt more alive in this moment than she'd felt for seven years, two months, three weeks and five days—and God, it felt good. So, "Fine," she said.

"Oh, Veronica, I'm going to need more than an easy 'fine.' You don't want to want me, I don't want to want you—but the want is there. If we're going to exercise it, we need to go hard, so don't just acquiesce. *Tell* me you want me to touch you. *Order* me to do it."

A little thrill ran through her. Oh she was so ready for this. "Okay, touch me. Touch me now. Do it. Feel how wet I am. Taste me if you want," she said and almost before the words were out, his hand was under her dress, fingertips whisper-soft against her bare mons. She had to force herself to stand there and let him—not because she wanted him to stop but because she wanted to grab him by the lapels of his jacket and order him to do more.

"Open for me, Veronica," he said and, with a little gasp, she shifted her legs apart. In one sudden, dramatic move, two of his fingers speared into her—and it was as if a switch had been turned in him, so that he started to shake. "Wet as a fucking storm," he breathed. "I knew it."

As suddenly as he'd thrust his fingers into her, he drew them back out. "Okay," he said, rubbing her moisture between his fingers, then bringing his fingers to his mouth, sucking them, eyes closing. Veronica got the impression he was trying to calm himself down, but watching him enjoy the taste of her was making her the opposite of calm.

"What about *your* underwear?" she said.

His eyes opened. "What about it?"

"I want you to take it off before I get there. It's called parity. Or let's put it in money terms, shall we, and call it getting rid of the gender pay gap. What you're paid, I'm paid."

He smiled. "That's my girl."

"I'm not your girl. I won't be that ever again. All I want is for your underwear to be off by the time I get to the cottage so *I* don't have to rip it off *you*. Got it?"

"Got it," he said and held out his hand. "Now seal the deal."

She put her hand in his. It was as though this really was a deal—a business deal. Except that every sense she had was on high alert and there was a pulse between her thighs that was insisting an hour was too damn long to wait no matter how businesslike it was supposed to be.

And he must have thought so, too, because he tugged her into his arms and crushed her against his chest. "Can you feel what you do to me?"

"Yes."

"So you want to talk gender pay gap? I've had my taste. Now it's time for yours. What do you want me to do to you?"

She choked down a bubble of hysteria at the thought that in the chapel she'd told herself he'd be shocked if she wrapped her legs around him! *This* Rafael looked ready for anything.

But she knew what she wanted—what she'd wanted all night—and maybe that would be as much a shock to him as if she demanded he strip naked.

"I want you to kiss me," she said.

If she thought he'd be disappointed at such a tame request, he quickly proved her wrong, pulling her in more tightly, *breathing* her in, as he slowly, slowly, lowered his face until he was hovering over her, a mingled breath away, so close...

And then, putting the lie to that slow hover, his mouth connected with hers in a hard, fast swoop. No holding back, no easing in—just his mouth smashing against hers, his tongue surging into her, licking deep and sure, his teeth biting at her lips.

It was everything she'd been missing—but also more. Familiar but also new. The same…yet different. The heat, the taste, the need were all there—but it was more demanding than a kiss from him had ever been. Like a harbinger of something else, something wild and dangerous, to come. She wanted that danger. Needed the wild. Longed to feel the physical need again. Revenge, she reminded herself. That's what this was all about. Her revenge.

And then what?

The question came unbidden. What would it prove to make him shake with lust for her the way he was daring her to do? What would she gain by trampling over him, making him work for every moan and pant he won from her, making him beg? Suffer? She'd given him every piece of her once, she'd *loved* him— and she hadn't been enough to keep him. What made her think she was enough now to inflict any damage on him all these years later?

She pulled away as a shiver shook through her, telling herself it was the drop in air temperature that caused it, not a premonition of disaster.

Catastrophe scale, she said to herself.

But just at that moment she couldn't think of anything worse than not having him.

Except, perhaps, falling in love with him again.

CHAPTER EIGHT

Rafael groaned long and loud when he stepped inside the cottage and the seductive scent of vanilla grabbed him by the dick. He had forty minutes to wait until Veronica arrived and each one was going to be interminable with that smell impregnating the air.

He walked quickly through the two downstairs rooms. A spacious living area, which opened onto a pretty garden, and a well-stocked kitchen/dining area with a pay-as-you-drink collection of booze. A flight of stairs—with one squeaky step—led up to two bedrooms. Each bedroom had an array of mismatched, vintage-but-not-antique furniture—a four-poster bed, a bureau, a vanity table with chair, a wardrobe and an armchair—and a very basic attached bathroom.

It was a cute cottage, but so unlike the luxury surroundings Veronica was used to, it was hard to believe she'd opted to work from here for two weeks when she could have checked into a five-star suite in London. Even if she was set on staying on the estate, she could have moved to the sumptuous dower house once Romy and Matt left on their honeymoon.

But what did he really know about her living arrangements? He'd just assumed her place in Manhattan would be like her parents' glamorous interior-designed penthouse apartment, which he'd visited a couple of times. Maybe with a dash of the timeless elegance of the Johnson "family seat" in Kentucky— site of the mind-bogglingly lavish party thrown for her parents' twentieth wedding anniversary.

Other than that, all he had to go on was that three-bedroom town house they'd shared in DC, and *that* had been furnished eclectically with a mix of trash and treasure, for all that the house itself belonged to her Vanderbilt-ish parents. Probably because Veronica had insisted that anyone living in the place operate along the lines of *mi casa es su casa* and add whatever they wanted to the ambience. So Romy's ancient cookware, Matt's student-digs couch, Rafael's tattered collection of vintage Colombian photography and Veronica's designer bookshelves all jostled for equal space. It worked, too. It just... worked.

He shook the memory away, uncomfortable at how thinking about that house made him feel. When he'd first moved in he'd been so angry about the rent issue. That undercurrent of anger had never left him, so it didn't make sense that he should feel so...so *homesick* for the place. Homesick for the way they'd lived and loved, even for the fights they'd had. He wondered if they'd still be together now, living, loving, fighting, if she hadn't bought that motorcycle.

His dream bike and he'd so desperately wished he

could accept it. But when he'd reached for the ring in his pocket, *his* side of the bargain, he'd caught a flicker of doubt in her eyes and known the bike was a test—a bit like that special look her mother blitzed the girls' boyfriends with. And what Veronica had said during the fight over the caviar zoomed into his head—that her parents had said he'd have to come to terms with her money or they were going to end up fighting their whole lives. He'd seen his life laid out as a series of tests and fights and capitulations, and he'd known if he was going to have a forever with Veronica, he had first to leave, get his shit sorted, then come back for her—a better man with a better goddamn ring!

All of which he'd intended to say. He'd started strong, telling her he loved her, that he'd love her forever. But all those other words, the important words, dammed themselves up behind a wall of pride. How did you tell someone you were leaving because you wanted too much to stay, and sit, and heel, and beg for her? He'd told her he had something important to take care of, that she should head over to the postgraduation party at Flick's without him, that he'd meet her there…and left it to Matt to say sorry he wasn't coming after all, that he needed to get his head straight, that he'd call her when he'd done it.

Test failed. Candidate dismissed. No option to resit the exam.

Ah Jesus, enough!

Those days were past.

This was a new era. The rules were set. Two weeks.

A business deal. They each knew what they were bringing to the table and what they were taking away.

He checked his watch. Twenty-six minutes until she arrived.

He took off his jacket and his shirt and smiled at the emptiness of the wardrobe as he hung them in there. Veronica always overpacked, which was probably why the prospect of *un*packing was so daunting she never did it—at either end. It surprised no one that half the time she couldn't find what she wanted in the two gargantuan suitcases she always traveled with, and the other half she located things she had no use for.

Rafael, however, was a neat traveler and careful with his things, so even his shoes and socks, once removed, were neatly stored away in their proper places in his suitcase.

Then he dug out the panties he'd stashed in his pocket, which had been burning his leg since she'd walked away from the mausoleum. He spent a minute fighting the temptation to lick them and in the end had to shove them back in his pocket to stop himself. For added insurance, he stripped off his pants and folded them up with those panties still in the pocket, then put them out of sight in his suitcase.

By that time he was sweating from an excess of about-to-be-slaked lust, so he figured a shower was in order—he'd always liked to be fresh and clean before touching her. He whipped off his last item of clothing, the pale gray tee he used as an undershirt, which he folded and placed on the chair.

As he entered the bathroom he found himself assessing the shower dimensions to ascertain if Veronica would fit in with him, and the idea of taking her under the spray made him so horny he decided on a cold shower. Sure, he'd told her to make him beg, but he didn't want to go down on his knees the minute he saw her!

After an emphatic scrub of every body part beneath a drench of adrenaline-boosting icy water, he concluded the thing about cold showers tamping down sexual desire was a fucking myth, because he was bigger and harder and hornier than he'd been at the beginning.

Fortunately there were only eighteen minutes to wait or he might have given in to the compulsion to jack off. He was even degenerate enough to consider saving time by greeting her at the door stark naked. All very alarming, given he'd planned a languid seduction beginning with a restrained kiss, followed by a ceremonial procession up the stairs to the bedroom, a slow undressing, and an hour of foreplay before the main act.

He grabbed a clean T-shirt out of his suitcase and yanked it on, furious with his body for its treachery. Jeans came next. A pair identical to the buttery-soft pale blue ones she'd never been able to keep her hands off. He couldn't yank *them* on, though—he had to zip them up v-e-r-y carefully over his rampant erection. He finger-combed his damp hair then checked himself in the mirror on the vanity.

"You'll scare the shit out of her if you look at her

like that!" he said to his reflection. "Get it the hell together."

Back downstairs. A glass of wine to help take the edge off, consumed faster than normal, after which he was still too ready, too willing, too aching. But at least there was only five minutes to go.

He stationed himself inside the front door, his ears twitching like a crack-smoking Spock for sounds of her arrival, but those five minutes passed with no sound.

Breathe, he ordered himself. *Breathe nice and slow and even.* Give or take ten minutes, she'd said; that gave her another five minutes before she was officially late. And if she took longer? Well, so what? He'd been waiting seven years, two months, three weeks and five days for her; surely he could wait another ten, twenty, even thirty minutes.

"Jesus," he said out loud, tearing his hands through his hair. "Can you hear yourself? *Seven years, two months, three weeks and five days?* How about adding some hours and minutes and seconds to that tally just to make yourself sound even more pathetic?"

Pathetic. The magic word, obviously, because there it was: the sound of footsteps on gravel.

And then nothing except the sound of his blood roaring in his ears like Niagara Falls.

The footsteps restarted. He counted those hesitant steps, using them as a method of control. One, two, three, four…four…foooour…?

Where the hell were the five, six and seven needed to get her to the damn door?

His fingers stretched with the need to yank the door off its hinges, his unrestrained cock was surging like a wild thing in his jeans, his brain had snap-frozen on the thought that she wasn't going to come in, even though he knew that was stupid because this was *her* cottage.

"Fuck it!" he said under his breath and wrenched open the door to find her standing a few feet from the door—gazing at the cottage, as snap-frozen as his brain.

"You're late," he growled and came straight for her.

"I had to call my sist—"

And he swooped, kissing the words out of her like some violent bird of prey.

On the walk from the hall, Veronica had tried to work out how she should enter the cottage and what her first words should be to telegraph that whatever Rafael had said about exorcisms and going hard, the process should nevertheless be orderly and controlled. This was two weeks, not one night. Plenty of time.

But as Rafael barreled toward her with that half-feral, half-anguished look on his face, there was room for only one thought in her head: that she'd been waiting too long for a man to look at her exactly like that.

Two heartbeats—wild and wicked—and he was kissing her. An instant, drenching wetness had her jamming her thighs together—an instinctive reaction.

"Don't close me out," against her mouth.

"You don't understand, I'm so wet, so…wet."

"Oh God," he groaned. "God, *God*!" And he kissed

her again, so savagely she had to grab onto his T-shirt to stay upright. "Come," he said, and took her hand to pull her inside.

Whizzing, stumbling, world-tilting moment. And then she was inside, her back against the door, being kissed once more, his hands cradling her face, then moving to her shoulders—dislodging the strap of her evening purse so that it clattered to the floor—and then down her body.

"Open your legs," he said, dragging her dress up with one hand and unzipping his jeans with the other.

"Okay, but hurry, hurry," she said.

He shoved his jeans roughly down. "Okay, hard and fast, no foreplay this first time. Just say yes, say yes. Or…or say no but say it now. Say it in five, four, three, two—"

"Yes," she cried. "Yes, yes!"

"Fuck."

And bang! He was all the way inside her. He stopped then and she could feel him throbbing as he kept himself rigid. "You okay?" he asked.

"Yes," she gasped. "Yes, I want this, so do it, *do* it."

He pulled out of her, paused for a split second, as though he'd stop himself, but then his hips flexed and he was inside her again. Out, then in. Out, in. Another stop, a garbled cry.

Oh God, he couldn't stop. She'd die if he stopped. "What?" she asked.

"Esto no me puede estar pasando de nuevo," he said, panting through the words. "No, no, no."

She wanted to ask *what?* What couldn't be happening to him again? But he kissed her, kept kissing her, over and over, licking into her, lashing at her, deep, drugging tongue kisses, so she couldn't speak, could barely think. There seemed to be an almighty battle going on inside him, a drawn-tight tension in his rigid body that suggested he was caught between two hells—no heaven in sight. It made her want to hold him closer, to tell him he could have whatever he wanted, that she'd give in to him, give him everything, she would, she *would* if he'd just tell her what he needed. But in the end the only word she could find to fit between the breaks in his endless kisses was "Please." Both surrender and entreaty, as she surged against him.

"Don't ask, you never have to ask," he said, and grabbed her hips to move them against him. "Take anything you want, show me how you want me to be."

As her hips took over the rhythm, he brought his hands up to cup her face again as he kissed her even more deeply. It was as though he were claiming property he'd once lost—and yet whatever he was finding in her wasn't what he remembered. He wanted more. And so did she, she realized. Even though this *was* more.

"Go harder, harder," she said. "It's driving me mad to want you like this."

"I *want* you mad," he breathed back at her. "I want you crazy for me. I want you hungry and straining and sweating and mine, mine, mine, mine, *mine*, even though I know you're *not* mine. Damn you to hell, Veronica."

"I *am* in hell. You put me there, you know you did, and I hate you for it," she said, the words coming out like angry sobs. "And I hate you more...for making me want you still."

He gathered her closer than ever, she could feel the tremors running through him—or maybe they were her tremors, but she didn't know at this point where she began and he ended. There was only the two of them, locked together, taking and giving the way he said it would have to be. No mere acceptance here. She'd expected his passion—it had always been a part of him, the heat and physical need. But this was more. Hotter, harder, laced with an almost palpable need for more and more, as though what she gave would *never* be enough. It was like a deep, dark despair—and she felt that despair. Her constant companion. The love and hate entwined, the urge to both soothe and punish, to possess and fling away, to end whatever it was between them and yet need it like air. To be alive again...and know it had to end. God help them both.

She threw herself at him, but still he went for more, grabbing one of her thighs, yanking it up his hip, opening her so he could wedge himself inside her just that little bit farther. She gasped and he sucked it right out of her mouth. "This is what I want." Kiss. Thrust. "Mine. Like this." Kiss, out, kiss, in. "This is *all* I want—it is, it *is*, I'll make it all." Kiss, kiss, kiss, and his mouth slid to her neck. "¡Ay, Dios mío! Too fast."

"Rafael," she said. "Pleeeease, I'm so close. Please hold on."

He shifted her, just a fraction, brought her thigh a little higher.

"Yes," she said, on fire. "Oh yes, yes."

He was gasping, struggling for breath, shuddering, shuddering, shuddering, as he slowed down, holding back for her. "*Verónica, mi amor, dime cuándo.* Say when, tell me when."

One thrust, two, and she felt it. Racing, bursting. "Now!" she screamed. "Now, now."

He cried out and let go, three hard thrusts, and the shock of his sudden explosion as she came with him stole her breath. She slumped against the door, a shaking mess, as he pulled out of her for the last time, as he lowered her thigh from his hip, as he rested his forehead against the door above her head, his body twitching, his breathing erratic.

A moment, two, and then somehow she wasn't slumped against the door anymore but in his arms. "Shh, *mi vida.* Don't, please don't," he said.

She realized that her breaths were heaving like wrenching sobs, even though her eyes were dry; there were no tears, there *could* be none.

And that, she reminded herself, was why she hated him. Because he could make her want to cry for him and yet he'd stolen her ability to do it.

CHAPTER NINE

MI VIDA, HE'D called her. "My life." His fucking *life*.

And it was true.

His life had been shaped by her from the moment he'd first seen her, his heart swelling with a hopeless, helpless longing to give her whatever it was she was looking for, to *be* what she was looking for. He'd wanted her to the point of madness. Wanted her so much he'd almost lost himself for her. So much, he'd have gone straight back to her the day after he'd left her if she'd so much as crooked a finger, because that first night without her was hell.

And even by *not* crooking that finger, she'd continued to shape him. Her first marriage was responsible for turning *Catch, Tag, Release* from the overly sentimental love story it had started out as into an annihilating bestseller—wedding present, courtesy of his scorching jealousy. Her second wedding present was *Liar, Liar*—an ice-cold excoriation of loveless marriages.

And now, with *Stomp*…?

Well, *Stomp* was the jewel in the crown. A vicious

tale about what the churn of old love and new hate could do to a person. A story of obsession and revenge. A story about what she'd done to him. Proof that she was still shaping his life—but also that he intended to finally kill her power over him. And because he wanted an unsubtle symbolism for that killing, he'd written a death for the ironically named heroine, Hope. Ringing the death knell over the hope he'd cherished that he would one day get Veronica back.

Good plan. Except it had taken only one thrust inside her to make him realize he wasn't ready to ring the death knell. And he had no idea what he was going to do about that, other than keep reminding himself this was not a romance they were indulging in. The intention was to overdose on her—the sexual equivalent of smoking a million cigarettes—so he could stop craving her.

She pulled suddenly out of his arms. *"Esto es una locura,"* she said.

"Crazy, yes," he said. He swooped to pick up her purse off the floor—and as what she'd said registered, he straightened slowly. "You speak Spanish now?"

"Words, phrases, that's all," she said.

And then she blushed—which she almost never did—and he felt something unfurl in his chest. She'd learned *Spanish*. For him. Had to be. But why, when she'd never intended to see him again?

He unsnapped her purse, lost in that question, and blinked stupidly at the contents, wondering why he'd opened it. Then he saw the flash of pale pink and remembered. She always carried a silk square; she seemed to think it passed for a handkerchief. He took it out. "Here," he said gruffly, holding it out.

She tugged the skirt of her dress down to cover herself, then whipped the handkerchief from his hand and tore it in two. "I don't need it," she said—and he saw that she was right: there were no tears.

She grabbed her purse from his other hand, stuffed the two halves of silk in it, and threw the purse back onto the floor, as though giving her assertion an exclamation point. "What happens now?" she asked coolly.

Okay, no tears and apparently no explanation for what the non-tears actually *were*. He looked for a clue on her. Found nothing. And then he realized he was *really* finding nothing—no remnant of himself on her. He looked harder, needing a sign, however minor, that what they'd done had had an impact on her aside from the actual orgasm. Infuriating that she could look perfectly restored before the sweat on him was dry, leaving him nothing but the memory of those sobbing breaths and a line of Spanish.

He was going to have to up his game, obviously.

"Now you put your hands on me," he said.

"Where do you want them?"

"Do you really need suggestions?"

"Anywhere I want?"

"Choice is yours."

"Good," she said and raised both hands to cup his face.

His heart lurched in his chest—unfair—and he snapped his head back so that her hands dropped. "Not like that."

"You said anywhere I wanted."

"This is about sex."

"I think about sex when I touch your face."

Oh God, she knew how to get to him! "Think a little lower," he said and one of his hands moved to stroke his cock through his jeans.

Her eyes dropped, exactly as he'd intended. She licked her lips and he thought he might explode at the thought of them wrapped around his cock.

"You zipped yourself up prematurely if that's what you want," she said, reading his mind effortlessly. "So should I unzip you or do you want to do it?"

"You do it."

"All right then—"

"*After* you take off your dress."

Unhesitatingly, she turned her back to him, wordlessly offering him access, no hint of shyness, no uncertainty. Never. He slipped the tiny button at the nape of her neck from its loop then slid her zipper slowly down—but when she started to turn toward him he stopped her and leaned down to kiss the back of her neck, once, twice, thrice. Payback for the way she'd touched his face. But although she drew in a too-careful breath, she didn't flinch—of course she didn't; she'd never flinched, no matter what.

After only the slightest of pauses, she turned, shrugging out of her bodice then pushing the dress down, over her hips, off.

"Wait," he said as she stepped out of it, testing his own restraint.

She was as beautiful to him as she'd always been.

Small and slender. Stylish and classy. Nothing about her screamed, everything whispered—the only color coming from her were her turquoise eyes. Her bra was nude-colored and so were her high heels and her barely-there stockings, which were held up by lace bands at the top of her thighs.

She shifted slightly, and at last he saw evidence that he had indeed been there. Those lace bands of her stockings were stained with his cum.

She saw where his eyes were and moved again, smiling as she opened her legs—evil queen peeping out from behind the princess. Her stockings weren't the only cum-soaked things on her body, the very tops of her inner thighs were gleaming with it. Evidence he'd been there with his cock. That he'd be there again, and again, during the night.

His…*cum*…

He drew in a sharp breath. Okay, they had a problem.

"The pill," he said. "Are you taking it?"

"Yes," she said and then her eyes went wide. "Oh."

"Did your husbands wear condoms?"

"No. But we had blood tests."

"Were they faithful?"

"Yes."

"How can you be sure?"

"Because I know them."

"You know me, too. Know I always was."

"It doesn't matter what you were, only what you are. So this…tonight…what we did…no condom…? It can't happen again like that."

"And if I tell you the only person I've ever had my

naked cock near was you? Because if it will make a difference, let's go find the Bible they always have tucked in a drawer somewhere in these places and I'll swear my Catholic soul away on it."

She looked at him, one heartbeat, two, assessing. Then, "Not on a Bible," she said. "For all I know, you've become an atheist."

"I haven't changed."

She shook her head, laughed. "Swear on your mother's life and I might believe you."

Without hesitation he grabbed her hand, placed it over his heart, laid his palm over it to keep it there, and looked directly into her eyes. "I swear on my mother's life."

"I'd accept that," she said.

"Good."

"I'd accept it *if* you hadn't told me you'd love me forever five minutes before you walked out on me." She pulled her hand free. "So what I require is either an all-clear STD test result or condoms, or you'll be getting hand jobs for the next two weeks and not much else. So see if you can find a condom, and I'll wait for you in the bedroom."

With that, she turned on her high heels and ascended the stairs, regal as an unfucked monarch despite the fact she was practically naked. Even the squeaky fourth step didn't faze her.

Rafael's instant reaction was to stride over there and yank her the hell back down. He even took a hasty step toward her. But then he saw an imperfection that stopped him. A very *minor* imperfection:

a fine ladder down the back of her left stocking, almost imperceptible except as a faint silvery sliver of a line as the light hit it. And even though he hadn't caused it, it suddenly made her more real to him. Less…untouchable. More his.

"Veronica," he called out as she reached the top of the stairs.

She stopped but didn't deign to look back at him.

"I'll find a condom if you keep the stockings on."

He waited as long as his dick would allow—three whole minutes.

She'd left the bedroom door ajar but not open. There was some kind of symbolism in that, but it was as much as he could do to control his body let alone his thought processes, so he wasn't going to try to figure out what it meant.

"Rafael?" she called from inside, letting him know she knew he was there.

He pushed open the door and stepped inside.

She was standing in the middle of the room. She'd taken down her hair and it was gleaming, as beautiful as he remembered. And then he thought it was bizarre, and maybe even a little concerning, that her hair should have been the first thing he wanted to touch, because the *second* thing he noticed was that she'd taken off her bra and was now naked except for those stockings.

Her breasts were small and round and perfect, her nipples the delicate shade of coral pink he'd lodged in his brain like a Pantone chip, jutting out like bullets. His mouth dried. His cock went diamond-hard. He knew he would have *triple*-sheathed himself for her if that's what she demanded.

He ripped off his T-shirt, his hands going to his jeans to start the shedding process as he hurried to the bathroom. Condoms. He knew he had them. He dropped his jeans, kicked them away, fumbled in his shaving kit for a condom, put it on faster than he'd ever done in his life. Grabbing a handful of spares—and he wasn't being ambitious, he was going to use every damn one—he went back into the bedroom.

He thought, belatedly, he should have checked what he looked like in the mirror on the back of the bathroom door, but maybe it was just as well he hadn't—if he looked as wild as he felt, he'd probably have tried to reorder his features into something less threatening and that would have delayed him when he didn't want to be delayed.

It didn't matter, anyway. Whatever he looked like, it didn't seem to worry Veronica, who came striding fearlessly toward him.

"Bed," he said, stopping her with that one word, and she nodded and changed course. Clearly she wasn't going to waste time talking, either.

They reached the bed simultaneously. He used one hand on her hip to keep her where she was as he tossed the condoms in his other hand onto the mattress, and leaned in for a brief, hard kiss. And then he sat on the edge of the bed, both his hands on her hips now.

She prepared to straddle him but he said, "No."

She blinked at him. "No?"

"Not yet," he clarified and pulled her between his thighs. "Put your hands on my shoulders and lift your left foot onto the bed beside me."

She did as he asked, and the smell of sex and vanilla slid into his nostrils and he wanted to lick her, fuck her, suck her, mark her—everything all at once.

"If this is about taking off my stocking, just tear it off, I don't care about it," she said urgently, dragging him out of the black hole of desire he was swirling in.

Tear it off—yes!

He toyed with the idea of doing that then flipping her onto her back on the bed and sinking his cock straight into her. But if he did that he'd be the animal and she'd still be the princess. And it was her turn to be desperate.

His slid his hand down her hip to the top of her stocking, fingers sliding beneath the band on the outside of her thigh. Next, his other hand...to her moist inner thigh. Slowly he eased the stocking down, down, down. He reached her foot, worked the stocking over it and off, then gripped her toes, circling each one between finger and thumb before stroking his hand back up her leg, enjoying the goose bumps prickling her skin in his fingers' wake. He squeezed her thigh—a signal to her to change legs—and as she did so, she leaned toward him.

He breathed in as the scent of her intensified for that moment, and before he knew what he was doing, he'd hooked a finger in the nylon of her other stocking and was tearing it all the way down and off her as he took the tip of her breast into his mouth and sucked.

She whimpered and he moved his mouth from her nipple. "Too hard?"

"No. Perfect."

"Tell me what you want," he said and then he licked her nipple, kissed it, licked again, sucked more gently now.

"I want you to keep doing that. Sucking my nipple until it hurts. And then I want your cock inside me."

"Good answer," he said against her tight nipple as he grabbed her hips to pull her down as he thrust up just far enough to sink his cock halfway into her, giving her nipple a long, hard suck.

"Oh my God," she panted, and then she let out a long, low groan as he caught her thigh to stop her moving off him and sucked her nipple again.

She mewled something indecipherable in the back of her throat, and then, more clearly, through a series of gasps, "Please...let's just do it...now, now, now... *God*, Rafael!"

He pulled out and then thrust into her again, to the hilt this time. Stop.

She cried out and he jackknifed as the fuck of what he was doing, the unadulterated *fuck* of it—lust and punishment—had him so breathless he had to release her nipple from his mouth to take in air.

He gasped against her breast, fighting for control as she did her best to move on him. "No," he said.

"Yes," she pleaded.

"I said no!"

It took superhuman willpower to lift her off his dick, and although he did it, he couldn't quash an ago-

nized groan at the separation. Half crippled, he got off
the bed and grabbed the stocking he'd removed from
her. Before he could think twice, he looped it around
her wrists, tying them together, and then turned her
toward the bed and knotted the stocking around one
of the end posts.

Leaving her there, he strode to the bathroom.

Veronica's heart was pounding, her nerves thrum-
ming—lust and excitement.

This was new territory, to be helpless, to wonder
what he had planned.

He could only have been gone for a few seconds,
but every one of them was a torture of anticipation, so
that when he returned carrying the giant jar of vanilla
oil she took wherever she went, she actually twitched.

"What are you going to do?" she asked—and she
could hear both excitement and a tiny thrill of something that wasn't quite fear in her voice.

"I'm going to work as much of my cum out of you
as I can, and then I'm going to suck your pussy," he
said, grabbing her other discarded stocking and soaking it with the oil. "I seem to be saying this a lot tonight, but open your legs."

She shivered deliciously as she obeyed him and,
as he dabbed the scrunched-up stocking between her
thighs, her hips flexed, relaxed, flexed, in a wordless
fuck-me routine that she *could not* control.

He edged up close behind her. "Every time you
wear stockings for some other man, I want you to
remember that I had you like this, tied up for me

and hot as hell." He licked her neck as he kept up the pressure between her legs, dabbing at her opening, then stroking the length of her, then circling her clit.

The slight crunch of nylon again her intimate flesh had her gritting her teeth against a wanton moan. She was so close to ordering him to drop to his knees and lick into her right that second. She felt him push inside her, using a section of her nylon stocking. He kept it there, fingers twisting against that heavenly spot that always brought her climax on fast, while the fingers of his other hand returned to her clit and circled there. He kept at it, until she could barely tell the touches apart—the stocking, his slippery fingers, inside, outside, everywhere, working her fast then slow then fast, relentless. She could feel the orgasm coming, desperately tried to slow it so she could have more, but it hit her hard and sent her rigid. Rigid... then limp, sagging against the laddered stocking that tethered her to the bed as she tried to catch her breath.

"I'm going to make you come again," he said against her ear in a voice that seemed to answer the throb in her. Then he shocked her by shifting the vanilla-saturated stocking so it was against her asshole. And then, hoarsely, "Say if you don't want this."

"I do want it," she said, because *oh God*, did she want it! She wanted everything he'd done to her before this night and everything he hadn't dared. She wanted him to take her as high and wild as she could go, obliterating everything except what he was doing to her body.

He moved, his fingers in the mess of drenched

nylon, pressing against her, probing gently but firmly, entering her with no more than a sheathed fingertip, waiting as her body adjusted to the intrusion. "I'm going to lick you here, Veronica. Give me permission."

"Yes, yes, please. I want you to lick me."

With a groan he dropped to his knees behind her. "Open for me," he commanded, and she shifted her legs further apart. He spread her cheeks and she bowed her head against the wood in supplication. She was past wanting this—she *needed* it.

He dropped the stocking, went in with his tongue, rimming her. She jerked with each lick of his tongue, frantic for more, and he gave it to her, one finger sliding into her. Tight. So tight she squirmed.

"Veronica," he said—and she heard the craving in his voice.

"I'm okay, okay, don't stop," she urged, and forced herself to relax despite the desire coiling in her like an ever-tightening spring.

He drew his finger out. She protested but, "Shh," he said, and moved in to lick her once more.

She moaned out a long "Ooooh," relaxing her muscles. His finger—no, two fingers—slid into her again.

"Me vuelves loco," he groaned, his left hand snaking around her to come at her from the front, and she could only agree because he was driving *her* crazy. Fingers of his left hand flying over her clit, fingers of his right hand slowly stretching her asshole. *"Te poseeré, te poseeré."* And she thought in that moment he did. He *did* own her.

"Rafael," she cried.

"Let go, relax, let me have this," he urged.

Easing in, out, in, until she screamed her frustration.

And he was up, on his feet, yanking at her legs, sliding inside her pussy now. Another time, she thought. Two weeks—surely now they'd started they would finish it.

And then his words, in her ear, wrapped around his panting breaths. "I will take you every way I know how…before I'm done with you… I will fuck you until you can barely walk… I will replace every old memory you have of me…with new memories…and for every man who comes after me…you'll think of me…"

A vow—as though he were saying it to himself—but she made the same vow in her heart, to replace every memory he had of her with a new one, so that he would never stop thinking of her.

His left hand came around in front of her, his fingers circling her clit, rubbing, pinching.

"Come," he ordered.

But now she wanted to see his face, to see what she'd done to him. So, "No!" she said, "not until you untie me."

"Come, damn you."

"No!"

And with a curse, he was untying her wrists, turning her, yanking her against his chest and kissing her as he slid his cock into her again. Once, twice, thrice. Again, again, so hard she landed on her back on the bed, him on top of her. Moments only, until she felt herself convulse once more, squeezing around his cock, and a split second later, he shouted her name as he came.

* * *

Breaths. Hearts beating hard. Another thrust even though he was spent, because it made it somehow… more. Made it real, to feel her against him in the aftermath.

Then silence. Shocked and heavy.

And somehow…desolate, though he didn't understand it.

Or maybe it was that he didn't want to.

"I didn't hurt you?" he asked, too tentative.

Her answer was to reach her arms around him, kiss him deeply. And then, "No," she said, as though knowing he needed to hear the word.

He gave in to the weakness of being held by her for too long a moment, and then eased himself off her. "I'm going to get rid of this condom, then get clean for you," he said. "Get into bed. I'll want you again in a few minutes."

And maybe, he thought, when he was clean and she was his again, he'd understand why what they'd just done still wasn't enough.

CHAPTER TEN

FIVE O'CLOCK.

Veronica had lapsed into her usual sleep-coma two hours ago, at which point Rafael had gotten out of bed, prowled restlessly around the cottage, collected her dress and purse and brought them upstairs, and noted she hadn't moved so much as a muscle while he'd been gone.

That was normal: she'd always slept like she was in a coma. In their first month together he'd held a mirror to her mouth no less than four times to check she was still breathing. A wave of nostalgia swept through him, making him almost smile as he slipped back into bed beside her. He wished she'd roll into him and wake herself up—then maybe he could stop thinking and just…

Just what?

Just talk to her? About what? Hadn't they said everything they needed to say to get them through to the end? And if he had nothing new to talk to her about, what was the point in her being awake? To fuck her again, obviously. As long as she wasn't too tired. Or too sore. If she was either of those things he could just kiss her and tell her to go back to sleep.

At that point in his musings, it became obvious to him that being close to her without having an actual body part inserted in her somewhere was dangerous. *I want to fuck you*—that's what he'd said to her at that mausoleum, what had kick-started the whole damn thing. Not, *I want to kiss you and tuck you up and hover over you like a nursemaid making sure I wasn't too rough last night.*

I want to fuck *you.*

Was it still considered "fucking" when your chest ached with melancholy the morning after because whatever you'd gotten from a woman, it wasn't enough, and you knew it even if you didn't want to acknowledge it?

Was it really considered "fucking" when dread was creeping through your veins because you knew that even if something changed in the next two weeks and you both decided that not only was the sex just as good as it had always been but you wanted to keep going, and going, and going, that the most you could ever hope for was one more week? Because that was when she'd get your book, and when she read your book she'd give up sticking pins in the voodoo doll she'd made of you and stick them right into your actual balls?

He should never have bargained for the two weeks—he should have stuck with just one night. He'd be putting his suitcases into his car right about now if he'd done that, and heading for the airport, and he'd be no worse off than he'd been yesterday.

Except that he *would* be worse off. Because he would have had last night—one more night—to grieve over the loss of her.

What a mess.

He wished he could go back in time and *not* leave her in that what-the-fuck-am-I-doing moment. And yet he knew it was only by leaving that he'd made himself good enough, successful enough, to have her—and, Jesus, wasn't *that* a twist and a half of craziness!

What he really wanted was…the impossible. To merge two time periods and cut out the in-between. To have been the man he was now back when he'd had a chance of keeping her.

Fuuuuuck. Two weeks of such mental gymnastics and he'd be in a straitjacket.

She stirred, and he looked at her face, expecting her to wake. But all she did was murmur his name in her sleep. "Rafa…"

Rafa, not Rafael. Such a small thing to move him so terribly. She wasn't the only one to call him that and yet when she did, she was the only one in the world.

He knew what was coming when she said that in her sleep, and braced for it. But even expecting it, even preparing himself for it, a lump still formed in his throat when she reached out a hand and patted his chest, as though making sure he was there, then left her hand resting over his heart. He'd missed it so much, and *resented* missing it, and wondered—of course he'd wondered—if she was doing exactly that when she was asleep in bed with first Piers then Simeon. Feeling blindly for them, reassuring herself she wasn't alone, that they were beside her, keeping her hand over their hearts as though the beat of them was a talisman to keep her safe. And the weird thing was that he'd wanted her to have the comfort of it, but hated the thought of her sharing her one, her only, her *secret* vulnerability with anyone but him.

So *of course* he'd had to go and give that quirk to Hope in *Stomp*. Except he'd turned it into a pretense—a *manufactured* vulnerability, a siren's trick. Hope wasn't really asleep when she used it on Alejandro (Alejo, she called him)—just pretending to be, because she knew Alejandro, with his towering need for her to belong to him, would trust her gestures more if they were coming from her subconscious.

How could he lie beside her with her hand on his chest knowing he'd used this private moment in his scathing book? And he hadn't just used it, either. He'd stripped it of its authenticity, adulterated it, turned it into a manipulation. That Veronica didn't know she did it and therefore wouldn't recognize it when she read it somehow made it worse—like he was telling the world her most personal secret. *His* secret, too. And he couldn't shake the feeling that once the book was published, he'd ruin his own memory of it and never forgive himself for doing so.

A sense of urgency, a need to rip it out of the book, gripped him.

In fact he needed to reread the whole book with fresh eyes and see what he'd done to her, ask himself if she *deserved* what he'd done to her, while there was still time to change it.

He took her hand, desperate now that she *not* wake up, tucked it carefully beside her and got quietly out of bed. He grabbed his washbag from the bathroom, picked up his suitcase and his briefcase, and made his way into the second bedroom to shower and dress before settling himself into the armchair with his manuscript and starting to read.

One chapter in, he knew he was going to need whiskey—maybe drunk straight from the bottle—and he headed down to the kitchen.

Veronica opened her eyes slowly, not trusting the feeling that she was exactly where she was supposed to be, even though she was more than three thousand miles from home.

She eased cautiously up onto her elbows to look around, but she already knew Rafael wasn't in the room. If he were, she'd either hear him in the bathroom or he'd be wrapped around her in bed.

Which meant she could safely indulge herself by grabbing his pillow, snuggling her face into it and breathing him in. She could pretend they were back in their DC town house, on a typical Sunday, and he was out for his usual morning ten-mile run. She'd be "sleeping" when he got back—an excuse to be waiting for him in bed. He'd know she was faking it but he'd leave her alone and go shower off—always so

fastidious about being clean before he touched her—
and then get back into bed with her. A tug to bring her
against his chest, a kiss below her ear, a murmur in
Spanish—*Te amo*. I love you—before making slow,
gentle, welcome-to-the-day love to her.

It was a lovely memory, but at the moment she
was more interested in the reality of now—which
was not so much slow and gentle as wild and tough.
He'd gone for her last night as though it were his last
day on earth and he needed everything, all of her,
urgently, frenziedly, before the chance was lost. Just
thinking about it made her breathless.

Breathless…and something else. Something per-
ilously close to happy.

Well, damn, she deserved to be happy, didn't
she? So she'd *be* happy. Even if it was to be only
two weeks—well, thirteen days now. She'd make it
enough. Take him a million times, gorge herself on
him the way she'd gorged herself by eating twenty-
three cupcakes at Phyllida Graeme's eleventh birthday party—she'd thrown up all night, and she'd never
eaten a cupcake again!

She gave Rafael's pillow one last, long sniff—de-
li-*cious*, he really, truly was!—then tossed it back
onto his side of the bed, stretched her arms out and
up, and leaped out of bed with a laugh that quickly
turned into a groan as her legs almost collapsed
under her.

"Whoa!" she said and grabbed for one of the four
bedposts to steady herself. Rafael hadn't been kidding
when he'd said he was going to fuck her until she could

barely walk! Every muscle in her body was aching—muscles she didn't know she *had* were aching!

Glorious.

She leaned into the bedpost, rubbed her cheek against the wood. This was the post he'd tied her to. He'd probably thought she'd protest that treatment, but she'd loved every single thing he'd done to her—so much so, the remembrance sent a tingling throb all the way through her until it arrived with a zap between her thighs before spreading backward and zapping her where he'd licked her so thoroughly.

Was it right to feel so powerful when you were tied up?

Maybe that was something she should discuss with Scarlett.

Hmm. Or maybe not. Scarlett had been so suspicious when Veronica had called her to relay that the catastrophe scale had worked, that she hadn't killed anyone, that she'd had a civil conversation with Rafael (because, hey, it had to be classified as civil when she hadn't killed him, didn't it?) and that everything was under control. She wasn't sure a segue from "civil conversation" to being tied to a bedpost with her own stocking wouldn't have Scarlett planning an intervention and catching the next flight out of New York. And since she was a full thirteen days away from needing an intervention, she'd rain-check the call to Scarlett until she was back home.

And anyway, it *was* under control. Even when she'd been tied to that bedpost, and she'd known he was intent on…on *conquering* her somehow, he'd let her be in control, and she'd swear he hadn't even realized he was doing that. She'd wanted to be untied—he had therefore untied her. Simple.

Was she crazy to have let him tie her up in the first place? Was she crazy to believe she could control what happened to her *despite* being tied up? He was altogether harder, tougher, stronger, more demanding than her Rafael—and yet her Rafael was in there, too. He had to be, or she couldn't have trusted him.

Would he trust her to tie *him* up?

Now *that* was an interesting question.

She decided she liked these control games. She wanted to push it, push him, and be pushed herself. She liked the combination of danger and trust. Liked the feeling that she was off the leash, alone with him, with nobody to get in the way of their sexual odyssey. It was like a…a *honeymoon*, almost.

Okay, honeymoon was a step too far.

She let go of the bedpost and made her way gingerly into the bathroom, compiling a list of ablutions to make herself ready for seduction.

Brush teeth
Shower
Wash & blow-dry hair
Apply makeup—lipstick not required
Dress sexy

Halfway through step one she realized she couldn't see Rafael's washbag, so she turned to see where he'd put it only to be distracted by the sight of herself in the full-length mirror on the back of the door.

Her vigorous tooth-brushing slowed. Slowed. Stopped.

"Wow!" she said.

She looked like she'd been manhandled. Mauled, even.

There was a sizable love bite on her neck, the sight of which made her feel weird—but weird in a good way, a *sexy* way. She'd always thought a hickey was a thing you got in high school from an overenthusiastic boyfriend. But she didn't feel like a schoolgirl when she saw that circle on her neck—she felt like tasty vampire bait. He'd bitten and sucked her all over, but this was proof that Rafael had lost control for once in his life because he'd never marked her before.

And it wasn't the *only* proof, either, because her nipples were erect and they had been all night, because he'd sucked them on and off from the time he'd joined her in bed until the time she'd fallen into a sex-drenched oblivion. So relentlessly had he gone for them, she suspected they'd be sticking out for the rest of her damn life! *And* she had beard rash. Not only on her breasts but also on her mons—one of the joys of waxing everything off was that she could see the abrasions—and that did something weird to her, too. Weird and fantastic. She felt like the most desirable woman on the planet, remembering how many times he'd burrowed his face down there, how he'd slid lower, deeper, sucking, licking, kissing.

Ooooh God, she was freshly wet now, needy as

hell, wanting him to come into the bathroom, bend her forward and lick her some more.

She was shaking as she returned to the sink to rinse out her mouth and then, as though spellbound, she returned to the mirror because she needed convincing that it was really her she was seeing. She leaned in close, focusing on her face. Her mouth was swollen and it was a darker pink than normal. Her eyes looked positively sultry, her eyelids heavy and slumberous. More beard rash—her cheeks scraped to blush-color from his regrowth. Her hair was a tousled mess of silvery gold.

"Wow," she said again—not caring that her vocabulary wasn't as expansive as usual this morning.

She looked sooooo sexy. A snowdrop that had been turned into a wild orchid. And she smelled just as exotic. Vanilla, salt, sweat, the musk of arousal. And Rafael's cum, because that last time he'd been caught off guard, ejaculating on the lower part of her back before he could get the condom on. And even that little mishap was thrilling, now that she thought of it.

Okay. *Okaaay.* When he'd said he wanted to fuck her, she'd known he was going to fuck her *good* and she'd wanted that. But it seemed now his intention had been to fuck her *bad,* and if this was what being fucked bad looked like, felt like, smelled like—like you'd been savaged, half devoured—then she'd take it, by God.

In fact she'd not only take it, she'd *give* it—lob whatever he gave her right back at him twice as hard.

She'd fuck him not only off his damn feet but into *orbit*! She'd bring him to his knees and make him beg, just like he'd dared her to do.

Revenge—served *sizzling* hot. And she would count her path to success in the mirror image of her body every morning when she woke up tenderized and love-bitten.

So for now, she wouldn't wash the smell of him off her. She'd leave everything on her for him to see when he returned from his run, and let things unfold from there.

She went digging around in her suitcase for a come-fuck-me-immediately outfit, but had to admit a swift defeat: there was nothing in there that would incite anything but fashion admiration. How could it be that she had only one immodest item? And she hadn't even packed it—it was an old, pale blue T-shirt of Piers's that he'd refused to throw out even though it was threadbare, a leftover from one of their weekends away.

She slipped it over her head and returned to the bathroom mirror. After a gazillion turns in the washing machine, it was thin enough to be almost transparent, so that not only was the jut of her nipples against the cotton obvious but the color of them was vaguely visible, too. The hem hit above mid-thigh and the neck was so wide it slid completely off one shoulder. It gave the illusion of being both there and not being there. And she figured all she had to do was leave off her bra and panties and Rafael would be on her in a split second.

"Okay," she breathed out as she left the bathroom—and that's when she noticed the hot-pink flash of her evening purse. She distinctly recalled dropping it on the floor downstairs but now it was placed neatly on top of a perfectly folded gray T-shirt on the armchair—Rafael's T-shirt, the color he always wore under his dress shirts. The sight of the two items sitting so innocently together made butterflies erupt in her tummy, ruining her femme-fatale buzz. She told herself it was no big deal that her purse was on top of his T-shirt. But it felt...wrong. Because it felt...right.

She looked around the room, looking for other evidence of domesticity, but there was nothing. Unless he'd brought her dress up, too...? If he had, he would have hung it neatly in the wardrobe. So...

She approached the wardrobe the way someone would look for a concealed serial killer, which she knew was ridiculous, but she couldn't seem to help it. She paused with her fingers on the door handle, telling herself it didn't matter if her dress was in there. Then she opened the wardrobe—and decided it mattered all right, because it was hanging next to Rafael's shirt.

Her hand came up to rub over her heart. It was somehow more shocking to be confronted by the non-sexual intimacy of their clothes hanging together in a wardrobe than it had been to be tied to the bed. It hurt her to see it. Made her...homesick. And there was *no point* in missing what they'd once had because that had been a TV sitcom fantasy. Her dreams of riding off into the sunset with him on that motorcycle had been so…so *stupid*! As if it would ever have lasted! It couldn't have lasted. It couldn't. It *couldn't*! She truly believed that, she *had* to believe that, because otherwise… Ooooh God, otherwise, she'd made a terrible mistake.

It hit her, quite suddenly, that *that* was the real reason she was here in this cottage with Rafael. Revenge—yes. To take a walk on the wild side once more—sure. To feel alive, to…to have him again—of course. Closure—absolutely. But more than anything, she needed affirmation. She wanted *not* to have made a mistake in letting him go.

Her legs were giving out once more, sending her staggering over to grab that bedpost again. But her eyes were drawn inexorably back to the open wardrobe. One shirt, one dress, two lives.

Te amaré por siempre, Verónica.

I will love you forever.

She could still see his stricken face as he'd said it.

She remembered that first phone call he'd made the next day. How every drop of blood in her had coalesced in her heart, swelling it until it almost burst as she'd let the call go to voice mail before deleting the message unheard.

She remembered burning his letter, blocking his emails. She remembered that fledgling seed of hope, germinating in her dying soul, after her first divorce, wondering what she'd say if Rafael tried again to contact her. The long, deafening, agonizing silence that eventually convinced her she'd lost him forever.

Scarlett's painful sympathy. The rush into a second marriage while she was still mourning…

No!

She pushed away from the bedpost, went over to the wardrobe and closed it. She'd make sure Rafael knew she didn't need him to pick up after her the way he once had. She didn't need to…to *mingle* with him. She just needed him to fuck her—and not good but *bad*.

To which end—where was he? They had thirteen days and she was going to use them, goddamn it—starting now!

She hurried from the room, down the stairs…and pulled up short as a series of low curses in Spanish floated out from the kitchen.

She visualized the room, which was separated into two distinct areas by a granite-topped island bench: a small cooking space and a larger dining area dominated by an old scarred table with four chairs. Where would Rafael be? In the kitchen making the strong coffee she could smell, or at the dining table drinking it? Not that it was important, except insofar as she wanted to position herself for maximum power over the moment.

More Spanish—most of it indecipherably fast—but three phrases she could translate. *Ella es patética*—she is pathetic—*Esto es una mierda*—this is bullshit—and then *Ella me va a matar*—she's going to kill me.

Which sounded like a perfect line upon which to enter.

Up went her eyebrows. On went her smile. She took a deep breath, inhaling fumes from her body that were probably akin to the stench of an eighteenth-century whorehouse, and in she went.

"Morning," she said as though she'd spent every night since he'd left her in a sexual foment and it was therefore no big deal to see a hot guy in the kitchen in the morning.

Rafael, who'd obviously been intent on rising from his chair at the dining table, jerked as though he'd been Tasered and promptly collapsed back into it—score one for Piers's T-shirt, and two for her nipples, which snagged his immediate attention and held on fast. Excellent!

"Holy fu—sh—he—" he said as she reached the table. But instead of finishing that thought with the "fuck," "shit" or "hell" he was obviously trying to choose between, he swallowed hard, gave his head a small shake and dropped his eyes to the two piles of paper in front of him.

The pile on his left had the type faceup, the one on his right had the type facedown—so he was reading what had to be his manuscript left to right. Brilliant deduction, Dr. Watson.

"*Stomp*?" she asked, and came forward to take a seat opposite him.

He jumped in his seat. His eyes came up as far as her chest then dropped again. He started shuffling the pages together. "Yeah but… I'm not…sure I'm happy with it."

"I can read it today if you like."

Up came his eyes again—all the way to her face. "What?"

"Um, I can read it?" she said. "As in it's my *job*? You know, as your editor? I can give you an opinion, make some suggestions, write you some notes…?" She stopped there because he'd moved past startled and on to appalled. Regroup. "I *am* going to be editing the book in three weeks. You *will* get revisions. Unless it's the Mona Lisa of manuscripts—an untouchable masterpiece. Don't tell me you've never had revisions before!"

"No—yes."

"Con-fu-sing."

"I mean *yes*, you're going to be editing it and *yes*, I'm expecting revisions. But Bryan's reading it and so I'd rather… I'd rather wait for his feedback and then if I have to make changes…" He trailed off, cleared his throat. "What I'm saying is I'd rather give you the *next* draft."

She watched him for a minute as he kept shuffling the pages. What he said made perfect sense…and yet it didn't. She was here and he was here and the book was here, and she'd read his stuff all through college—so what was the real problem? "You used to let me read your early drafts," she said.

He stopped shuffling but this time didn't raise his eyes. "That was in college. College…was a long time ago."

"Seven years, two months, three weeks and six days, to be precise," she said dryly. "But I can still recall you and I having an animated discussion about

Catch & Keep, which I'm *guessing* became *Catch, Tag, Release*. That was two days before graduation. And you were stuck at chapter fifteen with a case of writer's block."

"I'm not…stuck."

"I thought you said you weren't sure how the epilogue was going to come together."

"It's more a choice of…alternatives."

"Maybe I can help you choose."

No response, except for him putting the manuscript pages, all in one pile, facedown on the table.

Oh for fuck's sake! "Okay, the offer's there," she said, giving up. "If Bryan finishes early and you change your mind, let me know."

"He won't finish early. He…he's going to talk to me when he's here for the Harrogate Crime Writing Festival next week—the twenty-fourth."

"Fantastic. I'll come along. I don't know why I didn't think of going myself."

He shifted in his chair. "I thought you wanted to keep things between us confidential."

"Yes, but all Bryan needs to know is that I'm editing your book—he doesn't need to know what else we're doing. We could be just…well…old college friends, both in the business, both here post-wedding, who decided to go to the festival together."

"He'll know," he said.

"Not if we don't tell him."

"Don't be so fucking naive, Veronica."

"Huh?"

"I'm looking at you sitting there, and you know what I'm thinking?"

"No," she said, but that throb between her thighs was calling her a liar.

"I'm thinking I should be writing erotica, because I can see myself dragging you over here and unzipping my jeans and impaling you on my cock. I'm thinking of the sex scene I just read in *Stomp*—the hero, Alejandro, bending Hope, the heroine, over the couch and taking her from behind—and wondering if perhaps I should try it with you just to refresh my memory of what it was like when I did that to you that night in DC when we had the place to ourselves.

"I'm thinking of taking you out into the moors and laying you down on the heather and putting my head between your legs and licking you until you come. I'm thinking about you in the shower with me, sucking my cock, and watching you swallow my cum. I'm looking at that love bite I left on your neck and I'm thinking I'd like to rip that T-shirt off you and suck your nipples even harder than I did last night and mark you there, as well. I'm thinking about taking you every damn way you could possibly imagine, and if you think anyone who knows me is going to see me with you and not realize that…?" He laughed. "Well, let's just say Bryan isn't an idiot."

He stopped there—and it was just as well because they were both breathing hard and she dared not move or she really might have crawled across the table to get to him.

She cleared her throat. "I still don't see why that would be a problem if we—"

"He knows your father, Veronica. What will you do if he drops a hint there?"

She held her breath. Would she care? No. Would her father care? Hmm. Yes, actually, because he'd wanted to beat Rafael to a pulp for hurting her in the first place. "You win," she said on that blown-out breath. "I won't come. Happy?"

"Ecstatic!" he said and got abruptly to his feet. "I'll make your coffee—there's one of those fancy pod machines."

As he strode into the kitchen, she had to admit he had a point about people being able to tell what was going on, because if anyone saw her watching his ass in those pale blue denim jeans that fitted him like a second skin, with two fingers over her mouth to stop her tongue from rolling right out of it? Well, she figured they'd know all right.

A minute and a half later he slid a cup across the table to her and then lingered on his side of the table as though undecided whether to sit.

She took a tiny sip, discerned it was her usual double espresso with the tiniest drop of milk and precisely half a teaspoonful of sugar. The simple fact of his remembering how she took her coffee had her closing her eyes, remembering other times when they'd sat drinking coffee and talking about books—and more specifically *Catch & Keep*. Going through it chapter by chapter, her giving him suggestions, all of which he'd consider, some of which he'd push back against, some he'd incorporate, some he'd ignore. How could he remember how she took her coffee yet forget the ease with which they'd worked together on that story?

She could only have closed her eyes for a brief moment, but when she opened them, he was back in the kitchen. She looked to where *Stomp* had been sitting on the table and saw it was gone. Hidden away.

He returned to the table and put a plate heaped with toast slathered in peanut butter down in front of her. Another memory—this was the usual Sunday breakfast he used to prepare for her. Energy food, he'd say, because he'd always want to go back to bed afterward.

She looked at it and found she didn't want to eat it. "If you'd woken me when you came back from your run," she said, "I'd have made bacon and eggs while you were in the shower."

"A few problems with that. No run. I showered at five o'clock. The destruction of the planet wouldn't have woken you. And you can't cook."

"Like you said, college was a long time ago."

"What does that mean?"

"It means when you set up house with someone, you learn to cook."

"You set up house with me and you didn't cook."

"I set up house with you but also Matt and Romy when we were *students*. And with Romy there... Well, you know what she was like. The kitchen was her domain."

He looked toward the window then back at her.

"You're saying you learned to cook for your husbands."

"For *myself*," she corrected. "And, to be honest, I'm not great at it, but the basics I can manage. I can certainly make bacon and eggs—*scrambled* eggs, anyway. When I fry them I always break the yolks. I can make pancakes, too. Although Simeon says—"

"I assumed you'd have a home chef," he said, cutting her off.

"Really?" she said, bristling. "Well, it wouldn't be the first time you made a wrong assumption."

"Your parents have a chef."

"That's their choice and mine is not to. But if it's important to you that the woman you're having a *two-week fling* with—the woman who's sitting across from you all but flashing a Let's Fuck sign at you— knows how to cook and therefore doesn't need a chef, I'll prove it to you. I'll cook for you every night we're here. How's that?" She threw up her hands. "So come on, place your order. Don't ask for beef Wellington or coq au vin or osso buco Milanese. But good old American meatloaf, grilled steaks, spaghetti Bolognese I can manage. Or maybe you'd like—"

"What did *they* like?"

"Who?"

"Piers. Simeon."

"Piers likes chili. Simeon is more into—"

"Chili's fine. Chili is just. Fucking. Fine."

Pause. She saw that his hands had clenched into fists on the table, and those fists were practically pulsing— clench, relax, clench, relax.

"What's wrong, Rafael?" she asked.

"Nothing," he said, and shoved himself away from the table. "Every fucking thing is just fucking fine."

He got to his feet and stalked into the kitchen, where he stood rigid with his back to her.

Veronica's first impulse was to go to him, to put her arms around him from behind and just hold on. But she battled the urge back because that's exactly what she would have done back when she'd loved him. And she didn't love him now. She *didn't*. She *wouldn't*. She hadn't spent the past seven years, two months, three weeks and six days kissing that voodoo doll on the mouth and saying *There, there, I won't hurt you.* She'd stuck pins in it, wanting to inflict the pain, to pass her pain *on* to him, because it was his fault she was in agony!

So she stayed where she was and the moment stretched while she tried to find a response. And when he sighed and turned toward her looking *so* tired, she felt her resolve waver and knew she had to attack or she'd lose this battle.

"Well, it's a good thing nothing's wrong, Rafael, because I'm calling my boss tomorrow and after that, this deal of ours will be set in stone from my perspective.

"So let me say this—if you have an issue—any issue at all—with me working on your book—and I've got to say that's the impression you're giving me this morning—now's the time to tell me. If working with me is the problem, I'll get another editor assigned to you. But if it's the Johnson half of the

Johnson/Charles connection that's worrying you, and God knows you never gave my father the time of day, so I'm guessing that's a hot contender here…" She shrugged—shoulders and hands. "Then we have some serious renegotiating to do.

"Because the way I see it, we're one night in and I've already started fulfilling my side of the bargain. I said no to nothing last night, not one thing. Now don't get me wrong, a book's forever whereas what we've got happening is short-term, and I'll understand if you've changed your mind and want to take your book elsewhere, go to auction with it, whatever." She leaned across the table. "But if you *have* changed your mind, I'm going to want to know how you propose to pay me back for last night. Because—sorry to labor the point—college, long time ago. At *college*, I was with you out of love. Last night, I didn't do what I did for love, I did it for *Stomp*."

"Oh I know that. Believe me I know that very well," he said, stalking back to the table and looming at her across it. "You must want my book *bad* to fuck a guy you hate as enthusiastically as you did last night."

"Just doing as asked. Not mere acquiescing, right? Going hard? Exorcisms Anonymous? And you see, I've learned to compartmentalize, Rafael. Sex and love—they're different things. These days I *can* do sex without love."

"Fair enough," he said, and sat, all hard-edged business. "So why don't we *do* some compartmentalizing? Set some boundaries? A schedule maybe?"

"You mean like divide the day into work and sex?"

"Why not?"

"Why not *indeed*! How *perfect*. How do you want to structure it? Work all day, fuck all night?"

"Sure," he said. "A lovely home-cooked meal together at seven each evening, then I get use of your body from eight until…say…four o'clock in the morning? How does that sound?"

"Depends what happens at four."

"Gotta get some sleep, right? That gives you sixteen hours' recovery time. Is that enough?"

"Recovery time? What makes you think I need recovery time?"

"The fact that you fell asleep at three—an hour before I was ready to stop."

"Maybe that was boredom," she said. Madness, but what the hell?

He raked her with his eyes—from the top of her messy head to chest, where his gaze stuck. A tic jumped to life in his cheek and she found herself breathing in time with it. Endless moment. The air was thick with anger, but it was also ripe with the scent of sex. On her, she knew, but it was more than that. Every molecule in the room seemed to be pulsating with lust.

"Are you saying I left you unsatisfied?" he asked low and silky.

"And if I am?"

"If you're horny, all you need to do is beg me, and I'll see what I can do."

"I thought you were the one who was supposed to beg."

"I'll beg when you *make* me beg. But I'm here now, if you're horny, so *ask me nicely* and you can come on over." His hands went below the table; she heard the zipper of his jeans come down.

Ohhhh. *Ohhhhhhhh!* She was so glad she'd resisted that urge to put her arms around him. It was time to give her voodoo doll a jab—and she knew exactly where to stick a pin. Right up its ass.

"Well, it's tempting, Rafael, very tempting," she said, and paused, head tilted to the side as though considering that offer. "But…on balance, no. I'm *kind of* horny, but not so horny I can't wait. When I said I didn't need recovery time, I meant—and sorry if this hurts your feelings—that what you did last night didn't exactly cause any undue stress on my body and therefore only the briefest period of recovery was necessary." She got to her feet. "Let's see if there's a comparison I can think of… Hmm… How about draining a cyst under local anesthetic as opposed to triple bypass surgery? One you can go home same day, the other you need a week in hospital."

"My dick being the cyst? Better than an amputation, I guess."

And of course she laughed—she simply could not hold it in—and try as she might to bury that giveaway snort, it was there in all its ghastly glory, defeating her eyebrows à la Johnson.

He laughed, too, and that took her breath away so that when she said, "Don't push your luck," it came out all girly and flirty, which wasn't at all what she'd intended.

His laughter faded to a smile and their eyes locked, and his face softened as though he were remembering exactly what she was remembering—when laughing had been so easy. "Yeah, well, my dick is what's getting you the book, so be careful what you do with that voodoo doll of yours, okay?" he said, and the crush of melancholy in her chest for what she'd lost made her want to cry, with real tears, if only, *only* she had them.

But she didn't have them—and that was his fault.

Whatever they'd had at college—the sex and the fun and the books and the laughter and the loyalty—it hadn't been enough because he'd left her and she'd let him go, and there were *reasons* for that, there had to be. Which meant she had to harden her heart against those insidious memories and concentrate on the here and now. On getting the book and saying goodbye.

"Oh, I'll be *super* careful," she said. "It won't be *my* fault if the book deal falls through. I intend to earn every page of that manuscript if I have to bang the brains right out of your head after every damn dinner I cook you to make sure the deal is watertight. So I suggest *you* get some rest—I'll need that cock of yours in perfect working order by eight o'clock tonight."

And with that, she picked up her plate, took it into the kitchen, stacked it in the dishwasher and headed for the door.

She stopped halfway, looked at him over her shoulder. "And you might want to set up the second bedroom as a study, an office, whatever you want to call it. That way you won't be distracted by my goings and…er…comings."

She bent over, as though to examine a spot on the floor, knowing her T-shirt was riding up and exposing not only her ass but a perfect rear view of her pussy.

To make doubly certain Rafael was getting a royal eyeful, she hunched up her shoulders, letting the hem climb further. She knew he was watching because he sucked in a very audible breath then let it out slow-slow-slowly.

And then she straightened, looked at him over her shoulder again. "Sorry—did I distract you? I thought there was an insect on the floor but it's just a scuff mark."

CHAPTER ELEVEN

IT WASN'T UNTIL Rafael was barricaded in the second bedroom, having closed the door with a definitive I-am-in-control-goddamn-it click, that he took a proper breath. If you could call the great, slurping gust of air he sucked in then blew out with a "Fuck" attached to it an actual breath.

He threw his manuscript on the bed and proceeded to tear at his hair until his scalp hurt.

She'd had to walk into the kitchen just as he'd finished reading the damn death scene—more vibrant, more badass, more seductive, more *everything* than the inadequate Hope his moronic Alejandro was tormenting himself over in *Stomp*—and slay him where he stood. Or where he sat. Hell, he couldn't remember what he'd been doing. Sitting? Standing?

Drooling, either way, his dick twanging like a divining rod in her direction all through that conversation in the kitchen.

So what had he done?

He'd set. A goddamn. *Schedule!*

Good job, *imbécil*.

No idea how he was supposed to fuck her out of his head within two weeks when she was off-limits to him for sixteen out of every twenty-four hours! And it wasn't like she was going to let him play happy families with her for the other eight hours—which was the point she was making with that strategic bend-over at the end.

Insect? Scuff mark?

"Give me a fucking break," he muttered.

She'd known *exactly* what she was doing. Almost-wearing that goddamn T-shirt as a goddamn *dress*, which was obviously a cast-off of one of her moth-erfucking husbands. Talking about earning his book, banging his brains out.

And the really sick thing about the whole situation was that everything about what she'd said and done in that kitchen encapsulated why he'd fallen so hard for her in college. Because she moved in whatever kind of line she had to, to get what she wanted—straight or curved or twisted—but always forward, never backing away.

He'd been a fool not to predict she'd cut him off at the knees when he'd left, no matter how many emails he'd sent, calls he'd made or letters he'd written prom-ising to come back. He just…just hadn't expected her to do that when she loved him as much as he loved her. Hence the books. A form of therapy to get him past the anger and hurt—and still, he'd never come to terms with it.

Yet now, years later, all it had taken was one mo-ment, her bending over in a kitchen, for him to not only understand why she'd done what she'd done, but to actually *admire* her for it. She'd made a straight-line decision because he'd taken the curved-and twisted-line options away by leaving without telling her why he was going or even *that* he was going.

Hope in *Stomp* wouldn't have had the strength to kick him to the curb so decisively!

Which is why he was falling way out of love with the languishing Hope. So out of love, he was going to rewrite her. Make her kick more/kiss less ass.

He picked up the manuscript, took it over to the window and thumbed his way through to the part where Hope touched Alejandro in her fake sleep. The murmur...the hand reaching out...settling over his heart...stupid Alejandro being glad that she was so weak for him, not guessing it was subterfuge.

Subterfuge—not something anyone would ever accuse Veronica Johnson of. When she faked sleep, she made it damn obvious. She used to do it every Sunday when he'd get back from his run. Stretching seductively, letting the sheet slip so a breast, a leg, one ass cheek, *something*, was exposed, looking like she was about to burst out giggling but keeping her eyes closed.

He started laughing.

Well, fuck. Ripping that whole scene out of *Stomp* was a good place to start rethinking the book. Then he could rebuild Hope's character so that when she died of that broken heart she did it in a "take that, asshole" kind of way instead of her current woe-is-me style. Hell, he'd go through the manuscript line by line, starting now, and write himself some revision notes.

He pulled out his computer, set it up on the vanity table and got to work.

Of all the things Rafael had said in the kitchen, one line above all others kept replaying in Veronica's head. *I'm thinking of the sex scene I just read in* Stomp—*the hero, Alejandro, bending Hope, the heroine, over the couch and taking her from behind—and wondering if perhaps I should try it with you just to refresh my memory of what it was like when I did that to you that night in DC when we had the place to ourselves.*

Not only because hearing that scene described dredged up the actual memory, although of course it did, but because of the part about him having just read it in *Stomp*.

I should be writing erotica, he'd said—but he *wasn't* writing erotica. He was writing a literary novel. So why was that scene in there? And how had he used it?

Questions without answers until she got her hands on the book.

The disquiet she'd felt at the mausoleum came trickling back, the sense that something wasn't quite right, the frustration that she didn't know the right questions to ask. Add that to his reaction this morning when she'd asked to read *Stomp*, and the way those pages had literally disappeared off the kitchen table when she'd closed her eyes for longer than a blink, and it didn't take a rocket scientist to figure out she was in yet another book—apparently bent over a couch this time.

Not that that was the end of the world. It was his memory as well as hers—why shouldn't he use it? And she'd be unidentifiable—she'd have to be. Otherwise it would take some mega-size *cojones* to agree to sell it to Johnson/Charles, because that was one book her father would definitely read. Rafael would need one hell of a catastrophe scale to get through a meeting with Holden Johnson after that. And then Scarlett would sic her enforcer onto him for a knee-cap removal service. And her mother would harvest those kneecaps, grate them over a bowl of Veronica's spaghetti Bolognese in lieu of Parmesan cheese and force him to eat them.

Okay, given all that, she couldn't *possibly* be a main character. A glimpse of her in a secondary character, perhaps—no problem with that. A cameo, fine. The couch scene? Who cared as long as the female participant wasn't a short, skinny blonde with greenish-blue eyes?

That was how he'd written Julie in *Catch & Keep,* which she knew in her bone marrow had become *Catch, Tag, Release*—although his words had been "petite," "willowy," "platinum" and "turquoise"! Talk about seeing someone through rose-colored glasses. Veronica had made him change Julie to a golden-eyed, statuesque redhead. And she had to assume those changes had stuck, because nobody had recognized Veronica in that character or for sure she would have been tipped off.

Nobody had recognized her and yet as she heard her sister's voice in her head telling her to read his damn books, her heart started to thump because she knew the time had come.

She had to stop reading at Chapter 16 of *Catch, Tag, Release*. Which seemed prophetic, since that was where he'd stalled on the first draft of *Catch & Keep* two days before graduation, but was really all about getting dinner started because her chili needed two hours' simmering time.

She figured she'd get back to reading the book once the chili was on the stove. But as she dumped the ingredients in a pot, then arranged the sides in dishes to be stored in the fridge, scenes from the book kept popping into her mind—scenes that hadn't disturbed her while she'd been engrossed in reading, but which were now taking on a slightly sinister cast—and she started having second thoughts about continuing.

Julie was the problem. *Julie*, who insisted she didn't want to be swallowed whole by the privileged life that had been mapped out for her since birth… but whose actions seemed to run counter to that goal. Julie, who was getting her wild on with the hero of the piece, the financially challenged Eric, but seemed to be hedging her bets and encouraging wealthy investment banker Niles.

Still, Veronica had to admit it was possible she was overinterpreting because she knew she was Julie and

Eric was obviously Rafael, so she made a decision to
read on as far as she could before dinner.

She made it halfway through Chapter 17, stalling
after a scene involving a bottle of champagne and a
teeny, tiny jar of caviar that was straight out of her life
with Rafael. There was no way to misinterpret what
it meant. Rafael had first thought about leaving her
the night *before* graduation—right in the middle of
making love to her, if Eric the not-much-of-a-hero's
thought processes were to be believed.

Ooooh. She was going to make him pay for that.

CHAPTER TWELVE

VERONICA HAD SET out all the sides on the dining table and was transferring the chili from the pot on the stove to a serving dish when she heard Rafael come into the kitchen at precisely seven o'clock.

She tried to picture what he was seeing. Just the back of her—her ponytail tied with an innocent pink ribbon, her back demurely covered in black, her lower half shielded by the kitchen island.

But it was amazing what could be done to the hem and neckline of a little black dress with a pair of kitchen scissors and a hotel sewing kit.

She finished transferring the chili and picked up the dish. But when she took a deep breath to steady herself for the reveal, she felt something suddenly give at nipple level. A look down had a startled giggle erupting, which she choked back down. She'd known she'd attacked the neckline of her dress a little too vigorously and had hoped the frill of lace purloined from her white silk top would preserve some modesty—but there were her nipples, sitting all the way up and out.

She had a lightning-fast debate with herself over whether or not to put down the dish so she could shove her nipples back in, but decided they could stay exactly as they were, nestling in that frill of lace like two plump berries floating in cream. She could think of no punishment more apt than flaunting herself at Rafael when he had to wait until eight o'clock to touch her—that would show the schedule-setting bastard that she wasn't a woman to be messed with!

"Can I help?" Rafael asked—probably wondering why she was standing motionless making choking sounds.

"Table's all set, as you can see," she said, strangling the words out. "Just take a seat, maybe pour us some wine—the bottle's open on the table, the glasses are next to it. Better taste it, though—I'm not familiar with that label."

She heard the wine glug into the glasses, then took another deep breath and got control of herself by counting down seconds to guess when he would have a mouthful of red wine…

Aaand…

"Right," she said brightly, and turned. "I'll just bring this—" Breaking off and biting a quivering lip: he had, after all, just sprayed a mouthful of wine across the table. "Oh no! Is there something wrong with the wine? Choose another bottle if you like."

"There's nothing wrong with the wine, Veronica," he gritted out, putting his glass carefully on the table and dabbing at the mess he'd made with his table napkin.

"Then what's the problem?"

"You *know* what the problem is."

"No, I really don't think I do," she said, and waited for him to put down the sodden napkin before coming out from behind the island holding the bowl full of chili.

"Fuck!" he said, and took a reeling step backward. "Fuck, *fuck*."

She reached the table, put the dish of chili down. "Fuck? But it's not eight o'clock."

"What the…the fuck are you wearing?"

"Oh, this old thing? I always cook in this," she said, perjuring herself without compunction as she took her seat.

"You always cook wearing a top as a dress, stockings and a suspender belt, and your…your chest on display?"

"My *chest*?" She laughed. "You know, my mother always *said* you were the classy one out of the two of us. Finally, I see she's correct, because I'd call what I'm showing off tits and ass."

"Bullshit," he said.

"You mean I *wouldn't* call it tits and ass? I assure you I—"

"I mean your mother. She didn't say that. About… about me being classy."

"Oh yes she did! Girl Scout's honor! *You* wouldn't have been sent off to finishing school." She held out her hand for him to pass his plate. "By the way, if Deanne Cahill in *Catch, Tag, Release* is supposed to be my mother, I'll have to give you a fail on characterization. You always *did* get my mother wrong. She's not the Antichrist. Now… I need your plate please."

He picked up his plate and held it—almost like a shield. "So you read it."

"Half of it." Pause. "Are you going to hand me that plate or are you determined to snap it in half?"

He looked at the plate in his hands as though he'd never seen it before and then passed it to her. "I didn't think you were going to read it," he said.

"I wasn't so sure myself," she said, and started piling chili onto his plate. "But I make it a rule never to work on Sunday and since you were holed up in the second bedroom all day, I figured I may as well relax with a good book. Except 'relax' isn't really the right word is it?"

"What *is* the right word?"

She handed his plate back to him. "Instructive— which is exactly what you said it would be. I've definitely been *instructed*." She smiled thinly. "Who knew you saw me as New York Barbie?"

"I don't."

"At least I come with all the accessories. The house, the pool, the convertible. Camper van, pony, a Jet Ski! Even caviar and champagne. I wonder if a 1952 Vincent Black Shadow motorcycle will turn up—I mean, somewhere other than in our garage in Kentucky, where the one I bought you currently resides."

"No, it won't. The motorcycle isn't in the book."

"Hey, you're supposed to say 'spoiler alert' before you give those details!"

"You asked."

"Heard of the word 'rhetorical'? Well, I'm sure there'll be an *allegorical* motorcycle in there somewhere."

"Julie's not... She's not... *Mierda*."

"Not *shit*? Because she seems a shit kind of person to me," she said. "But I guess that's what happens when you load up your character with only bad traits."

"I mean she's not you. Not...really."

"How can you *say* that after I dressed the part for you?" She looked down at herself, then across at him. "This *is* something Julie would wear, isn't it? She seems so desperate to have as much sex as she can before she's forced into that dreary life in a New York penthouse apartment with Niles the banker!"

He must have recognized the martial light of challenge in her eyes, because his whole demeanor changed, like he'd suddenly picked up a flung gauntlet. "Julie wouldn't wear a maid's outfit—if that's what you'd call what you're wearing!"

"Only because that's what her *maid* would wear I presume?"

He inclined his head—his only answer.

"You don't like her much, do you?"

"All I have to do is understand her. It's Eric who loves her."

"Oh, Eric!" she said, and pulled a face.

His jaw moved, like he was grinding his teeth. "What's wrong with Eric?"

"Eric doesn't have the balls to be with a woman

who doesn't need him to survive. If she's not bare-foot, pregnant and broke, he runs."

"He doesn't have the balls because she's cutting them off! 'Eat caviar, Eric. Drink champagne, Eric. Let me pay for dinner, buy you an Armani suit, get you a better cell phone, a new computer, Eric'!" He half rose from his seat, hands on the table, glaring across at her. "She was paying for him like he was a fucking male escort! What the hell was he sup-posed to do?"

She matched him stand for stand, stance for stance. "Stay, that's what! Stay, fight with her about it—fight *for* her! Find the courage to not give her up, since he said he loved her so fucking much!"

Long, searing moment and then his face shut-tered. He sat back down. "Yeah, well, when you get to the end of the book you'll see Eric's days of hav-ing his balls handed to him on a plate are over the day she—" He cut himself off, shook his head. Not going there.

"She what? What happens to Julie?"

He watched her, narrow-eyed. "No spoilers, right? So I'll just say she gets the life she always wanted." Long moment of stillness, and then he took a slow breath and started spooning sour cream, pineapple and carrot onto his plate indiscriminately. "How about we talk about something less bloodthirsty, like serial killers? Tori's book—is it the Murder Eight series? She won an Edgar for the last one, didn't she?"

Subject effectively changed. And they kept chang-ing subjects every time a barb flew.

A brooding kind of tension brewed between them until it felt as though they'd set a metronome on the table, ticking away the seconds and building an almost palpable dome of lust around them as eight o'clock crept closer.

At the twenty-minutes-to-go mark, the conversation dried up completely.

Seventeen minutes, and the air was crackling with electric anticipation, expectation robbing the space around them of oxygen.

Thirteen minutes—clear the barely touched plates of chili.

Nine—serve the chocolate mousse.

When there were only eight minutes left, Rafael put a condom beside his plate and Veronica started to tremble as her excitement level rocketed up.

Seven minutes.

He was examining his mousse as though it were a plate of dirt, without making any attempt to pick up a spoon to eat it. His hands rested on the table on either side of his bowl. The long, elegant fingers of his left hand drummed insistently on the tabletop. Those on his right were curled up tight into his palm.

"I told you I wasn't in Romy's league," Veronica said with a failure of a laugh—just something, anything, to break the tension.

"Huh?" was his unhelpful response.

"You barely ate any of the chili, and you don't seem interested in the mousse. I know it's kind of lumpy. There's something about the temperature of the eggs or the chocolate having a seizure or...or something that I always get wrong, but I can never remember what it is."

He made an impatient chopping movement with his left hand—it seemed he was no longer capable of conversing—and then curled those fingers in to match the right fist that was all but vibrating against the tabletop.

Two minutes.

And then he lifted both fists a few inches and brought them down on the table in a controlled thump.

He pushed his chair back. "It's almost eight o'clock. And given I've been staring at your nipples—exactly as you planned—for an hour, and I'm horny as fucking hell, I think we'd better decide on a safe word."

"A *what*?"

"A safe word. Something you say that will stop me before I hurt you."

"You won't hurt me."

"Humor me on this, because just at this moment…" He raised a hand as though to protect himself, then dropped it. "Humor me, okay?"

And just like that, her anger flared. Humor him? Why the fuck should she? "How about 'Niles' for the inoffensive banker in *Catch, Tag, Release*? Or…or Piers? Not that Piers is an investment banker but—"

"Believe me, you saying Niles or Piers is more likely to spur me on than stop me."

She threw her napkin on the table. "Then how about *Liar, Liar*?"

"Good choice," he growled. "*Excellent* choice!" He glanced at his wristwatch. "And just in time."

She stood.

"Stay where you are," he barked at her.

"But—"

"Stay in that chair, I want to show you how much I love chocolate mousse."

"*Now* you want to eat dessert?" she said, but she sat because she knew this wasn't about mousse.

"Yes, now I want to eat dessert. So reach into that bowl in front of you and scoop up some mousse. I want you to coat your nipples with it. Do it."

She couldn't repress the wild tremor that shook her—didn't want to. This felt like a showdown. A physical continuation of the conversation about *Catch, Tag, Release* they clearly weren't prepared to explore to the bitter end. Working out boundaries—what each of them could and could not accept.

"Should I take off my dress?" she asked—a test, an offer for what they were about to do to be his call.

"No."

"Okay," she said, dipping her fingers into the lumpy mousse, "but the chocolate will ruin the lace, so if you want to see this dress again—"

"I don't want to see the dress again—and *I'm* going to ruin the lace, Veronica."

"That's not like you," she said, and placed a dollop of mousse on each nipple. "You've always been so fastidious."

"College was a long time ago, remember? Now shut up and rub that mousse in—no, *roll* it in the way you like it when it's me doing it."

She gasped as she obeyed him, then moaned. She

was squirming on her chair, remembering what he'd said this morning about dragging her over and unzipping his jeans and impaling her on his cock, wishing he'd do it now.

"Tell me how they feel," he said.

"Hard. Ready. Aching. Needy."

His hands disappeared below the table. She heard the zip of his jeans go down. "Hard, ready, aching, needy," he repeated, and reached for the condom, tore open the packet. His hands disappeared beneath the table again, presumably to slide the condom on. "Just like my cock."

She moaned again and this time it galvanized him so that he was on his feet.

"Hands off," he said, "my turn."

And he came around to her side of the table, his jeans gaping open, and positioned himself behind her. He scooped up more mousse, dabbed it on her, then his fingers delved into the narrow band of lace, forking around her nipples just hard enough to squeeze without impeding his hands from sliding up and down. "Jesus," he groaned, and as though he couldn't wait one more minute, he dragged her up out of her chair, spun her to face him, head lowering, mouth diving to lick then suck the mousse off her right nipple until she cried out.

"You know the safe word," he said and then sucked again. "If I'm too hard, say it, stop me."

"I'm not saying it. I want it exactly like this," she said, and his fingers fumbled for her other nipple, clumsy in their haste to touch her so that the lace she'd sewn on tore free of the dress, exactly as he'd predicted.

He pulled back, breathing hard, and when she looked down to see what he'd done she had to admit she'd never looked so ready to be fucked in her life. Torn lace on one side exposing her nipple completely, the other side with a chocolate-stained frill and reddened nipple peeping through. She looked like the personification of sexual excess.

"Is it the same?" he asked. "Am *I* the same? Do you still think I don't have the balls for you?"

"Why does what I think matter?"

"Because it fucking *does*!" he said, and spun her to face the island, pushed her toward it, crowded in behind her. She felt the back of his hands against her bottom, knew he was shoving his jeans and underwear out of the way, and then his fingers returned to her nipples, rolling them tight and hard. "Safe word. Now."

"No."

He shoved a knee between her legs, kicked her feet apart. "Trust fund, finishing school, Manhattan penthouse, Kentucky horses, society parties…the perfect life…yet you don't even make me lift your dress to get to you," he breathed against her ear and shoved his cock between her thighs, rubbing it against her clit.

She pushed her bottom back, egging him on. "Two bestselling books, movie in the works, TV-star date, looking like a god, you could have anyone…yet I'm *still* the one you want to fuck," she shot back at him. "Now put up or shut— Ahhhhh." As his dick went deep into her.

"I'm not moving until you tell me who you think I am. That it's me you want, me you see, me you feel. Only me. Me as you see me now."

"All right, okay, it's you! It is!" she cried, and it was a sob of need as much as an answer. "You, Rafael." Another sob—surrender. "You."

"¡No me llames Rafael!"

"Wh-what? But that's your name."

"Dime Rafa como siempre lo hacias."

"Rafa," she said. "Rafa, all right, Rafa, Rafa."

Another string of Spanish words as he pulled all the way out of her and then thrust all the way back in, and her hips hit the counter.

She cried out from the force of it.

More Spanish as he instantly pulled out of her, too fast for her to translate. He turned her into his arms. He kissed her, gentle now. *"Ah, perdón, perdón, mi amor,"* he said.

"No, no! It's okay, you didn't hurt me."

"I don't want to do it this way," he said, taking her face between his hands.

"It's okay."

"No, it's not."

Breathing hard into the silence. Both of them poised as though on a precipice. Lust and fear and need and something else. Something from the past, like a sort of sorrow.

"The book," he said. "Those two… Julie and Eric, they existed in my head, a punishment, but they're not real."

"I don't want to talk about the book."

"Just…let me say this. I wrote it angry."

"Yeah, that much I could tell," she said, her voice thick.

"I lost sight of you in my anger. I did it to hurt you."

"I know—so the least I could have done was read it when I was supposed to, right? I'd be over it by now!"

He laughed softly and then bit his lip and smiled down at her at the same time—a rueful expression so at odds with the harsh way he'd seemed intent on taking her. "So let me *not* hurt you in the kitchen, hmm? We won't do it like this."

She wanted to bury her face against his chest and pretend she hadn't seen that look on his face, block her ears and pretend she hadn't heard the gentleness in his voice. Because it was loneliness she was seeing and hearing. Loneliness and longing, and sweetness and an aching sadness. And something else. Something that was a lot like love. And it was too late for love. Way too late. She couldn't risk love, wouldn't believe in this time, couldn't survive it going wrong again.

"Come, upstairs," he said. "It's safer in bed."

"I don't *want* to be safe," she whispered—but the words were suddenly just words because the safety he was offering would make what they were doing something other than dirty, dare-you, raw sex. And that was more dangerous than shoving her against a kitchen island. Bruises you could see were safer than ones you couldn't.

That look again, making her heart stumble. "Don't you, *mi vida*?"

No. No! She didn't want him to understand her or to comfort her. So she undulated against him, urging him on, and when all he did was kiss her too damn gently, she lifted her leg against his hip, then undulated again.

"Veronica!" he said—a caution in it that she *would not hear*!

"No!" she snapped and with a hoarse cry lifted herself so he instinctively supported her weight as she wrapped both legs around him, and when he ground out something in Spanish, something that told her she was everything he wanted, she pushed herself onto him so that his cock sank all the way inside her. It was his undoing—no holding back now.

The madness built, the desperation to take, the jerking of hips and slap of flesh. A gasp, a long, low moan, and she screamed as the orgasm came for her, slumped as he followed her a split second later. His face was buried against her neck as he said over and over, *"Mi vida, mi vida, mi vida."*

She screwed her eyes shut. "Don't say that," she whispered. "Don't."

He pulled her in closer, hugged her tight. "What do you want me to say? Tell me, I'll say it. I will."

She unclamped her legs from around him, let them slide down until her feet were on the floor and she was standing in the circle of his arms. "Tell me you want to fuck me, that's *all*. That's all I need."

He kissed the side of her neck. *"Tú me perteneces,"* he said.

"No I don't," she cried. "I don't belong to you. I

never did. You're not like me, you don't lose things that belong to you. If I belonged to you, you would never have let yourself lose me. You'd never have left me."

He said nothing, just held her. She could have pulled free; instead she opted to drive the point home with a little voodoo-style viciousness using her teeth as pins. But when she turned her face into his shoulder, intending to bite through his T-shirt like a savage, something in her brain went haywire so that she kissed him there instead.

"Come to bed, *mi amor*," he said.

Don't call me that, she screamed—but only in her head because he was kissing any words she might have said away.

And then he lifted her in his arms and she knew she was in trouble because she wanted him to call her that again.

CHAPTER THIRTEEN

He kept coming back to that fucking death scene!

Rafael paced around the second bedroom—as much as he *could* pace now a desk had been delivered from Tremenhill Hall for his temporary use, and all his worldly possessions had been relocated by Veronica from the main bedroom while he'd been out for his run this morning.

He'd laughed when he'd seen his suitcase. When he'd opened the wardrobe and found his shirt. Not that it was entirely unexpected since at 4:00 a.m., as he'd leaned in to kiss her, she'd reminded him she was off the clock and in "recovery mode," so he should probably take himself off to the second bedroom to sleep if he couldn't keep his body parts to himself.

He'd duly gotten out of bed, picked up the jeans and T-shirt he'd left on the armchair, and taken himself to bed in here…where he'd tossed and turned all night thinking about the way he'd portrayed himself in *Catch, Tag, Release*: Eric, the cast-aside lover too willing to accept his fate but who turns cruel by the end—not a pretty picture.

He'd written Alejandro gutsier from the start in *Stomp*—appropriate, since Rafael was now a strong, successful twenty-nine-year-old! If you could call it gutsy to be a vengeful asshole, wreaking havoc on those you think have betrayed you. Stomping on the heart of the woman you loved because she dared to move on.

Three hundred thousand words in total: one man's quest to get a woman out of his head.

And yet she was not only still in his head but in the marrow of his bones.

He sighed as he set the manuscript down.

So much for fucking her out of his system—all it had taken was two nights and he'd fucked himself back into love with her.

No, that was a lie.

The truth was, he'd never fallen out of love with her.

The truth was, what he'd really intended to do when he'd gone after her at the wedding was to show her not what she'd been missing but who he'd become—a match for her at last, someone she could love again.

The truth was, he was going to go on loving her when their two weeks were up and she left him—and she *would* leave him, because he'd written three caustic books about her and she wasn't looking especially forgiving after the first half of *Catch, Tag, Release*. The most optimistic spin he could put on her reaction was that she'd seemed to accept he'd written it in anger. Anger was something she'd always readily understood, given her own firecracker temper. And at least she hadn't kicked him out of bed. He smiled suddenly—well, okay, she *had* kicked him out of bed, but not until four o'clock, by which time she'd worn him out.

As for *Liar, Liar*? He might get away with that one. For one thing, he wasn't in it himself, even in disguise. For another, "Emma" could be any New York socialite, and Emma's husband "Martin" was a step away from a caricature, drawn out of Rafael's jealous anguish. It was unlikely Veronica's marriage to Simeon had been seething with the sexual frustration and miserable boredom he'd ascribed to that of Emma and Martin.

But *Stomp*? Well, she was in *Stomp* right down to the eye color.

And he was writing it *now*—not as an angry young man in the early throes of a devastating breakup, but as a man who should have at least tried to get over his broken heart the way she'd tried to get over hers. Because she *had* tried, he had to accept that; she'd blocked him and she'd gotten married. All he'd done was write crap about her to share with the world—and in *Stomp* he'd turned her into something she not only would never understand but would despise: a woman who wouldn't think twice about letting herself drop dead of a broken heart.

Which brought him back to the dread certainty that even if by some miracle he managed to hold on to her past the two weeks they'd negotiated, once she read *Stomp* everything would come to a screeching halt.

Talk about irony! *Stomp* had been his way of extricating her from his life—and yet it had taken *Stomp* to get her back into his life—and *Stomp* would ultimately be responsible for taking her so far out of his life. *Stomp* would end up being a self-fulfilling prophecy and driving him fucking insane because he'd forever wonder what could have been if he'd never written it.

He sighed deeply and went to stare out the window at the moors, touching a hand to the windowpane as though he could feel Hope's ghost through the glass.

Something about Alejandro's despair at that moment reminded him of Heathcliff in *Wuthering Heights*.

Veronica's favorite book—she'd read it aloud to him once upon a time. He could still see her face as she'd read that scene where Heathcliff begged Cathy not to leave him, to haunt him, to drive him mad if she had to…

"'I cannot live without my soul,'" he said, and now both his hands were on the window. And God knew that was Rafael's own problem—turning himself into a madman because he was living without his soul.

"*¿Por qué no puedo sacarte de mí?*" he murmured. "Ha, good question. Why *can't* I get her out of my soul?"

And as though Heathcliff's ghost had slapped him around the head, the solution was there, fully formed.

It didn't matter that he couldn't get her out of his soul—what mattered was finding his way back into *hers*! All he had to do was make her fall in love with him again!

Okay, it was going to be tricky since she'd told him not once, but twice, that she hated him. But she couldn't hate him as much as she wanted him to believe, because she came apart in his arms every time he touched her—*and* she gave as good as she got. Lack of attraction sure wasn't an issue, and where there was attraction there had to be hope.

Of course, he had time constraints. He only had twelve days at his disposal. *But* it had taken only a minute to fall in love with each other the first time around, and that was in a crowded bar. This time they were completely alone together, on neutral ground in a can't-hide-yourself cottage neither of them owned, and the rich girl/poor boy dynamic that had caused so many fights no longer applied.

Which left only the one obstacle. *Stomp.*

"Hello, moron," he said out loud and laughed. "You're the fucking author. Don't revise it, *rewrite* it! Give yourself a happy ending. Get the girl. Keep the girl."

A burst of manic energy had him hurrying to the desk, composing an email in his head for Bryan to flag that a rewrite was necessary, for which a detailed synopsis would shortly be under way, so to go no further with reading *Stomp* Mark I.

But when he opened his emails he saw Bryan's name in his inbox, which had to mean Bryan had already finished reading it. He hoped Bryan didn't love it, because if he did, the poor guy was going to be disappointed.

And then he took in the subject line—Kill That Bastard Alejandro—and burst out laughing.

Odds were he was about to make Bryan happy. He read on.

Rafe
Finished reading *Stomp*.

Two things to think about—and please remember these words are coming to you from a place of love.

Alejandro sounded interesting when you talked to me about him, but on the page he's out-Heathcliffing Heathcliff. He needs to grow the fuck up—being unlucky in love isn't enough of an excuse to turn into a complete asshole, and we don't want your female readers to hate his guts. Rewrite him, redeem him or kill him off. The way it currently stands, I want him dead.

Your sex scenes need work. Mawkish in first third, brutal in the middle third—no wonder Hope decided to die. The flashbacks about them in the final third are mawkishly brutal. Quite a feat. What the hell happened to you? Either reread *Catch, Tag, Release* or read some romance to refresh your memory of how it's done, otherwise the only prize you're likely to win with *Stomp* is *Literary Review*'s Bad Sex in Fiction prize.

Other than that, the writing is tight and the pacing is good.

See you next week. Looking forward to talking about Melissa Charles, who called me today!!!!! BL

Those five exclamation points at the end were… interesting.

But not quite as interesting as the feedback on the novel.

"Kill the asshole and have more sex—check and double-check," Rafael said and burst out laughing again.

CHAPTER FOURTEEN

THE FRUSTRATING THING about having to keep yourself aloof for sixteen hours a day when you were a sex maniac for the other eight hours was that it was almost impossible to keep the boundaries intact.

Veronica had nevertheless done her best in the face of extreme provocation.

She'd reverted to dressing stylishly but demurely as befitting a Johnson who'd been beautifully "finished" at the Koller school. But all Rafael had done was smile and look through the damn clothes as though he could not only see her skin but her internal organs, as well.

She'd gotten her industrial-strength concealer onto that first shocking love bite, the second one that had appeared on her left breast on Monday night, and the third and fourth (right hip and inner thigh) from Tuesday night, expertly enough to make a Hollywood makeup artist proud. But he'd merely examined all those places from a distance as though figuring out where to deposit the next one.

And she'd adhered to a strict personal timetable

that had her hurrying through breakfast while he was out for his run, hidden away in the shower when he returned, and working in the living room by the time he was eating his breakfast. She'd thought the message was obvious: hands off until 8:00 p.m., so he might as well close himself in the second bedroom and curse at his computer (and she *knew* he did that because this was a small cottage and sound carried).

Unfortunately, Rafael didn't seem to get that message. He'd taken to wandering downstairs and into her space whenever he damn well felt like it. Bringing her cups of coffee, making her lunch and depositing it on the coffee table in the living room for whenever she was ready to eat it, and popping in to ask for editorial advice she was quite certain he didn't need.

Occasionally, he'd refer to *Catch, Tag, Release*— the purpose of which seemed to be to gauge if she'd read the second half (she hadn't been able to bring herself to do so thus far) and suggest that he'd provide context when she did (and she was very sure context would be a bad idea—she didn't want to be put in a position where she'd either forgive him or kill him).

He spent an inordinate amount of time during these excursions reaching his arms over his head— ostensibly to stretch out his "computer-hunching" muscles, but coincidentally straining his T-shirt over his superb chest. As if that wasn't bad enough, on Wednesday afternoon he stripped the damn T-shirt off, right in front of her, because apparently he needed to go into the garden to do something—not that she

knew what it was he actually *did* out there because
she was not going to look!

With her nerves fraying, Veronica slipped on one
of her diamond engagement rings before dinner on
Wednesday night. She told herself it was to remind
herself she wasn't a young, in-love college girl anymore and therefore wasn't susceptible to falling for
Rafael a second time, but she couldn't quite suppress
the thought that it was more about needling Rafael
into doing something she could resent. He'd always
had a deep vein of jealousy, and if she could use it
to jolt him out of the frustrating calm that seemed to
have descended on him, it might drive a much-needed
schism between them and remind them both what this
time together was supposed to be about.

Of course Rafael noticed the ring—it was such a
whopper it was hard to miss—and as his lips tight-
ened, she thought he was on the verge of an explosion… But then his hand went to the right front pocket
of his jeans, his eyes closed for a brief moment, and
when he opened his eyes, the moment was gone.

He picked up the bottle of red wine she'd put on
the table and poured out a glass. "Are you happy with
the wine they've provided?" he asked.

"Um…yeees. Why?"

He handed her the glass. "Because I'm going into
Leeds tomorrow. I've run out of clothes and can't
work out how to use the washing machine so I'm
going to buy a few things. You can come with me,
if you like…?"

"No! No. No! No."

He seemed amused. "No?"

"No!"

"Okay. Anything *at all* you need me to get for you? If not wine, how about food?"

"I got some groceries from the village today, so we're set."

"You did?"

"Yes. I have a few new recipes to try."

"Oh," he said, and stared into his bowl with a look she couldn't interpret. "And tonight it's spaghetti, I see. Great."

Just because he was in love with Veronica didn't mean he had to love everything she did—and Rafael most certainly did not love her cooking.

He was starting to wish he hadn't made that crack about the chef on Monday morning, because when they were living together in real life they'd have to hire one.

Living together in real life.

God, he liked the sound of that.

He'd certainly been pulling out all the stops the past few days to get her to imagine that life with him—and, okay, he'd struck some pretty demeaning poses as he went about it, but he was working with what he had. Still, gratifying though her nonverbal responses were—the blinks, the change in her breathing, the quickly averted eyes—his main aim was for her to imagine life *outside* the bedroom, since they both already knew that inside the bedroom was as perfect as it could get.

Coffee, lunch, laughs, conversation—these were going to be the key. Which meant his priority now was to get them off that dumb-ass schedule that tied them to working hours and therefore gave too much emphasis to the eight-til-four sexfest. He was on hyperalert, watching for any trigger he could use to shift them into a more-cruisy/less-full-throttle life. Normal—he wanted normal. The kind happily married couples lived.

As things transpired, the trigger came that night.

He'd just finished a prolonged session of cunnilingus, which he enjoyed immensely—not only because he loved the way Veronica tasted but because he'd wrung a seemingly endless stream of orgasms out of her.

Appetizer, he thought, smug as hell, and reached over to the nightstand for a condom because it was his turn to come—and by God did he need his turn—only to find…no condom.

CHAPTER FIFTEEN

HE SCRAMBLED OFF the bed, checked on, under and behind the nightstand.

Nope. No condom.

Opened the nightstand drawer.

No condom.

Raced to the spare bedroom to check in his suitcase—nope. Into his bathroom, where he rifled in a panic through his washbag. No condoms. He'd used them all up.

Back to *her* bathroom to check in *her* toiletry bag, even though he knew she wouldn't have any because Piers and Simeon—those fucking assholes—hadn't had to use one.

Shell-shocked, he robot-walked back to the bed.

Veronica had sat up, drawing the sheet coyly up to cover her breasts. "No condom?" she asked.

He shook his head, bereft of speech.

"Oh, *silly* me! Of *course*! We used the last one at three o'clock this morning." She was doing her best to look sympathetic and only managing to smirk. "If you'd told me, I would have bought some when I drove

into the village today." She sighed—way over the top—
the wretch. "That's it for tonight, then, I guess...?"

He was caught between an instinctive urge to howl
like a wolf, an almost irresistible compulsion to laugh
at her pathetic attempt to look sympathetic, and a desire to throttle her.

But then she said, "Although I suppose a hand job
is doable."

Hand job.

He remembered Veronica telling him she needed either an all-clear STD test result or a condom if he didn't
want the next two weeks to be all about hand jobs.

Fate.

Because he'd be in Leeds tomorrow.

And tonight?

Well, there were hand jobs and then there were
hand jobs.

"Let go of the sheet, Veronica, and come here,"
he said.

"What are you going to do?"

"I'm taking you up on the offer of a hand job."

She laughed as she flung off the sheet and got out
of bed. "So where do you want it?"

"Where do *you*?" he asked.

"In the bathroom, I guess? Or at least, I want to
use my vanilla oil if you're okay with that."

"I'm *definitely* okay with your vanilla oil in the
bathroom. Can we watch ourselves in the mirror?"

"Suuure," she said, leading him to the bathroom
but sounding as though she was at last realizing they
might not be talking about the same thing.

She watched him warily as she tipped some oil into her palm and rubbed her hands together. And then, "Are you ready?" she asked.

"I am," he said—but when she reached for his cock, he stopped her, even though it half killed him to have to do it. "But you've got the wrong idea."

Her alert eyes went to his. "I don't under... ssstand...?"

"The hand job is for you."

A heartbeat's worth of staring, and then she laughed again—breathlessly now—as he positioned her to face the mirror, with him at her back, watching over her head. "Touch yourself," he said.

"But—"

"Touch yourself. Play with yourself. Let me watch."

"So I'm giving *myself* a hand job? What do I need *you* for?"

"I'll chime in," he said, and kissed the top of her head, "starting...here..." His hands came around her to cup her breasts, his thumbs grazing across her nipples. "I promise I won't leave you wanting, so give me this gift."

"Gift," she said as though that were an alien concept, and he realized then how few gifts he'd given her. He'd been too focused on not accepting *her* gifts, because he couldn't give her anything to equal them. "All right," she said, and she offered him a tremulous smile as she slid a hand down her body and slipped her fingers between her thighs. "I'm already wet from your tongue, but the oil feels good."

He groaned; she laughed.

"Sure you don't want to do it?" she asked huskily.

His turn to laugh, very, very shakily. "I'm very sure I *do* want to do it…and I will, very soon." He thrust his cock against her lower back "But if I'm going to have to suffer, I might as well share the suffering and make you wait."

He watched her small fingers with their delicate pink-polished nails sliding against her clit, listened to the sounds surrounding them—the swish of oil, her own quick breaths, his pounding heart—and it was erotic to the hilt. So hard to stay as he was, his agitated fingers plucking at her nipples in time with the movement of her fingers. So hard not to take over. She'd let him, he knew she would, but he also knew there would be time for him tomorrow.

"Open wider," he said, his voice hoarse in her ear. "Make room for me."

"Already?" she said, but parted her legs eagerly.

"It's an obsession, the way I want you," he said, "too hard to wait."

He sent one hand down to open her labia while his other continued to play with one of her nipples. The scent of her became so sensually intense it brought on the shakes and he didn't care because as she slumped back against him he felt something similar racking her body and he loved that they were in sync.

They were on a whole new plane of arousal, watching their hands working together between her legs. He was attentive to her slightest shift, so in tune with her movements he seemed able to read where her fingers would be even before she knew, ensuring every pleasure point was covered to maximize her arousal. He alternated between directly caressing her and trailing his fingertips across her own stroking fingers, so that at any given instant, her clitoris was circled or stroked.

Knowing he couldn't last much longer, he dipped inside her to spread her moisture where he wanted her to concentrate. He kissed then licked the side of her neck as he jerked rhythmically, helplessly, behind her. He knew he had to get this done before he came on her back, which he was *not allowed to do* because this *was not about him*. He lowered his other hand, reaching between her legs.

"Play with your clit, Veronica. Bring it on so I can feel you squeeze my fingers."

"Your fingers?"

And he slid two fingers into her so that she understood, and she arched her back for him, then flexed her hips, seeking more.

He looked at her, his eyes fierce in the mirror. "Look me in the eye. I want you to know it's not only me, it's us."

She nodded, kept her eyes on his, her fingers flying now. Flying, gliding, slick and fast, and then she lay right back against him, and while one of her hands kept up the pressure at her clitoris, the other came up and reached behind his neck, pulling him in and holding on—and *that* was his gift, the trust she had in him. He could feel her climax coming, both fast and slow, wild and relaxed. Voluptuous, to be held by her like that, to have her display herself, to watch three hands between her legs.

He saw her eyes start to close as the peak raced for her, but she forced them open, kept them open, and then said his name. "Rafa."

"Yes, yes, *mi vida*, I'm here. I'm here, let go."

It was his permission to close her eyes, and as she did so, the orgasm came, wrenching her enough to make her shudder, hard enough for him to feel that shudder all the way through to his heart.

Waiting through her recovery, knowing she would have fallen if he hadn't been there for her to rest against. Loving her with everything he had. She opened her eyes and he had to wonder if she could see that love because it was so obvious to him. She smiled sleepily, and he realized she *couldn't* see it—maybe because he'd always looked at her like that so there was nothing new to see, maybe because she didn't want to see it. In either case, he still had a long way to go.

He lifted her in his arms, carried her out of the bathroom, to the bed, lay her down then turned to leave.

"Where are you going?" she asked groggily, and he turned back to find her up on her elbows, frowning at him like a rumpled kitten. "It's not four o'clock."

"Go to sleep, Veronica. I have one more hand job to attend to."

"But I—"

"No, I can do it. I'll be gone early in the morning, so I'll see you tomorrow night."

CHAPTER SIXTEEN

RAFAEL WAS HAPPY to see a box of condoms beside his wineglass when he entered the kitchen for dinner on Thursday night. But when Veronica came to the table, bringing a tureen with her and putting it beside the box, he was even happier to be able to say, "Not needed."

She checked briefly. "The soup?" she asked. "You didn't eat the spaghetti last night. You're going to starve if you don't start eating more."

He repressed a shudder at the memory of the over-salted Bolognese. "I wasn't hungry last night," he lied. "And anyway I'm not talking about the soup—" glancing into the tureen and repressing another shudder "—I'm talking about the condoms."

Something like panic chased across her face, fast as quicksilver, before her eyebrows arched up like a shield. "I see," she said coolly. "Fine by me. But just so you know, Melissa has spoken to Bryan."

"I know."

"What I'm saying is that I've held up my end of the bargain even if my services are no longer required."

"Er—"

"And it's not my fault last night was disappointing!" Slopping a ladle's worth of soup into his bowl.

"Um—"

"I mean—what?" Another ladleful of soup "Am I supposed to be in charge of dinner *and* condoms?"

"Ah, I think you're laboring under a misapprehension, Veronica. The reason I don't need the condoms isn't because I don't want to have sex with you—" easing up to remove a piece of paper from the back pocket of his jeans "—but because of this."

She dropped the ladle into the tureen and took the paper from his hand.

"Test results," he said.

As she unfolded and read the page, he gamely picked up his spoon to try the soup, hoping her preoccupation with his all-clear results would distract her from any gagging he might be betrayed into. The tiniest taste told him it was worse than Monday night's chili, on par with Tuesday's overcooked steak with the horrendously gluggy gravy she'd buried it under, and better—but not by much—than last night's spaghetti Bolognese. He put the spoon down. "I got tested in Leeds today."

She looked at him. "So you're definitely not leaving me?"

"Do you want me to?"

And when the merest hint of a smile touched her lips, he decided that was enough of an indicator for him to push his chair away from the table and that disastrous soup, pull her onto his lap and make his case.

"If I admit to being an idiot, and beg you to take pity on me, can we give up on the timetable?"

"Beg on your knees?"

"I'll beg any way you want me to beg," he said huskily—and he hoped she got that what he was really doing was conceding defeat.

"How about in Spanish?" she asked, and even though she was stringing things out, the way she was rubbing her core against him told him the end was inevitable.

"Te ruego que no me hagas sufrir más y te entregues a mí," he said promptly. "And I'll say it in English, too, if that'll speed things up. I beg you to put me out of my misery and give yourself to me."

"What about saying it in—?"

"Veronica! Either say yes or get off my lap before I come in my underwear."

"Yes, in that case," she said, with a breathless laugh. "Yes, because I want to stay here. Yes…as long as I can have more—and I'm not talking about the soup."

"Definitely not the soup," he said, shifting her on his lap so she was facing the table away from him and pulled her in tighter, higher, until she was leaning forward, hands on the edge of the table to brace herself. God it felt good to have her jammed up hard against his cock.

"I'm going to be embarrassingly quick," he warned.

"Me, too, and I want it to be like that. I want to come fast and hot and bright like lightning."

"Then beg me, the way I begged you."

"Rafael!" she cried.

And he laughed—torture and surrender in one. "That'll do it—you see how easy it is for you to do what you want with me?" He reached down a hand to free his cock and used his chin to nudge her hair away from the back of her neck so he could fasten his mouth there and suck, and suck, and *suck*. He wished he could keep sucking until she bled into his mouth.

One hard grind edged her thighs apart and he wanted to weep at the heat of her as she moved restlessly on his lap. He imagined her on her knees ready for him, knew he was going to take her like that tonight, and as she pushed back against him, he slid a hand under her dress, tugged her panties to one side, and eased into her.

He stilled for a moment, positioning his hands on her hips to guide her as she moved on him, going deeper, deeper still, raining kisses over the back of her neck, murmuring to her in Spanish, words he hoped she couldn't translate because they were about his need for her, his unending love, his hungering soul.

But when she came a scant moment later and cried out his name—not Rafael but Rafa—he wished he'd said those things in English, too, so that there was no doubt she understood every word.

Veronica wasn't quite sure how it had happened, but the moment they'd ditched the schedule and the condoms, everything else changed.

It started with him taking over the cooking the night after that fateful Leeds trip.

She'd arrived in the kitchen ready to make meat-loaf, only to find him there before her, bending low to look in the open oven door.

"What are you doing?" she asked.

He closed the oven door but kept peering through the glass. "Isn't it obvious?"

"Um, yes. Looking at what I *think* is a chicken."

He stood and faced her. "Correction. I am *baking* a chicken. And potatoes. And I've already prepared a salad, which is currently residing in the fridge."

"But it's my job to get dinner ready. Part of the deal."

"Hmm, how to break this to you…" He sighed. "You can't cook, Veronica."

"Yes I can! I've been *cooking* since Sunday night!"

"You've been putting ingredients together—not quite the same thing."

"But…but… Piers and Simeon never complained about my cooking."

"They were clearly besotted with you. Or they had cast-iron stomachs. Or no taste buds. Or a combination of all three."

"How do I know *you* can cook, smartass?"

"You'll find out tonight. But if you want advance reassurance, cast your mind back to our DC days and you'll remember that I occasionally shoehorned Romy out of the kitchen to prepare my mother's Arroz Con Pollo, and it rivaled Romy's paella for Cordon Bleu status. Not to mention beating the crap out of Matt's overspiced hot-sauce omelets." Pause. "And I worked as a fast-food cook for a while after college, so I learned a few things."

"Oh you…you did?"

"I did."

"What else did you do? After…after college?"

"Lots of things."

"I guess… I guess you wrote about that period. I haven't read *Liar, Liar* yet, so—"

"I'm not in *Liar, Liar*, Veronica. It's not like *Catch, Tag, Release*."

"But I thought you said it was about what happened when the tagged fish got a new lease on life. Wouldn't that mean—?"

"I'm not the fish in question," he said, heading off any questions by bending down to look in the oven again. "But back to the chicken… It's looking good. Smelling good, too."

"All I can smell is you," she said, and tried to laugh as though nothing was wrong as he automatically straightened to lift his arm for a sniff. "Gotcha!"

"Yes, you've got me."

"I… I only meant I c-could smell the lemony aftershave you use. I mean… Well, you know you're paranoid about being clean."

"Clean for you, yes, because I love the way you smell."

"Rafael!" she said—a plea to pull back, because she knew there was something beneath the words she wasn't ready to hear.

He leaned back against the counter and looked at her with that…that look. The rueful smile, his lip caught between his teeth.

She took a step backward, because even though

he didn't make even one move toward her, it was as though he were prowling around her. "I'll let you take some of my vanilla oil when you fly home."

"I like the vanilla oil, Veronica, but what's underneath it is what I'm interested in, so if I could take that home…?" He trailed off, leaving a question hanging between them.

"Sorry," she said with an airless little huff of a laugh, "peeling off a layer of skin to send along with it is a little too *Silence of the Lambs* for my taste."

"Maybe you'd better make me a voodoo doll, then. Twist a bit of your hair around its head, dot a couple of turquoise chips on its face, dab some vanilla oil between its legs, and I'll be all set."

"I'm not sure I should encourage you to stick pins in me."

"You know it's not pins I want to stick in you, Veronica." And now he came for her. Step, step, step. But he didn't touch her. "And you?"

"Me?"

"Are you still sticking pins in me?"

She swallowed as her face heated but she didn't play coy. "No," she said. "I don't want to hurt you. I… No."

He touched her face with his fingertips, then leaned down to kiss her. That's all—just a kiss. No jerk into his arms, no tongue. A kiss leading to *nothing else*. And then he took her by the shoulders, turned her toward the door and gave her a gentle push, with an instruction to be back at seven o'clock.

After that, she couldn't find a way to get things back on track.

So when his washbag found its way back into her bathroom, and his clothes found their way into her wardrobe and bureau, she said nothing.

When his emptied suitcase turned up in her room, neatly positioned beside her own cases, she left it there.

When he stopped disappearing to the other bedroom to sleep, she never kicked him out. Even if they only did it once, even when they didn't do it at all one night, he'd simply curl around her and...well, stay curled around her.

They ate breakfast together before he went to the second bedroom to write and she took herself off to the living room with her laptop to edit. They told each other if they were going out—whether it was just for a walk around the estate or driving into the village.

He still ventured into the living room for any number of stupid reasons. She found herself seeking him out, too, asking questions about things she didn't need answered just because she missed him, and questions about *Stomp* she *wished* he'd answer but which he always managed to brush aside. It was strange to see him sitting at the big desk he'd had installed, when in college they'd worked together at the dining table— but it felt *right*, that they each had their own space. Like real life. Like *now* life, not *then* life.

Was it only nine days ago that she'd watched Rafael across the dance floor, feeling stuck in a time warp while she waited for that defining moment when her life might begin again? How strange to know that the moment had become a series of moments—a progression so gradual she didn't immediately realize her life *had* begun again.

In one way, she and Rafael had reverted to the couple they'd once been, but what was happening felt like more than that. They never talked about the past, or the future, and even their present was missing full and frank disclosure, because she hadn't finished *Catch, Tag, Release*, hadn't started *Liar, Liar*, and had finally given up asking about *Stomp*. But it didn't seem to matter that the world was spinning without them. It was like she was living an idyll, and if she could just hold everything and everyone at bay, if she could just keep Rafael in this cottage alone with her, that idyll would become the rest of her life.

All that soul-searching she'd done on the subject of whether or not she'd made a mistake seemed obsolete. Because that was then and this was now and he was hers again. She knew what Scarlett would say because she'd said it after Veronica's divorce from Piers when Veronica had started thinking Rafael might come back for her.

I gotta tell ya, Veronica, lots of women whose partners have left them have a moment when they want to take him back, have another go, whatever. They think the sharpest pain is gone and they've grown as people, and because they're going back on their terms, it's going to be different. But you know what? It almost never is. A guy who cheated on you is prob-

ably going to cheat on you again. A guy who's lied to
you is probably going to lie to you again.

She'd replayed that so often in her head, she could
practically *be* a therapist…and yet it didn't seem to
fit her situation with Rafael. Because he'd left her
for a *damn* good reason and they hadn't consciously
decided to get back together, it had just happened—
like fate.

Everything was perfect.

Until, suddenly, it wasn't.

CHAPTER SEVENTEEN

EARLY THURSDAY MORNING, Veronica emailed her suggested revisions to Tori Jayle and packed away her laptop.

At a loose end, she snuck upstairs and listened for sounds from the second bedroom, but an absence of cursing and the quiet clacking of Rafael's keyboard warned her to leave him to it. The epilogue. *Stomp*.

It had shocked her when he'd raised the subject of *Stomp* with no prompting from her during dinner last night—almost as though he'd wanted her to ask him about it. She hadn't asked, though—how bizarre was that, when he was finally giving her an opening? And so the conversation they could—maybe should—have had started and stopped with him telling her he needed to get it to Bryan ahead of their meeting in Harrogate tomorrow. Once it was gone, he'd said, he would teach her how to make chocolate mousse— which she could take as an indication of just how happy he'd be to see the last of the damn thing, because the thought of letting her near even one ingredient was enough to prematurely age him.

She smiled as she remembered how he'd laughed when she'd called him a smartass. Then how he'd looked at her when she'd suggested she wear her maid's outfit for the cooking class. Then what he'd done when she'd asked if he wanted to bend her over the couch for some writing inspiration…

Whew!

She crept quietly back downstairs, and as she paused with her foot raised above the fourth step—the one that creaked when you stepped on it—she felt suddenly nostalgic for this cottage. Which didn't make a lot of sense, given they weren't leaving for three days!

Or maybe it did make sense, because they definitely *would* be leaving. And they'd given no thought—and certainly no voice—to what would happen on Sunday, but they'd have to soon.

Squeak.

She imagined Rafael upstairs, hearing that telltale sound, his fingers poised over the keyboard—and for no apparent reason she heard Scarlett's voice in her head telling her to read his damn books.

"I *can't* read *Stomp* until I read the others," she whispered, as though her sister was standing right next to her on the stairs and they were trying not to be overheard.

And then she rolled her eyes—she was losing her mind, obviously!—and trod purposely down the last three steps, then into the living room, then out into the garden.

The garden was beautiful. A drench of color and scent. Beds crammed with geraniums, black-eyed Susans, dahlias, fuchsias at the front, and at the back, scented stock, lavender, hollyhocks in every imaginable shade, delphiniums in variegated blues, sweet peas, lupine, phlox, red-hot pokers.

Veronica sat on the stone bench picturesquely situated beneath an arched trellis dripping with jasmine. It was an ideal spot for reflecting on life…and books you may or may not be in…and love.

Love—because it was time to accept that she would always love Rafael. If only she'd accepted it seven years, three months and one week ago, she would have saved herself an awful lot of heartache.

She shivered suddenly, even though it wasn't cold. Damn it, she was so over these premonition-style chills down the spine.

Read his damn books.

"It's going to be my *job* to read *Stomp*, so stop it," she told an imaginary Scarlett.

At least, it was probably going to be her job. She'd know when Rafael came back from his meeting with Bryan in Harrogate tomorrow if the deal was really going to happen. And if it didn't happen…

Well, so what?

Another shiver had her banging a fist on her thigh.

Okay, *okay*, so she didn't want to read it. And she didn't want to finish *Catch, Tag, Release*, and she didn't want to read *Liar, Liar*, either.

Rafael's voice in her head this time. *You used to be braver than this, Veronica.*

Great! All she needed was to hear her mother's voice suggesting she ask herself why she kept marrying men she didn't love when the man she *did* love was single and available—as she'd done so calmly over cocktails after Veronica had signed her second divorce settlement agreement—and she'd know it was time to check into a health resort!

Or Teague telling her there had to be a reason for buying that motorcycle.

"Oh for God's *sake*!" she muttered, and went back into the house to scribble a note to Rafael to tell him she was going to the mausoleum—where she might actually get some peace and quiet. "I'll read his damn books if you'll all shut up!"

Rafael hit Send on his email to Bryan, to which he'd attached the detailed synopsis he'd written—and re-written—and rewritten—for *Stomp* II, and felt as though a humongous weight had been lifted from his shoulders.

He emerged from the second bedroom, calling out, "Veronica? Time for your cooking lesson!"

Silence greeted him.

He came downstairs and found her note—typically minus any mention of the time she'd left or the time she'd be back. It was a mark of how comfortable their relationship had become that those important omissions from that note made him smile instead of panic that she wasn't coming back. Even the thought of having only two more days with her, once you deducted his day in Harrogate, didn't alarm him. He was just so certain that what was between them wouldn't actually stop.

It wasn't until 6:45 p.m. that he heard her come into the cottage. Although he'd known she'd be back, he nevertheless breathed a quiet sigh of relief and relaxed.

He waited expectantly for the dinner routine to get under way. Her popping into the kitchen to ask if she could help, flustered because she was late. Him suggesting she pour them each a glass of wine. Her sitting at the dining table while he finished cooking. The two of them talking, laughing, serving, eating…

But when he heard the creak of the fourth step, which told him she was going up to their bedroom instead of coming into the kitchen, his smile dropped off his face. Something was clearly wrong.

He thought about downing tools and following her upstairs, but he was making risotto—one of Veronica's favorite meals, so of course it was fucking hard work—which made leaving the stove undesirable. Not that they couldn't go the village for a pub dinner if he ruined it…but no. Two days left to have her all to himself; he wasn't subjecting their precious new relationship to the outside world a second before he had to. So he was stuck, at the stove, stirring the pot like a Shakespearean witch, waiting for her to come to him and tell him what the fuck had happened. And she would come. She would. She *would*. She had to.

At seven o'clock he heard the squeaky step and breathed another sigh of relief. But when she came into the kitchen and he saw that her face was pale and shuttered, he knew they were in for a rocky night.

As she poured their wine, he brought their bowls

over and sat in his usual place opposite her, trying not to make it obvious that he was watching her. But when she raised her left hand to lay it across her forehead as though checking her temperature and he saw she was wearing one of her engagement rings, his eyes pierced her like a hawk's. He'd thought they were past that defensive crap, but apparently not.

She lowered her hand and looked at her fork as though gathering her energy reserves to lift it—and they might as well have been back at that first night, choking down chili as they waited for eight o'clock to roll around when they could touch. He knew, instinctively, she wasn't going to welcome any touch from him until she'd settled whatever it was that was troubling her.

What the fuck had happened? Had her sister called? Her mother? Her father? Melissa? One of her fucking ex-husbands?

He forced himself to make inconsequential remarks as his mind raced around possibilities. The Harrogate Crime Writing Festival, the intricacies of making risotto, the change in the weather that was expected to bring thunderstorms tomorrow night. She offered nothing—all she did was eat and nod and smile, and worry the life out of him.

When she did finally say something, as he put their bowls into the dishwasher, it came as announcement. And it was *way* out of left field. "I've decided to leave Johnson/Charles."

He froze, then straightened. "What?"

"I've decided to leave Johnson/Charles."

"Why?"

"Because it's time to step outside my comfort zone."

"So...what will you do?"

"I'm going to speak to Phillip Castle about a position at Smythe & Lowe as publishing director of their new romance imprint."

"London?"

"Yes."

"I...see."

"I'm not grafted onto New York you know."

"Nooo."

"I'm not! And...and I'm, not a fixture at Johnson/ Charles, either. In fact, it will be good—great—to get a promotion without everyone assuming I got it because of my father."

"Who'd assume that?"

"You."

He drew in a slow breath. Okaaay, they were about to get to the crux of the problem. "Once, maybe," he said. "Not now."

She waved a listless hand. "It doesn't matter."

"Yes, Veronica, it does."

"If you're worried about *Stomp*—"

"I'm not!"

"—don't be. I guarantee it'll be cherished like a baby. And I... I've been thinking there's going to be a conflict of interest with...with me and...and *Stomp*, anyway, so it'd be for the best if another editor took it on."

He let the silence settle and then said, "Do you

want to read *Stomp*, Veronica? Because you can read it now, right now, if you like."

"No!" she said, sounding like he'd suggested going on a shooting rampage.

"Then tomorrow, when I'm in Harrogate."

"Maybe," she said and pushed back her chair as though she'd flee on the instant.

"Dessert," he said, changing tack to keep her there. "Not chocolate mousse, obviously."

"Sorry, I…" She cleared her throat. "Sorry."

"It's okay. I'm pretty sure my chocolate would have had a seizure anyway."

She smiled—a dredged-up effort. "So what are we having?"

"Zabaglione."

"Oh! I love that."

"I know. That's why I asked Romy to teach me."

Silence. During which he found it hard to suppress a sigh. This really felt like he was back at square one. Had she not joined even two dots? He'd laid out such a generous scattering of the things for her to work with, *surely* she had to at least suspect he was in love with her!

And then she said, "I guess that would have been about the time you were writing *Liar, Liar*."

Uh-oh. "Ye-ees," he said cautiously.

"Martin makes it for Emma."

He pretended to be preoccupied with separating egg yolks as he weighed answers, but he knew all he could do was give her the bald truth. "Yes, he does. And yes, I learned how to make it when I was writ-

ing *Liar, Liar*. I was in New York for a meeting with
Bryan, and Romy was there for your wedding." He
added Marsala and sugar to the egg yolks. "I thought
you were going to finish reading *Catch, Tag, Release* first."

"I *did* finish it, and then I read *Liar, Liar*."

Adding a dash of vanilla, a sprinkle of cinnamon.
"You had a big day."

"I'm a fast reader."

He grated some lemon peel and added it to the
metal bowl, bracing himself for the discussion ahead.
"Did *Catch, Tag, Release* finish as you expected?"

"Well, let's see... Eric enjoying humiliating Julie
when she threw herself at him once he hit the right
socioeconomic bracket, sending her back to her old
life where she unhappily married the right man while
Eric soldiered bravely on alone. I'd say it finished as
you expected."

He rested the metal bowl over the pot on the stove
and picked up a whisk. "Of course it finished as I
expected. I'm the author. But it's a work of fiction,
Veronica."

"But Julie—"

"Yes, yes, we both know Julie is based on you, but
she *isn't* you. And I don't know Piers at all, so if you're
saying Piers is Niles..." He started whisking, nice and
easy, positioning himself so Veronica wouldn't see his
unsteady hands. "That's probably some kind of pro-
jection of your own feelings about him."

"And Simeon?" she asked.

"What about Simeon?"

"I know that's him in *Liar, Liar*. Martin—the passionless man Emma marries but doesn't want."

Whisking, whisking, whisking. "Did someone force you to marry Simeon?"

"I... I... No."

The whisk stopped. "So let me get this straight. You're telling me your husbands, neither of whom I've ever met, remind you of the most pathetic, insipid characters in my books, but that nobody forced you to marry them."

"They're not pathetic."

"They are in my books."

"I'm the one who chose them, so what your books are really saying is I'm the pathetic one."

"Do you *think* you were pathetic to choose them?" he asked.

"I did what I had to do."

He released the whisk and faced her, his temper starting to build. "You didn't have to do a damn thing, Veronica. You weren't broke or pregnant or beholden to them in any way. So I have to wonder why you *did* marry them." He waited...waited. Prompted, "Going to tell me?"

"You wrote them into your books very cleverly without me having to say a word!"

"As I said, I'm an author," he said, carefully tamping down his anger. "I make stuff up. But by all means tell me about them so I'll know if I got them right."

She glared at him, but he didn't back down. He'd invented those husbands based on the type of men he *assumed* she'd marry, and the fact that she recognized them so easily pissed him off for exactly that reason! If they were going to have this discussion—and God knew it was probably time for them to get everything out so they could move the fuck on—he was through pretending she hadn't cut his heart out with those two marriages. She wanted answers? Well, so did he. She'd wanted Eric to fight for Julie? Then *he* would fucking fight for *her*. He wasn't letting her send him back to limbo *without* a fight.

"No," she said.

"Why not?"

"Because it would be...disloyal."

He sucked in a rage-fueled breath. "Disloyal? What about your loyalty to *me*?"

"I owed you nothing!"

"So did they know about me?"

She swallowed but said nothing—and he had his answer.

"Did you let them stick pins in me?" he asked, and knew this was a fight that had been brewing not for the eleven days they'd been here but for all the years and months and weeks and days and hours and minutes and fucking seconds they'd been apart—unstoppable. "In my head, maybe, to torture me with thoughts of them with you?"

She jumped to her feet. "Stop!"

"Or maybe in my heart? Because it's been hurting for a hell of a long time. Or what about in my dick? Because the first time I tried to touch a woman after you was the night you got engaged to Piers and I couldn't get it up. I finally managed it the night of your wedding. She was five feet eight in her six-inch heels, and she had pale blond hair. She was wearing turquoise contact lenses and a pink dress, drinking Kir Royale." Bitter, bitter laugh. "Something for Scarlett to mull over. Especially since I *still* didn't want her. I didn't want her, but I did it anyway, and I've done it countless times since. And every fucking time it was like I was being unfaithful to you, and I hated every one of those women for *not being you*. Now *that's* pathetic."

"What do you want me to say? That I hated my husbands because they weren't you? Because I *didn't* hate them and I *won't* hate them. And I don't hate you for looking for companionship."

"But you do hate me? Still?"

"No! I just don't want you to…to blame me for getting married."

"Well, I do blame you!"

"Two men. Only *two*! When you confess to countless women?"

"It's not about how many men you've had sex with, Veronica! You could have slept with a million men and it wouldn't have stopped me from wanting you, from loving you. But you *married* them! And marriage took you out of my reach, even when finally I was *within* reach!"

"You took *yourself* out of reach—all the way back to LA!"

"You were supposed to *wait* for me! I was coming back for you!"

"When? *When* were you coming back for me?"

"When I sold my book!"

"And if you *didn't* sell your book? If you were like 99.99 percent of aspiring writers out there and *never* sold a book, or like 99.99 percent of authors who *do* sell a book and make enough for a sandwich and a cup of coffee? How long did you expect me to wait?"

"I wrote you a letter spelling it all out!"

"And sent it to *Matt*."

"I knew you wouldn't open it if it came straight from me!"

"Well, I sure as fuck wasn't opening it when it came via Matt! Did you really think I would? You had to know I'd be too *furious* to read it! That I'd tear it up and burn it. I didn't want a letter, Rafael, I wanted you!"

He recoiled, stunned. "You burned it?"

"What did you think I'd do? Press it in a book with a dried flower and knit you a fucking scarf while I waited for you?"

"You didn't wait long enough to knit me a scarf!"

"Why should I have waited? You had three and a half years to marry me and you *didn't*!"

"I couldn't!"

"Why *not*?"

"Because of this!" he said, digging his fingers into the coin pocket of his jeans and wrenching out the old engagement ring. He held it aloft so she could see it. "You bought me a motorcycle, and *this* is what I got you! You can see the problem, can't you? Or maybe you *can't* see it, because you'd need a magnifying glass to make out there's a diamond in this ring, but that fucking bike was pretty damn obvious."

She started to stretch her hand out for the ring but then that strange dry sob tore out of her and she covered her mouth instead as though to force it back. Her other hand came up then—clearly one wasn't enough to check the outpouring.

God it hurt to see that massive diamond on her ring finger. It ricocheted him right back to the day she'd given him the motorcycle, setting her apart from him. Only it was worse today, because he was holding out *his* pathetic ring, which looked like it cost only half as much as her manicure.

"Don't want it? Don't blame you," he said. And without waiting for her to confirm or deny, he tossed it onto the kitchen island, watched it spin, spin like a children's toy, then settle. Anticlimax—he should have thrown it across the room.

She kept her eyes on his as she slowly lowered her hands. "Why have you kept it all these years?"

"As a reminder that I was right to think you could do better. Because, lo and behold, you did do better. Two rich, society husbands."

"It wasn't like that."

"Then what was it like?"

"Punishment. One to punish you. One to punish myself."

"That is not enlightening."

"What I'm saying is neither of them was a real marriage."

"So you *didn't* marry them? Those fancy New York weddings were parties and nothing more?"

"I *did* marry them but—"

"Then I'm not sure what the problem is with defining them as 'real.' Unless you're saying they were marriages of convenience."

"No. Well, yes, in a way, but—"

"So they needed green cards?"

"No, it's just that—"

"Are you saying you slept in separate beds? Lived separate lives? They were like your brothers? That they never kissed you? Never fucked you? Never introduced you as their wife! As their fucking *wife*?" He grabbed the dish of zabaglione off the stove and threw it into the sink, so violently the mixture spattered halfway up the wall. His hands went digging into his hair. "You burned my letter! I *begged* you in that letter. I laid myself out for you in every way I could think of. I wrote you a fucking *poem*. And instead of reading it, you married. Someone. *Else*."

"Because of *you*! You're the reason I got married!"

He felt a roaring in his ears. A flash flood of fury. "If you had any idea what those marriages of yours did to me, you wouldn't dare to say that to me! Bad enough that I have to see that goddamn ring on your finger that *I didn't put there*."

She ripped the diamond ring she was wearing off her finger and threw it over her shoulder. "There! Is that better?"

"No!"

She picked up the ring from the island, shoved it on her finger. "Does this make it better?"

"No!" he said, even though his chest was tight with yearning. "No, no. God!"

"Do you know *why* it's not better? Because it's a *thing*! Nothing but a thing. You left me because of two *things*! A bike and a fucking ring. And you talk about blaming me for two *marriages*?"

"Veronica—"

"Well, I'll tell you what I'll do! I'll give you one more thing! Who knows, it might even make an extra-special scene for your next damn book." Up went her eyebrows, on went her finishing school smile. "When you're ready to collect it, I'll see you in the bedroom."

Rafael cleaned up the mess he'd made because he needed to do something mundane, something to let him think. But in the end he couldn't think past one question. What the fuck had he done?

He went to sit at the table, buried his face in his hands, trying to piece together how things had spiraled of out of control.

The letter she hadn't read, the husbands she hadn't even wanted—so what, when these two weeks with her had been the happiest he'd ever been.

Holy shit!

Ho-ly shit. They really were the happiest he'd ever been. Happier even than the three and a half years he'd had with her.

Because that was then…and this was now.

And he was a fucking idiot.

He raced from the kitchen, taking the stairs two at a time, pausing for a heavy bounce on the fourth step, just to make sure she knew he was coming.

CHAPTER EIGHTEEN

VERONICA WAS TWITCHING with fury as she prepared the room for Rafael's arrival. Covers off the bed. Those scissors she'd never returned to the kitchen on the vanity, two pairs of her stockings on the spindly chair before it, her jar of vanilla oil on the nightstand. Her clothes off, Piers's old blue T-shirt on.

When she heard that fourth stair squeak, she took up her position on the bed—on her back with her legs open wide and her arms stretched up and out. Starfish style—what an innocent word for what she was going to do—each limb pointing to a bedpost.

He came into the room. Stopped.

"Lo siento, Verónica," he said. "I'm sorry. Please, get off the bed—all I want to do tonight is kiss you."

She felt a quiver in her heart at his words, his voice, but she wouldn't back down. "Don't worry, I'm not staying like this," she said. "This is just a demonstration of the way I want *you*."

"The way you—?"

"So look closely, carefully. I want you laid out exactly like this."

"What's going on?"

"I'm helping you get my husbands out of your head by giving you the chance to one-up them. You sold this deal to me as a chance to take revenge on you—but it was really about taking *your* revenge on *me*, wasn't it? Me, and Piers, and Simeon."

"No. The deal was to get you back."

"That's what I said. Get me back. Revenge."

"Get you back as in *win* you back. Because I love you."

She jerked once, suddenly, and scrambled off the bed. "You'll love me forever, I suppose," she sneered.

"I will."

"Then prove it. Get naked on your back on the bed."

"Veronica, let me expl—"

"Words of one syllable. Shut up, get on your back on that bed or get out. The choice is yours."

He held his hands up—surrender—and did what she said, stripping, laying himself out on the bed.

She examined him, made a slight adjustment to one of his legs, then collected the stockings from the bed end.

"See these stockings?" she asked, using one to tie one of his wrists to a bedpost. "Red ones. Black ones. Piers always went for these colors when he bought me things, even though he knew my favorite color was pink, because the woman he loved—who was *not* me—used to wear them almost exclusively." She came around to the other side of the bed and tied his other wrist.

"Piers is a doctor," she went on. "*Not* an investment banker. A very good doctor. He's passionate about baseball, and horses, and that woman he loves—whose name is Mirabelle." Tying one leg now. "Unfortunately his parents didn't approve of Mirabelle, and he made a mistake putting their wishes before his own." Moving on to his last leg. "So there we were, Piers and I, in love with people we couldn't have, thinking we might as well give it a shot. That's essentially it—oh, except that I knew you'd hate it, so it was a way to punish you."

"I accept my punishment, *mi querida*."

She blinked at the endearment as much as at his placid acceptance of what she'd said, then covered it up by nodding at her handiwork. "Comfortable?" she asked.

"No."

"If I untie you, that's it—no more. It'll be over."

"Then don't untie me."

"But I'd better give you a safe word in case you change your mind?"

"I won't change my mind."

"How about we make it…voodoo. As in my doll."

"That seems appropriate."

"Repeat it so I know you know."

"Voodoo."

"Good," she said as she picked up her vanilla oil from the nightstand.

"Veronica, I love you."

She closed her eyes to stop him from seeing the way that hurt.

"Veronica…"

She opened her eyes. *"¡Váyase a la mierda!,"* she said, and tipped some of the oil low on his belly as though she hadn't heard him. "There. Some Spanish for you. Go fuck yourself!"

She put the bottle back on the nightstand and started to massage the oil into his skin, into his pubic hair, into his cock.

"¡Ah, Dios mío!" he groaned.

"You don't like it?" she asked, all innocent.

"You can see I do."

"I can see your *body* does, but don't strain too hard against those stockings or you'll hurt yourself."

"I want to touch you," he said.

"Touch? But that's *nothing.* Piers and Simeon both *touched* me."

"Then let me touch you, too."

"No. Now where was I?" she said as she kept massaging. "Ah, yes, Piers. Piers and I tried, but in the end, he couldn't live without Mirabelle. So, of course, I set him free and they lived happily ever after. At least I assume they will. But as for me—" tipping more oil "—alas, no. I was still in love with you, you see."

"Veronica," he pleaded, "I'm going to come if you keep rubbing my cock like that."

She stopped. "Sorry."

"Not sorry. Just a public service announcement."

"Thank you. We don't want it over before I really begin. I just like the way your cock feels in my hands, Rafael." She leaned over him and licked the pre-cum from the tip, and both his arms and both legs jerked against their restraints as he gave an agonized groan. "I like the way you taste, too."

"Then lick me again," he suggested.

She laughed and stepped back. "So, Piers and Mirabelle—happy, happy, happy. Me? Not happy. Want to know why?"

"Yes."

"Because I thought you'd come for me. But you didn't. You *didn't*, you bastard!"

"Ah, Veronica. How could I after writing that book? All I could do was hope you'd be so angry with me you'd come and find me. Do you have any idea how much I wanted you to come to me, for any reason at all?"

"I almost did. I almost *did* come to you! Instead, I waited, and waited, and learned Spanish for you! And now I've read *Catch, Tag, Release* I see what you would have done to me if I'd come groveling to you and babbling my Spanish love words."

"That book is fiction, Veronica."

"It's you! And me! And Piers. And *Liar, Liar* is me, my life, miserable with Simeon, because *you didn't come back for me.*"

"Untie me, Veronica, and I'll grovel for you in any language you want."

"I'm not untying you until I've finished my story," she said. "So, Simeon. He owns a gallery. His mother's a famous sculptor and his wife—Jeanette Wilkes, you may have heard of her—was a talented painter with a brilliant future ahead of her. When she died in a car accident ten years ago, he didn't really recover. He said he could never fall in love again—and that was perfect for me. Here's a newsflash for you, though—if my parents didn't want me to marry Piers (and I assure you they didn't) they were absolutely aghast at the idea of my marrying Simeon. All that money, all those connections, and he is nice, decent, kind—but my parents were only concerned with my happiness. What a shock, huh? Rich people caring about their kids! My mother went so far as to urge me to find *you* if I wanted to get married!"

"Smart woman, your mother."

"But I figured I was lonely, and he was lonely, and I... I didn't *deserve* to be happy after what I'd done to you. I deserved to be punished for my mistake. What I didn't expect was that Simeon would fall in love— not with me. Another artist, a sculptor."

She picked up the vanilla oil again, got onto the bed, eased one leg over him to straddle him, her knees on the bed holding her above his body. She poured more vanilla oil into her palm and this time used it on herself, bypassing her clit and heading for her asshole.

She saw he knew what she was about because his eyes went wide. He was struggling in earnest now, arms yanking at the stockings, emitting little grunts and groans as she massaged herself.

"Are you okay, Rafael?" she asked.

"No," he ground out.

"Safe word?"

"Fuck!" he said.

"That's not the safe word. Do you want me to re- mind you what it is?"

"All…all I want is…is you," he said, and he was actually panting as his hips started thrusting off the bed.

As she kept massaging herself, fingers moving in and out of her body, Rafael thought he was going to die of a stroke. But he couldn't die happy until she let herself hear that he loved her.

His arms strained at the ties even though he knew he wasn't going to be able to break them. It was instinct to try to touch her. It had always been instinctual with her. Like breathing. But if he couldn't touch her, he'd have to find another way to reach her—not easy when you were spread-eagled, tied to a bed and about to expire from an excess of lust.

"Ready?" she asked.

He nodded.

"You have to say it out loud."

"Ready," he said—well, he croaked it.

"Okay," she said, "but I want you to stay very still and let me take my time and set the pace. I've never done this before—see, I'm a virgin all over again for you, aren't you lucky?—and I need to control it, take it slowly."

"Yes, control it, control me. For you I will be as immovable as the Sphinx. For you I'll do anything," he said, and was fiercely glad that in this small way he could show her what she wouldn't hear. She could trust him to cede control to her; and because he loved her he would control himself.

She shook her head as though those words were

buzzing unwanted in her ears, and focused on getting more oil on him, *in* her... And then she put the cap on the oil and tossed it aside. Repositioning herself, she used one of her hands to hold him and the other as a brace on the bed beside his hip, then she lowered herself carefully onto his cock. He saw that she was breathing super slowly, trying to relax. He stayed deathly still and knew he would stay so even if it killed him.

Quarter inch by quarter inch, she took him in, keeping her eyes on his, her lids fluttering closed then open as she absorbed the feeling of him. She was biting down on her lower lip, he could feel her body shaking, and he thought he might burst with the emotions rampaging through him. Love, desire, need. Despair that she was giving this to him in a moment of defiance, not love—and self-disgust that he didn't have the strength to say no, even so.

He wasn't going to last. He knew it. The sight of her, the feel of her, the knowledge of what she was giving to him. The fact that he was tied added to the rush of it. It thrilled him that she'd bonded him, that she was taking him, that she was controlling him, that she trusted him to do what she asked and let her set the pace.

"*Mi amor*, it's coming," he warned. "Stop if you want."

She shook her head, violent, and sank a little lower onto him, taking him further than he would have expected, surely as far as she could, and he spilled himself inside her with a hoarse cry. And he hated himself, because he knew it wasn't her intention to take an orgasm for herself or she would have left his hands free.

She stayed still, took it all, limbs trembling either side of his hips, and then, when he thought she'd drained him of every ounce inside him, she laid herself flat out on top of him.

He said nothing, staying still for her for as long as he could bear it, because she needed to claim this victory. And then, "Untie me, *mi amor*," he said. "I want to touch you."

She sighed, got off the bed, went to the vanity and returned with a pair of scissors.

He laughed feebly as she looked at his dick. "I hope you're not thinking of using those scissors on anything but the stockings."

She smiled but it was perfunctory. "We still have two days of our agreement, so no."

"It's not an agreement anymore—it's just you and me," he said.

Her response was to proceed to cut each stocking in turn until he was free. "There," she said. "Now you have a part of me nobody else has had. Revenge, huh? Served hot." She held the scissors out to him. "So finish it."

"What do you mean?"

She gestured to the T-shirt she was wearing.

"What?" he asked, confused.

"Use the scissors. Get symbolic. Cut this T-shirt off me. It's Piers's, you know."

"I don't need to cut it off you, Veronica. Wear anything of theirs you like, you'll still be mine."

He went to take her in his arms but she stepped back.

"Then I'll do it," she said. Throwing the scissors on the bed, she reached for the neckline of the T-shirt and ripped it down the front, then tore it off her body.

Standing there naked except for his ring on her finger, the tatters of her ex-husband's T-shirt on the floor beside her, his heart burst with love and pride. If she could accept that pissant ring without losing one iota of what made her who she was—and wear it like a fucking queen what's more—why couldn't he accept a 1952 Vincent Black Shadow motorcycle and stay exactly who he was?

Talk about epic moments in life.

And then she seemed to collapse a little before his eyes without actually moving. "I feel dirty," she said into the silence.

And without looking at him again, she went into the bathroom.

Veronica flattened herself against the wall of the shower, wishing she could disappear into it before Rafael came in—as she knew he'd do.

If only she could go back, handle that talk in the kitchen differently. Without the anger, the accusations, the recriminations. Except that then, of course, she might as well have been with some other man. Rafa was the only one she could let go with and fly all the way into the harsh sun knowing he'd still love her. And she *knew* he loved her. But love had never been the problem, and sex had never been the problem. It was the other stuff that had gotten in the way—and that boiled down to their need to find their place in the world.

She'd been looking for freedom and had tried to buy it with a motorcycle; he'd been looking for security and had left her so he could find it. *Of course* he was going to come back for her. So why hadn't she let him? That was the burning question.

She heard the bathroom door open, and then felt Rafael get into the shower behind her, but she was so sad, so drained, she couldn't make herself face him.

He brushed a hand down her hair. "I don't want you to feel dirty."

"It's not because of what I did, but how I did it. To punish you again. Or maybe to punish myself."

"How can I make you feel clean again?" he asked.

"Unless you can time-travel with me back to graduation day so I can fix everything I did wrong... nothing."

Another stroke of her hair. "I'd go back with you... except that I love you more today than I did then."

"If you love me after everything I've done, you need psychological help."

"Ah, but I love you *because* of everything you've done. We weren't meant to be back then, *querida*. But I think, now, we are."

"Can it really be that simple?"

"We can make it so."

She turned then, stepped into his arms, under the spray. "I wish I'd read the letter, Rafael," she whispered.

"I'll write you another," he whispered back.

CHAPTER NINETEEN

Saturday.

Second-last day.

A few seconds to soak in the quiet, followed by a check of the clock on the nightstand.

Nine o'clock.

And she was alone.

She swung her legs out of bed then stopped as she saw a note on the bedside table.

She picked it up with trembling hands.

Below is a list of computer passwords and file names. You're going to want to kill me after you read *Stomp*, so please use those pins freely on Little Rafa while I'm gone to work out some aggression so when I get back from Harrogate you'll at least kiss me before you stick the knife in my chest. Lots to discuss about the new book…

It took nineteen reads of the note for Veronica to determine she didn't need the aggravation that was *Stomp* and was therefore *not* going to read the damn thing.

She pulled on one of Rafael's gray T-shirts and went downstairs for coffee, managing to valiantly resist the lure of the second bedroom for two whole hours.

At which point she threw her fourth cup of coffee against the kitchen wall. The kitchen walls were going to have to be repainted at the rate she and Rafael were throwing things.

Okay, so it seemed she *was* going to read the damn book.

But first she had to…prepare.

She took her time over the preparations—showering, washing and blow-drying her hair, rubbing vanilla oil over every inch of her skin, dressing in an almost-new Prada suit she would have worn to the office in London, and applying her makeup with extra care. Ridiculous, given all she'd be doing was sitting in the cottage on her own, reading, but she felt in need of armor.

And then she took a few deep breaths and made her way to the second bedroom.

It took her only a few minutes to find the manuscript, and she figured she'd know within three chapters if she had anything to worry about. If all was well, she'd close the computer and pretend she hadn't given in to temptation.

At seven o'clock that night, she hit Page 422 and stared at THE END for a disbelieving three minutes.

What the fuck had she just read?

Wuthering Heights fan fiction at its absolute worst. Brooding hero, erratic heroine, doomed love.

Sex scenes so execrable she would have let him bend twenty other women over a piece of furniture just to save his readers' eyeballs from exploding!

And the characters! Had he seriously thought getting Hope to give up her *entire fucking fortune* for Alejandro was a good idea? It was positively *archaic*! And then to kill Hope off, in that disgustingly soap-opera-ish, my-heart-is-broken way *halfway through the book*? Fuck that. And fuck the way Alejandro spent the second half of the book wallowing in misery over it, too.

And while she was having a rant, where was the all-important epilogue he'd been slaving over for almost two weeks?

She rested her fingertips over her tired eyes and ran that note Rafael had left her through her aching head. She was going to hate it—yep, spot-on there. But it was the last line that was troubling. Lots to discuss about the new book...

Like...what new book?

Hadn't he tortured her enough in the three books he'd already written? Because there was absolutely no doubt in her mind that she was Hope! What new ground could there possibly be to cover? He'd done their own relationship in *Catch, Tag, Release* as well as her first marriage, her second marriage in *Liar, Liar*, and now the final vengeance story in *Stomp*. What more was there to do? Only these past two weeks and what was there to say about—

Oh!

Oh! That bastard. Was that what these two weeks

were about? Getting more raw material? And to think she'd said last night that what she was doing to him would make an extra-special scene in his next damn book! Was he taking notes in his head all through it?

Oh God, she couldn't breathe. She was back in that metaphorical coffin, desperate to get out, to be free.

She ran downstairs, out into the garden, looked wildly around.

Pretty. Colorful. A place to reflect.

But she didn't want to reflect. She wanted to rage and scream and tear things apart.

She looked around, seeking an escape, and saw the stone fence that separated the estate from the moors.

Next minute she was running.

CHAPTER TWENTY

RAFAEL WAS BUZZING by the time he returned to the cottage and pulled his car in next to Veronica's—a hot-looking Jaguar sports car, because *of course* it was.

When he got out of the car, he took a moment to look at the cottage despite the fact that it was raining. Funny that he'd come to think of this modest cottage as theirs over the past two weeks. As home. Or maybe not funny. Maybe perfect. Because Veronica was here.

He hoped Veronica had read *Stomp* I because it would make it easier for him to explain *Stomp* II. So many things to discuss, ideas for the story, ideas for other stories, ideas for their life.

But when he opened the door to the cottage, shaking the raindrops from his hair, he knew she wasn't in—he could feel the emptiness.

He turned on the main light and searched the lower floor anyway, cast a look into the garden as a just-in-case, even though he couldn't believe she'd be out there in this weather, called out a general "Veronica?"

No answer.

He headed up the stairs, stopped on the landing. "Veronica?"

No answer.

Into their bedroom, relaxing as he saw her suit-cases, as a quick examination of the bathroom showed her toiletries in their place.

He pulled out his cell phone, dialed her number and heard the muffled sound of her phone ringing—which might have been comforting if it hadn't been coming from under her pillow.

Okay, no need to panic. The fact she hadn't taken her phone with her meant only that she wasn't far away. But where? He had no idea. She'd have needed her car to get to the village. And the rain was sheeting down—this wasn't weather for a stroll around the estate.

He came out of the bedroom, headed for the stairs, stopped.

Second bedroom? She was such a sound sleeper it was conceivable she'd fallen asleep in there and hadn't heard him hollering her name. Not that he could figure out why she'd be in bed before him or why she'd sleep in there, but at this point...

He didn't bother finishing that thought; he simply headed into the room.

No sign of her, except the scent of vanilla, and his open computer.

He took the jeweler's box out of his jacket pocket, checked the gift he'd bought her. That settled his nerves enough for him to become convinced she'd walk in any minute. He'd go downstairs, get a bottle of wine breathing, practice what he intended to say. And wait. Just...wait.

But when he looked out the window for a weather

update and saw not only the torrent of rain cascading down but caught a flash of lightning, he knew he wasn't going to wait.

Veronica didn't know how long she'd been wandering over the moors like Cathy's ghost. She didn't know what time it was when she'd clambered back over the low stone fence and into the estate grounds. She didn't know how she'd found her way to the mausoleum, either, but it seemed fitting to end up there on this stormy night.

"Catastrophe scale," she said as she walked up the steps to the platform. "Zombies. Aliens. Or something simpler—say, like dropping dead of a fucking broken heart like some pathetic loser!"

Maybe Rafael would be the one to find her. He knew she was drawn to this place, so when he got home tonight and wondered where she was, he could conceivably come looking for her here. Serve the bastard right if he found her dead.

The only problem with that was that it might give him license to go the full Heathcliff, beating his head on a tree trunk, railing at fate and declaring his undying love. That would be enough to make her come back from the dead just so she could tell him to get over himself.

Heathcliff! *What* an asshole. Resenting a woman for what she'd done when he'd left her, plotting his revenge, inserting himself back into her life, and then getting all accusatory when she dropped dead.

She looked out at the moors, imagined Rafael as

Heathcliff roaming around out there with a lantern. Restless, angry, searching for something—because he *was* searching for something.

At least…he'd *been* searching for something. But last night she'd really thought he'd found it. Found *her* again. Loved her again—only loved her *more*. That's what he'd said. *I love you more today than I did then… I love you* because *of everything you've done.*

But then, Heathcliff had loved Cathy and hurt her anyway.

"Damn you, *Wuthering Heights*!" she yelled into the wind and rain. "And damn you, too, *Stomp*!"

Well, she wasn't going to go all Cathy/Hope and grieve herself out of the novel of her life halfway through it. She was a Johnson and she gave zero fucks and the precise *way* she was going to give zero fucks about having her heart broken *twice* was by not giving up her damn money and not dying, damn it!

"Zero fucks," she said out loud. "As in ze-ro!"

And that was when she realized she was crying. Real tears. Hot tears. Mingling with the cold rain on her cheeks. And despite the way her head was throbbing, her muscles were hurting, her heather-scraped legs were stinging and her heart was aching, she felt like she was achieving closure at last. She loved him, she always would—but she was going to say goodbye to him and she was going to cry as long and as hard as it took to do it.

"You're a fuckhead, Rafael," she said. "And Heathcliff is, too."

She sat on the platform, leaned back against a pillar and let the tears flow.

CHAPTER TWENTY-ONE

IT WAS ONLY a silhouette. Darker than the night but not by much. A form sitting on the platform, knees up, head leaning back against a column.

"Please God, please, please, please," Rafael breathed as he hurried toward the mausoleum, but he knew it was her.

Up the steps, falling to his knees before her, dragging her into his arms, onto his lap, kissing her hair. "Jesus, Veronica." Kissing her cheeks. "You scared me to death." Kissing her forehead, her eyes. "I've been out of my mind!" Kissing her stubbornly unresponsive mouth.

He pulled her to her feet, stepped away from her but only to take off his jacket and throw it to the ground then rip off his T-shirt. Wiping at the mascara-streaked tear tracks on her cheeks with his T-shirt, not believing he'd once wanted to mess her up—no, mess her *down*—to make her less perfect. When what he really wanted was to have her any way she came. Rich or poor. Perfect *and* imperfect. Smiling and scowling. Hot and icy. He wanted her feisty and fuck-you, with her eyebrows of destruction any way she wanted to arch them, wanted her snort-laughter and her fierceness. Wanted everything about her and loved everything that had made her who she was.

This was the hour of reckoning. The knowledge that settled into his soul just at the sight of her. That if you loved someone, you just loved them.

Which was just as well, since the first words she said to him were, "You're an asshole."

"Yep," he admitted. "Going to try not to be from now on, though."

"You're a bastard."

"Yep—same thing, going to try not to be from now on."

"I'm going to cut the dick right off that voodoo doll with the bluntest, rustiest knife I can find."

He winced. "Okaaay. I must love you to distraction to risk that, but you go right ahead. As long as you come with me now and let me explain."

"I don't want to talk to you."

"Then I'll talk," he said, pulling his T-shirt back on. "But can we get into the car and dry off first? I don't want you dying of a chest infection midway through the story."

"You already killed me off."

"Sorry about that."

"Despicable."

"I was channeling Heathcliff."

"Heathcliff's an asshole."

"Yes, I know."

"Heathcliff's a bastard."

"Yep."

"I hate *Stomp*."

"I thought you would—and quite rightly."

"Is that all you have to say?"

"Um, the book sucks? I did warn you."

"So why did you write it?"

"I call it a college boy's obsession with trying to mold a woman, trying to own a woman, when it was the fact the woman couldn't be molded or owned that he loved the most. Come on, it was bound to suck!"

"Is that why you made me give up everything for you in *Stomp*? To mold me, to *own* me?"

"Hmm, strictly speaking, Alejandro did that."

"Alejandro's an asshole."

"Yep."

"Alejandro's a bastard."

"Yeah, but it's not entirely his fault, because when the author wrote it he was a dick. Sorry to be repetitive, but the author's going to try to not be a dick anymore."

"For the record, I'd never give up my money for a man like Hope did."

"I'm glad to hear that because we're going to need a chef, and a house in Yorkshire."

"And I'd never drop dead of a broken heart, so stop *s-stomping* me to death. *Stomp!* Fuck that book title!"

"Hey, I killed you *once*! *Metaphorically*. And I've decided to kill myself off, as well, if that helps. Plus I'll let you choose how we go. Till death do us part, like that old married couple interred in this mausoleum. Hell, I'll even throw a mausoleum into the book if it'll please you. But can I short-circuit this conversation by reminding you that you're still breathing? And I'm still breathing? And that's real life, not fiction?"

"But aren't you planning another book about me?"

"Er…no."

"Isn't that why we're here? So you get raw material for a new book?"

"Jesus!" He burst out laughing. "We're here because I love you to a ridiculous degree, and I wanted you back, and kidnapping is illegal!"

"So there'll be no more books about me?"

"No more books about you—well, not unless you want one. Say, an erotic rom-com. Second chance at love, rich girl gone bad, poor boy made good—all the tropes. A brooding Heathcliff-type hero, a feisty voodoo-doll-wielding heroine. Good enough for Smyth & Lowe's new romance line! The happiest ending ever to not end."

"As long as you know I'm not going to do any languishing."

He burst out laughing again and pulled her in for a quick, hot kiss. "God, I love you. And I promise, *promise*, not to make you languish, and not to break your heart, and never, ever to let you go. Not in books and not in real life. I'll stick pins in Little Rafa for you, I'll write you a book of love poems, I'll let you tie me up every night, I'll eat caviar even though I really truly don't like it, and drink all the champagne in the world if that'll make you happy."

"Caviar!" she spat, pulling out of his arms and

glaring at him. "You knew that night you were going to leave me, even before I gave you the motorcycle."

"What the fuck?"

"Eric told me!"

"Yeah, well, Eric's an asshole. And a bastard. And a dick. I should know because I created him."

"Eric made love to Julie the way you made love to me the night we had a fight over the caviar. Like he was escaping the demons of hell even as he soared to heaven."

"Yeah, I may have gotten a little dramatic that night."

"That was a goodbye fuck."

"Ah, Veronica," he said, dragging her in again. "I wasn't trying to leave you, I was trying with everything in my soul to keep you!"

"You were?" she sniffled against his chest.

"I was. Now can we please go home?"

"What if home turns out to be London?"

"I love London. But it can be New York or LA or Yorkshire or Bogota—shit, you're loaded, I'm almost-loaded, we can have a place in each of them, can't we?"

"What's the point of that?"

He kissed the top of her head. "No point—except that my home is wherever you are. But can I make a suggestion? That we call the cottage home for this last night and get the hell out of here? My T-shirt's wet and I'm cold!"

She put her arms around him and drew him close. "Is that better?"

"Always. But I have a present for you in the car, so if we could get at least that far, I'd be grateful."

"I don't want a present. I'm New York Barbie, remember? I already have all the accessories."

"Oh if we're going to go that route, I'll be Colombian Ken—and the best thing about Colombian Ken is he comes with his own motorcycle—a 1952 Vincent Black Shadow."

"Huh?"

"I'm telling you I want my motorcycle."

"Huh?"

"Motorcycle. I want it. I want you. I love you. I'm desperate to get you naked. And I'm about to drag you to the car because I'm not molesting you at a mausoleum. Decorum, Veronica! What would you parents say?"

He grabbed her hand and dragged her through the rain to where he'd parked, bundled her into the passenger seat, then ran around to the driver's side and got in.

"I can't believe you're wearing a dirty T-shirt," she said, as he turned on the interior light.

"Yeah, well, times change," he said, and started laughing. "And that's a great title for chapter one of a new book: Rafael and Veronica start afresh—or at least, start dirty." He reached across her to the glove compartment, extracted the jeweler's box he'd stored there and held it out to her. "Take it."

But all she did was bring her clenched fist to her mouth and look at the box.

"Take it, Veronica!" he said again.

"If there's a huge diamond ring in there I'll go ballistic, just so you know."

"Ballistic over a huge diamond?"

"Not the diamond, the principle," she said, taking the box at last. "You going one better than my other husbands."

"As it happens, I'm only marginally less in love with your husbands than I am with you. They will be nightly in my prayers for the rest of our lives for keeping you well enough occupied that you didn't fall in love with someone else, and for getting the hell out of your life at speed so I could get back into it." He grinned at her. "And, also, they're responsible for my two *New York Times* bestsellers." He leaned over and kissed her. "But the third bestseller, according to Bryan, with you and I killed off, will be even better." Another kiss. "And incidentally, smartass, it's not an engagement ring in that box."

"So you don't want to marry me? *Again?*"

"I do want to marry you. Again. The difference is that this time I'm going to do it, because *this* is the right time. And also, because I already *gave* you a ring—which you're already wearing. The miracle is you didn't fling it into the wilderness after you read *Stomp.*"

A look of surprise came over her face. "I didn't even *think* of doing that."

"Which I consider a good sign that you're accepting my proposal despite hell not having frozen over."

"So you're proposing?"

"I am."

"But it's *not* a ring in the box."

"It's an engagement bangle, okay? Now open the damn thing."

She opened the box. Took out the diamond-studded platinum bangle, read out the engraving: "'Whatever our souls are made of, his and mine are the same,'" and started crying again.

"Why are you crying?" he asked.

"Because I've got closure."

Panic shot through him. "Oh no you don't! Oh no. You. Don't. You *love* me."

"Yes, but—"

"You love me!"

"I know that. It's just—"

"What the *fuck*, Veronica!"

"Oh for God's s—" But she cut herself off there, grabbed him by two handfuls of hair, pulled him in and kissed him hard. "Now!" she said, when she released him. "Will you shut up?"

"Okay," he said meekly.

"I'm not crying because I don't love you, I'm crying because I do, you idiot! I love you because I *can* cry, because it feels like forever since I felt anything enough to cry, because it's been a thousand forevers since you left me. So let me warn you now, this is the new forever. If you try to get rid of me again, I'll write a book about you and turn you into a swamp monster. I'll send Scarlett's enforcer after you."

"Enforcer? Seriously?"

"And I'll get a thousand new pins, thicker ones,

longer ones, sharper ones, and torture you one body part at a time! What do you think of that?"

She was crying in earnest by the end of that speech, so he dragged her out of her seat and onto his lap and kissed her so deeply he figured she could barely breathe let alone weep. And when he released her, he cupped her face in his hands and said, "Do you a new deal. Tell me you love me in Spanish, and I'll be your modern day Heathcliff and read *Wuthering Heights* aloud to you to seal the forever deal."

"Heathcliff!" she said in disgust, then buried her face against his chest and started to cry again. "Oh God! I've gone right off *Wuthering Heights* these past two weeks, you bastard."

"No you haven't," he said. "I know you're secretly in love with Heathcliff or you not only would have tossed the ring, you'd have thrown that bangle at me."

"What am I going to give you as an engagement present?" she snuffled.

"A matching bangle. Well, maybe we'll make mine a bit chunkier. All you have to do is pick out a Heathcliff quote. I'm kind of partial to 'Drive me mad' because I know Heathcliff says that at some point and I'm pretty sure that's what you're going to do to me. But if you want something a little more romantic, how about that old chestnut, 'I cannot live without my soul'? Because I don't want to, you know. I just want to live with you."

She raised her head then, gave a sniff or two, then asked, "What about my family?"

"Hmm," he said, prying the bangle from her and

snapping it onto her wrist. "If we have to get bangles for all of them, you're going to have to provide the quotes—I've reached my *Wuthering Heights* memory limit."

She laughed through her tears as she ran a delicate finger over the platinum band. "I meant what'll we do about you not liking my family?"

"What's not to like? Your parents had *you*, didn't they? And if your mother told you to come find me, she's obviously smarter than either of us. As for Scarlett… Well, she's got such bad taste in men she has no business being a therapist if you ask me, but even so—"

"What do you mean, bad taste in men?"

"Hey, the drug addict, an enforcer."

"The enforcer's a client!"

"But *even so*, I'm going to make her love me. And your father, too!"

"You can't make people love you."

"You just watch me try," he said. "I got you to love me twice, didn't I?"

"No," she said. "You got me to love you once. I never stopped. *Yo siempre te he amado.*"

"Ah! Now we're getting somewhere! Spanish!"

"It means I've always loved you."

"You don't say! Keep going. I can take it."

"Okay, *mi amor.*"

"My love. Good."

"Tú me perteneces. Siempre me pertenecerás."

"I belong to you, and I'll always belong to you. No contest there."

"Te amaré por siempre."

"You'll love me forever."

"I will," she said, and laid her hand against his cheek. Till death do us part, I'm afraid."

He covered her hand with his, and smiled into her eyes. "Afraid? No you're not, my darling. And neither am I."

"So what are you waiting for? Let's go home."

* * * * *

COMING SOON!

We really hope you enjoyed reading this book. If you're looking for more romance, be sure to head to the shops when new books are available on

Thursday 29th November

To see which titles are coming soon, please visit
millsandboon.co.uk

LET'S TALK
Romance

For exclusive extracts, competitions
and special offers, find us online:

f facebook.com/millsandboon

🐦 @MillsandBoon

📷 @MillsandBoonUK

Get in touch on 01413 063232

For all the latest titles coming soon, visit
millsandboon.co.uk/nextmonth